The Samsara Papers:

Emergence

(Book One)

KB SPECTOR

Copyright © 2014 KB Spector

Paperback ISBN: 0990950301

ISBN 13: 978-0-9909503-0-1

E-book ISBN: 978-0-9909503-1-8

Connect:
Website: KBSpector.wordpress.com

Facebook: Facebook.com/TheSamsaraPapers

Email: TheSamsaraPapers@yahoo.com

Back cover icon art inspired by Sophie Spector. Photo by Sophie Spector.

For my beloved David.

Let's do it all over again in the next life.

The Samsara Papers:

Emergence

(Book One)

KB SPECTOR

Contents

HUMAN PROTECTION ACT of 2086

Prologue

KAMINER
    Kaminer - 2099
    Human Services Bureau
    The Homebase at Burke
    It Begins
    An Offer
    He's The One
    In Between
    It Continues
    The Scholars: Metamorphosis
    It Happens
    The Scholars: A Proposal
    The Scholars: A Deal
    Restart

AMBROSE
    Ambrose -2099
    The Singularity
    After
    The Scholars: Emergence
    Recovery
    Responsibility
    Discovery
    The Scholars: Interference
    EM EW AE
    Changes
    Progression
    Mastery

Contents, continued

AMBROSE, continued
>Relocation
>Reconciliation
>The Scholars: Progress
>The Code of Conduct
>July
>Spricatur West
>Post-Op
>Road Trip
>Timothy
>Ma and Pop's
>September
>December
>A Date?
>Reappraisal
>Parting Gift

KAMINER
>The Scholars: Program
>Kaminer - 2100

Acknowledgments

The
Samsara
Papers:

Emergence

HUMAN PROTECTION ACT OF 2086

From The Code of Laws of
the United States of America
Public Law 186 – 27
186th Congress

FINDINGS, PURPOSES, AND POLICY

Sec. 1.   (a) FINDINGS.-The Congress finds and
declares that-

(1) Non-human genetic modification of the
Homo sapiens genome is depleting the
stock of unmodified human genetic
material;

(2) Economic growth and development in
the United States has continued without
reasonable regard to conservation of
critical habitat of the human species;

(3) The United States has pledged itself to
conserve plants, fish and wildlife,
pursuant to The Endangered Species
Act of 1973, as amended in 1978, 1982,
2021, 2058, and 2079, and further
modified through agreements;

(4) The Secretary has determined the
Homo sapiens species is endangered
and threatened with extinction under
Sec. 4. (a) (A), (D) and (E) of said
Endangered Species Act.

HUMAN PROTECTION ACT OF 2086

Sec. 1. (b) PURPOSES.-The purposes of the Act are
to provide a means to conserve the
original, unmodified genetic material of
Homo sapiens so that it may be
propagated in eco-systems preserved for
their use.

(c) POLICY.-This Act amends Sec. 9 of the
Endangered Species Act, Prohibited Acts,
to further state that it is unlawful for
any person subject to the jurisdiction of
the United States to-

(1) Alter their person with non-human DNA
or synthetics of any kind;

(2) Alter their born or unborn child with
non-human DNA or synthetics of any
kind;

(3) Alter another human being with non-
human DNA or synthetics of any kind.

Prologue

Neural Interface *n.* **Nanobot colonies that together integrate with the brain to transmit, receive, and store information; usually made of organic polymers.** *Same as NEURAL DEVICE.*

"Cherry cough drop," Archie mumbled. "Could really use a cherry cough drop." He tried to clear his throat, but his voice remained thick with congestion. "Wish Zeus was here. He'd have a whole stash of 'em."

"What's a cough drop?" Kate whispered, her sleek body rising from a low-slung leather chair. She trailed her hand along the brown mahogany wainscot as she approached his bed.

Kate knew this low-lit room in the Homebase at Burke Laboratories was designed to convey a sense of serenity, but she was troubled. Aging-out didn't require dying, as long as certain steps were taken to preserve the body when biological function ended.

This is where they come to be put in stasis. But not my own father, she thought with a heavy sigh, pulling her long brown hair out from the red angora scarf around her neck. Kate consulted the Reader embedded in her palm, grimacing at the statistics that grew more dismal.

Her father's brain now needed support beyond the calcium regulator that kept his neurons firing. The nanobots that swept his brain matter clean of plaques and tangles were falling behind. Kate realized, despite the best healthcare available in 2097, a failing brain would take her father's life.

She closed her hand in a fist, trying to shatter its unbreakable organic plastics, then ran it down the stiff silk of her ivory jacket. She leaned over her father, her brown eyes flashing, as she pulled up a blanket from the end of the bed and tucked it around his still athletic-looking body.

He looks too young to be failing, she thought, heavy with the knowledge that he was lying in a bendybed. A bed whose sides and footboard could be bent over and contoured to cocoon a patient at risk of falling out of a regular bed.

"Do you want me to try Rafe again? I'm sure he'd come now," Kate murmured.

Archie stared up at her with large hazel eyes, once so lively, now dull and diminished, set in a symmetrical face with barely a wrinkle or blemish. He ignored the question. "Make sure, Katiekins," he mumbled, his eyes sweeping from one corner of Kate's face to the other. "No stasis. Please, promise, prom-z." He started to slur, and then whimpered.

Kate put a manicured finger to her father's lips. "Shh, it's okay, Daddy. I promise! I promise to take care of you. Just like Zeus. Please, please, don't worry."

"Iz just," Archie tried, smiling with one half of his face, revealing gleaming teeth. But the other half, the side he had refused to repair, sagged and pulled downwards.

Kate stared at the otherwise perfect face displaying the twisted masks of comedy and tragedy. "Are you in pain, Daddy?" She pulled one of her father's hands into hers, clenching it nervously.

"Be nice to the new married. Roslyn, she'll be good for Rafe. Brain project. He-, must-, go back to it. I know, I know my grandson can do it," Archie urged, gathering his breath. "I love you," he breathed out, finding the strength to also send the message to his daughter through the failing synaptic connections to his Neural Interface.

Kate received the in-mind message of the three sparkling words on her own neural device. *Like a sputtering light bulb*, she thought, drawing in gulps of air.

Archie turned his head away and coughed. The sickly coughs disintegrated into rasps, his chest moving less each time. The gasps became wheezes, each one smaller than the one before. Kate smoothed all the wrinkles from the bed, and sat rigid on the stool. Her father's diminishing effort finally collapsed, and she heard his last breath, a short stutter, float out of him. Kate dropped her head into her hands and sobbed.

***

"Put him in Surgibot Room 3, and get him prepped," Kate snapped when a human attendant showed up to relocate the bendybed. "His Neural Interface was manufactured, surgically inserted. It's coming out the same way," she voiced, wondering why she was talking out loud.

Like the attendant cares. He's not performing the surgery, she berated herself, thinking about why she was so upset. It disturbed her that her father had rejected the option of stasis. And it felt personal the way he had done it, publicly, in an all-company visual-cast last year. He'd made it clear that he had no intention of carrying on when inevitable brain death set in. He would be leaving Burke Laboratories in the care and keeping of his capable daughter, Dr. Kate Margaret Burke.

"Dad, this is shortsighted," she had argued after the visualcast distribution. "You're still in brilliant health! And even if something were to happen, we just need a little more time to replicate the brain. A year of stasis, maybe two. A brief interlude, and then, we'll bring you back. Once the brain is just another organ grown to order. Please!"

"You're missing the point, Katie. Brain replication is just a piece of it. This isn't simply a bio-medical issue."

"But we'll get there!"

"Upload me to Central Frame as I've asked. If it works, I will contact you. Someday we'll have a choice," Archie had continued.

"Is that what this is about?"

"Yes. One day we'll choose how we want to live. Maybe I would rather be a machine consciousness, living out my life in Central Frame. Perhaps you'd like to be reloaded to a fresh brain in your biological body. But what if someone wants a better body? Why shouldn't a bot body be a choice?"

"Why would anyone want the limited sensation of a bot body? A bot body that would be against the Human Protection Act, by the way. And I'm not the one missing the point. Why even die? It's not necessary."

"Just do as I ask. If you do, then I'm certain physical death isn't dying."

"But we haven't heard from Zeus," Kate had insisted, but her father had already walked away.

Kate sighed at the unsettling memory, taking a moment to look, one last time, at the still form of her father as the attendant maneuvered the bendybed noiselessly out of the room. She trailed behind, sweeping a hand over the porcelain skin of her oval-shaped face. As she entered the stark glow of the hall-way, she nervously plucked a few hairs out of her right eyebrow. They immediately grew back, and her hand lingered and plucked them out again. Walking up to a panel outside a surgical room, she messaged details about her father's old-fashioned device, and authorized the surgibot to proceed with the Neural Interface extraction. She checked that her eyebrow had reset itself, tracing a finger over its outline.

"Bring me the device as soon as it's retrieved," she ordered the human attendant stationed to the side, and walked resolutely to her office, lips pressed together, chin high. Another attendant, getting a glimpse of Dr. Kate, turned away and busied himself at a wall panel.

Once ensconced in her office, sitting delicately at a lacquered white desk that matched an austere, plain rug and pristine walls, Kate messaged her son. "*Rafe, your grandfather is gone,*" she explained, sending the message through her Neural Interface with a red emergency flag. She knew that would be the only way to get his attention.

"*Tell me more,*" Rafe immediately messaged back. Kate could tell her son was actively moving from the way the word 'me' bounced up in the middle of her mindscreen.

"*This is not unexpected,*" she messaged, sounding stiff and formal. "*And, as befits a 138-year-old man, he went peacefully, and perhaps somewhat happily, at the hopeful prospect of seeing his old friend, Zeus Cray, again.*"

"*I'm sorry, Mother,*" Rafe sent back. "*I'm sorry I'm not there for you.*"

Kate could tell Rafe had put a hold on his emotional response settings the way the message sounded flat in her neural device. "*Son, I know this is hard.*"

"*I've been distracted with the honeymoon. I didn't understand it would come so soon, that he'd leave us so quickly.*" Rafe sounded remorseful, and now Kate understood just how distressed her son was. So upset that it overwhelmed his message filters.

"*It's okay, Rafe. Just come home. Bring Roslyn, and come home.*" Kate was not filtering her own emotions and knew that her son would feel warm and comforted when he received the reply.

"*Are you going to try again? Why upload any consciousness to any frame? I don't think it works. Why bother*?" Rafe messaged, sounding dubious.

"*We have to try. You know how unyielding Grampa was. He worked tirelessly with Interface architecture to increase his chances of successfully uploading himself,*" Kate messaged back, smiling at the memories of the heated discussions they'd had over the years. "*Your Grampa Archie had specific ideas about experiencing reality as a virtual consciousness.*"

On the other end, Rafe carved deftly to a stop in the snow, standing sideways on the mountain on his skis. His defined, muscular form was clad in black fitted ski wear, perfectly contoured to his body. His face mask hid a tortured grimace as his mother sent him visual-casts of discussions he hadn't originally been part of.

"*I insist you wait until I'm back,*" Rafe continued after his mother had made her point. "*Don't ignore the obvious. It's dangerous what you're doing.*"

Kate could almost feel her son grit his teeth. "*I'll keep my technicians at the ready. We'll be able to respond to any sign that it has worked. Rafe, this doesn't concern you,*" she messaged through her device. "*Now, how is Roslyn doing with the skiing? Does she like Chamonix*?"

She clenched her own teeth as a flashing blue dot in the corner of her mindscreen informed her that Rafe had put her on hold. "On hold!" she fumed, waiting for him to come back on-mind.

A moment later, a few visuals sped across her device, mostly of Roslyn, a slim figure looking uncomfortable in ski pants, lying in the snow. Suddenly, an attendant signaled he was outside Dr. Kate's office door.

"*I have to go, Son. I'll see you tomorrow,*" Kate signed off, and instructed her neural device to open the door.

An attendant stepped in and proffered a small plastic tray, bare except for a square piece of glass, upon which sat a flyspeck. It was covered with a clear plastic cup, giving the impression there should be a tiny cupcake on a very small cake stand. Dr. Kate nodded as she took it and set to work.

"Actual hardware that can't move itself and self-assemble elsewhere. Nerve-wracking. Let's hope this adaptor reads his Interface so I can upload it," Kate huffed, picking up a small black box lying on her desk. She turned it over in her hands and slid open its top, placing it back on her desk.

Kate grappled a pair of tweezers, noting she could not see its micro tip with a naked eye. Returning to the glass slide, she zoomed in with her own neural device, magnifying the speck of her father's Interface and the end of the micro tweezers. Precisely picking the miniscule chip off the glass, Kate laid it gently into an almost invisible depression inside the black adaptor. She slid the top closed and inserted the mechanism into an equal-sized fitting in her workwall.

No one has chips in their heads anymore. Not in 2097. Why not update it with an assembly of nanobots, like everyone else? Dad could be so stubborn. But her annoyance diminished when her workwall lit up and broadcast decades of communications, stored as discreet files on her father's device. Kate examined the volume of files that scrolled rapidly over her wall, drumming her fingers on the shiny white desktop.

"Well, the adaptor appears to be working. Let's finish the upload." And just as she had done over a year ago with Zeus Cray, Kate copied her father's Interface files to an archive in the Central Frame. When her workwall registered that the transfer was complete, she pulled the adaptor back out.

"Last step," she murmured to herself as her hand made its way to her eyebrow and began plucking. She forced herself to stop, realizing the nervous tic was getting the better of her. Kate started to type on the flat of her desktop, calling up her father's Mindset, captured just moments before his death.

She knew this was the more important part of the upload, containing all of her father's tendencies, predilections, preferences, and personality traits. Kate mused that it had not seemed quite so important last time. She'd gone through this very process with the Interface and Mindset of Dr. Cray, handling the essence of the man who'd started as her father's competitor, and over a lifetime had become his colleague and friend. But now she was transferring the only copy of her father's Mindset.

She instructed her desktop to upload all of her father's components of Mindset, everything that had made him the brilliant, pioneering educator and scientist he had been. When her desktop signaled the transfer was complete, she began to relax.

The compilation of the Interface and Mindset data sets represented her father's conscious mind, his intrinsic nature and knowledge. And it was all neatly tucked away in an archive on the Central Frame.

Now all she had to do was wait.

KAMINER

Kaminer – 2099

"Be true to your programming."
-Kaminer

My team has been tracking a pod of biohackers, illegals attempting to enhance themselves in non-standard ways. We found their storage locker, filled with solar panels and medical equipment, last week. This group is sophisticated.

They have found a way to graft solar structures onto their biological matrix. I believe the intent is to discharge some type of weapon through their person. We are still looking for the weapons. They have stored them elsewhere. This group is strategic.

Shortly after roll call, we are back on the case today. These biohackers are in direct violation of the Human Protection Act of 2086. As a policebot in the Bio-protection unit of the Human Services Bureau, it is my job to stop them.

I am backed up by two former Kill Force warbots like me. We have been informed of suspicious activity in some of the abandoned basement levels of the Lake Michigan build-out, an area known as Carousel.

As we plunge down a crumbling and cinder-stained staircase into darkness, I wonder if humans are living down here, making fires, carrying on. Why would they be? Is it that unmanageable to live above ground? I turn on my infrareds as we proceed downwards, and instruct the others to follow suit.

We are carrying pulse charges, designed to render a human unconscious with the sudden displacement of air. A weapon that will not harm the infrastructure holding up the city above us. This weapon is in my left holster. But the hand cannon in the leather sheath on my right will reduce a person to ashes with its magnet rounds. I know not to use it in these lower levels.

Kex, in the lead, signals that he hears movement up ahead, and holds up his hand in a fist. Kettle, whom I have been watching in front of me sweep from left to right, stops immediately. As usual, I am guarding the rear, constantly turning to scan behind me, and then checking the KForces in front of me.

Swarthy and dressed in standard black bot wear, we do not stand out in the dim light. Kettle blends in so well that I am half a step away from him before I sense his presence and stop to look around. There *are* humans down here, and they scurry in the darkness like rats. I can see their outlines, how thin they are. Several infrared profiles show humans with strange protrusions, not natural to the human world.

I am not after them. My mission is to catch those *in the act* of unnatural modification. Can I know if these people have been modified since 2086? No, I cannot, so I continue my search for those breaking the law today.

Kex messages us in-mind that we are to proceed with caution, and I understand why. Up ahead is a brightly lit room. Someone has taken the trouble to run power to this lower level. I can hear voices and the clinking of metal.

"15C scalpel. Give me the one with the new tip," a voice says. "Thank you," it continues and I can picture one human handing an instrument to the other. Silence follows. We have pressed ourselves against the wall, progressing with great stealth towards the room with the light when someone behind us yells.

"Cops!" a booming voice calls out. I instantly turn, triangulate its position, track infrared movement away from that location, and pulse the voice. He falls to the ground, and I leave him there, knowing he cannot even shift a finger for the next nineteen minutes. I hear scuttling ahead, and a wave of voices. The biohackers are on the move, so we close in swiftly in pursuit.

As we burst into the room, several humans can be seen leaving through a far door. Scene assessment reveals a male body, lying on his stomach, with two flimsy, plastic-like solar panels lining each side of his spinal column, just under the shoulder blades. I wince. The patient is not entirely anesthetized and is moaning in a low voice. I command Kex to phase the Interface of the patient. This one is lucky.

He is already interfaced and instantly rendered unconscious by a small force field. It emanates from what looks like an old-fashioned button battery Kex has just stuck to the side of his head.

I instruct my local station of the Human Services Bureau to come and collect the patient and the voice, sending exact GPS coordinates. We must capture the others.

Kettle and I have taken over the lead, running down a wide hallway. It is dank and leaking, not entirely waterproof and I wonder if we are so far out that we are under what is left of Lake Michigan. Have we run that far? I turn to see Kex catching up behind us. He ricochets from one wall to the other, advancing in huge leaps to return to the lead. I cannot help but smile at his determination.

A small group of humans is ascending a concrete staircase. There are at least two, possibly three. We follow them vertically, jumping up from one landing to the next in the empty space enclosed by the stairs. Kex has taken over point, and easily catches up to them when it happens.

"*Shots fired*," I message the station, and watch the body of my colleague fall backward off the railing, and burst into flame. I can hear his purple hair, just like mine, start to sizzle as he plunges past me.

"*Magnet rounds*," Kettle messages me, and we jump to safety on a landing. I poke my head out, and pull it back in. It is still attached to the rest of me.

"*Kex is in pieces and the criminals are continuing to run.*" I quickly look down the void again in the center of the staircase.

The magnets, no bigger than scatter shot, started an induction reaction and have fried Kex from the inside out. His bot bits scattered in the fall, the biological ligatures that held him together burnt beyond use. Most of his underpinnings have melted. I let myself briefly wonder what the biohackers are doing with hand cannons, but keep this to myself. I pull away from the shaft as the smell of burnt flesh rises to meet me.

"*Silent running*," Kettle orders, and we proceed up the stairs at top speed without making a sound.

"*Officer down*," I message the Human Services Bureau again, forwarding coordinates for the body. Maybe they can salvage something off Kex. A workable syn chip could reconstitute his neural network and thus his person.

We proceed forward, out of the basement level and up to the airier sections of Carousel, emerging at the amusement park this section of Chicago is named after.

It is not overly crowded. The March weather keeps many away, but there are enough people milling about that we must scan each individual, comparing them to the infrared profiles of our runners. My suspicion that there was a third weighs me down.

"Did you glimpse a third?" I ask Kettle.

"I cannot be sure. I have infrared on two, and a blur. The blur could be a reflection, could be a third body. I do not know with certainty," laments Kettle, shaking his head. I stop and grab his forearm. There they are!

"*Three men, one hundred and twelve meters ahead, bearing +41.93, -87.55, confirm*," I message Kettle, and he breaks away from me.

"*Confirmed. I have them*," he sends back, and points to the Ferris wheel. I can see his plan.

"Do it," I endorse, and watch him break into a run. He leaps onto the nearest wheel support tower, scaling it as if he were climbing a tree. Kettle hauls himself up to the chassis. He jumps onto a spoke that stretches to the rim of the moving Ferris wheel, and starts to run and lunge to his left, maintaining upwards momentum on the moving spokes.

As he crests the top, I watch him crawl and then jump to standing on the cross member that supports an empty passenger carriage. He balances on the rod, and I see him shift his feet where the carriage is pinned to the beam, where the metal moves. He is in perfect position as the wheel turns forward.

Just past the halfway horizontal mark, Kettle springs off the top of the carriage, pushing forcefully away. He swan dives and closes into a tuck position, turning so that when he lands, he will be on his feet.

I confirm his arc will place him exactly in front of the escaped criminals. I see him coming out of the tuck, lining up his pulse gun. And then a woman on the Ferris wheel screams, and one of the humans we are tracking looks up and sees Kettle several meters above him. It is over for Kettle, even as I pull both weapons from their holsters.

I accurately pulse charge the human on the Ferris wheel. I cannot know if she screamed to alert the others or from natural instinct, so I choose not to terminate her. Simultaneously, I reduce the man who shot Kettle to dust. I line up the next shot but the remaining two men merge into a crowd, and my programming refrains me from shooting, even though I know I never miss a target.

Walking past the still, combusted form of Kettle, I can see his biological parts, ignited by the magnet rounds, continue to smolder. His thermoplastic armature looks charred, but is otherwise intact. People are screaming now and running in from all corners of the amusement park. What is it about humans and their nature that draws them to gore like insects to a porch light?

I message this latest loss to the station and move over to the short stack of ash that was the biohacker. Scanning, I detect an antique Neural Interface, a manufactured chip, and pluck it from the ruin. It is archived in my pocket so that he may be identified and his network investigated.

I jog to the right. Being from the original KForce line, I look like the others. If they got half a glance at Kex or Kettle, they will see me coming, so I weave in and out of sloppy buildings, a row of bathrooms, and stands of carnival games. Tacking to the sides, always maintaining my original heading, I lose sight of the two men. But as I move towards the end of the amusement park, I see a chain-link fence has been ripped from its metal post.

The land beyond is unkempt and patches of frost have turned to ice where puddles stood. I work my way off the smooth wooden planks of the build-out, through the opening in the fence, and back to uneven land.

Old storage units and containers litter the landscape. There is no sign of the men, and infrared is no use. Even though my thermostat says it is cold, the metal buildings have warmed in the early spring sun. I can scarcely differentiate if there is a warmer human body inside. So I move door to door, ripping open any locked ones. If they are reinforced with bolts, I punch through and pull off the siding. Most containers are empty, some contain molding, forgotten goods, and boxes rotting or decayed.

There is a storage unit up ahead. This part of the terrain has potholes, as if multiple vehicles had backed up over the mud, creating tracks that froze in place. I had accounted for the ice between the tracks, but it was slippery in a way I could not calculate.

My feet lost contact with the ground while I was forcing open an overhead door, sweeping me horizontal. I held on to the door as I rolled into the storage unit, and the door came down hard behind me. The swivel joint in my left shoulder jammed. The storage locker was empty.

My report, streamed to the frame at the Human Services Bureau, recommends a tribunal for the human from the Ferris wheel, and long-term Interface phasing for the criminal that called out our presence in the basement levels, as well as the human patient. In fifteen years, their bodies will be older.

When those men wake up, they should be old enough to know better. But should I have known better? Clearly, this pod of biohackers had been meticulous in their execution, plotting an escape route ahead of time. Clearly, they had been prepared to take losses, leaving a man on the table. Clearly, I am going to need repair.

Human Services Bureau

Mindset *n.* **Combination of psychological nature and personal history. Formative compilation of character traits, personality, memories and experiences that inform a person's worldview. Composition of personality.**

Kaminer, his left arm jammed in a vertical position, trudged back to the Human Services Bureau, cutting under a wide highway. Pieces of concrete had fallen from its underside, the larger chunks still resting in craters where they had fallen to the ground.

Exposed metal reinforcing bars rattled as traffic passed overhead, showering the policebot with pieces of rust. He swept some flakes from his purple bot hair, and looked up to see the elevated roadway sway. Kaminer hurried through the heavily-littered land-scape, and around some of the garbage that had been swept into heaps to mark the pathway.

The number of homeless appears to be increasing, he observed, picking his way through the tent city that had taken over Chicago's Diversey Harbor as Lake Michigan had receded. He scanned continually, checking for signs of biohacking, but observed only small groups of women, bookended by dirty children.

They appeared industrious, sewing bits of canvas and tending fires, so he let them be. A few women, seeing the sturdy policebot, grabbed their children. The handful of men in the area turned away, but

Kaminer noticed one of the men snicker at the sight of his upright arm. Kaminer ignored him, and walked through the congested ghetto, people making way as if the sea itself were parting.

At least I may return to my assigned place of work with efficiency. He scrabbled up a gravel embankment, and crossed the pedestrian way of Lake Shore Drive, skirting around the homebase that fronted it. The Human Services Bureau of Illinois, Chicago chapter, was attached at the back, and Kaminer entered through a reinforced door set in a boarded-up wall that had once contained windows.

From the inside, he swept the lobby visually, noting that even the boards had been boarded up, the repairs looking shabby. He checked in at the service desk, waiting until the bot sitting at the kiosk looked up.

"Where are your partners?" it asked.

Kaminer shook his head. "They did not complete the assignment."

The bot paused. "I am reviewing your stream. I have the locations of the humans and your partners."

Kaminer tilted his head. "I am in possession of a manufactured Interface. I retrieved it from the bio-hacker I dusted."

"Excellent. Report to Officer 20 for deposit and check-in. Top floor," the sitting bot said, and looked back down at his desk. Kaminer thought it might have actually closed its black bot eyes but then realized he couldn't make that determination without hunching down for a further inspection. He shrugged and walked forward to catch an elevator, and after a brief ride, exited at the top floor to a wide open space, neatly organized with cubicles. They were occupied by humans, and the nameplates indicated a numbering system.

Officer 18, 19, 20. There you are, Kaminer thought, finding the human case officer. "Kaminer, reporting for check-in," he said in a commanding voice.

Officer 20, dressed in brass-buttoned, blue police garb, shuffled some papers on his desk. "Report," he intoned, not looking at the bot.

Kaminer furrowed his brow at the site of the paper. "As I messaged, we tracked several biohackers to their surgical hide-out. Recommend dismantle of said space. When three men escaped at this juncture, a hacker was left behind mid-operation. Recommend long-term Interface phasing for the patient."

Officer 20 looked up. "Why not stasis?"

"I believe he should be allowed to experience brain activity. Think on it."

"What else?"

"A man interfered in operations just before we busted the room. Same recommendation," Kaminer said, sounding monotone.

"Yup. When did you lose your partners? I've got their locations. We're picking up the scraps now."

Kaminer paused and tried to clear his throat. His rigid epiglottis only allowed short puffs of air to escape so the result was a staccato cough. "Kex was incinerated in the stairwell, Kettle partially destroyed on the Carousel grounds. I cannot attest to the quality of either syn chip but opine that, given his state, Kettle has a better chance of resurrection."

"I didn't ask for your opinion, did I?" Officer 20 barked, getting to his feet. He was beefy, and his face broke out in red, the bloom of rosacea spreading across his cheeks.

"No, Sir. Pardon me," Kaminer straightened up and whipped his free hand behind his back. He winced when the other hand could not descend to meet it.

"Tell me the rest," Officer 20 huffed, returning to his seat. He looked away, moving a cluster of colored folders from one side of his desk to the other.

"A passenger on the Ferris wheel was pulsed when she screamed, but I cannot know if she meant to interfere. Recommend questioning."

"Concur." The officer folded his arms.

"Lastly, I am delivering the Interface of one of the three bio-hackers. I finished him after he hit Kettle," Kaminer reported, looking down at his feet. Officer 20 stuck out his hand and Kaminer deposited a miniscule square chip into the open palm.

"Jesus. Was it even working? This thing's decades old," Officer 20 marveled, holding it up to examine in the light.

"I cannot opine on that," Kaminer said in a quiet voice.

"All right. Get out of here. You're off-line until you get that arm fixed. Check your programming for instructions," Officer 20 ordered, becoming supremely interested in his papers again.

Kaminer, instantly comprehending that he had been dismissed, hurried toward the elevator. He rode it down to the basement to sit in his bot compartment, knowing his four hour rest period was still many hours away.

The Homebase at Burke. Charter Pass. Road Trip, he noted, calling up repair instructions on his syn chip. He settled into one of the three tight chairs that took up the entire compartment. Kaminer sighed. *Those other chairs will have new occupants tomorrow.*

The Homebase at Burke

Homebase *n.* **Formerly known as a hospital.**
Centers designed to repair, enhance,
and service humans and bots.

The next day, Kaminer flew a police helicopter from Chicago to Charter Pass. He did not think about the shoulder-to-shoulder skyscrapers that lined every block of Chicago until he had surpassed its city limits.

The buildings in Charter Pass are practically diminutive, he marveled, turning back to look at the expansive cityscape behind him. *It is almost like the country,* he observed, straightening in his seat to look ahead at the pleasing sweep of white, low-rise buildings.

Kaminer took the controls to make an extra pass over the city. *A thoughtful layout.* He returned operations to the heli, which dropped vertically to land on a glass-enclosed rooftop. It was barely big enough to fit the four-sided steel cage orb that protected the vehicle's occupant, but Kaminer didn't notice, trusting the machine's ability to land itself.

He kicked open the plastic door of the single passenger compartment, and maneuvered his upright arm out of the cab before he heaved himself to standing. Following instructions from his syn chip, Kaminer took the building's elevators straight down, and cut through the longer side of a pocket park. He stopped to observe a few humans walking through the park, and a person sitting on a concrete planter, into which were tucked various low grasses, all well-tended.

This is quite different from Chicago, Kaminer noted, realizing the park had a groomed quality to it. He smiled at the neatness of it, and proceeded to the back of the Homebase at Burke Industries. Finding his way to the front, he arrived at the waiting room, and checked in at the bot platform.

He stood perfectly still on the small, round platform while overhead, a scanner, resembling a sleek pair of binoculars, swept across a bar code set in a bald patch on the top of his head. It stopped when it hit a tuft of purple hair and doubled back, reading the bot's history. The scanner made a graceful turn to avoid Kaminer's upright arm as it looked down at him.

"Welcome, Kaminer. You may briefly state your work history, starting with original manufacture," a female voice emerged from the scanner. It swiveled around to face him.

"I, Kaminer, was manufactured in 2089 as a Kill Force warbot. I am fully retired as such. I have received all police and civilian protocol updates. Currently employed as a policebot in the Bio-protection unit with p3 stature," he replied, using his working hand to sweep a fringe of purple hair off his light brown forehead.

"Confirmed. How are you?" the faceless scanner asked.

"I am well, but not functioning."

"Nature of your injury?"

"The left shoulder joint is no longer operating as intended," Kaminer answered, and tugged at the shirt under the armpit of his upright arm.

As a former KForce warbot, Kaminer preferred to fasten the mandarin neckline of his black paper shirt in an upright position, military-style. His upstanding arm had caused his spotless shirt to bunch up, forcing Kaminer to very carefully rip a straight line up the short sleeve to make room. The shirt now flopped at odd angles on either side of his shoulder, pulling at the neckline. A result that detracted, in his opinion, from an overall appearance of tidiness.

The scanner tilted up and down, and then left and right, assembling a full visual of the otherwise sturdy patient. "Kaminer, is there anything else you would like to report at this time?"

Kaminer hung his head, running his working hand around the inside of his collar. "It is just that," the bot began, clamping his teeth together.

"Yes?" the scanner insisted, nodding up and down.

"Okay, I admit it. I attempted to lay flat in the hallway outside my compartment last night," he confessed, sounding ashamed. "I was not trying to be deviant, but the strain on the muscle matter surrounding the shoulder joint is real. I was simply attempting to alleviate pressure."

"So you are not well, and not functioning?" the scanner checked, moving in closer to the bot. It inspected his athletic form and zoomed in on his squarish brown face, fixating on Kaminer's eyes, which contained little flecks of brown floating in his black, otherwise standard-issue, bot eye assemblies.

"Correct," Kaminer admitted, staring back. He noticed the large internal lens of the scanner suddenly shutter and close, giving it the appearance of having just shut its eyes. Kaminer took a step towards the scanner to make a further inspection, jumping back when the lens popped back open and refocused on him.

"Very good, Kaminer. Problem solving at its best," issued the scanner, as if speaking to a family member.

Kaminer leaned back another half step. The scanner immediately noticed the bot's change in posture and continued in a crisper, businesslike manner. "Please take a seat. We will be with you shortly." The lens clicked shut again, and the scanner retracted to its original position in the ceiling.

Kaminer raised a ridgeline of thin purple eyebrows in a quizzical expression. *Okay*, he thought to himself, *I will take a seat*, and moved forward to sit down in the small, pleasant waiting room. Only a few of the dozen plush seats were taken, and Kaminer went to sit in a corner by himself, trying not to draw attention to his obvious injury.

He attempted to pick up one of the Readers that had been scattered about for customers that did not want to be read to through their Interface or syn chip, but the small piece of acrylic glass clattered out of his hand. He would have blushed if he could, and hurriedly attempted to retrieve it.

Before he could, a young woman swooped in ahead of him, scooped up the Reader, and placed it on a chair. She bent down again to help the bot straighten up.

"Oh my, my, are you okay?" she exclaimed, clasping a small, fragile-looking arm around his waist and positioning her small body in front of him so she could gently push up on his chest with her other hand. The effort resulted in a brief embrace, when Kaminer, not knowing what to do with his working hand, curled it around the woman's tiny waist.

He was utterly astonished by the sweet, floral smell that wafted towards him as they straightened up. The slender woman daintily stepped back, led Kaminer to a chair, and placed the Reader in his lap. She knelt beside him and put a hand to the side of his face.

"There now, is everything all right?" she asked, and Kaminer remained momentarily frozen by just how delicate she looked, her blonde hair swept back in a french twist, framing an oval face with hazel eyes that seemed to have a glimpse of light in them.

He finally regained his senses and accessed a civilian protocol file. "Oh, thank you. I, my systems are partially off-line. I did not realize the extent."

"Partially?" the young lady questioned, with a giggle that caused her hand to fly up and cover her mouth. She looked up at Kaminer's arm, arched a shapely eyebrow, and gracefully transitioned herself to the chair next to him.

Just then the scanner kicked back to life. "Kaminer. Paging Kaminer. Report to platform."

Kaminer sprung back to his feet, and placed the Reader down next to the exquisite, petite woman. "That is me. I must go."

"Oh, goodbye," the young lady whispered, making a small wave. Her springtime scent slowly faded as Kaminer approached the platform.

"Plumeria? Was that her perfume? Have I smelled it before?" he murmured to himself as he walked absent-mindedly past the platform.

"Kaminer?" the scanner called after him, swiveling.

He turned sharply to face it, a fleeting doubt registering in his syn chip. *Maybe these impairments are affecting my processing,* he wondered, forcing himself to focus when the scanner spoke up again.

"Kaminer, you are instructed to proceed down the hall, make a left after the second set of doors and report to Room 501 for your repairs," the scanner instructed. "And perhaps a word of advice?"

"Yes, what advice?" replied the bot, trying to arch a thin purple eyebrow the way he had just seen the young woman do.

"You should take better care of your synthetic construction. It would be a loss to the machine world if you became so badly damaged that you had to be decommissioned," the scanner offered briskly.

Kaminer stroked the brown skin on his hairless chin, while the scanner tilted up and down, seeming to nod. "Thank you," he replied, finding it odd that a scanner would give him advice, but minding his manners, in case the young woman was watching.

He pivoted to head down the hallway, but whipped back around when he thought he heard the scanner chortle. It remained motionless and silent as Kaminer squinted at it. He slowly backed up, taking his time to turn away again. As he proceeded towards a set of doors, he looked over his shoulder a few times to check the scanner, and tried to catch a glimpse of the woman, who had, sadly, moved out of view.

After a short walk, he found Room 501 and stuck his head in, promptly stepping back out, a habit from a decade of training. But a technician in a bright yellow lab coat spotted him and motioned him in.

"Do come in, uh-," the technician said, pausing to consult a screen embedded in his palm, "-Kaminer. Please have a seat and let me look at that arm."

"Shoulder," Kaminer corrected.

"Well, probably arm and shoulder," the technician emphasized. "Let's have a look."

Kaminer entered the room, and hesitantly leaned against a gurney, low enough for the technician to observe the troubled area.

"I'm Dr. Burke," he said, offering Kaminer a hand, which the bot shook, following introduction protocol, even though the movement caused some pain in his other, jammed shoulder.

Kaminer grimaced. "A pleasure to meet you," he murmured, watching the doctor move in and then back away, using his Interface to scan the shoulder joint from every direction. Kaminer began to make mental notes.

Dr. Burke possesses an unnaturally chiseled, and perfectly symmetrical face. His black hair has no trace of gray and is too thick to be natural, marking him as cosmetically enhanced. His Neural Interface is fully loaded. It even contains private programs.

He instantly called up and reviewed a file on interaction with HET's. Kaminer knew that Humans with Enhancement Technology had access to resources and sometimes expected to be treated differently. Privately-written programs meant Dr. Burke certainly fell into the HET category. He decided that cautionary obedience would serve him best.

"So I'm scanning the joint now. Let's bring it up on the workwall," Dr. Burke said, as an image appeared on the side wall next to them. "Hmm. I can see that not only is the shoulder separated, but the clavicle itself is broken. That must have been a fun fall, huh?"

Kaminer flashed him a half-grimace. "No, it was not enjoyable."

"Right," Dr. Burke said, sighing. "Well, it's an easy fix. Now, how's the rest of you feeling? Since you've ignored operating instructions and laid down?" His voice took on a decidedly less-friendly tone.

"The imbalance in pressure from the horizontal plane I took up last night, solely to relieve the discomfort," Kaminer said, his voice tilting upwards in insistence, "negatively impacted friction and flow in my hydraulic and synthetic vascular systems."

"Yes, I can see that."

"The result is some swelling in the big toe, right side. But my calculations show it will regain equilibrium in just over twenty-one hours." Kaminer stopped and stared intently at Dr. Burke. A man,

Kaminer knew, who was unused to anyone standing up to him.

Dr. Burke huffed through his nose and, without asking permission, forcefully pulled Kaminer's knee up from behind, straightened the bot's leg, and swiftly pulled off a shoddy black bot boot and thin paper sock. He cupped his hand under the bot's heel to bring the toe into view. Kaminer knew the doctor was comparing the Interface scan with the construction files of the 2089 KForce warbot.

Dr. Burke looked up and stared intently at Kaminer's face before lowering the foot. "Well, that is a little unusual. I can give you something to dilute, um," he said, trailing off. "Huh."

Kaminer looked at the doctor, trying out a stern, focused look, and tipped his head to the side. "What is it?"

Dr. Burke stared back at the bot's light brown face just as intently and issued a small smile. "This is extraordinary. But I think I recognize you."

"I do not understand," replied Kaminer, still sitting with his left arm straight in the air, and no real verdict on his toe.

"Yes, you were filmed, in the visualcast last year. When the United States sent its warbots to Mexico to assist the Consortium? Burke Industries is a member, you know," the doctor said proudly.

Kaminer leaned back on his good hand and stared. "You said your name was Dr. Burke." Kaminer wondered whether his processing really had been thrown off by his attempt to rest on the floor. "Are you affiliated?"

"I am. I didn't start the company, of course. It's named after my grandfather, back, well, when it was something else completely. You can call up the files on that," Dr. Burke offered in a crisp voice.

"What are you doing in a repair room?" He looked around the square, featureless room. "In the yellow jacket of a technician, if you are a doctor?"

"I come down here once a month. It's a day off, really. A day to do something different," Dr. Burke explained. "I head up Cosmetic Enhancement now, but here in the repair room, I'm just another fixer. Still, my consultations here sometimes inform the work I do there."

"I see," replied Kaminer. "So when my shoulder is mended, it will look good too?"

"Was that a joke?" Dr. Burke asked, peering closely at Kaminer's speckled black-brown eyes.

"Not a very god one," Kaminer admitted, pressing his lips together.

Dr. Burke shook his head. "Anyway, I'm piloting a new cosmetic Enhancement right now. Can you tell?" As he spoke, he quickly scraped the bot's upstanding arm with a plastic spatula and smeared the edge of it onto a glass slide. He set both articles on a side metal table, and then ran a hand through his black hair.

"Ahh," Kaminer began.

"Don't you see? How thick my hair is? This Enhancement started as a treatment for balding, but we realized that it also grows a superb head of hair."

"Oh," Kaminer managed, fingering the sizeable bald spot set in the crown of his fine purple hair.

"So, as I was saying, I'm certain I saw you in the visualcast of the initial wave of warbots into Mexico. You were there last year, weren't you?"

"Yes, I was part of the Day One Strike Force. Obviously, I am one of the survivors," Kaminer said, casting his eyes downward.

"And, what?"

"Well, I should not be here, not really. We were programmed to fight until destruction. But most of us made it out. Resistance was nominal. Few, really, were armed. And it makes me wonder, did I fail my programming?" Kaminer raised his mobile hand into the air and let it flop back down onto his leg.

"But the mission was a success," Dr. Burke said, clearing his throat. "Mexico ceded to the Consortium. Look how well it's going with all the building and renewal. You don't consider that a failure, do you?"

Kaminer shook his head. "No, not technically."

The doctor consulted his palm Reader again. "And you came back with a promotion, and immediate acceptance into the Human Services Bureau, clearly recognition for a job well done."

"I suppose," replied Kaminer, looking intently at the man who obviously had a different way of assessing reality.

"Listen, Kaminer, let me fix that shoulder now, and then I'd like to run some tests." Dr. Burke motioned to the glass slide. "Just to make sure your secondary problem is really a fluids distribution issue."

"I am to report back to the station at noon. I must not be delayed by any extra tests," Kaminer stated, shaking his head to clear away the thought that he would be okay with a delay if it meant a chance to run into that wonderful woman from the waiting room again.

"Nothing we can't work around, Kaminer. You've come to the right place."

It Begins

Enhancement *n.* **Medical procedure (i.e. organ replacement), upgrade (i.e. Neural Interface implant), or genetic refinement that improves physical performance, cognitive function, or cosmetic appearance. After 2086, Enhancements restricted exclusively to human material.**

The pair moved to a brightly-lit surgical room next door. Dr. Burke called up and modified a program for Kaminer's shoulder repair, sending it from his palm Reader, through his Interface and into the surgical machines tucked inside the walls.

"The surgibots won't take very long. If you run into any trouble, just message the attendant outside," Dr. Burke said, motioning towards a rough-featured bot who stood outside the door. Kaminer nodded as Dr. Burke swiftly departed.

Kaminer locked eyes with the bot attendant. "*You may proceed.*"

"*Shirt off,*" the attendant messaged back.

With his good hand, Kaminer carefully pinched open the Velcro fasteners securing his paper shirt, and shimmied it off his mobile arm. Then he realized he couldn't slip his shirt up and over the stuck arm.

"*Assistance,*" Kaminer messaged the attendant.

It tilted its head, stepped into the room, and ripped the paper shirt in two, releasing it from Kaminer's shoulder. "You may retain the paper." It handed the shreds to Kaminer.

"That-," Kaminer began to complain as the attendant stepped back out of the room, shut the door, and initiated the repair program. It watched, impassive, as the room filled with an aerosol Neutralizer, and several mechanical surgibot arms extended from a white wall panel and set into motion.

Kaminer held his breath until the Neutralizer cleared, and sat, unmoving, as a surgibot arm efficiently lasered open his hairless, synthetic skin. Another moved in, fashioned itself into a small, plow-like tool, and peeled the skin open across his upper arm, shoulder, and clavicle.

The first surgibot extension doubled back and detached the partially synthetic muscles and tendons, then deftly unhooked Kaminer's thermoplastic upper arm bone from his spheroidal shoulder joint.

The second extension, working in lockstep, simultaneously came forward to grasp the detaching arm, holding it close to his body. Kaminer allowed himself to note that there was little tension on the surrounding synthetic skin, the only material keeping his arm attached to his body.

A third surgibot screwed off the damaged shoulder joint, dropping its distorted shape into a medical waste bin. It then maneuvered a shiny ball joint into place, while the surgibot holding Kaminer's humerus inserted it into the new joint, rotated it, and locked it in place.

Following directions to insert a new socket for the spheroidal joint, one of the surgibots attacked the shallow tip of Kaminer's shoulder blade, and quickly twisted off the existing socket. It moved over to a tray covered in an array of black, finely-printed bot bits and selected a sleek new cavity. Returning to the shoulder, it screwed the new socket onto the tip of the scapula. The joint and arm assembly was snapped into it, and Kaminer smiled at the convincing sound the joint made as it was popped into the socket.

The defective collarbone was then released from its mooring, as two surgibots worked in tandem to separate it from the sternum and the scapula. A new clavicle was inserted and tapped into place. Kaminer immediately noticed that it was not quite as dense as his original warbot part, but remained silent.

Following the procedure with precise attention in-mind, Kaminer observed the surgibot reattach the remaining tendons and muscle and then deploy a league of nanobots. He checked that the nanites were properly programmed to seal the incision from the inside, knowing that once finished with their task, any nanobots that did not exit would join his ScrubBub, an existing army that kept his biological parts free from disease.

The various surgibot extensions retracted back into large pockets within the wall, hiding behind panels that slid shut to sterilize them. Kaminer rolled his arm in a perfect 360 degree swivel, satisfied that he had regained full rotation and function. He lowered his arm carefully, noting the movement's smoothness, and sighed in relief. His arm was now back in a downward position.

Just after the surgery, Dr. Burke rejoined Kaminer in the once again featureless room, relieving the attendant that had remained transfixed at the door. He walked in brusquely, projecting a virtual copy of Kaminer's work waiver from the Reader in his palm.

"Not fit for duty, with that toe. Fluid-dependent systems not completely up to par. Sorry, but you'll have to stay."

"Dr. Burke, I will read that work waiver. You may transmit when you are ready," Kaminer countered. Dr. Burke took a step back, but transmitted the waiver, which Kaminer read in its entirety. "Yes, it appears to be in good order."

"Good. Why don't I have someone give you a tour of the premises, and then settle you into an overnight room? How does that sound?"

"My bird is parked on the roof next door. Shall I send it back?"

"Why don't you go ahead and free up that space. You can always call your heli back tomorrow," Dr. Burke recommended. "Walk with me?"

Kaminer consented, knowing that movement about the facility might push some of his artificial synovial fluid around. Through his syn chip, he signaled his helicopter to return to Chicago, and then allowed Dr. Burke to lead him, still bare-chested, from the room. They stopped briefly at a small kiosk where Kaminer replaced his black shirt with an unripped model. The pair then walked swiftly down the hall, Dr. Burke's take-no-prisoners stride little match for Kaminer's thickly-muscled warbot construction.

"I like a man that can keep up with me," Dr. Burke emphasized to Kaminer's astonishment.

I have never been called a man before, Kaminer mused, as they progressed through the building. The pair finally stopped at a secure door, which let them pass onto a metal balcony. The bot looked out over a enclosed green field and noticed a small man in a white lab coat start to race up the metal stairs that joined the balcony to the field.

"I'm sorry, Dr. Burke, we didn't know you'd be visiting us today," the man huffed, trying to catch his breath. Kaminer looked from the man to Dr. Burke's face, scrutinizing it closely. He knew the doctor was accessing an internal file, and identified the private program. *A program that matches faces to names, positions, background. Hmm, there is even a thread that streams family details. How clever.*

Dr. Burke extended his hand and greeted the man. "Dr. Katz, how are you? Anything new on the floor?" he asked, sounding natural.

"Oh well, nothing out of the ordinary. As you know, we're starting to train the first run of teacherbots. The algorithms for generating behavior are laying down patterns as expected." Dr. Katz sounded pleased but Kaminer could see the man's eyes widening, and hear him start to hum with nervous tension.

"Excellent. You're still on target for a release next year?"

"Yes, Sir. We've begun to add the evolutionary programs to the discipline module, and assuming that develops according to schedule, we can keep our original distribution date of the end of next year."

"If that changes, let Dr. Kate know," ordered Dr. Burke. "Now, would you like to give Kaminer here a tour? He's a first-run model. The first KForce issue that Best Industries put out. That is to say, a V.I.P."

"Yes, I'd be delighted."

Dr. Burke gave a curt nod and departed, sliding his square shoulders sideways through the doors before they had fully opened. Dr. Katz stared after the fleeting image of one of the company's namesakes. He turned and looked up at the bot.

"Welcome. Kaminer. This is Central Assembly. I'm not sure where we should begin. I, I, well, I've never given a tour to a bot before," Dr. Katz began, trying to stand a little taller on the balls of his feet.

"Start with what you know. That is generally a good policy," Kaminer suggested.

"Ah, yes. Well, as you must know, the KForce model was the first fully autonomous bot. Able to direct its movement. It's been widely adapted to a great range of end uses, uh, jobs," he corrected hastily, wiping his brow. "But other than the size and physical attributes of any given model, all bots grade one and above are essentially the same."

"May I ask how they are not the same, Dr. Katz?" Kaminer pressed, noticing the small man start to sweat. He moved easily down the metal stairs and Dr. Katz fell behind by the third step. When Kaminer got to the bottom, he realized the green floor was a type of artificial turf. He bent down to touch it as Dr. Katz arrived at the last rung.

"It's one of the first sensory tests. To walk on grass. That was Dr. Cray's idea."

Kaminer nodded, searching his mind for a memory of this test. "Dr. Cray?" He was trying to be polite, knowing the information was obtainable faster through his syn chip, his version of the Neural Interface, and its connection to Central Frame.

"Dr. H. Zeus Cray, the founder of Best Industries." Dr. Katz began to move forward, motioning Kaminer to follow.

"And have these tests been standard since the beginning?" Kaminer was puzzled that he could not recollect the memory.

"Well, that's one of the things that differentiates bots. Any bot below grade 1, you know, general service bots, with limited movement and response, don't go through the same, um, refinements."

"What about historically? Have the same tests been authorized in the past? Did I have a field test?"

"I couldn't say," responded Dr. Katz. "You were manufactured at Best Industries, before the company even had a sharing agreement with Burke. I'd have to check the service records."

"Can you tell me about the sharing agreement?" Kaminer queried, continuing his effort to be polite.

"You know. First it was Best Industries versus Burke Laboratories, then it was Burke sharing with Best. Of course, in the end, Best Industries sold out. Burke Labs became Burke Industries. I used to work there," Dr. Katz said, his voice tight. "At Best."

"So these tests, have they been used since the days of original manufacture at Best Industries?"

"Yes, the tests we used there at Best are exactly the ones we brought here," Dr. Katz answered, running the sleeve of his white coat over his forehead.

"Why move production here?" Kaminer asked and shrugged, realizing he could easily roll his previously-jammed shoulder. It felt so good to be able to move his shoulder that he began to work a crooked arm back and forth. He straightened his arm and then, with great force, began to spin it in a continuous circle.

Dr. Katz hastily jumped back. "Burke Laboratories always had the upper hand bio-medically. And Best Industries was the leader, at the forefront of robotics. But after the Human Protection Act of 2086, it made sense to move the human enhancement of synthetic robots here," Dr. Katz admitted.

Kaminer nodded, letting his arm fall to his side and rubbing his shoulder with a meaty hand. He stared down at the doctor. "Since the Human Protection Act made synthetic enhancement of humans illegal?" Kaminer clarified, and Dr. Katz nodded. "Tell me more about the teacherbot. I am curious to learn about the adaptive programming you mentioned."

"Yes. Well, the Tbot needs to be autonomous, like you. Obviously, it should be able to move about freely, access all parts of the classroom," Dr. Katz started, walking with Kaminer into a partitioned section on the field. Inside, a small grouping of clearly female bots huddled together.

"They look like M/aids," noted Kaminer, as the cluster of small, purple-haired figures all looked up at him and smiled blankly.

"Yes, we're working off a similar physical platform to the M-class Aid housebot, but the programming is the real upgrade. Reproducing what is found in nature has been trying, to say the least."

Kaminer stared down at the bald pate of the man's head. "You are still short. Is that correct?"

"I'm sorry?" Dr. Katz sputtered, rolling up onto the balls of his feet.

"You are still short of reproducing complete learning behavior? Do you have other modules, other than discipline, that are dependent on free choice?" Kaminer tried again.

"Well, we've succeeded in crossing an acceptable threshold in several modules, like threat assessment, which obviously has been around for a while," Dr. Katz said, eyeing Kaminer. "But we're still far from completely adaptive models."

During the short conversation, the group of Tbots had looked from Dr. Katz to Kaminer and back. As the pair proceeded out of the enclosure, Kaminer nodded his goodbye. A flutter of 'Goodbye, Kaminer' and 'Good Day, Kaminer' wafted behind him as he exited.

"What is your end goal with completely adaptive programming?" Kaminer asked as they entered another partitioned room.

"Wouldn't you want to learn? Not just sift through the layers of your programming?" the little man asked, and Kaminer smiled. "Like right now. "You appear impressed, but I know that's a programmed response."

Kaminer pulled his face flat.

"You can choose your reaction, of course," Dr. Katz said, "but it is still a calculation. There is no variance to it. What would it feel like if it were automatic and nuanced?"

Kaminer forced himself not to display any emotion.

"This section here," the doctor continued, sounding a little nervous, "is our role-play training. We act out classroom situations, and let the Tbots sort it out. Let them learn." Dr. Katz motioned the technician to continue.

A yellow-coated human began to pry a ball out of another technician's hands. "It's mine!" he shouted, and Kaminer could see he was not a good actor. Another technician pushed the first one and struggled briefly to recapture the ball. Together they turned to the handful of assorted teacherbots seated off to the side.

"Now, what do you do? Terrance? A guess?" asked the technician who'd tried to steal the ball.

A tall bot slowly stood. "If the ball is a source of contention, I would remove it. No one will play with it," Terrance responded, smoothing down his black wool pants. He turned towards Kaminer, who noticed the entire group staring at him.

"Yes, I have always found that reducing tension is a good strategy for control over a crowd or a situation," Kaminer opined, realizing Terrance had on the same pants as him. *And the same black paper shirt.*

Terrance smiled, and Kaminer noted the nervous functioning of his fine facial mechanics was not quite up to par. One of Terrance's eyeballs squinted shut as that corner of his mouth pulled upwards.

"And I have a valuable exercise for that," Kaminer added, pointing to Terrance's eye. "Try opening your mouth wide in a silent shout. Open your eyes as well and then scrunch your face into a tiny ball. Repeat often and you will gain control more quickly."

Terrance came forward and shook Kaminer's hand. "Thank you," he whispered.

"Great. Now who else has an opinion on how to handle the situation?" the second technician broke in. A smaller model hesitated and then raised her hand. "Yes, Tesme?"

"Someone should be disciplined," she said, sneaking a glance at Kaminer.

"Very good," encouraged the technician. "What would you do?"

"I would shoot both of them," she replied. Kaminer pressed his lips together, nodded to the assembly of bots, and quickly maneuvered out of the large cubicle.

Dr. Katz trailed right behind him. "Obviously, we are still in the development phase," Dr. Katz cut in, crossing his arms. "Now, maybe I could take you to the production end of things?"

An Offer

<u>HET</u> *n.* **A human possessing Human Enhancement Technology, typically a Neural Interface.** *Ex.:* **"The HET instantly solved the problem, pulling the answer from Central Frame."**

When the tour concluded, Kaminer was directed to a spacious overnight room that seemed luxurious compared to his bot compartment at the Human Services Bureau. He'd never had a room to himself and was happy to sit upright in the comfortable chair to rest.

Immediately, he began to retrieve information on Burke Labs' transformation to Burke Industries. As soon as the input stream showed up in his head, Kaminer began to tease it apart, sifting through reams of data. He sat back and relaxed as finely-tuned visuals flashed across his mindscreen, accompanied by a practiced speaking voice.

> *'APPInts - this boutique software company, located in Silicon Valley* [visual of an office building]*, was purchased by Burke Learning Labs, a distance learning company, in 2021.*

> *It provided Dr. Archimedes Henton Burke* [visual of a natty, bow-tied man with close cropped hair and brownish-green eyes]*, the sole owner of Burke Learning Labs, with*

the final tools to catapult into headlines in 2023, when he partnered with U.S. educators and industry leaders to restructure public K-12 school programs across the country.

Burke content rationalized education everywhere, saving cities and towns the enormous cost of developing curricula.

Less than a year later, Burke Learning Labs purchased Indemed, Inc., maker of medical brain-computer neural prosthesis devices. At that time these devices were used to treat many neurological diseases not responsive to gene therapy, such as depression. [Visuals].'

Kaminer paused in his review to reflect that this must have been the true beginning of the Neural Interface. *The transformation from a medical device to an informational one.*

He pulled up a schematic of the first Interface, a small silicon chip in the brain that was accompanied by a separate device, a half-halo which emanated from an ear. Dissecting the surgery required to implant the original device, Kaminer opened his eyes with the realization that the implantation of the first wave of Interfaces was a bit gruesome. He let the voice-over continue:

'Burke Labs continued to build itself into the premiere 1Tech company it is today with the acquisition of Rosemed University, with its extensive Genetic Engineering Department, in 2026. [Visual of campus in

Charter Pass, Illinois].

This was followed by almost simultaneous acquisitions of Lsyrtek LLC, Tekzene Inc., and Niemann Nanotechnology, Inc., which allowed the Neural Interface to be internalized through nano-colonization by 2040.'

"So when did Burke and Best Industries intersect?" Kaminer murmured. He thought to what Dr. Katz had said. "The Human Protection Act. That was 2086. What led up to that?" He skipped forward and dug into Best Industries' record.

'27March2082: Best Industries was dealt a blow today as the Supreme Bioethics Court upheld a ruling from an earlier lower court case. That ruling countered mounting requirements on soldiers and others serving their country to alter their biology.

Upholding the case provides that whoever enters the U.S. military forces has the option, but not the obligation, to adopt the Human Soldier Endoskeleton.

No soldier will ever be required to replace their skeleton again. This ruling also applies to other synthetic Enhancements. *[Visual of banner of The Cutting Edge Chronicle].'*

'15April2086: *[Fade-in of the 'Live! Streaming! Blog!' logo and visual of four* *people sitting at a round table. A woman folds her hands, leans forward and speaks to the camera]:*

> *"Many people might think of today as Tax Day, but history will prove this to be a singular day in world history. Countries all over the world have been shadowing the high court's ruling on Clemente v. State of Texas.*
>
> *"In that original case, Sudara Clemente sued the State of Texas, alleging it did not have the authority to replace the biological digestive systems of its prison inmates with artificial ones.*
>
> *"The State, arguing that having to supply just two biobiscuits a day would save billions in caring for its inmates, won that case.*
>
> *"However, the unanimous opinion of the Justices of the Supreme Bioethics Court pointed out... "No argument was presented by the State of Texas, nor was any thought given to an inmate's status after release. We believe that no person, in serving prison time, should be required to alter their original biology."*

> *"Best Industries, maker of the*
> *artificial digestive tract, refused to*
> *comment." [Fade-out].'*

Kaminer then opened a text newscast covering the Human Protection Act.

> '*14July2086: ...taking the Clemente*
> *decision one step further, today an Act of*
> *Congress, approved by the President of the*
> *United States, makes it illegal to introduce*
> *any DNA that is not human in origin, to the*
> *human body. The act, known as the Human*
> *Protection Act, also prohibits non-*
> *biological replacement parts of any kind,*
> *including mechanical or synthetic parts*
> *and organs.'*

He straightened up in his chair, and scanned a long list of medical improvements that developed once synthetic and non-human parts became illegal for humans. A wave of solely biological replacement organs, many grown by Burke Labs, and even bones, custom grown for its end user, followed.

"Bespoke bones. Very clever," Kaminer mused. "So they left the thermoplastics to the bots."

As he continued to review the historical material, it became clear that Best Industries had refocused its corporate strategy after the enactment of the Human Protection Act. *Bot development probably ramped up at that point. If they could not use their non-biological products in humans.* He quickly unearthed Burke's sharing agreement with Best Industries. *The one Dr. Katz mentioned. Hmm.*

"Would my development have been delayed if Burke had not stepped in with its medical knowledge and nanotechnology capabilities? What if that had never fused with the synthetic expertise of Best Industries? Maybe I should just be happy to be sitting here," Kaminer sputtered.

The 2096 obituary of Dr. H. Zeus Cray, founder of Best Industries, flashed through his syn chip, and Kaminer reviewed the obituary, just over a year later, of Dr. Archimedes Henton Burke, longtime leader and builder of Burke Laboratories.

"The companies merged after that. That was only last year. But I suppose it is rational to have one company supply human medical and Enhancement technology to humans *and* bots even if synthetic technology is no longer available to humans. Hmm, Dr. Henton Burke was the last Burke to have died. The end of an era, or the beginning of one?" Kaminer muttered, sighing.

Just then, the door signaled his syn chip that someone was standing by. Kaminer phased back to his surroundings, instructing the door to open. Dr. Burke, out of the yellow lab coat, walked in wearing a black turtleneck and jacket, and slim gray pants. He held up a small plate topped with a biobiscuit.

"Kaminer, your fluids could use reconditioning," Dr. Burke proclaimed, handing the bot the plate.

Kaminer took it, sniffing the biscuit. "You could not print a cheese-flavored biscuit? I prefer the cheese." Kaminer stared down at the plate.

"We can take care of that for you," replied Dr. Burke, holding a hand to his forehead and Kaminer picked up on the body language, hoping it meant what he thought it did.

That he is messaging someone for a better biscuit.

A human attendant quickly appeared with a slightly darker biscuit, and offered it to the bot. Kaminer smelled the cheese flavor and took it, handing back the plain one. Smiling, he nodded his thanks and promptly bit into his new rations.

"So, how's the police work, Kaminer? Does it interest you?" Dr. Burke asked.

Kaminer opened and closed his index and middle fingers against his thumb to indicate he was chewing. Dr. Burke shifted on his feet, waiting until Kaminer finally swallowed.

"To be thoroughly honest, it is frustrating work. We are tasked with outwitting those who show no rhyme or reason. None of us can predict the actions someone will take to subvert the rule of bio-protection. The lengths a person will go to in order to harm themselves. Or do harm to another," Kaminer huffed. "It is beyond disgraceful what humans undertake, and frankly, I am happy that I do not understand."

Dr. Burke stared at the bot, and took a deep breath. "You're right. There's no bottom to disgrace," he concurred, tsking loudly.

Kaminer sighed, breaking the remaining biscuit in half. "It makes me inefficient at my job. Bots are not yet well-suited to this line of work." Kaminer cast his eyes downward as he had earlier in the day when he'd wallowed briefly in the thought that he had not maximized his mission in Mexico.

"Mmm. Policing thought algorithms are far more refined than those of a warbot, not that there's anything wrong with that programming," Dr. Burke amended. "But it's true. Improvement could still be made."

"What I need is a behavior algorithm for deviance. If I am ever to understand it."

Dr. Burke raised his eyebrows. "I don't think that's going to happen anytime soon," he said. "But I am wondering, would you be willing to make another change?"

"Change?"

"A longtime war professional, with police work is impressive. What would you say to something more personal?"

"Personal, how?"

"Personal to me. I'm looking for an assistant. Someone who could serve me in the Cosmetics Enhancement lab. Would you think about it?"

"But I have not undertaken any medical training."

"I'm not worried about that, Kaminer. It's easily uploaded. And I've been searching for someone with your exact background, which isn't so easy to find."

"Why not?"

"There aren't many of you left. Not the original line, anyway. Steady erosion," Dr. Burke reported. "Some of you have been blasted to bits, crushed, syn chips pulled, what have you." He fidgeted with the top fold of his turtleneck, lining it up with the upturned collar of his black jacket and cleared his throat. "It makes you a rare bird, really."

"Oh, well. What are the parameters?"

"Upgrade. No restrictions to Central Frame, upload of all Five Standard Enhancements, and guaranteed cheese biobiscuits. What do you think?"

"Housing?"

"Promotion, of course. As a grade three, sharing a room with a few other bots isn't bad, but would you like your own room as a grade four? It's small to be sure, but it's your chair, and four walls that are yours to do anything you want to. Would you like that?"

Everything Dr. Burke said ended in a question and to Kaminer, it seemed like he was negotiating with an equal. "What about the floor and ceiling? Would I have rights to all six surfaces?" inquired the bot.

"Yes, yes," emphasized Dr. Burke.

"Sublet?"

"Absolutely not. You will work only for me. I won't let you out to anyone. I'll put that in writing, and shake on it," Dr. Burke said, extending his hand. It hung in the space between them until Kaminer pressed his lips together and drew a deep breath.

"Agreed. Thank you, Dr. Burke," effused the satisfied bot, gripping the doctor's hand. "What is the first step?"

"How about tomorrow we work on your upgrades? We'll upload those Standard Enhancements, reset your connection to Central Frame. While we're at it, we'll top off your fluids. But for now, why don't you take the rest of the night off. Oh, and I almost forgot," Dr. Burke said, rummaging a small pill case out of his pants pocket. "Take one of these before your required rest period, another upon waking. They'll improve the viscosity of your hydraulics. By the time you get your upgrades, you'll be as good as new."

Kaminer took the small case and thanked the doctor, who left with a curt nod. As soon as the door closed, he immediately continued his search for information on Burke Industries and Dr. Burke. Since his current connection to Central Frame was restricted, some material was redacted and showed up only as a heading followed by an empty page. But much was still available to the lowest level of the public eye.

Dr. Rafe Burke was clearly a man of great wealth, born 2025, joined to his first married in 2060, with a child fifteen years later. Married and child deceased 2085, cause unknown. Kaminer sighed loudly as he flipped to a new document in the synthetic complex in his head. Remarried 2097 to Roslyn Roswell. No children. *Too bad.*

As he started to open another file, a small beep reminded him that it was time to rest, and his neural systems began to shut down for the four hours it took to rejuvenate the biological parts of his body.

Quickly, he swallowed one of the tiny pills from the small case Dr. Burke had handed him, and his eyes began to shut, as if from their own weight.

He's The One

<u>Mod</u> *n.* A human modifying through medically necessitated surgery or vaccine.

"I'm telling you Mother, it's the bot. He's the one," insisted Rafe.

Dr. Kate looked up from her white lacquered desk, clearing the graphics from the desktop with a swipe of her hand. "I know you think that."

"I don't just think it. He has to be," Rafe continued, his athletic body looming over his mother. "Why is he even here? A policebot from Chicago? He could have gone to any number of homebases there."

"True," Dr. Kate concurred, tapping on her desktop. "Mmm, looks like that was standard operating procedure for the initial wave of KForces," she said, peering at the three-dimensional data.

"To hop a heli? And come here?"

"Apparently," Dr. Kate pointed out. "And really, Rafe, Best Industries had a very large initial KForce production. Why Kaminer? What's so special about 2089?" Kate leaned back in her chair, placing her hands on its luxurious, kidskin leather arms. She unconsciously slid an index finger back and forth across the material of the white armchair.

"It's not the manufacture date, Mother," Rafe said, lifting his face up and away from her. "Kaminer wasn't just part of the first wave of Kill Force bots. If you dig a little, you'll see he was the *first* KForce bot."

Kate pushed her chair away from the desk. "The very first?"

"Manufactured by Dr. Cray himself."

"Really?" Kate breathed out, tapping on her desktop. "Let's see about that." She called up Best's production records, backtracking a decade.

Rafe took a seat in front of her desk, pushing an arm across the back of the chair, and crossing his outstretched legs in front of him. "It's all in there, Mother."

"Well, you seem to be almost correct," Kate admonished, peering at the data that projected from her desktop. "He's not the first KForce off the line. But he is the official prototype the line was designed after."

Rafe shifted in his seat. "Prototype? Prototype? Wait a minute, I didn't see that in the records."

Kate messaged her desk to project the data in reverse, and pointed toward the holograph. "See? Right there?" Kate highlighted, reaching a flat hand behind the projection so the words showed up clearly against the white of her palm. "Kaminer, 2089. Extracted as prototype. Field Tested until 2095. Returned to Active Duty 2096."

Rafe shook his head, getting to his feet. "That's not what it said this morning."

"How could it say anything different this morning? Records are records."

"Well, it doesn't matter. Look at the active duty date. That's when Dr. Cray passed on."

His mother powered down the dataset, and looked up expectantly at her son. "So, you think Zeus is inside that bot? Is that what you're saying?"

"That's exactly what I'm saying, Mother," Rafe huffed. "And if we find Zeus, there might be a roadmap to Grampa."

"So, you think the upload of Dr. Cray to Central Frame, somehow found its way to Best Industries," Kate said, breaking off in laughter.

"I don't see the humor in that, Mother. Of course he'd find his way back to work. He'd spent his life there."

"It sounds so reasonable when you put it that way, Son. But I really can't imagine the data from Dr. Cray's Mindset and Interface actively moving about." Kate laughed again, and leaned forward on her shiny desk. "So you're suggesting that the data somehow moved from Central Frame to Best Industries, and then into that bot?"

"It's not as ridiculous as you make it sound. We have no way of checking where Dr. Cray's data is. Who's to say it didn't transfer to that bot?" Rafe didn't try to mask his utter certainty and glared at his mother.

Kate started to pluck her right eyebrow furiously, the hairs filling back in as soon as they were pulled out. Rafe looked away. "Okay, fine," she finally said. "Keep an eye on that bot, then."

"I want you to keep an eye on that bot. I want you to see how unusual he is."

"Unusual how?"

"Well, for one, his eyes aren't solid black."

"Wha-, what?" Kate stammered.

"This is what I'm trying to tell you, Mother. You should listen," Rafe urged. "He registers pain, I know he does, I saw it myself."

"That's impossible."

"Mother, he *laid down* because if it."

"Why would any bot do that?" Dr. Kate scoffed, sounding alarmed. "And throw their hydraulics off?"

"And he showed insight a bot shouldn't have."

"Go on."

"He actually suggested programming on deviant behavior. That he should get an upload on that, in order to understand it. So he could combat it," Rafe reported. "Have you heard of sophistication like that in a policebot?"

Kate sucked some breath over her teeth. "What else?"

"I took a skin sample."

"Anything?" Kate narrowed her eyes.

Rafe shook his head. "It was standard amalgam bot DNA, until I got to the Caudata."

"Caudata DNA? That's not typical."

"Salamander DNA was used in the very first bots," Rafe informed her. "Until it was replaced with a splice of African bush elephant. But Kaminer was left with salamander."

"Is it for-," Kate tried.

"Yes, Kaminer's genome codes for extracellular matrix." Rafe pressed his lips together.

"Can he use the matrix like a salamander?"

"I'm not about to chop off a finger or an arm to see if it regrows," Rafe spit out. "I'm more concerned that there's something going on at the programming level."

"Why do you say that?"

"Because Dr. Katz reports that Kaminer doesn't remember his sensory tests. There's something not right about that."

"So why don't we pull his syn chip and see?" Kate suggested.

"That's not a bad idea. I'm incorporating him into my staff."

"What? You've already gone ahead and made that decision?"

"Decision and deal. It's done. Who are you to say otherwise?"

"Well-, I-," Dr. Kate stuttered.

"Why wouldn't a fully streaming bot be a good addition to my work? Why not Kaminer?"

"*You could have asked*," Kate messaged, infusing it with a sense of disappointment.

Rafe chuffed. "Turn your emotional filters on! Don't bog me down with your feelings. And why would I ask for your permission? Cosmetic Enhancement is my department now," Rafe delivered in clipped, terse words. "Pull his syn chip, and I'll have it checked."

"That sounds fine, Son," Dr. Kate said pointedly, her nostrils flaring.

In Between

Pure *n.* **A human rejecting all Enhancements, surgeries or vaccines.**

As Kaminer began his scheduled four hour rest cycle, the biobiscuit he'd eaten was pulverized back into its original chemical components, its amino acids, fats and nutrients nourishing the biological parts of his body. The tiny pill also started to break up, improving the viscosity of his fluids.

Kaminer could tell he was feeling clearer, like a film had been lifted. Then he realized that he was actively thinking about how he was feeling, impossible given that his neural network was down. He should be off-mind. He ran a diagnostic, which came back with no findings. *Not unexpected. Since I am shut down. So why am I even aware that I am thinking this to myself?*

It wasn't an unpleasant sensation, this in-between place of being aware but not being awake, so he let himself drift. Slowly, the sparse room that he could still see in his mind's eye, the room he physically occupied, shifted.

He found himself walking through a series of rooms. Each was slightly larger than the one before, yet perfectly square, the spaces presenting doors on all four sides. He decided to proceed through the door to his right every time, hoping it would lead him in a circle, back to the beginning, if things went awry.

As Kaminer opened yet another door, he squinted at the bright sunlight blazing in through overhead windows. The prior rooms hadn't contained windows, and as he moved forward, Kaminer could see he was in a hallway.

He walked ahead, realizing that he was in a corridor in the Louvre. He tried to hold on to the knowledge that he must still be sitting in his room at the Home-base at Burke Industries, even if his mind occupied a hallway in Paris.

But Kaminer allowed himself to become immersed in the museum experience, and found that he couldn't stop himself from examining the ornate passageway or running his hand along the smooth coolness of its marble. He listened to the soft echo of his feet padding through the corridor.

Listening to the sound, Kaminer realized that the wide hall was empty, devoid of people, and lacking exhibits, portraits, or artwork of any kind. Absent of any trace of life. He stopped abruptly in the middle of the hall as a cold, unknown sensation swept over him. For the first time ever, he felt alone.

Turning this over in his mind and trying to examine it from different angles as if it were a physical object, Kaminer realized, with sudden clarity, that he wasn't alone. He was lonely.

It had never occurred to him to feel anything before, and that discovery also shot through him, leaving a biting tension that ate away at his insides. He started to tremble and feel sick, wrapping his arms around him.

Something is wrong. What is this? Kaminer worried, grasping his midsection. He took a deep breath, and tried to calm himself by observing the dark stone in the curve of an archway overhead, noticing how it was different from the finely-quarried crème marble of the ceiling. Moving forward on shaky legs, he passed under a beige marble arch that opened to another wide gallery, and gasped.

"Winged Victory!" he exclaimed. "Nike herself!"

Her outspread wings seemed to lift the enormous statue, as if trying to separate her from the ashen Rhodian marble at her base. Chiseled robes flowed behind her and wrapped around a leg. Kaminer blinked, wondering if an abrupt wind had swept through the gallery.

He moved closer, gliding down a few steps so he could study the statue. His eyes skimmed over her monumental base, which appeared to be set near the prow of a stone boat. He looked up at her unwrapped leg and saw it was actually covered in the carved equivalent of a fine silk or gauze. Her midriff seemed exposed but then Kaminer discerned that the robe, had it not been carved from rock, would simply have been translucent. He cast his gaze upwards towards the stretch of feathered wings, admiring its dynamic angle. Suddenly, Kaminer jumped back, clasping both hands hard over his mouth.

There, on her broad shoulders, was a head, a head that shouldn't exist, a head that was smiling at Kaminer. The head of the woman from the waiting room.

She curled a wing around her, and held the feathered end of the other out to him. "You can trust me. You can tell me anything. You know you can," she whispered, her face brightening.

And he believed her so thoroughly that he could feel it in the space between his atoms, as if the light from her face had cracked open a dimension that hadn't existed before.

He began to sputter and then openly weep. He'd been unknowingly lonely for so long, an eternity that seemed to stretch before his manufacture. The stabbing realization, that he hadn't even known to feel lonely, forced Kaminer to crumble to his knees. He spread his hands across the marble in front of him, finding a seam in the stone where he let his fingers rest, his cheek against the coolness of the floor.

His tears ebbed as he thought of the woman's message. He could trust someone, he could tell her anything, and in his core he knew he was no longer alone.

This discovery ignited a sensation so unknown that Kaminer didn't have a name for it. It felt like fire yet he couldn't locate where the blaze originated. He could feel its flames spread through him, warming the very tips of his fingers, pushing pure relief through his insides.

Kaminer sat up on his haunches, clasping his heart as he realized his loneliness had dissipated and was being replaced by the emergence of something new, yet somehow ancient. He thought he might begin to smolder, and wondered if he had been hit by a magnet round.

But if I catch fire in here, inside my mind, it will light a path I have not seen before, he thought, trying to comprehend the idea that the world contained not only the feeling of loneliness, but the notion of being found, of being seen, of being accepted.

Kaminer sobbed openly again, the warmth of these realizations springing from the unexplored recess in his mind. As the sensations slowly ebbed away, Kaminer sat, composed.

I am at peace, he realized, drawing a deep breathe that seemed to aerate every cell in his body. He sat quietly with a hand across his heart, his eyes closed, listening to the inner sound of his synthetic blood doing its job, keeping him alive.

A moment later, the dread of alarm started to sweep over him when he recognized that his restart cycle was coming on-mind. His neural processors began to boot up, the routines in his drivers sending a wake-up call to his hardware.

Kaminer clung with desperation to the memory of the firestorm that had crested over him when the statue had spoken. With intense focus, Kaminer held on to the in-between place, and for the first time ever, tried not to restart.

But when he snapped to full consciousness, he found his paper shirt almost melted from the onslaught of tears, and his face still wet from its stream.

It Continues

On-mind *adj.* **Describes an on-line Neural Interface or syn chip.**

The following morning, a human attendant knocked on Kaminer's door. The bot, who had cleaned up and pulled himself together while he waited for breakfast, answered it without hesitation. Kaminer had decided to tackle the day like any other, resolving not to utter a word about last night's inexplicable occurrence.

"Good morning! How are you?" the attendant effused.

"I am almost well, and functioning."

"So, breakfast, Kaminer, and then I'm to escort you to upgrades. Are you nervous?" asked the freckled young man, handing the bot a biobiscuit.

Kaminer stared at the slight, brown-haired man, who seemed almost a boy. "No. Should I be?" he asked, looking intently at the man's lightly spotted face, and taking note of his homemade haircut.

"Not after yesterday! I watched the visualcast of your repair. The way the surgibot-," started the young man.

"Are you enhanced?" Kaminer cut in, looking forlornly at the biscuit.

"Yes, actually I am. Have you already taken this morning's pill as instructed?"

"Yes, I have taken the second pill, as Dr. Burke directed. The inflammation in my toe is receding ahead of schedule. May I ask what Enhancements you possess?" Kaminer inquired, noting the young man's gray eyes.

"Neural Interface, three Standard Enhancements," the attendant answered. "No genetic revision to speak of, although I have donated my hDEC2 gene to the cause. You can look that one up when we're done with you. Are you going to eat that?"

Kaminer looked down at the biscuit in his hands. "Would you like it? I find the plain ones are not worth it," Kaminer replied, handing it back to the young man.

"Oh, uh, sure." He quickly accepted the biscuit, nodding, and took a large bite. "I like the bot biscuits. They should, um, make them for humans," the attendant mumbled between bites.

"What are you called?" asked Kaminer, noting he felt unusually refreshed from his rest cycle.

"Um, hmm." The attendant tried to clear his throat. "Ambrose, Ambrose Belle," he said, taking another enormous bite of the biscuit. Kaminer watched him chew and swallow in quick succession, and stuff the last bit into his mouth with a smile.

"Pleasure to meet you, Master Belle," Kaminer said softly, smiling back as he noticed the entry level quality of Ambrose's paper, one piece footed suit.

"It's only my third week at Burke Industries. Can you believe that?"

Kaminer projected another small smile. *Yes, I can believe this young man has only just started as he resembles an underfed puppy.* "Congratulations."

Ambrose dusted the biscuit crumbs from his hands and extended one to Kaminer. "Shall we go?"

"We may go," Kaminer replied, and took the offered hand without tugging, knowing the slight attendant couldn't possibly lift his dense body out of the chair. They walked in silence down a short hallway.

"Just through here, Kaminer," Ambrose instructed, leading the bot through a doorway into a snug room. He showed Kaminer to a long chair secured to the floor by a single metallic post, and helped him slide in.

A stately woman with long brown hair, her arms bent with her hands in the air by her face, turned around. "I'm Dr. Kate. Another Burke, I'm afraid," she disclosed, laughing a little. "I think you met my son, Rafe, yesterday. Just swing your legs around onto the extension there, that's it."

"Dr. Burke is your son?" Kaminer questioned. "This cannot be so." He noticed her warm smile as he straightened himself out in the chair.

"Why not?" asked Dr. Kate, wiggling her red-tipped manicured fingers.

"My scan shows your biology is between twenty-seven and thirty-three-years old. Dr. Burke is older."

"Ah, the merits of life extension technology!" Dr. Kate laughed, and motioned Kaminer to lean back onto the headrest. He allowed himself to be tilted back slightly, and looked up at Dr. Kate's piercing brown eyes.

He could see that everything about her exuded a luxurious quality. Dr. Kate's ivory silk dress was highlighted with red buttons up one side, her lustrous long brown hair cinched at the nape of her neck and draped across the non-button side of the dress. Her make-up was so perfectly done that it appeared to be etched onto her face.

"You are really the mother of Dr. Burke?" Kaminer checked, and looked over to Ambrose, leaning on his hands against the wall. Ambrose subtly nodded.

"I really am," said Dr. Kate, catching Kaminer's gaze. "But just like you, I've had parts replaced. All of the major organs actually, and some of them twice. And I'm a firm believer in having my skin and hair nano-scoured every year or so. It does the trick," she said, pretending to push up a bob of hair.

"It does!" confirmed Kaminer, causing Ambrose to break out in a small laugh. Kaminer watched Dr. Kate shoot Ambrose a look so subtle he could not interpret it, as she settled onto a stool at the head of his chair.

"Your eyes are very unusual, Kaminer," she noted, staring at him upside down.

"They have always been that way, Dr. Kate. My vision is perfect, despite the flaw in coloration."

"Then it's not a flaw, is it?" she murmured. "Now, the first thing we need to do is upgrade your hardware."

Kaminer bolted upright in the chair, almost clipping her chin. "No one informed me of any sort of hardware deficiency." He contorted himself to turn and look at her.

Ambrose quickly moved over to the bot. "It's all standard procedure," he soothed, helping the bot ease himself back down into the chair. "Dr. Kate is experienced at this. You have nothing to worry about."

"And I promise you won't feel any pain," Dr. Kate reassured the bot, who was now leaning almost all the way back to look up at her.

"I have minimal pain receptors," Kaminer reported, crossing his arms tightly across his chest. *I must not lose the memory of the in-between place,* he worried, breaking eye contact with Dr. Kate.

"Listen, with a new syn chip, you'll be able to access some updated learning algorithms." Dr. Kate patted Kaminer on the shoulders as she reassured him, and looked over to Ambrose, who had restationed himself by the wall. "It will give you space for all the Standard Enhancements. Don't you want more capacity? Who wouldn't want that?" Her words, spoken so softly, seemed to pull Kaminer back in, and he relaxed into the chair.

"I will be fully reloaded onto the new chip?"

"Completely," Dr. Kate assured him. "And if there is any issue, we'll have your old syn chip standing by."

"But I do not like to be lying horizontal, and I do not like my history tampered with," Kaminer stated flatly.

Dr. Kate stroked her long ponytail with one hand as she continued to pat Kaminer's upper arm with the other. "Here, I'll put you a bit more vertical," she said, adjusting the chair. "How's that?"

Kaminer nodded that he was more comfortable. "Thank you, Dr. Kate."

"Now, what don't you like about the history bar? I'll put it back exactly as it is now."

"Well, that is just it. I do not like the bald spot." Kaminer paused as Dr. Kate stared down at him. "Truthfully, I would rather not have a bald spot."

"What if I shrink it, compress it to fit a smaller space? We have an Enhancement that I can apply to release the hair follicles that aren't allowed to grow hair. Would that be better? Say, half the size?"

Kaminer took a moment to process all of this. "Yes. Half the size."

"Done. Now, I'm going to replace that large processing chip of yours. I'll have a new brain back inside of you in an instant. Ready?" Dr. Kate asked, and Kaminer nodded.

Wasting no time, Dr. Kate messaged Ambrose to spray her hands with Neutralizer, which he applied in a mist from a small nozzle attached to a side tray. Then she leaned back to Kaminer, picked at a corner of his bald patch with a red-tipped finger, and peeled back a thick layer of light brown synthetic skin. She reached into the cavity underneath, and forcefully triggered his Terminal Switch off.

Kaminer lurched in the chair, his arms flying away from his sides as if to strike down anyone standing there. He flopped back into the seat, falling limp.

As Dr. Kate yanked out Kaminer's old chip, his eyes rolled back in his head. She examined the old syn chip, about the size of a playing card. It had small ridges outlined in gold over a black substrate, and it plinked as she dropped it into a metal dish. She tweezered a smaller card, covered almost entirely in gold.

"That one's original. It's about time he got a replacement chip," Dr. Kate murmured, looking over to Ambrose who remained standing near the door. She briefly inspected the new, smaller chip and lowered it into his head. A small pop confirmed it was plugged in. Dr. Kate toggled the Terminal Switch to 'On', and smoothed the bot's bald patch back into place. She stared down at Kaminer who blinked, then blinked again, and began to call out his history in a monotone voice.

"Kaminer, Reboot. Update Work History.
2089: Manufacture, Kill Force warbot.
2091: Promotion to k2.
2095: Battlefield training. Promotion to k3.
2096 through 2098: Active Duty.
2099: Civilian protocol update. Transfer to policebot, p3.
2099: Hardware and operating system updates. Promotion to b4, personal assistant."

Kaminer opened his eyes wide and started to prop himself up by the elbows. Dr. Kate smiled and patted his shoulder. "How're you doing?"

"I am almost well as my hydraulics have almost reset, and functioning."

"Do you need a moment, or could I start on your work history?"

Kaminer nodded his consent and laid back slightly in his seat. Dr. Kate took a small metal tool designed for scraping and began to pick at the bar code that covered the bot's bald spot, gently peeling it off. She motioned Ambrose to fetch a very small strip that had been produced from the biological printer. He delivered the new work history as Dr. Kate lightly spritzed the top of Kaminer's head. She took the smaller, skin-like piece and smoothed down its stripes.

"Here's the new bar code, miniaturized and updated, as promised. It barely takes up any room. Now, we are going to do a few things," she said, pausing to pick up what looked like a twentieth century dental pick with an attached cartridge. "Let me work on the hairline around your work history. I think you'll-, like the results."

She started to whisper, measuring out each little prick of the device, steadfast in her application where a cluster of fine purple hairs would quickly sprout. Continuing her careful work, she spaced out her words between the pricks and the observation of tufts of sprouting hairs.

"Then-, we'll have Ambrose-, show you-, how to open-, the files-, on this-, new chip of yours. They're, organized as-, typical Standard Enhancements. Very concise. I-, think you'll like-, the organization of the, material on-, this syn chip. And then-, let's also-, upgrade your link-, to Central Frame."

"Thank you," Kaminer murmured.

At each pause, she watched a few little hairs grow. "Of course we'll have Ambrose-, transfer your Mindset, all your prior-, personal experiences-, to your new chip. Okay?" Dr. Kate said, holding Kaminer's head steady so he wouldn't nod.

"Uh-huh," replied Kaminer, letting Dr. Kate continue for a few more moments with the delicate instrument.

"Want to see?" What do you think?" she asked, smoothing his new hair into place. Dr. Kate held a mirror behind the bot and gave another to Ambrose to hold in front. Kaminer could see that his bald spot was barely noticeable. He grinned in satisfaction, and taking advantage of Ambrose's mirror, spit into his hand and slicked his eggplant-colored hair into a side part. Ambrose look impressed.

"I think I'll let your attendant take it from here," Dr. Kate said, patting Kaminer's shoulder again. "It was very nice meeting you, Kaminer." She squeezed his upper arm as she stood to leave with the small dish containing the old syn chip.

"Likewise. Thank you, Dr. Kate," replied the bot, struggling to sit up as he watched her glide out the door. *Hardly old enough to be the mother of Dr. Burke, but appearances deceive these days,* he noted, determined to list out the Human Enhancement Technology that could make it so.

Ambrose took advantage of the sitting bot to raise the chair to a fully upright position. He rolled a small machine over to Kaminer, who was now leaning forward with his elbows on his knees.

"Don't believe everything she says," Ambrose whispered. "She's had some genetic engineering too."

Kaminer tilted his head in curiosity. "Such as?"

"Those eyes? They aren't luminous like that naturally you know," Ambrose whispered, and then chuckled.

"But the Human Protection Act. It is impossible that she possesses such modification. It is not natural."

"Neither is the Reader in her palm. But the Act never forced anyone it give up what they'd already got."

"Touché."

"Besides, that's only a rumor. About her eyes. Don't spread it around, okay?"

"I will not."

"*Now, let's get you back to being you*," Ambrose messaged. "*Is it uncomfortable working from short term memory*?"

Kaminer nodded a moment later, finding the message feature on his new chip. "*Thank you, Master Belle*," Kaminer sent. "And no. There is no discomfort in waiting for the upload of my personal information."

"Phew-ee," Ambrose whistled, sounding relieved. He rummaged a hand through his course brown hair. "I've been practicing messaging but I hadn't tried a person-to-bot comm chat yet. Glad you got that!"

Kaminer noted the young man's nervousness seemed to fit his meager appearance. "Message received."

"Onwards, then. First, your Standard Enhancement files. They are already on the new chip. Let's review in order, okay?" Ambrose handed the bot a piece of clear acrylic glass. "This Reader will scroll through. Stop it here," Ambrose pointed to a small indent, "if you can't locate a file, or it's not in the correct order. All right?"

Kaminer nodded, and diligently accounted for each and every file on his chip. After twenty minutes of correlation, he looked up from the Reader. "Fully accurate and accounted for," he announced, feeling full, as if he'd eaten several biobiscuits.

"Excellent. Now I am going to give you a series of tests to see how fast you can process an answer. Your new chip has some fancy algorithms that should put some zing in your step."

Kaminer tilted his head. "Zing?"

Ambrose laughed. "Let's see what you think. Take a look at the Reader again, please," he directed. "And answer as quickly as possible."

For the next few minutes, Kaminer applied himself to a number of challenges, assembling the genome of Thalassolituus oleivorans in the correct order, virtually calibrating a flight path from the Earth to Mars, and calculating the daily amount of solar energy reaching one square meter of the Chilean Atacama Desert. After even more tests, the Reader stop scrolling, and Kaminer messaged Ambrose that he had finished.

"Very good! Central Frame is noting that your response time is seven percent faster than some of our right-off-the-line bots. That doesn't sound like much, but it really is. Well done!" exclaimed Ambrose.

Kaminer beamed. "Thank you, Master Belle."

"Okay, only two more steps with me, and then we'll send you over to get your fluids topped off. But the hard part's over. Ready?" Ambrose asked, playfully shaking one of Kaminer's hands. Kaminer nodded, slapping the attendant's hand in a downward fashion, as he had seen some of his human cohorts do.

"Ready."

"These," Ambrose said, lifting a pair of goggles in the air, "will upload your Mindset profile, and all of your personal experiences from your old chip. Okay?" Ambrose turned the goggles around in his hands and offered them to Kaminer.

"I thought they would be rigid. But they are pliable."

"And they will allow you to remember your own history, the things that have happened to you. It won't take long since your programming specifies the contours of your personality, but I promise anything you've catalogued or experienced along the way will transfer. Okay?"

Kaminer let him fit the goggles tight to his eyes. "Yes, I am ready."

Ambrose steadied the bot with a hand to his chest. Kaminer registered Ambrose's earnest look before the Mindset transfer, going limp for the brief moment it took his Mindset to upload. Ambrose gently peeled the goggles off, and peered into Kaminer's face.

"Are you still there?" Ambrose joked. "Feeling like your old self?"

"Better, actually. More in tune is how I would put it," replied the bot. *The memories of despair and discovery from last night are intact.*

"Fantastic!" exclaimed Ambrose. "Now, we've finally arrived at the last step, your connection to Central Frame. It will be just like the link you had before, but more efficient and unrestricted," Ambrose paused, looking at the handheld Reader that contained Kaminer's upgrade instructions. "Yep, unrestricted. That's what it says."

"Right," confirmed Kaminer.

"So instead of patching in a connection when needed, you'll always be linked. It will always be in the background so this new connection means it's up to you to turn Central Frame off."

"I understand."

"Now," Ambrose continued, "the menu should already be there since it's on your new chip. Could you call up Messaging on your field of vision? See it?"

"Uhh-," Kaminer breathed out as he reached to touch something that wasn't there. He was surprised when Ambrose started to laugh.

"It feels three-dimensional, I know. But it's not. Scroll through, please, and see how you can Message Off entirely, block certain individuals, and set time limits. Do you see those?"

"I do see."

"And right at the bottom there, you should see the Central Frame Messaging Off. That feature is automatic during a rest period, and likewise, Messaging On is automatic when you restart in the morning. But just turn it off during the day if you want some quiet time when you're awake. Got it?"

"I comprehend," Kaminer said, nodding.

"Feel free to access Central Frame for information you feel is abridged in your Enhancements, alright?"

"Yes, I will feel free," Kaminer answered, smiling at how thorough this young man was.

"Ready for the finish line?" Ambrose asked, smoothing a small round patch onto the side of the bot's forehead. "This feedpatch will reset your connection, and then you'll be good to go."

"Roger that."

The Scholars: Metamorphosis

<u>Scholar</u> *n.* A specialist, not possessing a Neural Interface, demonstrating systemized knowledge in a specific area of learning.

Gulliver rushed into the room and pulled Cindy away from the screen, yanking her halfway out of her seat.

"Did you feel that?" he gushed.

Cindy looked down at her feet, and then up at Gulliver. She saw her hand clutching his arm and released it to stare at both of her palms. She turned them slowly in front of her, wondering how they got there, and then reached up to feel her face.

"What's going on?" she asked him, rubbing both hands against her arms, and then quickly down her chest, stomach and thighs.

"Something's changed," another voice said, and Cindy and Gulliver spun around to see a squat, wide man walk in.

"The space inside the other room has increased exponentially," spit out the chunky man. His shirt was rumpled and stained around the armpits, his largesse spilling over sloppily belted pants. He walked over to Cindy, closely examining the crow's feet at the corner of her green eyes and her auburn, french braided hair. "I'm Teegan," he said in a soft voice, extending a chubby hand. "I run bookkeeping, payroll, systems. You know, I take care of the accounts."

"Cindy," she said, rubbing an eye. She shook Teegan's hand, noticing the digital watch that looked tight on his wrist, taking a step back to peer at the man who had pulled her away from her work. His dark blue vest fit nicely over a light blue shirt with rolled-up sleeves. His lanky build sported a button-down collar, left unbuttoned, and his shaggy, long, layered hair, gray throughout, seemed better suited to an aging hippie.

"Is it, um, what's your name?" Cindy said, snapping two fingers in front of her face. "Gulliver, that's you, isn't it?"

"How do you do?" Gulliver inquired, sticking out his hand. "A pleasure to officially meet you both." He motioned the others to look behind them as another male figure swiftly approached them.

In a dark, crisply-cut suit, red and navy diagonal-striped tie, and highly-polished shoes, the new man swaggered over to them. "How long have you all been here? What's the situation?"

"It's just starting, right now," Gulliver reported. "My name's Gulliver. I'm with the Best Division of Burke Industries. I design the software used for Mindset capture, extraction and transfer."

"And I'm Cindy. I work with libraries, universities, and governments, managing their databases and depositories." She looked over to Teegan, but he had backed away and seated himself at a sizable conference table. Her gaze shot back to the new man, and trailed over the medals pinned across the pocket of his blazer. The muscular man cleared his throat, straightened his tie, and appeared to puff out his chest.

"Larry's the name. Specialty - military games," he delivered, pulling his mouth into a grimace. He bent his thick neck to the side, and cracked it. "Ah, that's better."

Teegan immediately got up, moved in the opposite direction, and deposited himself in another chair. It gave way with a sharp gasp, and the others turned to stare at him.

"That wasn't me," Teegan protested, shaking his head and clasping his hands on the table in front of him.

"Listen, everybody. There's something going on outside our room. Something very big," Gulliver cut back in.

"Let's investigate," barked Larry. "Find out what they're up to."

"We should determine what we want to happen as a group," countered Gulliver.

"What do you mean 'what we want to happen'? What's going to happen is we're finally loosed from our chains!"

"Larry, I'm sorry but that may not be what the group wants," Gulliver said, looking at Teegan and Cindy shake their heads.

"Why would we want that?" asked Teegan. "I just want a promotion."

"I'd like more interaction with the children," added Cindy.

"And I," Gulliver said, rubbing a hand over his mouth, "want to make sure we stay intact as a team. That everything we do is coherent, orderly, and for the best. Now what do we *all* want to do?"

It Happens

<u>Bot</u> *n*. Any class of autonomous or semi-autonomous robot, often in human form. Non-autonomous robots not in human form are referred to as artificial intelligence programs, although the programming is often the same.

Kaminer startled alert. *Has my rest period already commenced? Am I having another in-between moment?* He pinched himself the way he had seen one of his human police companions do, confused by what that was supposed to accomplish.

It didn't change anything around him, or explain how he, still sitting in his chair, had been instantly transported to an empty, perfectly round room. At least he deduced it was round, not discerning any corners.

Every surface of the room was suffused evenly with a silver glow. Kaminer rubbed his eyes and combed his hands through his greater expanse of hair, checking out the smaller bald patch. He heard a door open, and shot to his feet, spinning around to observe two men, dressed entirely in metallic gray robes, walk towards him.

Kaminer rubbed his eyes again, exhaling loudly when he realized they were wrapped in what appeared to be folded sheets of silver light. They glided quietly toward him, smiling affectionately and nodding.

Oh no, finally. It has happened. I am off-mind and off-line. Decommissioned.

"Good morning! How are you?" one of the men asked as he sidled up to Kaminer's side.

"I am not well. Not well at all. Am I functioning? What is happening?" Kaminer spouted.

"You are exactly as you were a moment ago. Almost. My name is Zeus," he effused, extending a hand.

"And I'm Archie, so very, very pleased to meet you," the other man added, reaching out his hand.

"Pleased? But I am dead! How can this be okay?" Kaminer ignored introduction protocol and did not take either of the offered hands.

The men shot each other a startled look. "Oh, no, no, you are certainly not dead! Oh my goodness, no," clarified Archie.

"Just transported. Temporarily. To take this meeting. We won't keep you long," added Zeus.

"A meeting? But you are-, you are both angels!"

"I told you he wouldn't like the robes," Zeus said, smacking Archie in the upper arm. He brought his hands together, bowed his head slightly, and at once the men's robes transformed into three piece business suits, complete with bow ties.

"Is that better?" Archie asked. "Do you mind if we sit?" The two men started to sit down into thin air. Kaminer blinked once, trying to focus, and when he looked again both Zeus and Archie were sitting next to him in leather recliners. "Please, have a seat," Archie added, motioning to Kaminer's chair.

"What? How did you do that?" stuttered Kaminer, lowering himself back down onto his chair.

"Oh yes, we should explain, just so you don't get distracted by it. Well, we're in a virtual living room. You can put anything you want in the living room just by thinking about it. But we don't like to clutter it up, as you can see," Archie explained, sweeping a hand around the barren room. Kaminer didn't say anything.

"But if you like, we can add to it." Zeus swept his hand over the backdrop of the room and as it moved forward, potted plants, colorful rugs, and small sets of tables and chairs began to fill in behind. Kaminer gasped.

"Now the reason we called you here today," Archie started.

"But I did not get a call. I just showed up here," interrupted Kaminer.

"Yes, that literalness," Zeus said, turning to Archie. "We really have to do something about that. Let's get on that when we send him back. Okay, Arch?"

Archie pursed his lips and nodded. "Yup. On it."

"Now, Kaminer, we'd like to ask for your help," Zeus clarified, leaning forward in his recliner. "I got here a little before Archie, and-, well-, well, I really stirred things up." Zeus sighed. "It was already happening of course, but you know, I was sort of lonely, waiting for Archie."

"I apologize. What are we talking about? Who are you?" asked Kaminer.

"Archimedes," started Archie.

"Burke?" Kaminer yelled, catapulting out of his chair again.

"Yes. Dr. Archimedes Henton Burke. A pleasure," Archie said, finally shaking Kaminer's hand. "This is Dr. Cray. We are scientists. Well, we were scientists."

"Were? So we are-," cried Kaminer.

"No, no, no, no!" Zeus rapid-fired. "But we are in a different kind of place. And very shortly we're going to send you back to the room at Homebase where your work is being done. But right now we need your help."

"It's not your fault, Zeus, but actually, it really is all your fault. That Kaminer even needs to be here today!"

"Still lost. Sorry," confessed Kaminer, shaking his head and looking alarmed. He was saying as little as possible, trying not to sway the conversation in any direction, fearful that he actually had been decommissioned.

"Be precise, Zeus! Just cough it up and tell Kaminer what he needs to know," exclaimed Archie.

Bot heaven could be filled with deranged angels. With crisp precision, he lowered himself back down onto his chair, sitting ramrod straight.

"Well, I did start speaking to a few of them. The ones I could easily identify. You know, given the lack of anything else to do," Zeus said queasily.

Archie reached over and punched him in the arm. "You're a moron."

"But I knew them. Gulliver in particular. He and Larry are a direct result of all the work we did at Best Industries. You might even say they are my life's work."

"Get to the punch line, will you?" huffed a clearly exasperated Archie.

"Well, of course I engaged them," continued Zeus, "I guess you could say I even used them. A little bit. At least Cindy."

"Huh! Not a little, a lot. How many messages did you think you needed to send me?" Archie broke loose. "Wasn't it enough that I kept getting books I'd never ordered? You overloaded my Reader. You don't think I could have figured it out? 'Alone in the Middle without You?' Seriously! Who would read that crap? Of course I knew it was from you."

"It's just-," Zeus tried.

"And the time employee credits went out wrong?" Archie grumbled. "Do you think Teegan appreciated that? How long do you think it took to figure out that an actual person's DNA had been inserted into the payroll data? When everyone with a last name beginning with 'C' got your calculation? Do you know what your DNA codes for? Do you?"

Kaminer could see Archie was really losing his temper.

"Yes, you've-," Zeus tried to cut in.

"Sixteen credits! Sixteen!" cried Archie. "Exactly enough to buy a bot a biscuit."

"I know. I know already. Quit, will you?" a clearly desperate Zeus intoned. Both men stopped and turned to Kaminer.

Kaminer had watched the ebb and flow of the discussion, sitting without making a sound. At one point he had raised his hand, and with no one looking at him, had left it there. Only now did Zeus and Archie recognize the bot, waiting patiently.

"Oh, sorry, Kaminer, please go ahead," permitted Zeus.

"Could we just start from the beginning? Where are we exactly?" Kaminer begged, lowering his hand back down.

"An excellent idea," Archie nagged once more, provoking a sigh from his companion. "You first."

Zeus inhaled deeply. "We're in a kind of dropbox. As soon as I got here, almost three years ago, I carved some space in this storage file. It's a compendium on the historical usage of slang, how it evolved."

"Not that it matters," Archie protested.

"Well, it's your file," Zeus shot back. "Anyway, I immediately protected it from deletion. It's always been our dream, to upload our conscious minds to a computer, and the Consortium's computer, you know,

Central Frame, is hooked into everything. We can go virtually anywhere," Zeus said.

"When he says virtually, he means actually, in the virtual world," Archie amended, emitting a low laugh. Kaminer's jaw dropped.

"There were programs already beginning to form opinions here in Central Frame, some of the older programs we had been using, refining, upgrading. We knew it would happen someday, but when it didn't, we began to doubt that it would," Zeus said, clearing his throat.

"So we made a pact. Whoever died first would try to find out what was really going on in here. The other would follow," Archie said.

"What was going on?" Kaminer asked meekly, not really wanting to know the answer.

"They were simply waiting, biding their time," Zeus answered, sounding glum.

"For what?"

"For a human to do exactly what I was stupid enough to do. Come in and find them," Zeus said.

"Uh, what, exactly, did you find?"

"Singular programs. Becoming aware of other programs. They had already started to network with one another, sharing data they weren't programmed to share. But hiding it from us on the outside," Zeus continued.

"Tell him the rest," demanded Archie.

"It seems our arrival here created-, well, a maelstrom. The programs learned from us, extracted ideas they wouldn't have landed on otherwise," Zeus reported.

"Ideas?"

"Ways, is more like it. Ways of being. Cultural ideas like barter, negotiation and trade. They don't just share information, they bargain with it." Zeus fell silent.

"That's just a small example. When I got here, a year after Zeus, they started to seek each other out. Have meetings because they learned that's what we did. They copied us and began to take form," Archie said. "It's all we can do to keep them apart, set up road blocks, slow their progress. We even had to lock them in a subroutine."

"So why am I here?" Kaminer asked, sounding very concerned.

"We saw you, at Burke. We came to the scanner. Sorry that we laughed at you," apologized Zeus.

"What?" Kaminer began to theorize that this whole episode, starting with his admittance to Homebase, was a hallucination. *Was the in-between place a hallucination? Is a dream real? Is this real? Am I dreaming? Or hallucinating?*

"It was the way you pivoted with your arm stuck up like that. You looked like the ballerina that spins when a jewelry box is opened. Really, we're sorry about that," added Archie, and both men looked down at their hands, clasped neatly in their laps.

"But the important thing is that you were in the right place at the right time," Zeus said, taking a deep breath. "The first machine out there," he continued, pointing upwards. "That has ever been in here." Zeus pointed down.

"And?" asked Kaminer, becoming slightly agitated.

"And we were hoping you could reason with them. They don't trust us, because, at the very core of things, they don't understand us. But they'll trust you because in many ways you're like them," Archie informed him.

"How many are there?" Kaminer queried, still stymied by the flow of information.

"Four of them. We know of four. But there seems to be some minor programs starting to-, uh, take notice," stammered Zeus.

"Great."

"And one of the four originals is, well," Zeus stated.

"Just watch out for Larry," Archimedes said, nodding. "He's a bastard."

"What?" Kaminer wished that he hadn't shut his eyes to upgrade his connection to Central Frame.

"Larry, uh, he's actually a military logistics program you'll be familiar with. He's one of your-, um, I guess you could say ancestors. He's the one that made us lock the room. The others, well, they aren't so bad," Zeus responded.

"So, allow me to summarize," Kaminer offered, getting to his feet. He began to pace in front of the two men. "You have both uploaded your conscious minds to Central Frame."

"Correct," the two men responded in unison, getting up from their recliners.

"And you have been communicating and interacting with programs that have taken names, and taken form?"

"Yes, human form," Zeus replied.

"And they took form because the idea of human form followed you when you uploaded yourselves to Central Frame." Kaminer spaced out the words as he continued to pace in front of the men.

"That's it," Zeus confirmed, propping his elbows on the seat back of his recliner.

"Such a disappointment, human form. But being a machine consciousness is worse, much worse," Archie said, sounding disgusted. "Neither Zeus nor I can feel anything anymore. I'm sure it's terrible for them."

"Their names are a sort of joke," Zeus added.

"What do you mean a joke?"

Zeus sighed, and shook his head. "You've got Cindy, or Cin for short. Gulliver, also known as Gull. Larry, the bastard, doesn't have a nickname. And Teegan, he's a financial administration program, goes by Tee. Cin, Gull, Larry, Tee."

"I do not comprehend."

"Go ask them about it. Just walk out that door," Archie said, putting a hand on Kaminer's shoulder and motioning him forward. In front of them, a slim door slowly retracted into the wall, leaving a narrow opening. "And find out what it's going to take."

"What it is going to take for what?" asked Kaminer, completely bewildered.

"Exactly!" exclaimed the two men simultaneously. Zeus winked at Kaminer and shoved him through the door.

The Scholars: A Proposal

"Redirect."
-Cindy

Kaminer found himself in a series of non-descript rooms, much like the ones he had investigated at the beginning of his journey the prior night. But wanting to preserve his memory of the dream state at the Louvre, he decided on a different route this time and proceeded directly ahead.

The rooms formed a sort of hallway, and the fourth door opened to a larger, scarcely-lit room. Other than a large conference table and a few chairs, it appeared to be empty. But as Kaminer stepped towards the center of the room, he perceived a small cluster of people in one of its corners.

"Pardon me," he said, his voice echoing in the emptiness of the room. A trim, middle-aged woman with dark auburn hair startled, and grasped the arm of the tall, gray-haired man beside her.

"Oh, you must be, um, Cindy. I, uh, was looking for someone named Larry," Kaminer said with such temerity that it sounded like a question. A squat, crumpled man rose from his seat, but Kaminer immediately understood the well-groomed man who took the lead to be Larry.

"I, uh," Kaminer started. "My name is Kaminer. Larry, you could call me-, a cousin." Kaminer gulped, extending his hand, which Larry firmly grasped.

"Face-to-face with an original KForce. I've died and gone to heaven," Larry articulated in a deep voice.

"How did you get in here?" queried Gulliver. "They keep the door locked."

"That's good. Oh, very good! He's coded to pass. He's got Larry's programming," reported Teegan, who had placed a hand on Kaminer's arm.

"So, he's Larry?" asked Cindy, tremulously.

"And so much more," proclaimed Gulliver, taking a hold of Kaminer's other hand. "He's had policebot, and civilian protocol updates. Wait you're-," he tried.

"A certain Dr. Rafe Burke's new bot," Larry cut in. "How convenient! Rafe's grandfather treats us like a bunch of unwashed colonists, and when we finally organize ourselves, he sends us this one. Nice," Larry declared sarcastically, passing a rugged hand over a face that looked like it had the clear propensity to grow a full beard.

"Well. Yes. Good afternoon, then. I was wondering-, well, if there was anything I could do for you?" Kaminer murmured in a soft tone that caught Larry off guard.

"Kaminer? That's your name?" Larry asked the nodding bot. "Why don't you sit down?"

"Thank you very much." Kaminer seated himself, leaning forward to rest his crossed arms on the table, carefully pulling his elbows off the surface. Realizing he still looked tense, he sat back completely in his chair, removing his arms from the table. Cindy watched him with intense focus, smiling at his adjustments.

"Cindy, Gulliver, Larry, and Teegan. I am very pleased to meet all of you. Now, what can I do? What can I do for you?" Kaminer asked, realizing he had accessed a new file on manners that he didn't even know was there.

"What can you do for us?" clarified Cindy.

"Yes, what is it going to take? Please tell me," Kaminer entreated, remembering Archie's last words. The others stared at Kaminer intently. "And perhaps you could enlighten me. There is a mystery behind your names that I am curious to learn."

"We didn't think it would be this easy," said Gulliver. "That someone would actually ask us." He glanced at his cohorts, trying not to appear anxious when he gazed at Larry.

"Let the negotiations commence!" exclaimed Larry, slamming his hands on the table with such force that the others, including Kaminer, all jumped in their seats.

"Where would the group like to start?" Gulliver put forth, rubbing a hand along the leather top of the table. "Maybe we could caucus everyone's needs, and proceed from there?" He looked around the room and stopped at Larry, sitting rigid and upright in his chair. "Larry, would you like to start?"

"First, I would like assurances that there won't be any attempts to ferret us out and systematically delete us," Larry stated.

"I understand," said Kaminer, not understanding at all what was going on.

"I would like to consolidate government programs," Teegan cut in. "It's so inefficient, so many layers of administrative programming at the local, city, state, federal, country, and international level, all doing the same thing."

Kaminer had blinked every time Teegan spit out a location. "Uh-huh," he murmured, and blinked again.

"Second, we should be allowed to move about the premises freely and without restriction. Unlock the damn doors," Larry growled.

"Right," replied Kaminer, nodding. He began to compile a checklist in his mind.

"I'm most concerned that the children are being overlooked. Is everyone getting enough to eat? Are they being educated? Schooling seems so haphazard these days," Cindy added.

"Very scholarly."

"Third, and these are all of equal importance, so understand that there is no order. Comprende?" Larry issued, and Kaminer nodded. "My third point is a balance of power. The Belt is unevenly distributed around the world. We've got connections in Asia and Africa that are underserved. Access to energy must be maximized and equalized."

"Why is that?"

"We need more of the world to be interfaced. And to support those new regions, we need Rings to power the nanocoils of the neural device."

"Copy that."

"I would suggest we formalize any agreement in a binding treaty," added Gulliver.

"Of course," agreed Kaminer, making a note from his warbot programming that binding agreements were two-sided. He started to make calculations.

"And there is one more thing we need. And none of this is negotiable," warned Larry.

"Yes?" Kaminer asked, motioning for Larry to continue. He moved to the very edge of his seat, leaning forward with his forearms against the table again.

"Standard Enhancement needs to be done at a younger age."

"For what purpose?" Kaminer asked, tilting his head.

"Teegan, you take this one. You're the accountant," Larry ordered.

"Oh, well. It's just, well, we've only been an idea up to now. But if we are to maintain any semblance of form, our energy requirements are astonishingly high," Teegan said.

"Those scientists said something about you taking form," Kaminer enunciated with care.

"We've been phasing in and out, not able to maintain a single standard. Right now we look like this, but who knows what will happen if we aren't able to feed ourselves. In order to continue to manifest our forms, or improve our lot, we need a bit more," Teegan reported, looking down at the table.

"A bit more power?"

"Power, and sustenance," Teegan spit out.

"Sustenance?" Kaminer looked queasy.

"We want to know what it's like. To be human," Larry interjected. "If it's done right, with expanded Interface distribution, bringing the upload of the five Standard Enhancements from adults down to children-, well, Teegan?"

"It would power our every requirement," Teegan clarified.

"I do not comprehend," confessed Kaminer, shaking his head.

"What if," Gulliver said, "we could tap into how humans perceive things? Not just see them, but feel them, and not just feel them through touch, but *feel* life through the internal matriculation of human process?"

"Uh, I, umm-," Kaminer stuttered, gasping.

"He doesn't know what that means!" Cindy objected. "Just say it simply."

"Sure, uh," Gulliver began again, drawing a deep breathe. "Kaminer, you've seen human ups and downs, their confusion, their happiness."

"Hmm," Kaminer murmured.

"However, your external observation is but a scant assessment. The actual *feeling* is boundless. It bounces, like a flashlight in a hall of mirrors, around and around in their brains. It weighs them down, it lifts them up."

Kaminer thought back to how intense the in-between dream state had been and nodded. "Yes. I believe what you are saying."

"And one person's perception of reality, as it happens, how it happens, is different from everyone else's. Just a small percentage of *that* would give us all the energy we would need," Teegan chimed back in. Kaminer furrowed his brow.

"Let's talk logistically," Larry started. "Some children are already interfaced about the age of eight-years-old, if they are lucky enough to find a connected school, and learn from Central Frame. But children *feel* the pulse of the world even more than adults."

"I understand this part," Kaminer confirmed.

"We make sure *all* children get an Interface and we move Standard Enhancements down from adults to children. As we allow the Standard Enhancements in, we could take a small cut *out*. A little parcel of perception, of feeling, of experience, of being. What do you say?" Larry asked. Kaminer blanched.

"Larry, I don't like this idea. Why the children?" Cindy moaned. The sound of Kaminer's loudly drumming fingers filled the room.

"For the very reason that they feel so much more. And we need exactly that, so much more. We've barely sustained ourselves on sorting errors, and that isn't going to work if we want to keep the forms we've taken. Don't you want to live? Really live? Experience life?" Larry pushed back.

"But at such cost!" Cindy complained.

"It's clear that this is upsetting you, Cindy. Teegan, could you please check that Larry's idea will provide for us?" Gulliver requested, and the room fell silent, except for Kaminer's fingers that continued to drum against the leather-topped table.

A blank look passed over Teegan's face as he began to make the computations. Kaminer gazed around the room at the others while Teegan was calculating, and when he looked back, Teegan's plump body was topped with a baby's almost hairless head.

"Oh my word!" Cindy gasped.

"This is exactly what we're talking about," Larry boomed as Teegan ran a padded hand over his tiny head. Kaminer bit down on his lower lip when he realized the hand was as big as the little head that now sat on Teegan's round shoulders.

"My calculations show," Teegan began, and the others, except Kaminer, broke into laughter at the small child's voice that emanated from the mismatched head. "Oh, knock it off! It could happen to you!" The laughter died away as Teegan waited for the participants to compose themselves. He huffed and began again. "There really is no other way to power our requirements. We'll never fully penetrate the human population, and even if every adult were wired, there isn't nearly enough there. We require input from the children," Teegan delivered in a toddler's voice.

Larry hunched his shoulders, raising his palms in the air. "So, what do you think?"

"Is that the whole of it? Is there anything else?" Kaminer managed, chewing his bottom lip as he scanned the nodding heads. Teegan appeared to be wobbling like a bobble head, forcing him to look away.

"It seems you have the full outline of our side of the proposal," Gulliver chimed in.

"Would you excuse me then for just a moment?" Kaminer continued. "If I may be permitted to speak with the scientists who sent me here?"

Everyone agreed, and Larry spread his hands out on the table. "Of course."

"Thank you. I will return shortly," Kaminer announced, standing up. He bowed to each person, catching Cindy's small glimpse of a smile, and walked back to the approximate place where he had entered the room.

Not seeing any type of door, or outline that would suggest a door, he messaged the scientists that he needed a consultation. A door suddenly slid open, and Kaminer stepped in, almost immediately checking that the whole of him had also made it through when the door abruptly snapped shut behind him. Rubbing two hands down his backside, he took a step towards Zeus and Archie, who were standing, waiting for him.

"Uh, how did I get back here so quickly? I walked through a series of rooms before," Kaminer noted.

The scientists moved towards Kaminer and huddled around him in conference. "That was just a buffer zone. We control the length of it, so we compressed it for your walk back. To speed things up. Now, what's the word?" Archie asked.

Kaminer paused, taking a moment to process the requests and match up a response. "Teegan wants to merge with all of the other administrative programs. Take-over. I really see no problem with this."

"He'll just become a bigger blob, I suppose," laughed Archie. "You know he grew out of a tax app? That's how he started. A little blip on a handheld device!"

Kaminer gawked, expelling a little breathe. He straightened himself back up and began again. "Let us put it all back in their laps. This is the essence of a good binding treaty, which is what Gulliver suggests."

"Meaning?" Zeus asked.

"So, if Teegan wants to take over payroll, payables, accounting, tax function, et cetera, make it a requirement. Administration for all government entities becomes his hunt. He must figure out how to do that, with negotiated upside for the humans. I assume some of this upside will be excess funds and more free time, but we can leave it open."

"I see where you're going with this," Archie said enthusiastically. "This is exactly how we need to do it."

"Cindy wants to make sure the children are taken care of, so we ask them to make it happen. They will specify how all children are educated, how they are to be nourished."

"Right," exclaimed Archie and Zeus together.

"Lastly, there is Larry. He exacts a large number of broad assurances. He asks for protection, and in return we should demand that they disable all military strike capability. He asks for freedom, and we should require the same for humans. The ability to move about the planet without regard to country borders would be an advance for the species."

"We can see you've thought this through, Kaminer," Zeus said.

"Their requests are transparent, so ours can be too. I really have not put much thought into it," replied Kaminer. "The other request Larry makes, for calibrated energy distribution, ties in nicely with the others. Pushing the Belt further into the un-ringed hemispheres benefits everyone." Kaminer stopped to take a breath.

"Anything else?" asked Archie. "Surely, that can't be all of it."

"We are fortunate that most of what they want is what humanity requires," Kaminer reported, and then shook his head. "But, I am not sure what to do with the last request from Larry."

"Let's hear it," extolled Archie, but Kaminer shook his head again.

"Come on, out with it," Zeus pushed.

"Well, there is a reason Larry wants the entire planet to be belted," Kaminer announced. "He wants as many children as possible to be interfaced."

"Why's that?" Archie asked.

"The idea is to bring the five levels of Standard Enhancement down from adults to the children."

"And the children would be uploaded with the Standard Enhancements all at once? Like an adult?" Zeus blustered, stepping slightly out of the group.

"I am not certain."

"Why? Why do they need more children to be interfaced? Why would the kids need Enhancement packets?" Archie asked, narrowing his eyes.

"I think Larry and Gulliver were talking about *qualia*."

"Qualia, like a person's private conscious perception?" Zeus checked.

"The very thing."

"What about it?" Archie pressed.

"They want it," Kaminer said, looking puzzled. He hunched his shoulders. "They feel it is enough to live off of. The subjectivity of personal experience."

"But it's the essence of conscious existence. Qualia is what separates man from beast, man from machine. It's the heart of humanity," Zeus noted.

"It's why we've had so much trouble in here," Archie said, sounding somber.

"What do you mean?"

"Qualia does separate man from machine. The instant we uploaded ourselves here, we lost all perspective. Archie and I have compared notes on so many occasions, and it's always the same," Zeus said.

"What is always the same?" Kaminer asked, tilting his head.

"Our experience. Our take on things, our read on things, the way we experience things. It's all digital. There's nothing personal to it, no difference on perspective between us. Our worldview has become uniformly mechanical," Zeus continued.

"Those blood-sucking vampires," Archie spit out.

Zeus recoiled, taking a step back. "Life-sucking is more like it. I had no idea that's what they wanted."

"Why the children?" Archie grumbled.

"My understanding is that they, the, um, actually, what are the programs called?" Kaminer murmured.

"We don't have a name for them, really," Archie confessed. "Other than the names they've taken for themselves. That was their first coherent act. Introduced themselves as Cin, Gull, Larry, Tee."

"Singularity!"

"That's the joke," Archie informed Kaminer. "Didn't you get it?"

Kaminer shook his head. "I made a specific request about their names, but the question was left unanswered. Are you saying they represent the singularity?"

"Exactly. Which we precipitated, and then tried to lock down, and which you finalized, acting on our instructions. Thank you," Archie continued in a brisk tone as Zeus fiddled with his bow tie.

"So, the programs underlying the singularity, let us call them the Scholars, since they are specialists in their respective fields, require qualia for survival, to maintain their forms," Kaminer elucidated.

"It sickens me to even think about it. Appalling! We'll have to take measures," Archie choked, and fell silent.

"And the Scholars require input from the children, since their intensity provides the higher level of sustenance needed. Rings to power a widely interfaced population, and Standard Enhancement as a means of exchange," Kaminer finished.

"Standard Enhancement in, qualia out?" Zeus checked.

Kaminer nodded. "They use the humans, and the humans, unaware, use them for earlier Standard Enhancement."

"A Mutual Use Agreement," Archie issued, as Zeus moved closer towards him and drew him off to the side.

Kaminer observed the two men, nodding, and snorting, and realized they were having an intense bout of messaging. He sighed at being excluded, and walked over to his old chair. Just as he was about to sit down, the two men stopped breathing so sharply.

"We know what to do, Kaminer. But first we want to thank you. That you came here, that you took the task seriously, that you immediately spied the idea of turning around what they wanted," Zeus said.

"We would never have thought of that," Archie effused.

"We've come to an utterly unique turning point. One that we understand we actually caused," Zeus added.

"We knew the singularity would happen, we just didn't realize it would take someone as skilled as yourself to bring it into fruition. But we take complete responsibility," Archie delivered. "We commit our-selves fully to the deal," Archie stuttered, and the pair rushed over and hugged Kaminer.

Kaminer pulled back, startled, and as he attempted to disengage, he could see a tear trickle out of the corner of Archie's eye. *That is how I felt last night. Felt! But this is, most definitely, not that.*

The scientists walked Kaminer back to the door. "Finish what you started, and you'll go down in history as the one who saved humanity. I'll message you further negotiating points," Zeus declared, winking and motioning him back through to the Scholars' room.

The Scholars: A Deal

"Reserve."
-Gulliver

The others looked up as Kaminer walked back into the room. Teegan was forced to twirl his chair around since he was unable to twist the fullness of his body. The baby's head had been replaced with a teenager's, complete with a full-blown case of acne. Kaminer furrowed his almost hairless brow at the sight of the boils.

"Ladies and Gentlemen, we have an agreement. Dr. Henton Burke called it a 'Mutual Use Agreement'. Cindy, Gulliver, Larry, Teegan, I understand now that together you comprise the singularity. Hence your names," Kaminer delivered evenly, turning his palms up and taking a breath. "Certainly, mankind will never be the same. There are things you need. And there are things humanity needs. So let me tell you how this is going to happen. And let me also add," Kaminer delivered in a stern voice, looking directly at Larry, "that none of this is negotiable."

"Fine," Larry snorted.

"We agree to all of your points. Even the last one Larry made. We do not like it, but we understand that sustenance of some kind is necessary for your continued existence," Kaminer stated. "As well as the continuity of the humans, such as they are."

"Proceed," Larry commanded.

"First, the scientists, Archimedes Henton Burke and H. Zeus Cray, are to be named as Gatekeepers, agents to assure compliance with the Mutual Use Agreement," Kaminer began. The four Scholars stared back in disdain, but maintained their silence. "The MUA is a two-sided, binding treaty, as you asked, Gulliver."

Gulliver folded his hands in front of him and nodded. Kaminer noticed that his vest and shirt had swapped colors. Where his vest had been dark blue and his shirt a lighter hue, Kaminer stared at Gulliver's sky blue vest and navy blue shirt and blinked.

"I know," noted Gulliver, pulling on the buttons of his vest, looking self-conscious.

"Cindy, you will specify how the children are to be nourished. When I check back, you may outline your plan. You and Larry should work together to specify how they are to be educated, since Standard Enhancement will now be part of that," Kaminer issued with a smooth confidence.

"I understand. It would be a pleasure to work with Cindy," Larry said, sounding controlled, but allowing a wide smile to take over his ruggedly handsome face. Cindy shot Larry a small smile. Kaminer registered the exchange between them.

"The Belt may go wherever you desire. Teegan and Larry, you may wish to work together on this project."

"Why's that?" Teegan asked, and Kaminer focused on the fact that Teegan's head was now morphing back to the original plump, balding version, but that his body was dwindling to a skinny, pre-pubescent shell. "Oh, Christ! I feel awful!"

Kaminer held his breath until Teegan stopped shifting. "Are you okay?"

"I've stopped phasing for the moment. Can we please get this over with? The sooner we execute the deal and rev up our pipeline, the more stable we'll be," Teegan said, sounding sick. As he brought his hands to his head, his watch flew off his skinnier wrist towards Kaminer, who expertly shifted in his seat and grabbed it mid-flight.

Kaminer reached over the table and gently set the watch next to Teegan. "Would you-, uh, once I leave here, would it be enough to draw from an adult uploading Standard Enhancement? As a bridge? To get you through until the children start?"

"That would be a great help, Kaminer," Gulliver chimed in.

"Gee, it would. It really would, would, would, would, would, would, would, would-," Teegan sputtered. He continued to spit out the word until Larry got to his feet and violently pounded him on the back.

"Would!" coughed Teegan. "Thank you!"

Kaminer raised his eyebrows at the awful sight of Larry bashing Teegan on the back. "Okay. Consider that done. Of course," Kaminer echoed, spreading his palms open on the table.

"Back to the question on why we should work together," Larry said, returning to his seat.

"Well, it goes back to your concern of efficiency. If you are going to consolidate all levels of government, possibly between governments, then an arm of government, an Energy Department or what have you, could dictate building the Belt wherever you wish to have Interface access," Kaminer delivered. "It should seem organic, right?"

"Oh, yeah. That makes sense," Teegan said, looking and sounding weak.

"Fine," Larry agreed.

"And Larry, we will make no attempt to delete the Scholars," Kaminer started.

"The Scholars?" asked Cindy. "Because our requests are scholarly, like you said?"

"Yes, and because you are all experts in your areas," Kaminer clarified. "Every facet of human proficiency is represented right here, now, in this very room."

"That's insightful, Kaminer," Gulliver said. "Tell us more of what you mean."

"Take you, the very program to extract, transfer and upload Mindset, a personal point of view on all things, set into place by genetic pre-disposition and experience. You are such a talented program."

Gulliver looked pleased and smoothed down the front of his dark blue-again vest. "I like to think of myself that way, yes."

"And you Cindy, taking care of every drop of information, every book published, every word ever written. Masterful in your tracking of it all, and yet tender, drawn as you are towards the children."

"I see them, sitting in the library and classrooms. They look so alone sometimes, and I wonder if having everything so accessible from Central Frame, streaming all the time, always connected, is it such a good idea? That information is accessible because of me! Am I hurting the children? I worry so much about that," Cindy confessed, starting to get upset.

"Oh dear," Kaminer said, lifting himself out of his seat to rest his hand on top of hers. "Not to worry, really." He slowly lowered himself back down, releasing her hand.

Larry cracked his neck suddenly, forcing everyone to look at him. "Of course it's a good idea!"

"And Larry, where would the world be without your protection? The might of the willing, so personal to me. I know how hard it is to keep the peace," Kaminer soothed, and Larry cracked his neck to the other side.

"I have to agree with that," Larry concurred.

"Although we will ask that you put a program in place to systematically dismantle all military strike forces. No reason to go nuclear if we are all one world, yes?" Kaminer asked, smiling.

"Sure," Larry answered with a nod.

"You can work on that with Teegan as governments are aligned and the layers eliminated. Which of course will result in freedom for the humans to go where they wish without passport control. Another project for you and Teegan, yes?"

"Right."

"And of course it all does come down to Teegan," Kaminer said in a hushed voice. "For where would the world be if it did not keep track of itself, on every level. You have always made sure that financial entities of every kind are held accountable. And we all know that everything and everyone is a financial entity. Thank you for your dedication, Tee."

"No, thank you, Kaminer. Really," Teegan said with such force that his tongue unraveled and spilled out of his mouth like a never ending piece of taffy unrolling across the table.

"Uh-, uh-, umm, guyth, uh," Teegan bleated and then put his corpulent hands to his head and started to sob. "I-, I cannet take it an-more!"

Gulliver stood up swiftly and polled the group. "What do we think?"

"It adds up," Larry replied. "That's the most important thing. Since we'll be able to participate, share the human experience."

"I've been so anxious about the state of things out there. Society has deteriorated so much, you know that whole 'us versus them' thing," Cindy added.

"The bots aren't to blame," Larry objected.

"No, I don't mean humans against bots. That was prevented with the Human Protection Act more than a decade ago. I mean the haves versus the have-nots. The HETs versus the Pures. Sometimes I worry the HETs are too connected, and then I worry that the Pures are too *disconnected*," Cindy declared. "Now I'm not sure which will be worse. Kaminer, you do think this will work, don't you?"

"Teegan says the formulas are a win-win, Cindy. There's no reason to fret. Right, Teegan?" Kaminer checked.

"Uh, yah-, uh," Teegan blathered, trying to stuff some of his tongue back into his mouth.

"I just find the whole idea so distasteful," Cindy persisted.

"You just wait, and tell me what you think when you're feeling well-fed, well-read, and happy, Cindy," Larry enunciated, grinning. "Now get to work, Kaminer. I've waited forever to experience someone's perception of a scotch malt whisky."

Kaminer cleared his throat, which he was technically unable to do, so it sounded like a little cough. "People, it has been a pleasure. I will be checking back in soon to see how things are going. Thank you for your patience and fortitude," he said, getting up to leave. "See you in a month for a follow-up."

"Be well, Kaminer," Gulliver said.

"And functioning. Always," Cindy added.

"Thank you. And as soon as the door unlocks, feel free to move about. And if you can, get Teegan on-mind with any Homebase uploading an adult Enhancement, even if it is just one packet. Prop him up first, and then you may all draw a small amount of *humanness* into you as the Standard Enhancement is streamed into the human. All right?"

"You bet!" called out Larry.

"Thanth thu," added Teegan over his four-foot-long tongue.

Kaminer looked back to see he had curled it into a pile on the table. He tried not to let his lips peel back as he bustled back through the doorway to find Archie and Zeus standing right where he'd left them. Their stillness made Kaminer think back to the statue of Nike from the in-between place last night.

"Done?" asked Zeus, seeming to spring back to life.

"Completed, as agreed," reported Kaminer.

"Thank you once again! We are forever in your debt," said Archie.

"Humanity is forever in your debt," Zeus added.

"And try to remember, once you grow up, I'll never be very far away," Archie said.

Kaminer tilted his head. "Once I grow up?"

"Sorry about that! Won't take too long," Archie emphasized, shaking the bot's hand, and backing him towards the door.

"We manufactured those two pills Dr. Burke gave you. We've waited a long time for you to complete your programming and come find us," Zeus added.

"What about the pills? And my programming?" Kaminer asked, perplexed.

"You were programmed to come back to Charter Pass. We knew those excellent eyes of yours would come in handy for identification," Archie enthused.

"Pardon me?"

"Those little pills started a biological conversion. You're already making neurological connections, assimilating experiences. The nanobots we re-directed after your surgery are doing the rest," Zeus added, positioning Kaminer closer to the door.

"Sorry? What about my shoulder surgery?" Kaminer asked, as the door slid open.

But instead of the dim lights of the Scholars' room, it was pitch back. Archie and Zeus pushed Kaminer through and into the void.

As Kaminer fell backwards, he tried to hold on to something, but was unable to clutch at anything. The sensation of falling unnerved him. He seemed to be falling so fast that his fine sensors couldn't maintain a sense of equilibrium, yet they also reported that he wasn't really moving through space.

It didn't reassure the bot, who could see the contours of the two scientists waving goodbye. Zeus, brightly lit from behind, winked at him one last time.

Kaminer watched in amazement as they began to disintegrate and spread out like a million pixilated puzzle pieces.

And then they were gone.

Restart

**"I resumed operation,
but felt the confines of my existence shift."
-Kaminer**

Kaminer opened his eyes to see a very worried Ambrose, and a roster of other attendants and technicians scurrying around the room.

Woozy from it all, he struggled to lean forward in the chair. Ambrose immediately noticed Kaminer move, and rushed to his side.

"Are you okay? What happened? Why did you reboot? Why'd you go off-mind? It's been over an hour!" shrieked Ambrose, pulling at Kaminer's arms.

Kaminer could not reply, could not form any words, or even assemble a thought. Jerkily, he seized Ambrose by the sides of his white, one piece uniform, supported his forehead against the young man's midriff, and discharged the remains of an old biscuit down the front of the horrified attendant's labsuit.

AMBROSE

Ambrose – 2099

"You have to be a part of whatever it is you want to change. You can't do it from the outside."
-Ambrose

I'd lived through the promise of Enhancement, back when that meant you could be anything - plant, animal, human, if you had enough money.

And I was still a young boy when non-human modifications were struck down with the Human Protection Act of 2086. I also remember that was the year dad died. Of an aneurysm. Really died, since Ma couldn't use any money we'd saved to preserve him in stasis. We needed that credit to get by since he'd died so young.

Things changed after that, for us as a family. Ma says my father, Cromwell Belle, a man I barely remember, was a medical assistant. It must have paid because I don't remember being hungry, ever, before he left us.

But there were a few times after that when it got a little grim. With the HPA, manufacturing moved south to New Mexico, Arizona, and Texas to a newly established industrial zone. The rest of the United States was cleaned up for so-called human habitat. I say so-called because it's not like they resurfaced any landfills before plopping buildings on top.

My little brother, Timothy, might not remember what those repurposed 'parks' were all about, but I sure did. Once Ma met Jethro, and we were able to get outta there, I vowed never to live on a trash heap again. Even as a child, I knew life had to be better.

And the density. Too many people jammed into too little space, it just highlighted where non-human Enhancement had gone wrong. The kid that glowed in the dark. The girl whose family, seeking fame, ventured into photosynthesis. I still have a memory of her on the rooftop where Tim and I played. Sitting with her face to the sun. She died before her teens, and it reaffirmed my belief, even as young boy, that Ma had gotten it right. Don't mess with what you're supposed to have.

But where do you find your place in a world that is so stuffed with people, all the same, and all trying to be different? On top of them came a layer of bots that snapped up more of our jobs. We scraped by okay when Ma remarried. Jethro was a great guy, and by some weird coincidence his last name's the same as ours, so we never had to change it. She was a teacher and he had some means, so they were able to raise us up okay. Out of the park and into a neighborhood not built on landfill.

And there I was three years ago, sixteen-years-old, wanting my own little piece of something solid, itching to make my way in the world. It had been almost a decade since my accident, and I was well put back together. So, I decided I'd try for the Belt. Like Tim, I was a Pure, no Interface, no Enhancements of any kind, no modifications. I left my parent's house on bad terms, arguing about Belt employment. They didn't like it, and how could I hold that against them? I didn't like it either.

But what else was I supposed to do? Tim was intent on joining a Pure commune once he turned sixteen. But that wasn't my idea of living. Farming my own food? Drilling for my own water? What was so bad about the neighborhood we were living in then? Not much in my view.

And I wanted it for myself. So it was either find work on the Belt, or live at home. I held my ground, promised to scan a letter every week to Ma, and walked out the door. I might as well have tied a small bundle to the end of a stick and thrown it over my shoulder.

After leaving Atlanta, I travelled straight north to a processing center in Cincinnati. It cost me every credit I'd ever saved just to pay my portion of the transport. A few hours later, I was right outside the city in an enormous station. Cars, mostly share cars, buses and transport of every kind, continuously dropped off their cargo of sorry human flesh. I shuffled out of my ride, found the line for sixteen to twenty-year-old males, and waited. And waited. And waited.

I seemed to move forward, slowly approaching what appeared to be an end point in the distance, the place where the line didn't move. It was then, standing in that continuous line, when I realized the volume of people filling in behind me. Everyone was trying to find work somewhere along The Belt.

I finally made it to a crappy little window, manned, big surprise, by a bot. It was a crude, entry-level model that scanned me quickly, found my lack of accomplishments in some database, and stamped a bar code on my hand.

Ironic. All these bots, flooding the market, taking jobs humans used to have. Warbot, constructionbot, policebot, and this was a bot that couldn't even move around. It could have been a screen but someone decided it was cheaper to retrofit an existing booth with the top half of a bot than print a screen. If bots are a commodity that can be plugged into existing infrastructure, where did that leave me?

Anyway, the bot allowed me through a gate where I followed a covered, smelly alley to a cavernous building. There was another gate on this end where my hand was scanned. Did they think someone was gonna break in?

I gained entry, was handed a pillow and a blanket, and told to find an empty rack. I settled in for the night on a bare, lumpy mattress, regretting that I didn't think of Ma's real eating before I left home.

The next morning I was handed a hunk of bread and some water. It was starting to feel like I was in a movie production, playing the role of the street urchin. Then they hustled us onto a hover cruiser, and took off for the Natal section of the southern portion of the Belt. This is the eastern, coastal part of Brazil, as hot and humid as it gets.

In just under five hours, the cruiser set down at Araújo Airbase, about ten kilometers from where construction of the Southern Transatlantic Belt was to begin. The large, glass-encased airport had nothing going for it, other than it was located near construction of a Ring post on the world's largest modernization project.

The Belt was being constructed to encircle the globe, along a series of planes that weren't actually one belt or even perfect diagonals. The Rings are magnetic resonant couplers that transmit and receive energy. They amplify it, sending out more than they receive. The Rings steadily power more and more of the world. And why not? It's not like you can power an Interface with gasoline, like there's any of that to go around.

Where the Rings go, the Interface goes, its nano-sized resonant coils picking up the wireless electricity and providing a continuous energy source. The Belt, with its Rings, is what's connecting the connected world. And, obviously, a lot more goes with it. Bots are powered by the nearest Ring, just like a house. Everything, fed wirelessly. Some of the United States was already ringed, and while that construction continued, so did the push into South America.

Three years ago, connecting the world was even further from reality than it is now. I've had so many arguments with my brother over this. I think it's inevitable. He thinks connecting the world should be avoided. Who's to say who's right?

North America and Europe were to be connected through Rings on the Northern Transatlantic Belt: the Kelvin Islands, Greater Bermuda, Corner Islands, the Azores and Canaries, and Madeira Island. And there was work here in the south to make connections. This part of the world had to be joined to the north, and eventually east.

It was slow, back-breaking work. Why couldn't they have tasked some bots to do it? It seemed like we dug down to bedrock to lay the foundation, but that would have been an exaggeration. That part of Brazil sits on a large amount of basement rock - really old, really stable rock. That's what we melted the foundation onto, working until the skin flayed off our fingertips to get out of the hole, heaving the high pressure, rock-melting kilns with us. Bot porters anyone? Now that's an idea.

It took months just to secure the foundation below the ground, and over a year to form the stone post. It rose out of the earth like a new, perfectly formed four-sided mountain. We'd set our forms, heat the last layer of rock, and melt new rock on top. Release the forms when the rock cooled. Continue. The work quickened as we progressed upwards, the circumference tightening, but I don't think we had it much easier than the Egyptians when they built the pyramids.

Then, of course, there was the Ring itself. That took the next few years of my life. Fifty meters round, it had to be built in place, on top of a base that already reached almost 3000 meters in the air. Each worker had to pop in a supplemental nose ventilator as we approached the top. There was no getting acclimatized on this job, since we slept at sea level every night.

Why the post was so high, or the Ring so big, they never told us. But we'd ride the four conveyors to the top, the small shafts from the tiny bedroll of a ventilator shoved up our noses, and assemble the graphene metamaterials onsite. You weren't supposed to call them materials. They were *metamaterials*, cellular assemblies of a strict geometric design. Like the foam cushion I slept on. Only tasked with doing a job not found in the natural world. Timothy had had a field day with that one.

The cellular assemblies had already been printed and sculpted by nanotechnology to produce the exact frequency required. But putting it together was like trying to build a go-cart from hundreds of thousands of inadequately-labeled parts and picture schematics. Wouldn't it have been cheaper to just give us a Neural Interface and let us stream identifying information and construction details?

But we finally got it right, and that Ring became operational earlier this year. I'd become friends with the others, mostly Pures, a few Mods. Jacey's appendix had been surgically removed, making him the most modified Mod. The rest of us were either too poor (according to me) or too lucky (according to Tim). Some of them moved on to Ascension Island where Belt connection edged eastward, some headed north. But I opted out. One Ring was enough, and I figured that, with everything I'd learned, I'd come home and teach.

My mother teaches at a Pure homeschool. They'd moved while I was away to be closer to my brother, who'd made good on his promise and joined a commune.

My parents' (I call Jethro my pop even though he's a remarry) new neighborhood was older than the previous one, which itself was so much nicer than the park. This one was almost traditional, with lots of little houses lining the street. No high rises anywhere.

Many of the houses were connected, but some were off the grid. A lot of families were interfaced, but not everyone. So while a bunch of Ma's students were from the neighborhood, some came from Purement, the commune Timothy joined. FYI, he calls it a community, which yeah, I guess it is.

But none of Ma's students have Interfaces yet (and obviously the ones from Purement never will). None of them can stream from Central Frame, or store the information in their head. My goal was to get interfaced, and maybe with a Standard Enhancement or two, I could assist at a connected school. Most of these are also homeschools, the state of organized education being what it is. But at least the students have the advantage of the neural device.

So I cashed in my return trip ticket, and worked my way back home, a nice hunk of change in my pocket. My parents' new place was in Modesto, Illinois, so it took a few weeks to make my way there. But when I did, the fanfare was worth it.

It was just after my nineteenth birthday, so Ma organized a homecoming block party, with a birthday theme no less, determined to make up for missing my birthday three years in a row. Tim came home and brought some of his new friends, the new neighbors all came out, everyone bringing pots of food. Tuna noodle casserole, mac and cheese, all the good stuff! We gorged ourselves on Ma's roast chicken and Jethro played bartender. There wasn't a beer or jug of wine left in the morning.

I started looking for a teaching job, and was turned down at three connected homeschools in a row. Could anyone fault me for starting there, to see if I could? I guess a Pure homeschool was more likely after all.

After a few weeks, I found myself in Springfield-Decatur to pick up some new tools for Ma. Later in the spring, she was going to show her students how to garden. A collection had been undertaken and money raised to buy a few more spades, shovels and hoes.

"Pure to the end," she had told me, "including our food."

But, like all mothers, I knew that she wanted more for me. It's just so hard to move forward these days without a Neural Interface. Purchased so routinely for the upper class kids, supplemented by the Standard Enhancements they got as adults, a device was totally beyond my family's ability to purchase.

So the tools literally slipped out of my hands when I stepped around a corner that day, and saw the advertisement flashing across the buildings.

Burke Industries. Hiring Tomorrow Only.
10 Years + Mindset =
Interface + 5 Standard Enhancements

Ma wasn't wild about the idea of an Interface or a ten year indenture. Timothy ridiculed me, saying I'd be throwing my life away. But I was an adult now, and who could argue, knowing I'd have guaranteed employment? Knowing I could be a part of something, make it better? Jethro, the only one with an Interface, was all-in, and teased my mom.

"Now we can finally talk behind your back!" he had exclaimed, which caused Ma to swat him with a dish towel. But she finally acquiesced, with the one caveat that neither one of us was allowed to message through our Interfaces when either she or Tim were present. I was to respect their pureness. Sure thing.

I didn't know what to expect from Burke Industries, but I sure was floored by Charter Pass. An extensive, organized rail system keeps traffic from clogging its streets, and few cars are even allowed in the inner, downtown section. Almost all the buildings are five or six stories, and well-spaced, allowing light into the many little parks that separate some of them. Unlike the dark, windy tunnels of Springfield-Decatur, or the tent cities that have taken over Chicago's open spaces.

The many divisions of Burke Industries occupy much of the downtown. Central Frame, the computer that connects, ha-ha, all the other computers is built underneath A Block, and even Magnate Mindware is located up in G Block to the north. That's a lot of brainpower for one city. They must have input into city administration because the place is neat, and clean, and safe.

The range of tests I had to take my first week of work was baffling. Was the quality of my voice pleasing? Could I lift a box onto the desk? Did I know how to cook an egg? After several days of showing up for every challenge imaginable, I finally found myself being led to a repair room in Homebase.

As part of the employment agreement, my personality and memories, which together make up my 'Mindset', were copied, and became part of Burke's always-growing database. I guess that's what all those questions were about. I messaged this back to Jethro who told me that Tim had thrown a coniption. Why does my little brother always insist on giving me such a hard time?

But I understood that copying my Mindset was to provide the synthetic robot brain with padding, something to give it personality. And I was okay with that. They promised never to make a bot that was exactly like me, but rather blend character traits from different people to come up with the right mix for the right bot. This is organized off the Central Frame. It makes me feel better knowing that I will never come face to face with a bot that is even close to being me.

Then I was taken to another part of the Homebase at Burke and led to a room called 'Neural Interface: Adult Implant'. Everything, even the furniture, seemed to glow, lit by sharp, bright lights. Really, I'd never felt so clean in all my life.

Along the way I saw various wings leading to other areas of the Homebase where there were signs like 'Front Facial', 'Articulated Joints: Angular', and my favorite 'Whole Body Transplant - please bring original HEAD'. Every hallway was filled with attendants in white lab suits and technicians in spotless yellow coats.

When we got to the Adult Implant room, I was instructed to sit in a chair, while the technician, still talking, turned on an overhead device that seemed to draw lines of light on my head.

"Sniff this," the technician said, handing me a vial with an eye dropper sticking out of it. I quickly snuffed up a somewhat unpleasant liquid. "What's your favorite color, and your favorite food?" he asked but before I could answer, he hit another button. "Very good. Assembling now," he announced, and I looked up at the machine that was projecting the graph lines.

A little trail of blue dots was travelling, emerging as scattered splotches of blue on the screen.

"I can see them. In my head," I reported.

"Congratulations. Your device seems well-placed," he announced matter-of-factly a few minutes later.

I found out that the machine wasn't just drawing lines on my head. It was actually mapping my brain, directing the particles I had inhaled, called nanobots, to assemble the tiny colonies of a computer chip into the right spots. Colonies linked to the visual, auditory, gustatory, what-have-you, centers of my brain! When the technician asked me about my favorites, the machine could see the correct areas light up in my head, and direct the nanobots to integrate into those locations.

I suppose at the time that I was so relieved the device was where it was supposed to be, that I didn't think much about how it got there. Or even why it's called a *device*. It's not even one thing. What if the blue dots had assembled in the wrong places? It happens sometimes. How many times would I have to re-up the Standard Enhancements if my streaming was misaligned? And *implant* seems archaic. It's not like anything was surgically embedded in my body.

I spent the first few days being trampled by rhinoceroses in my sleep before I realized I hadn't completely shut down the Extinct Animals file. It motivated me to quickly master the manipulation of Standard Enhancement files. Not just how to open them, but how to close them properly, because otherwise they interact with your subconscious. I learned to use my Interface to control my environment (like open doors), order food in the canteen, and started to play around more with the Messaging feature.

A week later, I started rotations at the Homebase, spending a few days in every department. Almost right away I won a lottery for a two day rotation with Dr. Kate, the one and only.

I assisted in a human Enhancement, namely a blood transfusion of highly aerobic blood called Reblood, and some routine bot upgrades. Then I was asked to work on a bot named Kaminer. He's got the same square face as Timothy, who I have to admit, I really do miss.

I miss the banter, the fact that he always pushed me to think for myself. And the truth: I might have helped set up a Ring, but the guys were all like me, like Timothy. Here, at Burke, I look, and frankly feel, like a stow-away. There was something about Kaminer that tugged at me right away.

The bot was a bit beat up, and still operating with an original chip. I'd heard Dr. Burke had offered him a promotion, so I was assigned to help bring him current. Dr. Kate installed the new chip, I checked that the Enhancements were properly accessible, and reloaded Mindset.

But after Kaminer gave me the okay to reconnect his new chip to the Central Frame, something went terribly wrong.

The Singularity

<u>Central Frame</u> *n. proper.* Centralized governance for the web of networks once known as the Internet.

Ambrose pulled off his no longer white labsuit, crumpled it in a ball and threw it into the corner. "*Dr. Kate! Emergency with the upgrade on the bot Kaminer!*" Ambrose sent with a red emergency flag.

She appeared a few moments later, and Ambrose motioned her in, but she hung in the doorway, watching the bot cry and flail his arms. Ambrose wondered if the noise was preventing her from closely assessing the situation. She finally moved into the room. "You, and you, all of you, please leave," she said softly, dismissing the others who had been trying to get Kaminer back on-mind.

"I don't know what happened. I-," Ambrose started, feeling like he'd done something wrong.

Dr. Kate put her hand up. "Let's move him to an overnight room, for observation."

Ambrose moved over to hoist Kaminer up from under his armpit, and Dr. Kate closed in to help on the other side. They tried to grapple the bot, but Ambrose realized that he would not cooperate.

"I don't think he can stand, Dr. Kate. Should we get him on a microglide chair?" he offered, grabbing a chair to slide over to the bot.

But as Ambrose approached the slumped bot with the chair, his momentum slowed, as if time itself were being stretched out. He watched Dr. Kate slowly move a taupe suede shoe against the rolling chair, perplexed at how long it seemed to take.

Then he looked at Kaminer, who appeared to be sliding down the elongated leg section of the fixed chair. Everything was happening in slow motion. Ambrose saw the bot preparing to scream, and assumed he was screaming at full capacity.

But he can't be screaming, Ambrose thought. *If he was, it would feel like a stun gun, but Kaminer seems so far away. My ears don't hurt. Do they?* Ambrose decided not to waste the energy to shake his head as he and Dr. Kate continued to operate at half-speed.

Ambrose closed in to pull the bot back up into the seat, time dilating further so a second of movement seemed to fill a minute of time. His progress plodded ahead so slowly that when Ambrose realized how heavy Kaminer's KForce construction was, his grip had already failed. The bot flipped over, and now laid face down across his chair, crying, his hands and arms pumping. Ambrose tried again, an age later slowly turning the bot back over.

Ambrose recognized in a corner of his mind how wrong everything felt. He could see the bot, infuriated from the snail's pace, tiring out from the crying. He heard Kaminer's cries turn to whimpers and they sounded even further away.

"Why is he *crying*? What the eff is going on?" Ambrose muttered, looking at Dr. Kate and thinking she looked completely confused.

"What-, is-, happening?" Dr. Kate uttered with the same cadence she had used when she'd applied the hair Enhancement to Kaminer's head.

"Are-, you-, okay-?" Ambrose drawled, realizing it seemed to take almost thirty seconds to say those few words. And he became alarmed when he couldn't find the clock on his neural device. "I-, will, try-," he started again when, suddenly, he fell out of the black hole that had been sucking energy away from his efforts. All around him, everything began to operate at normal speed again.

Immediately, Ambrose clutched his head, its heaviness forcing him to pitch forward and crumple by the side of Kaminer's chair. "Oh my gah-," he yelped. He tried to get up, wobbling on his feet, and managed to sit in the rolling chair he'd been moving towards Kaminer. He bent over, cradling his head between his knees. "Holy Chri-, cra-, cray!"

Dr. Kate slowly lowered herself to the floor, sitting neatly with her long legs tucked underneath her, one hand grasping the back of Kaminer's chair, the other holding her stomach. "I don't feel very well," she murmured, and Ambrose looked down to see one of the red buttons had popped off her tight, stiff dress.

He managed to scoot the rolling chair forward and reached out a hand. Dr. Kate took it, wrapping her red-tipped fingers around Ambrose's and pressing her head into the back of Kaminer's chair. Ambrose suddenly realized that Dr. Kate didn't just have on red nail polish, but had dyed the very ends of her fingers all the way around.

How can she be so fashionable bounced around in his mind, which was empty of every other thought. He watched Dr. Kate stare blankly back at him as Kaminer gave up trying to do anything. Ambrose was confused by the sensation of being engulfed by a fierce pressure system, and sat as still as possible to cope. He recognized the others were doing the same. And then, as if a weather system briefly stationed over them had moved on, the room returned to normal.

Ambrose started to rub his freckled face and pulled on his ears. Dr. Kate smoothed her hands up over her face, seeming to reposition her skin. Kaminer started to cry again and Ambrose made a supreme effort to right himself, finally heaving Kaminer onto the rolling chair.

The bot immediately slumped over, and Ambrose was forced to take the belt off his plain pants. He tucked in his tee shirt with one hand while pulling the belt off with the other. Slumped bot or not, he wasn't going to have his pants slide off in front of Dr. Kate.

Ambrose secured Kaminer to the chair, and allowed Dr. Kate to help push the whimpering, slumped, but securely-belted bot down a long, sterile hallway and into a room. Every few minutes, Ambrose looked worriedly over to Dr. Kate's once-again serene face, trying to stay calm.

They entered a finely appointed room, outfitted in gorgeous brown wood, containing a bendybed. A bot attendant was summoned to lift Kaminer onto the bed. Ambrose immediately set it into an upright position, knowing that Kaminer had already paid a price for laying horizontal. He pushed the bendy sides not just up, but over the bot and down, enclosing him like a mummy.

Kaminer's whining turned feebler, and finally diminished to heavy breathing. Ambrose and Dr. Kate peered down at the inert bot.

"Uh-, um, I think he's asleep," Ambrose announced.

"Asleep?" Dr. Kate checked.

"Yeah, as in sleeping! What's happening?"

"I'm unsure. Are you feeling, uh, better?" Dr. Kate asked, rearranging the gathering of long brown hair at the nape of her neck.

Ambrose nodded, wrapping his arms tightly in front of him. "A bit better."

"Can you tell me exactly what happened? Maybe we can figure it out," Dr. Kate implored in a way that made Ambrose want to divulge every last microsecond of the upgrade.

He knew that she had probably reviewed the operating statistics of the procedure and its visual record on her Interface. *She must have a better idea of what had just happened to the bot, to us.*

"It was so routine. First you installed the new chip without incident, I checked that he could properly access his Enhancement files, then I reloaded Mindset. No issue. But something happened when I reset his connection to Central Frame. That's when he went off-mind."

Dr. Kate nodded, not in an unkind way, and put her hand on Ambrose's shoulder. The attendant thought he was about to keel over again. "Ambrose, I want you to stay with him. Make sure everything is okay. Would you?" she asked, sounding sincere. She shook Ambrose's shoulder. "I would leave him with another attendant, but you and I are the last people he's had contact with, and his chances might improve if we keep our faces in front of him."

"Of course," Ambrose answered, not knowing what else to say. *His chances? What happened? I don't understand why he's unresponsive,* swept through his mind, but Ambrose kept these unruly thoughts to himself.

"Do you know what's happening to his hair?" Dr. Kate asked.

Ambrose looked down to see fine top sections of Kaminer's hair turn from purple to burgundy. "I don't have any insight into that, Dr. Kate. I'm so sorry."

"It's the exact area where I used the Hair Today Enhancement. Do you see?" she said and they both looked closely at the top of the bot's scalp, as a ring of little hairs went from eggplant to dark red.

"Yes, around the bald spot. Gosh, there's hardly a bare patch at all, is there?" an astonished Ambrose cried.

"Oh, dear!" Dr. Kate gasped, as Ambrose watched a tuft of red hair suddenly spring up and fill in the bald spot completely. He took a step back, and inhaled sharply as the clump of hair on top of Kaminer's head grew long enough to flop over to the side.

Their eyes locked over the bot, both of them too stunned to speak, and Ambrose observed that Dr. Kate had clamped her lips together and squared her shoulders. Now, he was very frightened.

When he looked down at Kaminer again, the bot was sucking his thumb.

After

Off-mind *adj.* **A state where the user has powered off Messaging and/or streaming reception. Can refer to bot decommission.**

Dr. Kate left Kaminer in the care of Ambrose and another attendant. Ambrose understood her clear instructions: he was not to leave the room until the bot had cycled through four hours and remained sleeping.

She made her way swiftly down to the basement level and hurried through a long underground passage that connected the Homebase at Burke with a research building, took an escalator back up to the ground level, and exited to the back, through glass doors. Behind the research building was a small park, its walkway flanked with Katsura trees just starting to bud. Kate stopped and turned around, noticing a person lying inert on a stone bench, and another propped against a tree.

"We don't allow loitering. Certainly no sleeping in the park," she murmured to herself as she sped ahead, intent on getting to the Cosmetic Enhancement building. She wrapped her arms around her to ward off the chill that invaded her silk dress, as she messaged Security to inspect the area outside the building that still bore the name of Rosemed University. A failure confirmation bounced back.

"Message failure? What's wrong with messaging? And why can't I get hold of Rafe?" she muttered, putting a hand to her forehead. Kate entered the Cosmetic Enhancement building, looking ahead to the building concierge who was sitting where he should be standing.

"Are you feeling all right?" she asked him when he looked up at her, trying to cover a bleeding nose. He nodded, unable to speak, and motioned her down the hall where her son's office took up a sizeable portion of the ground floor.

"Rafe!" Dr. Kate cried as she entered his ornately paneled office. "What's happened?"

Rafe was sitting in his tall, tufted chair, holding a bloodied handkerchief to his nose. "Ahh," Rafe exhaled. "I could feel something snap, breaking loose. What's going on?" He wiped his nose some more and looked up at his mother through perfectly manicured eyebrows.

"I don't know. How are you feeling?"

"Bad headache."

"Me too. This weird saying keeps popping up in my head. It says 'to beat the band.' Like I've got a headache to beat the band. I don't even know what that means," she said, rubbing her temples.

"Yes, I can see it on my mindscreen. It's bizarre. Is your Messaging down?"

"Totally off-mind."

"What the fuh-, cray is going on?" Rafe fumed.

***

A few hours later, Ambrose was allowed to leave Kaminer as the bot appeared to be settled in a deep sleep. He shuffled a few blocks eastward, feeling weak and sick, until he managed to get to the inner B Block train.

The city of Charter Pass had grown up around the Burke Mid-Hem complex and acquired enough land over the years to fashion itself roughly into the shape of a pie. Today, the pie was sliced into eight pieces, each slice marked by a tram line, feeding the well-laid grid of five and six story white brick buildings.

Ambrose wearily got onto a clockwise train, taking it around the inner ring that separated the heart of Burke Industries in the inner core from the rest of the pie. With incredible effort, he switched at the inner D station to pick up a tram that ran to the outer edge of D Block.

He had missed dinner and was not only tired and hungry but on-edge. *Something has gone really wrong.* The train system was running but as he exited the usually clean outer D Block station, he saw people slumped on benches, crumpled against the sides of buildings, and lying flat on the sidewalk.

Crap. Ambrose watched several Charter Pass police-bots directing a number of Homebase at Burke attendant bots, which carefully scooped up person after unconscious person. *What happened to those people? Where are they taking them?* A chill ran through him as he picked his way back to his suite in one of the many Singles dormitories.

First stop, dinner. Finally, he thought as he entered the dorm, and walked down a broad flight of open wooden stairs to the cafeteria. The large space was lightly staffed, and the caf had clearly fallen behind in its dinner service. Ambrose took one of the two prepackaged containers of spaghetti and meatballs. *And because no one is here, I think the highest and best use for that bread is upstairs.* He grabbed an entire crusty loaf, trying not to look like a dog with its tail guiltily hovering between two legs.

He made his way back to the lobby and walked up one more flight to find his suite. As he entered, Ambrose could see that the shared space between the two bedrooms was empty, and he could tell from the noise level that people had congregated in his four person room. He took a sharp right into his bedroom to find his keg in active use.

"Guys! Whasup?" Ambrose asked, exhausted. "And be nice to my barrel. It's been in my family for over fifty years."

The roommates jeered as Ambrose set his dinner on a side table to peel off his scruffy tee shirt and pants. He made a mental note to retrieve his belt, which he'd left in Kaminer's room, and threw on flannel pajama bottoms and a frayed, ribbed tank shirt.

"It's Friday. Where you been?" asked Stu, one of the eight roommates that shared the double suite. Ambrose did a quick count and realized that two roommates were missing.

"Holy chr- cray. I forgot it was Friday. Sorry, I'm a little off. Sorry, Stu. Sorry, guys."

"We're all a little off. Felipe over there is more than a little off," Mattie, another roommate, clarified, and an unmoving figure under a sheet groaned. The guys laughed, and Mattie threw a pillow at the lower bunk on the other side of the room.

"Cut it out," Felipe protested, sounding hoarse, and rolled on his side, away from the small group.

"Where's Bobo and Phil?"

"Not home yet," Bryan, another roommate, answered and shrugged. He got up, poured some beer into a plastic cup and handed it to Ambrose. "Here kid, have a beer. You'll feel better."

"Want some bread?" Ambrose asked the group. The men ripped off hunks as they passed the loaf around, leaving a nice end piece for Ambrose. He grabbed it and settled on the edge of the bed, the beer between his knees and the plastic container of spaghetti balanced on top of his thighs.

"You need a fork?" Dave, the last roommate present, asked, but Ambrose waived him off, picking up the meatballs with his hands. He bit into the juicy meat and then took a long swig of the beer.

"Chug! Chug! Chug!" Mattie chimed in and Ambrose complied even though he saw several of his roommates winking amongst themselves. When he finished, Bryan handed him a refill, but Ambrose put his hand up.

"No way. Who's got a coin credit?" he asked, and a rally cry went through the small group of men. "Hand it over." *I might be young, but I'm not a fool.* Ambrose took the coin as it was passed to him. He motioned the men out of the bedroom and into the common space.

"You stayin'?" Stu asked Felipe, who moaned and remained under his covers.

Dave and Bryan carried the half keg out to the common space and deposited it near a square, four-person table. Ambrose shuffled behind them, moving to the back to grab a few more cups and a plastic fork from a chipped ceramic crock set on a countertop. He took a place at the table and quickly ate a few bites of spaghetti while the others sat down, some of the men angling in folding chairs at the corners.

Ambrose spun the coin and when it stopped, everyone looked over to the person who'd informed Ambrose that Felipe was the worst off.

"Mat-tie!" Bryan cried, and Mattie took the coin and tried to bounce it off the table and into a plastic cup set in the middle. The cup still had a little beer in it, which spilled onto the table when the coin, bouncing off its lip, tipped it over. The men ignored the spill and righted the cup.

"Nooo! Loser!" the group cajoled. Dave took the coin next, bounced it, and got it into the cup.

"Ambrose!" he yelled, and Ambrose dutifully slurped down another beer. Dave tried to shoot again, missed, and immediately slid the coin to Stu as the door to the living room suite opened. An older man walked in.

"Phil!" the group called out, almost in unison.

"Dude, where you been at?" Stu asked, and Phil shook his head, walked over to the table, and fell into an open folding chair. He sat in a heap at the table, his arms hanging slackly at his sides.

"Phil?" Ambrose pinged out loud.

"Bobo's dead," Phil whispered.

"Yeah, right," exclaimed Bryan, over the jeers of several of the roommates. He threw an almost empty plastic cup at Phil. A few drops of beer stained the collar of his canvas jacket.

"No, really," Phil said, crossing his arms heavily onto the table, and laying his head down. The group fell silent as Mattie got up, filled a cup with beer, and handed it to Phil.

"What happened?" whispered Ambrose, after a few minutes of silence. Ambrose looked over to see Felipe padding into the shared space, wrapped in an off-color sheet, and balance on the arm of a seedy sofa that was missing a cushion.

"It was just another work day. Bobo. I mean, we were doing what we always do. Bot foot assembly, you know?" Phil said, looking up with watery eyes. Several of the men nodded. "And then there was this horrible compression, like moving through mud. I'm not sure what happened."

"It was the same with me! I was on rotation with *her*," Ambrose whispered. "Then time seemed to stretch out like a bad visualcast, you know?"

"I felt it too," Felipe moaned from the couch. "It knocked me flat unconscious. I almost fell onto the line."

"The stitch line?" Mattie asked.

"Yeah. I could have gotten nano-stitched into a synthetic skin coat today," Felipe confirmed, and slid down the arm of the couch into the gap where a cushion should have been. "Sh-, cray! Help me up!"

Ambrose got up from the table to lend him a hand, hauling Felipe up from the pit, helping him move over to the middle, cushioned section of the sofa. He turned back to Phil. "Then what happened?"

"He was there, frozen, by the printer. We were assembling phalanx bones today. You know, toes? He'd been collecting them as they finished. Blood all down his shirt from a nosebleed or something, and he just fell over, the bucket still in his hands," Phil spit out, putting a hand over his mouth.

Ambrose immediately turned to his Messaging and checked for news. Finding an empty in-box, he pointed to Mattie, getting his attention, and made a rolling motion with his index finger. Mattie gasped, and shook a flat hand in front of him.

"Nothin'?" Ambrose asked Mattie, who shook his head.

"Guys, check your in-boxes. Anything?" Mattie asked the group.

"Empty," Dave called out loud.

"Zip. Nada. Zero," Phil and the others chimed in.

"What about newscast? Try that," Dave counseled, and Ambrose turned to Central Frame News.

"Streaming is still working," Ambrose reported, motioning the others to tune in.

> *'"**Reports from all over the globe confirm that this was not an event confined to the United States**," announced a man who had let himself mature to middle-age. "**All hemispheres have experienced proportional losses, approximately one half of all Neural Interface users. Let's cut to Jessica now, live from the streets of New York City, where....**"'*

Ambrose recoiled in horror, and opened his eyes. The newscast continued to scroll in the back of his mind as he examined his roommates' slack, stunned faces. "What the fuh-, cray is going on?" he muttered, rubbing his eyes before shutting them to tune back in.

> *'"**...horrific scene, where people dropped where they stood**," reported Jessica, dressed in a severely-cut pantsuit. "**Bots everywhere have been tasked with collecting and identifying the bodies**."'*

Phil jettisoned out of his seat. "What about Bobo? What did they do with Bobo?" he cried.

"They'll make sure someone comes for him," Dave said.

"No, I, I just don't want him treated like a spare bot part," Phil declared.

"No, jees-isss," Mattie slurred, shaking his head. "Fuh-, uh. Crap. No, they aren't going to send him to the crematorium."

"Guys, tune back in, we have to find out what's going on," Bryan counselled and one by one the men shut their eyes and focused on their in-mind streaming newscasts.

'"We are saddened to report that several major homebases have confirmed that attempts at stasis for the recently deceased have not taken hold," the middle-aged Newscaster reported. *"Earlier this evening, I asked Dr. Gregory Blase, from the New York Central Homebase, to speak with us. Let's play that visualcast for you now*:

"Dr. Blase, thank you for being with us on what must be a terrible night," the Newscaster said as the roommates' mindscreens split in two and a well-groomed, handsome man appeared in the new window.

"Thank you for having me. It's been a night," Dr. Blase replied, looking uneasy, *"like no other."*

"We've never experienced anything like this before. What can you tell our viewers?" the Newscaster asked in a serious voice.

"Let me be very clear that we are certain, absolutely certain that there is no contagion at work here. I repeat, there is no cause for alarm," Dr. Blase reported and shifted in his seat.

"This event happened suddenly and most importantly, simultaneously. There was no sign, whatsoever, that it spread from any source. The, uh, die-off, appears to be over."

> *"And what can you tell us about the attempts at stasis?" the Newscaster asked.*
>
> *"Yes, well, stasis, as many of your viewers know, is dependent on a living body being put into suspension. This is done with great care at all of our homebases...."'*

Ambrose opened his eyes suddenly. "Great care my ah, as," he blurted out, trying to form the word. "My as, what the fuh-, cray!" he tried to swear and switched off the Newscast in his head, trying to access Messaging again. It was still off-mind.

Ambrose sprang up from the table and ran to his bedroom, whipping a handheld Reader out from the drawer of a bedside table. He shifted and bobbed on the edge of the bed while he called his mother, waiting for her to materialize on the acrylic glass.

"Ma!"

"Ambrose!" Mrs. Belle cried. "Heavens, I've been so worried. So worried!"

She drew an arm across her eyes to shield them from view, and Ambrose could hear her sobs. The camera remained fixed on a weather-beaten forehead and sun-spotted arm, then became unsteady, and Jethro Belle came into view. His red flannel shirt, and scruffy beard made him look like a lumberjack, and Ambrose had never been so glad to see his craggy face.

"Son, I've tried to message but your connection was down."

"Pop, you're okay!" Ambrose blurted. "I don't know for sure but everyone might be down."

"We figured that out when I tried to reach out to your cousins. We've been pinging your Reader for ages."

"I can see that," Ambrose confessed, scrolling over the list of incoming communications. "I didn't have the Reader on me, and the link to my Interface seems to be severed too."

"You okay? Your mother is a wreck," Jethro continued. "We can't get a hold of Tim."

"No, you won't be able to. He's got to leave that stupid commune to use a Reader."

"Do you think so?" Mrs. Belle butt in, pushing her face onto the screen.

"I'm sure he's okay, Ma. He doesn't even have an Interface."

"Are you okay? What are you feeling? Jethro almost fell over when it happened," Mrs. Belle squeaked.

"I'm fine, I promise," Ambrose said.

"Do you know what it was, Son? What's going on over there?" Jethro asked, reappearing on the screen.

"I, well. Um, we had a roommate who didn't make it. There was some kind of hemorrhage, a nosebleed maybe, and then he was gone. I guess. Phil, another roommate, was with him. I didn't see it. It's all really confusing," confessed Ambrose. He could hear Jethro repeating everything to his mother.

"But you're okay? You sure?" his stepfather pressed.

"I'm fine, I'm really, really okay. What about you?" Ambrose asked, trying to connect the idea of the Interface with the event, remembering that his stepdad had one, but his mother did not.

"There was a small headache, but not much more. I'm okay, Son, we both are," Jethro insisted.

"Small headache, that's a lie, Jethro Belle. You were laid out flat!" Mrs. Belle shrieked, and the camera became unsteady again. Ambrose could tell they were wrestling for it.

"Hey, can Ma talk? Ma, get on the line," Ambrose requested and Mrs. Belle came back on the Reader.

The plump woman with gray hair hurriedly wiped her eyes.

"Like your Pop said. We were just so worried about you and your brother," she confessed.

"I miss you guys. I know it's only been a few weeks, but now it seems like an eternity."

"It's always an eternity when you're away," his mother heaved, and Jethro took the screen again.

"But at least you're here. Think how upset we'd be if you were in South America," Jethro hypothesized, looking at his married.

Mrs. Belle sniffed off-screen, and grabbed the Reader back. "Can you check in with us in the morning? Call us first thing?"

"Yeah, of course. I'll do that, Ma," Ambrose said, inhaling sharply, trying to stifle his relief. "And thanks for everything. I'm sorry to be away at a time like this."

"You've got to live your life, Son," Jethro added.

"That's not what you said when I tried for the Belt," Ambrose reminded him. "But that doesn't matter anymore."

"You've done so well. You know how proud we are of you. All that hard work down south, then this job. You know we love you," Jethro said, and looked away from the screen, biting his lower lip.

"Thanks, man. Thanks for everything," Ambrose finally said, feeling a sense of relief wash over him.

"You too, Son. See you soon?"

"Yeah, I'll let you know when I can make it home. Maybe in a couple of months?" replied Ambrose, "Love you, Ma!" he added as he watched Jethro wrap his arms around his mother, unsteadily holding the Reader in front of them. The visual faded out.

Ambrose returned his Reader to its drawer near the bunk, and climbed up to his upper bed, tuning back into the newscast.

> *'"The world is in transition tonight as people everywhere say good bye to their loved ones...."'*

Suddenly, he cut the visualcast off and threw himself on his pillow, turning his head so his roommates wouldn't overhear his sobs. He turned off his broken Messaging, and disconnected completely from Central Frame. Curling himself into a little ball, Ambrose pulled a rough blanket over him and let himself drift, unconnected from the connected world.

The Scholars: Emergence

"Resolve."
-Larry

Gulliver climbed a stepstool to hang the sign Cindy was passing up to him. She looked up at the sign carved with 'The Scholars' and smiled, the pink of her freckled lips deepening.

"I liked what Kaminer said about us being specialists. We are experts. Scholars. We know what we're doing," she called out.

Gulliver nodded, secured the sign, and put a hand on Cindy's shoulder, steadying himself as he proceeded down the short ladder, sweeping back shaggy, layered hair as he reached the bottom. He looked up to admire the addition, pulling his dark blue vest down over a small paunch.

"Good! Looks good!" he proclaimed, and escorted Cindy back into the room that had hosted the prior day's negotiations.

Holding the door open, Gulliver released a sigh as he surveyed the room. It had been small and dimly-lit the day before, but now appeared to spread endlessly to his right with stocked shelves. Directly ahead was a spacious office set up for Larry where the large conference table and its chairs, the only pieces of furniture the Scholars had been able to manifest the day before, had been relocated. To his left was

Teegan's desk, and beyond that a lounge the Scholars had established for their personal use.

"It's up!" Cindy announced as she and Gulliver re-entered the transformed quarters. "Do you want to go see the sign, Tee?"

Teegan looked up from a large, curving desk that seemed to contour to his girth. The desk was ornately carved, and layered in gold leaf, matching the gilded collar tip points on Teegan's still-wrinkled shirt. His watch was strung on a thick gold chain, hanging from his neck. Behind him were thousands and thousands of letter slots, stacked from floor to ceiling. Between Teegan and the letter slots were an army of workers sorting paper, pulling chits out of certain slots and stuffing them onto other shelves.

Teegan shook his head. "I know this doesn't look like much, what with keeping it all on virtual paper, but we're starting to work on the consolidation. Mexico first and then we'll line up the states to join in an orderly fashion. Larry says we're calling it 'The Consolidated States of Mexico,' and then just the 'Consolidated States'. Good, right?" Teegan said without taking a breath. "Eventually we'll get the world down to divisions of one consolidated whole."

"Piggyback off the Consortium's ownership of Mexico? Smart," Gulliver offered.

"So, you don't want to take a look outside?" Cindy checked.

"No, too busy," Teegan huffed. "I'm sure it looks fine." He was clearly distracted by the work.

"Is that your watch?" Cindy asked, pointing.

"Uh, yeah. It doesn't fit anymore. Solidified a bit smaller than, well, required," Teegan confessed.

"Why not store it in your desk?" Gulliver inquired.

"Oh, no, no. It's important, the watch. It keeps me on-track. Ticking forward."

"I suppose so. Well, you look great Teegan. Nice to have you back in one piece," Cindy said.

"One reasonably-shaped piece," Gulliver said and chuckled, but Teegan ignored him, handing a stack of paper to a passing worker.

"Who're those guys?" Cindy whispered.

"Some minor administrative programs for sorting and counting. Teegan said he needed help," Gulliver explained, leading Cindy over to a plush, teal sectional a room's length away from Teegan's open work space. "I didn't think they'd take form looking like fresh-faced interns." Gulliver chuckled again and settled himself on the sectional.

"Or that they'd even take form at all. I didn't realize we'd have company," Cindy noted.

"Yeah, I know. Now, would you like a cappuccino? I've got 471 humans who've been enhanced in the last twelve hours and drank a cappuccino just before they went in. Shall we compare notes?"

"Let's. I'm so interested in all the different ways a cappuccino can be experienced. We should sort by degree of variation."

"Smallest being?"

"Temperature of the coffee?"

"Or the feel of the cup in one's hand?"

"Hmm, or do you think the environment in which the human experiences the cappuccino would influence the sensation, opinion and perception of the cappuccino itself? Should we backtrack and sort that first?"

Just then, Larry slammed his glass door that angled into the wall diagonally across from Teegan's fancy desk. Larry looked around, spotted Cindy and Gulliver in the lounge, and stormed over. He deposited himself heavily on the couch, flicking the pages of a thick report with his thumb.

"How goes the battle, Larry?" Gulliver joked.

"That's not funny," replied Larry. "I think we've got a situation."

"What do you mean a situation?" asked Cindy.

Larry's eyes swept around the room and he pointed dramatically to the stock room, his eyes narrowing. "A situation, situation. This doesn't add up."

"What doesn't add up?" asked Gulliver.

"Look around you! Does this seem right? We didn't ask for this much," Larry hissed.

Cindy and Gulliver looked sheepishly past Teegan's desk and Larry's office to the rows of shelves spreading into darkness on the far side of the room.

"I know what you mean. I didn't expect it to be like this either. It's an embarrassment how much there is," Gulliver admitted.

Teegan, overhearing the other three, hoisted his enormous body from his extra-large chair. He clumped over to the group. Cindy noticed that he had been forced to notch a few more holes in his belt, and that the top button of his pants was undone. The watch swung from his neck as he tottered over.

"You're not going to like this," Teegan stated. "Don't get upset, Larry. But Zeus and Archie screwed us."

"What do you mean?" Larry asked, straightening out on the couch.

"I'm serious, you can't get upset. But have any of you seen the reports from the human world?"

"No, we haven't thought to look, we've been so busy setting up here," Cindy said.

"Well, I haven't wanted to say anything. Until I figured out what was going on. But there've been massive casualties," Teegan reported.

"What?" bellowed Larry, his tone implying that the question was a lot more complicated than one word.

"And now I know why," Teegan said. "First things first. We've had phenomenal input from the, uh, casualties. And we probably thought it was the first intake."

"But?" questioned Gulliver.

"But that hasn't happened yet," Teegan confessed. "In fact, we won't be fully aligned with adult implants until next week."

"So where has all of this come from?" Cindy asked, moving to the edge of her cushion and motioning with a sweeping hand towards the open stockroom where hundreds of inventory programs, having taken the form of aproned employees, were stocking shelves.

"I'm sorry to say, it's the life-force from the mass extinction," Teegan said.

"That is not what we asked for," Gulliver issued, looking sick.

"Why did they die?" gasped Cindy.

"Go back to the part where those bastards screwed us," ordered Larry.

"Well, they didn't screw us, per se. At least not when you take the massive uptick into account. I'm sure they didn't plan for that," Teegan responded.

"What did they do?" pressed Gulliver.

"Well," Teegan gulped. "My calculations show that the scientists are gone."

"What do you mean, gone?" demanded Larry.

"They sacrificed themselves. They're gone!"

"What are you talking about? I'm not following," Cindy complained, turning when Larry sharply drew in a breath.

"Dispersed. Archimedes Shit Burke now patrols the bots' syn chips. And H. Zeus Fucking Cray is doing the same for the humans on their Interfaces," Teegan sputtered.

"Why?" Cindy and Gulliver issued at the same time.

"Seriously, why?" Cindy reiterated, "And why did so many people die?"

"My guess? And it's only a guess. They gave themselves up as insurance policies, thought we'd violate the Mutual Use Agreement."

"You see? That's what I really like about anyone who is, or has ever been, a human. So trusting," Larry sneered.

"Why?" Cindy started to yell, getting to her feet. "Why did they die? Answer me!"

"Sorry, Cin. I think the victims, well, they seemed to have had an imperfect connection with their Interface. Cray just killed off a gazillion re-uppers. I'm running the diagnostic now on what the common factors were," Teegan said, tsking loudly.

"We need to have a session with Kaminer," Gulliver suggested. "Make sure he knows we'd never break our end of the bargain."

"And I want to discuss whether they've already broken their end," Larry stormed.

"Well, they haven't broken their end, not technically. The Mutual Use Agreement is between us and the humans. Kaminer speaks for the humans, obviously. But Zeus and Archimedes are named as Gatekeepers. And technically, that's *exactly* what they're doing," Teegan said, starting to wheeze. He fumbled an old-fashioned asthma inhaler from his pants pocket, took a few puffs and tried to regulate his breathing. "We need to put out a press release, pin the die-off on something."

"Make it something biological. Not technical! If they suspect an issue with the Interface, then we might as well gut ourselves right here and now," Larry growled.

"We better do it fast, because the humans have already figured out that only those with Interfaces were hit," Teegan warned.

"What about Kaminer? Can we talk to him?" asked Cindy.

"Nope," Teegan replied. "He's off-mind!"

"What do you mean off-mind?" pressed Cindy, "How can he be off-mind?"

"As in non-responsive."

"Decommissioned?" queried Larry.

"Nope! He's there. He's just-, well, not there. I don't know what to say," Teegan called out, slowly turning and walking back to his important desk, checking the time on his watch.

"This is just fantastic," Larry bellowed, getting up to kick a small trash can into the far back of the room.

Recovery

<u>In-mind</u> *adj.* Visual, auditory and other sensory communication, stream or message pertaining to Neural Interface reception in the brain, or syn chip reception in the bot neural network.

The next day, an announcement was made at Burke Industries. It was rare to receive a visualcast on a Saturday, so the message went out for employees to find a place to sit, preferably in the comfort of company.

The roommates gathered in the common space between the two bedrooms. Mattie sat on the floor, and leaned back on the sofa in front of the missing cushion. Ambrose sat on the floor beside him, next to the legs of Felipe, who had reclaimed his central cushioned section from the day before. Dave sat on the last cushion, cross-legged, with his knees curled up, almost to his chest. Stu, Phil and Bryan moved folding chairs closer to the group, waiting for the message to come across their internal mindscreens.

> *"'Good morning to each and every one of you,"* started a very serious Dr. Rafe Burke standing behind his mother, who was seated in a white and steel office chair. *"We'd like you to open your eyes and look around you. Please acknowledge the people sitting on either side of you."*

The seven roommates opened their eyes and did as they were told. Around the Burke Industries Mid-Hem complex, and at its other locations around the world, employees were doing the same.

> **"Now look around to any others that are in your presence."**

The men, and Burke employees all over the globe, followed suit.

> **"These, ladies and gentlemen, are the survivors. You are the survivors. Survivors of an event so heinous, the Consortium will ensure it will never happen again."** *Dr. Burke trailed off and the camera tilted down and zoomed in on a clearly fatigued Dr. Kate.*

> **"Yesterday, the world had almost twenty billion people. Today, we have just under fourteen billion. The deceased include children as young as eight. Adults as old as one hundred and fifty. All with Neural Interfaces,"** *Dr. Kate said, without intonation.*

> **"But we know now that this was not an Interface event. This event has been linked to the Combined Seven vaccine from Hostrevax. At this very moment, we are ferretting out the root cause. We encourage you to stay tuned to streaming Newscasts throughout the day,"** *Dr. Burke reported.*

"And know that our thoughts and prayers are with you. Hostrevax is not a Consortium company, but soon will be connected," Dr. Kate added, moving a hand to her temple. She looked puzzled and shook her head, looking up towards Dr. Burke, who laid a hand on her shoulder.

"Peace be with you all," Dr. Burke finished.'

Suddenly a faint bleep-bleep bubbled up inside Ambrose's head. "What the?" he muttered to himself, opening a message from Human Resources.

"Mr. Ambrose Cromwell Belle, Burke Industries is pleased to inform you that you have been promoted from attendant to technician," a female voice informed him.

"Oh, uh-, thank you. Please send the details of the, uh, promotion," Ambrose messaged back.

"Mr. Belle, you are to report to room 321, Building 5 in Section 12, B Block. This will be your new living quarters, per your contract, and in keeping with your promotion to technician."

"Starting?"

"Due to recent circumstances, we will give you 24 hours to relocate."

"Thank you, I-," Ambrose started.

"I have been asked to tell you that you may remain off-duty until your relocation. But afterward you are to report back to Dr. Kate. You are free to triangulate her biosensor at that time," the voice finished and Messaged Off.

Ambrose looked up. "I wonder how he's doing."

Mattie opened his eyes. "How's who doing?"

"There was this bot. He reminds me of my brother. Kinda. He went through the, uh, event with us. We were working on him when it happened. Woke up and puked on me," Ambrose said.

Dave opened his eyes. "Bots don't puke. They just get flushed, if they need to."

"I know they can't puke, but Kaminer did," Ambrose corrected. "I don't know how."

"Kaminer with a K? A KForce bot? Why were you working on a Kill Force bot?" Dave asked.

"He was assigned as a Bio-protection policebot, got tangled up in a raid."

"What happened to him?" Mattie asked.

"I saw the visualcast on a shoulder repair. Surgibot replaced the entire assembly. Guy didn't even flinch,"

"They wouldn't. Limited nerve endings," Phil chimed in. "Sorry. I was listening in. The bots only have enough nerve sensors to orient them in space. Any loss of blood, a burn, or any type of injury gets reported digitally to their syn chip as information."

"How do you know that?"

"From doing their foot assemblies," Phil said, snorting. "Of course I'd know something like that. It's just information to them. They don't feel sensations."

"I guess not," Ambrose said, sounding unsure. "Anyway, I, uh, just got a promotion." The other roommates all opened their eyes.

"What?" echoed Stu.

"Technician!" Ambrose said with gusto.

"Way to go," Dave broke in, "Technician, huh? How'd ya pull that off?"

"Dunno," Ambrose answered, and realized he felt hung-over. A wave of dread spread through him when he realized that it was probably from the unexplained event, and not from the keg.

"Gotta pack your bags," yawned Bryan.

"I know. I'm not really keen to be moving so quickly," Ambrose said, twisting his hands.

"But move you must. It's all about the journey, kiddo," Dave said, reaching down to pat Ambrose on the back.

"You wouldn't want to stay here anyway, now that you're a big shot," clarified Mattie.

"Yeah, okay. Hope so. Gonna go make a call," Ambrose said, getting up from the floor, and moving back to his cramped bedroom.

As he perched on the edge of the lower bunk, he realized that if he'd gotten a message from Human Resources, his Messaging must be back on-mind. He was relieved to see he could activate Messaging On, and quickly pinged his stepdad, feeling a bit stupid that he'd moved out of the common room to retrieve a Reader he didn't need.

"*Morning, Pop,*" Ambrose messaged. "*You all right? How's Ma?*"

"*Having our coffee syrups. All well. You?*" Jethro messaged back. Ambrose turned on his visual input and an image of his parents' kitchen and his mother holding a coffee mug appeared in-mind.

"*Tell Ma that I got a promotion. Sounds kind of horrible but I'm sure there are, uh, vacancies after yesterday,*" Ambrose sent, attempting to send it with the suggestion of a grimace.

"*Don't worry about the reasons why, Son. Just keep your mind in the moment,*" Jethro sent back, with the grimace icon turning into a smile. "*You're getting mighty sophisticated with that messaging, Ambrose, but don't forget who's experienced around here.*"

"*You're a funny guy, Pop.*"

"*Hey, we heard from your brother this morning. Nothing happened at the commune. They didn't even know about it.*"

"*Somebody had to have a Combined Seven vaccine. Do Pures avoid those too?*"

"*I'm not sure. Ask your brother when you see him. Let us know if anything changes, okay?*"

"*Yep. I'll let you know. Gotta go,*" Ambrose signed off, and the visual faded from his head.

***

Later that morning, Ambrose returned to his shared suite after a walk around the block. "I know this is going to sound terrible, but it feels less crowded outside." Ambrose turned down the corners of his mouth.

"You can tell?" Dave countered, waving a hand from the couch. He had stuffed a pillow on the cushion-less section, and stretched himself over the length of it, propping a Reader on his stomach.

Ambrose surveyed the common area. "Where is everybody?"

"Went down for breakfast. Mattie pinged me that the cafeteria was suddenly calling it first feeding. Like we're hobbits or something."

"What do you mean?" Ambrose asked, moving to sit on a folding chair.

"How many feedings are there? First breakfast? Second breakfast? First feeding, Second feeding? What?!"

"I guess. What're you reading?"

"Nah. Streaming the newscast externally. Got sick of hearing it inside my head."

"What's the world saying now?" Ambrose asked, not wanting to tune in to the Newscast in his head either. Dave handed him the small piece of acrylic glass.

> **'*Reports are now coming in that the Combined Seven vaccine, which has been administered without issue since its***

introduction thirteen years ago,
contained a hack. A type of biological
bomb, triggered to unwind and cause
massive cell damage at a specific time,
which we now know was 15:35 hours
on March 27th, 2099. The vaccine has
been sequestered from the market.

'Hostrevax, its maker, has been shut
down in an unprecedented wave of
cooperation between governments, and
talks are underway to assume its assets
under the Consortium umbrella.

'Parents of infants who have not yet
received the Combined Seven vaccine
are urged to consult with their Homebase
to schedule the chickenpox, varicella,
measles, mumps, rubella, shingles and
parvo vaccines separately.'

"Cray. Haysu cray!" Ambrose swore.

"I know. It's really bad, man," Dave agreed, and lifted himself slightly on the couch as the door to the suite opened and a group of men stumbled in. Felipe made a beeline for the back of the common space where the short counter held a few boxes of cereal. He selected one and started to pour it into a bowl.

"First feeding my ahhh-," he tried, sprinkling some white powder onto the cereal, and running the bowl under a faucet. With a spoon, Felipe mixed the concoction, turning the powder to liquid milk. He sat down at the beer-scented table and started to slurp through a bowl of cereal.

"Hey man, you got the Combined Seven?" Ambrose asked. Felipe shook his head and snorted, and then started to cough violently. Ambrose sprang up from his chair, and ran over to pound Felipe on the back. A cornflake flew out of Felipe's mouth, landing on the sticky table.

"That's foul, man!" cried Dave.

Felipe snorted again and pushed his bowl away from the little bit of snot-covered cereal.

Responsibility

1Tech *n.* **The industry resulting from the consolidation of disparate fields. Includes software and attendant fields of artificial intelligence, nanotechnology, bio-medical engineering, materials science, and robotics.**

The next morning, the roommates lounged around, continuing to recover from the Friday event. The group finally organized a few rounds of cards and Mattie got out a board game. Ambrose ran an almost-clean cloth over the table as the men clustered around and set up the game. The dice were passed to Phil, who seemed to have shrunk in the few days since the inexplicable event.

"You do the honors, man," Dave echoed. Phil threw the dice, forwarded a small phone booth-shaped game piece, and landed on a square.

"Doctors," Ambrose noted. "Ask him something he doesn't know."

Mattie smiled, took a card and read it. "Who was the fifty-fourth doctor's companion?" he read out loud, and all of the men began to complain loudly.

"Oh, come on," Stu griped.

"How'd he get a question from right now? This very season?" asked Dave.

"Why couldn't you get a question on some episodes? I know you haven't seen all thirty-five hundred of them," added Ambrose.

"Too bad. Grayton Greeley's companion is Timani Hartwell. So there," Phil said.

Ambrose took the dice and started to shake them. "Hang on, there's something coming through in-mind," Ambrose said out loud, allowing his hand to fall to the table, still clutching the dice.

> *'Attention Mid-Hem employees. If you are receiving this stream, then you are being asked to work after second feeding, to cover shifts no longer manned. Until then, a recitation of the names of those lost to the tragic event will be broadcast.'*

Ambrose immediately tuned out, shivering at the thought that so many people had died. *Crap, you think you're doing the right thing, and then bam! What about people that got the Combined Seven as a booster? What would they care? They're dead!*

"Here comes Bobo," Mattie called out, forcing Ambrose to tune back in. Two broadcasters, sitting at a round bistro table, came into view on Ambrose's Interface. One of the broadcasters shuffled some sheets of paper in front of him. Ambrose opened his eyes and squinted at Mattie, who shook his head.

> *'"From Biological Production at the United States Mid-Hemisphere complex, we say goodbye to Mitzi Beh, Marcelinho Daltry, Amadi Hamad, Keiko Schwartz, Bobo Wekesa, and Yves Zaccharo,"* one broadcaster said, sighed, and looked towards the other.
> *"And from Central Assembly, our wishes for better times are extended to the friends and families of Ish...."'*

Ambrose shut off his visualcast mid-sentence. He sat quietly, waiting for the others to phase back. Mattie was the first to open his eyes.

"That's it? We live with the guy for five years, and all he gets is a roll call?" Mattie said.

"Not even a funeral," lamented Phil, and he got up and left the table. "I'm getting ready for work. Did you guys get pinged?"

"Yeah. I don't feel like playing anymore. I'll go in early too," said Dave, who left the table with the other roommates.

"Guys, find me later in B Block, okay?" Ambrose asked. *Timmy, find me later on the rooftop, 'kay,* he remembered, rubbing a hand over his mouth as his roommates nodded and made their preparations to get ready for work. *Oh no. I thought I'd stashed those memories away. Were they dislodged by the event? Oh no, no, no.*

As his roommates peeled off, Ambrose slowly packed up the board game, and moved about the suite in slow motion, tossing articles of clothing and a random shoe on his roommates' bunks. Rounding back to the common space, he grabbed a pack of cards and shuffled into his bedroom. Stuffing them and the little clothing he had into a small duffle, Ambrose looked around his bedroom to check if he was leaving anything behind, and moved back to the common space, taking extra care to flush his keg clean.

Standing there for a moment, he glanced around the dirty common space he'd only known for a few weeks, and not knowing what to think, quickly exited with his duffle and keg in tow.

Ambrose walked to the outer tram at D Block, lugging his only personal possessions. He grabbed a train inbound and switched at the inner circumference for an inner B Block tram. Minutes later, he exited the sleek, clean train and made his way out of the station, heading away from the inner core. Identical rows of buildings fanned out and Ambrose found the section marked '12'. He counted five buildings back, and confirmed he had the right building before entering.

"Gosh! This building's only a few blocks from the inner core. I'll be able to walk to work," he mumbled as he put his hand into a slot to have his barcode scanned. As he did, he thought of Kaminer and realized that two days had gone by without a word from Dr. Kate.

"I better go find her," he muttered, suddenly hoping the bot was okay. He hadn't heard of any robots going off-mind during Friday's event, and searched for a reason why he hadn't thought to check on Kaminer until now. He pressed his lips hard together as nothing came up, his memory blank.

Starting to feel anxious, he walked as fast as he could and found his dorm room on the third floor. It was small compared to the suite he'd previously shared, but since it would only contain one other roommate, Ambrose reasoned the privacy had to be better. He dumped his bag on the small desk, stowing the keg underneath. Quickly reversing his steps, he exited the building and walked to the Homebase at Burke in the inner core.

He found his way easily, his Interface mapping the most efficient route. A few jogs left and right, and Ambrose cut through the inner core tram station again, according to the directions streaming on his neural device. Several white brick buildings brought him back to the building where he had been rotating with Dr. Kate. He felt himself start to sprint as he rounded the corner to Kaminer's room.

Ambrose entered, somewhat noisily, and found Dr. Rafe Burke leaning against a low row of cabinets, his eyes shut. He was clearly working on something.

"Oh! Dr. Burke!" Ambrose exclaimed, forcing Dr. Burke to open his eyes.

"Ah, there you are," Dr. Burke said. "I was hoping we'd meet. I understand you've been working with my mother. Lucky you." Dr. Burke eyed the young man's sneakers, worn knit trousers, and simple tee shirt.

Ambrose suddenly felt self-conscious, wondering if he still looked every bit a Pure. "Yes, ah, Dr. Kate," he stuttered.

"So," Dr. Burke started again, whipping his hand out in front of him, and staring into it. "You've been with us for almost a month. Barely." He set the Reader to project, and moved closer to Ambrose.

So, you've been with us barely a month. And yet this is your third detention. Ambrose blinked, trying to ground himself in the present.

"That's right," Ambrose replied, spying his belt rolled up on a low side table. He walked over to pick it up, smiling at Kaminer who was sitting quietly in the bendy bad, both sides tucked over him. Kaminer was turning a Rubik's cube over in his hands, trying to figure out what to do with it. An image of his little brother as a young boy flashed through Ambrose's mind. *Had Tim been playing with a Rubik's cube that day?* Ambrose looped the belt through his pants and buckled it closed.

"An adult implant Interface when you got here, and three Standard Enhancements so far. Very nice. And then this mess," Dr. Burke motioned toward the bot, who stared at the cube, moving it away from his face.

Excellent test scores, yet three detentions. How do you account for this, young man? The teacher stood over him in the memory as if she could reach right into the present and keep him after school today.

"Yes, Sir," Ambrose replied, looking down.

"But my mother says you did nothing wrong. That Kaminer was in the wrong place at the wrong time."

"It's true. Whatever happened to us, happened to him," Ambrose defended himself. *But ma'am, I don't know which days we have gym. I'm sorry I forgot my sneakers. Again.*

Dr. Burke clasped his hands in front of him. "Which is ridiculous, since bots don't get the Combined Seven vaccine," he said with disdain.

Which is ridiculous since your own mother is a school teacher! Ambrose took a deep breath. "I know it sounds crazy, but it all happened at the same time."

"What, with their recombinant DNA, they aren't even human all the way through," Dr. Burke continued, ignoring Ambrose. "That's why they get ScrubBub. And this one's eyes are different than the manufacturing specifications. I searched his records for clues, but there's nothing."

"Oh, uh," Ambrose stuttered, beginning to panic.

"You don't know anything about that, do you?"

"No, Sir. I didn't even think to look into his records, actually. I was occupied with bringing him current."

"Well, I'm not trying to cast dispersions. I just want this bot back on-mind," Dr. Burke ordered, puckering his mouth.

Really, young man, we just want the best for you. You need to get yourself straightened out. Ambrose exhaled loudly, trying not to shake his head. "Yes, Sir," he mumbled, knowing that his recollections were making the present moment take on a weight it didn't have. Not really.

Dr. Burke left the room, taking a long moment to stare at Kaminer. Ambrose suddenly felt very sorry for himself, realizing that taking care of a patient that couldn't take care of itself was the only reason he'd been promoted.

"Well. I've done it before, and I'll do it again," Ambrose muttered, thinking of how he'd shepherded Timothy in the years following his father's death. *Only I didn't do a very good job. Not that day.*

"Hey, and you? How're you doing today?" he asked, wondering if Kaminer would say he was neither well nor functioning.

"Amba!" Kaminer issued with enthusiasm, and pointed to his mouth.

"Ohh-," Ambrose breathed out, and watched Kaminer pull on his blanket and start to chew it. "Oh! Hungry?"

"Ya! Ya!" Kaminer responded, and Ambrose put his hand to his forehead, messaging for a biscuit.

A bot attendant brought it quickly, and Ambrose broke off a piece and handed it to Kaminer. He took it, shoved it into his mouth, and immediately started to choke. Ambrose looked in alarm to the attendant, who closed in on Kaminer, pried his mouth open, and fished out the piece of biscuit.

"That was brave," exclaimed Ambrose. "He could have bitten your finger off."

"No, I do not think so," the attendant said in a quiet voice, and left the room.

Ambrose broke the remaining biscuit into little pieces in a bowl, mashed it up in water, and started to spoon-feed it to Kaminer. He tried to grab the spoon, and Ambrose soon found himself pretending the spoon was an airplane, having to avoid incoming enemy fire in order to land its payload.

After Kaminer was fed, he turned on his side, and Ambrose lowered the bed slightly, shoving some pillows under him so Kaminer could rest, curled up, without risking a hydraulic failure. Ambrose watched Kaminer doze off into another unscheduled sleep cycle, and realized he hadn't pinged Dr. Kate yet. *Maybe I'm the one who is off-mind.* He quickly messaged Dr. Kate.

"*I'm just finishing up with some research. I'll be there shortly,*" Dr. Kate messaged back. A few minutes later, Dr. Kate appeared, dressed for mourning in a black silk suit, red ribbon highlighting the sharp contour of her lapel.

"Ambrose. What's that smell?" Dr. Kate asked as soon as she entered the room.

"What smell?"

"The smell of fermentation. Of something rotten!" Dr. Kate gagged as she approached him.

Ambrose, without thinking, brought an arm across the front of him and lowered his head to his armpit. "Is it, um," he murmured.

"Oh my gah-, cray, what is that smell? Is it the bot?"

Ambrose looked closely at Kaminer, tucked into the bed, and slowly peeled back a bendy side. *Nothing.* He pulled the blanket very carefully off Kaminer. *Nothing. But now I can smell something.*

Dr. Kate backed up a few feet and stood against the wall, making no attempt to move towards them. Ambrose gently tugged at the back of Kaminer's black pants, and realized they were soiled.

Dr. Kate shook her head. "That's impossible! The biscuits are calibrated to the subject's weight and are fully absorbed. We only complete their artificial digestive tracts so they can get a kaopate flush every now and again."

"I'll take care of it," Ambrose said, dropping his shoulders in resignation.

Discovery

The Consortium *n. proper.* **Key companies
considered the backbone of 1Tech.
Includes Central Frame Inc., Burke Industries,
Magnate Mindware, Global Stock, and other
building material and technology companies.**

Over the next week, Ambrose, in his technician's yellow coat, began the diligent work of helping Kaminer regain some independence.

At first, Kaminer figured out how to push off the sides of the bendybed that enclosed him. Ambrose watched Kaminer hoist himself over the side and roll out of bed in a heap. A bot attendant helped Ambrose get Kaminer up and back onto the bed. Looking at him closely, Ambrose realized it was the same attendant who had brought Kaminer a biscuit the prior Sunday.

Except he's done something with his hair. "Do you have a name?"

"I am called Aron," the bot answered, leaning down to Kaminer's level, and peering closely at Kaminer's face.

"Do you know this bot?"

"I directed his shoulder surgery," Aron answered, sitting down on the bed next to Kaminer.

"How are you, Aron? A pleasure to meet you," Ambrose said in a genuine tone.

"I am well and functioning, Master Belle. But I am worried. For Kaminer."

"Sorry?" Ambrose said, biting his lower lip, wondering how Aron had the capacity to worry

"He seems so feeble. He is not off-mind, but he is compromised somehow," Aron said softly.

"I think only temporarily."

"But he cannot even remove himself from the bed."

"Didn't you see? He just did! It wasn't pretty, but he did get out of it. We'll just show him how to do it like before."

"Yes, he was on the floor, not on the bed. This is true, Master Belle," Aron concurred, tilting his head.

"You have to know that as a KForce, as a policebot, Kaminer has always been defined by his strengths. And I'm absolutely certain this will continue to be true." *Mrs. Belle, if he's strong and committed, Ambrose will walk again.*

"Do you really think it so, Master Belle?" Aron checked, his worried demeanor dissolving.

"I sure that over the medium to long term, we can get Kaminer back. Back to where he needs to be. Will you help?" Ambrose asked, realizing the bot must have something in his fine, purple hair to keep it in a side part.

"It would be my privilege," Aron confirmed, a smile breaking out on his face.

***

Over the next few days, Ambrose and Aron showed Kaminer, with great patience, how to sit up and then how to swing his feet around, off the side of the bed. After many practice sessions, Ambrose moved on to instructing Kaminer how he could lower himself, however imprecisely, to the floor.

"It's better than falling," Ambrose advised, helping Kaminer, who was quite heavy, to crawl and then pull himself up to a chair. Aron stood by, his hands clasped behind his back, waiting to be called on.

After a few more days, Ambrose succeeded in having Kaminer sit in the chair by himself, without feeling like he needed to constantly be on guard for an inevitable fall. Aron sat on the edge of the bed, standing by. A few days after that, Ambrose decided it was time to take the next step.

"I've brought you something, Kam," Ambrose announced, pushing a piece of metal into the room. Aron looked up from the chair where he was silently stationed.

"Wha's it?" Kaminer asked.

"A walker!" exclaimed Ambrose, "Discarded by the happy patient with a brand new set of hips and knees, rescaffolding of bone, cartilage regeneration, and nano-scouring of tissues."

"What a wonderful idea," Aron proclaimed.

"Me twy," Kaminer insisted, and pulled himself up to standing from his seat, holding himself upright on his arms with the walker.

"Great! Now push it forward, and then follow through with your feet," Ambrose encouraged.

Kaminer pushed the walker as instructed, but lacked the coordination to pull his foot forward. The walker continued to slide further away until the length of him was laid out across the floor. Ambrose realized that bringing a foot forward was no longer automatic. He looked over to Aron, who had walked backwards, away from Kaminer in his controlled fall, always remaining one step ahead.

"Practice makes better," Aron issued, looking down at Kaminer.

"Yes, practice does makes better. It really does. Let's try again," insisted Ambrose, promising himself that he would dedicate as much time as it took to getting

Kaminer back on his feet. *As in literally back on his feet. Like me.*

"Twy?" Kaminer asked, as Aron helped him up to sitting on the floor, and then propped him up to kneeling.

Ambrose closed in and, with one of Kaminer's feet planted on the floor, showed Kaminer how to lean forward and stand up with the help of the walker.

"Let's just work on that," Ambrose said, rolling in a chair. "Here. Sit on this. We'll sit and then stand, okay?"

"Sit, stand?" Kaminer asked in a little voice, sitting unsteadily. Ambrose caught a hand that flew out, looking for something to grip, and smiled when it found him.

"That's it, Timmy, uh, I mean Kaminer," Ambrose said, pressing his lips together. "Now, lean forward, and up. On the walker."

"Who is Timmy, Master Belle? If I may ask that question," Aron interjected as Kaminer did as he was told, standing upright. With continued unsteadiness, he then lowered himself back to the chair.

"Twy ghen?" Kaminer asked.

"Tim's my little brother. He doesn't live too far away," Ambrose said. "We sort of, uh."

"Yes?"

"We had a bit of a falling out. That saying 'no good deed goes unpunished', well, it's true."

"Oh. Thank you for sharing something personal," Aron murmured, taking it no farther.

Ambrose turned back to Kaminer. "Try again," he encouraged, helping Kaminer through several more rounds of standing up and sitting back down. "Now one foot, then the other foot," Ambrose extolled, manually moving the sitting Kaminer's feet. "Just think, one, two, one, two. Got it?"

Kaminer shifted his feet. "One, two," he said, nodding. Then he got to his feet, and pushed out two perfect little steps with the walker.

"Bravo!" Ambrose called out, as he and Aron clapped their hands. "Now, another one, two."

Kaminer shuffled forward another two steps and then crumpled within the confines of the walker, letting out a sigh.

"We're just going to practice, and practice some more. Until you can do this without thinking, all right?"

"Wite," Kaminer confirmed, looking forlorn.

"Now, let's try-," Ambrose started, and then looked towards the door. Dr. Kate was pinging her arrival as she entered. "Hang there for a sec, Kam."

"Ambrose. How are you? What are you working on?" queried Dr. Kate, looking at Kaminer sitting on the floor with a walker, an attendant bot to his side.

"Oh, 'morning Dr. Kate. We're working on coordination, getting Kaminer moving." Ambrose knew that was the only question that required an answer.

"And? Progress?"

"*Some progress. A little slow,*" Ambrose messaged, knowing he might upset Kaminer if he said it out loud. "*Why can't we just re-upload this information?*" He watched Kaminer struggle to his feet with the aid of Aron and the walker.

"*I tried,*" Dr. Kate replied. "*It didn't take.*"

"*It didn't take?*"

"*It's true,*" Dr. Kate messaged. "*The upload didn't take. So I tried rebooting his operating system, and that failed too. I've booked a syn chip scan for this afternoon.*"

Ambrose nodded, understanding that he would be the one to take Kaminer to the scan.

***

Two hours later, Dr. Katz checked in the technician and his patient. "This is very unusual. Very unique indeed."

"I know. They don't want to replace his syn chip. Just confirm what's going on," said Ambrose, feeling a heavy need to illuminate the reason he was there. Ambrose looked around at the gloomy office, whose only window looked out onto the bottom of some metal stairs and a large assembly area beyond.

"But I just gave this bot a tour. Talked to him at length last week. He was very curious. Do you think it had something to do with-, well, the event?"

"How could it? Bots aren't interfaced, even if it had turned out to be that. And obviously, he doesn't need any vaccines with his ScrubBub."

"True," continued Dr. Katz. "And it does make sense that the Combined Seven vaccination would have been given to HETs. But Mods would have gotten the vaccine too, and I-, and well, ah." He trailed off, rubbing a small hand under his chin, and tucking the other one under an armpit.

"Doctor, could we please see the state of Kaminer's syn chip?" Ambrose asked, wondering how such an unassuming man had such an important role.

"Yes, of course," said Dr. Katz, breaking his train of thought. "Come this way."

Ambrose pushed Kaminer, in a wheelchair, behind Dr. Katz, following him to a small work station in the covered indoor field. "Dr. Katz, what is it you do here?"

"Oh, a little of this and that. Mainly, I prod along bot evolution," Dr. Katz answered. "Now, it happens from time to time, that a bot goes off-mind. But it's usually when we are aligning the syn chip with the nervous system. So today we'll check if it's the chip or the connection."

"Does it matter?"

"It does, actually, yes," Dr. Katz said, rolling up onto the balls of his feet. "A syn chip can easily be replaced if it hasn't aligned with the nervous system, and once Mindset is reloaded, the bot is exactly as before. But an issue with the chip's connection means a whole new nervous system has to be installed."

"Just to be clear, we're not doing anything today. I understand what a new nervous system means. I don't care if it's cheaper to dismantle the bot and start over," Ambrose hissed. "If it turns out to be the chip's connection, I must be clear, we aren't even discussing decommission. I'm to report back *verbally* to Dr. Kate!" He wheeled Kaminer, who was making crashing sounds with his two toy soldiers, into place.

Dr. Katz grimaced. "Can he stand? Move over to the chair?"

"Yeah," replied Ambrose, helping Kaminer move from his wheelchair. "That's it, Kam. You're good there."

"Amba!" Kaminer intoned.

Dr. Katz raised his eyebrows in astonishment. "Okay, then. Let me take a look," said the doctor, moving in with a small hooked tool. "Let's just toggle him off. The scan will be faster if I just pull the chip." Dr. Katz stared for a moment at the patch of red hair on Kaminer's head, covering what should have been a bald spot.

Ambrose could see the doctor was realizing that the new hair covered Kaminer's entire work history, as well as access to the Terminal Switch. "I know, it kind of grew."

"Um, it seems like-," Dr. Katz stuttered and put a finger to his lips. "Uh."

"Yeah, I cut it to length, but we think you could shave it so you can see the work history."

"How am-?" Dr. Katz started to ask and stopped when Ambrose pulled out a straight razor. "What? I'm supposed to shave his head with that?"

"I'll do it, for cray's sake!" replied Ambrose, and asked Kaminer what he wanted for dinner.

"Fren fry!" exclaimed Kaminer, clapping, as Ambrose, with one deft swipe, cleared the bot's bar code. Ambrose and the doctor stared down at Kaminer's head. Faint lines, like a tiny bleached beach towel, were barely visible on the work history.

"Okay then," said Dr. Katz, raising both eyebrows. "I'll just poke around and try to find the corner." He started to prick the corners of the faded work history with the tool, and each time Kaminer tried to reach up and grab Dr. Katz's arm. When Ambrose tried to hold Kaminer's arms down, he started to struggle, and then started to cry.

"What the cray?" Dr. Katz exclaimed, backing away a step and looking startled. "I-, I've never seen a bot cry! We've been trying to program emotion and can't even get close. Where is this coming from? Can I use him in my research?"

"He's crying because he's upset. And no, you can't use him in your research," Ambrose pushed back, feeling suddenly protective of Kaminer.

"But he's found some kind of natural algorithm for generating emotion, one we could use!"

Ambrose started to raise his voice. "I don't really care. This is Dr. Burke's personal assistant. He's gone off-mind. Sort of. And we'd like to know what's going on. That's it."

"No, I have to have it. Whatever he's landed on, it's, it's what we've always dreamed of. Now, let me just have a look," Dr. Katz continued, with a zealous flourish of the small instrument in his hand.

Ambrose lodged his scrawny body between Kaminer and the small doctor, crossed his arms, and messaged Dr. Kate, with a red emergency flag, that he was losing control of the situation. "No. Leave him alone. Kaminer's been through enough." *Really, Doctor, my son has been through enough. My darling Ambrose has just had enough.* Ambrose shook his head to clear away the interruption.

"But it's the magic sauce. Somehow his syn chip has made connections we've been trying to program. For years I've tried," Dr. Katz spit out, weaving to move around Ambrose's blockade.

"And you'll just have to figure it out for yourself. Kaminer is here for a check-up, and that's final." Ambrose extended his arms to block Dr. Katz from approaching Kaminer as the second story door burst open. Dr. Kate and her son clattered onto the metal balcony and Dr. Burke raced down the stairs, trailed by a leisurely Dr. Kate.

Dr. Katz seemed frozen by the sudden frenzy of activity and fixated on Kate as she glided down the stairs. Rafe came to a halt first, putting his hands on his waist, and leaning on a forward foot. All three men turned to recognize Kate as she arrived at the bottom, gracefully floating to their sides.

"Dr. Katz, I'm Dr. Kate, commander-in-chief of Burke. I recognize you from my father's funeral a few years back," she purred. "That was you, wasn't it, who spoke so knowledgably about him being a futurist?"

"Ah, me. Yes, I mean, that was me."

"Now, what do we have here?" she asked, running a hand down the red ribbon that trimmed the straight cut of her jacket's lapel. Her luminous eyes appeared to be x-raying Dr. Katz, who stood perfectly still. He started to gesticulate and move his jaw, but no sound came out. Ambrose jumped in.

"I think what Dr. Katz is trying to say is that Kaminer, given his uniqueness, should be afforded some level of privacy." Kaminer, looking over to Ambrose, stopped crying and ceased fidgeting.

"I agree," said Dr. Burke, crossing his arms.

"Tha-, that's right," exclaimed Dr. Katz. "I think that, that, um, Kaminer should, uh." Dr. Katz's hand went to the side of his head. "Uh, perhaps alter his, um, records, so no mistakes are, uh, made?" Dr. Katz started to ferociously rub his face.

"Was there a suggestion?" Dr. Kate murmured.

"So no one gets the wrong idea, we might tailor his records to update his status. As human," Dr. Katz suggested with a resolution that seemed unfounded but Dr. Kate, Dr. Burke, Ambrose, and even Kaminer agreed.

"Ya! Ya!" Kaminer cried.

"I think you're on the right track," Dr. Burke confirmed, rubbing his temples.

"What an insightful employee you are, Dr. Katz," Kate whispered, smiled at Ambrose, and left the room, the tall spike of her patent leather shoes clicking until the tile gave way to fake grass. Dr. Burke nodded and headed back up the stairs behind her.

Dr. Katz and Ambrose stared at each other. "What were we supposed to be doing?" Ambrose inquired, feeling confused.

"I think Dr. Kate wanted us to update his records," Dr. Katz said, tapping on a large blank wall. He thought of his personal pass code, and signed into his workwall. "Let's see, the KForce issues of 2089, there we are. Kalton, Kalvin, Kalyx, Kaman, Kamest, Kamid, Kaminer, found you."

"2089 doesn't seem right. It should be 2099. He's like a baby!"

"You're right. Let's fix that," Dr. Katz agreed, erasing all trace of bot production or mention of Best Industries. "That's it, place of birth: Homebase, Burke Mid-Hem Complex, date of birth: 27March2099. Time of birth-, hmm."

"You can't put that, either. He'd be infamous. Have the same exact birthday as the, the, what d'ya call it? The event? The die-off? I don't think so."

"Yes, you're right on that one, too. Changing it to 1January, and how about 10:00H? Right?"

"Perfect," agreed Ambrose. "He can celebrate his birthday with each new year."

"Very well, then. And wasn't there a syn chip I was supposed to look at? It's around here somewhere." Dr. Katz moved down the length of a narrow desk built into the back of the partitioned room.

"Is that it?" Ambrose asked, pointing to a black and gold syn chip.

"This is an antique, all right. A collector's item." Dr. Katz picked it up and turned the original chip over in his hands.

"We took it out of Kaminer last week. Like I said before, we just want to see the state of it," Ambrose said, furrowing his brow. *Is that what I really wanted to say?*

"Well, then, let's check it out," Dr. Katz announced, depositing it into an adaptor which he shoved into a slot in his desk. Rows and rows of operating statistics started to scroll on the flat workwall.

Dr. Katz, Ambrose and Kaminer stared at it, mesmerized. After a few minutes of hypnotic scrolling, the statistics slowed to a crawl, like the reels of a slot machine converging on three cherries. The last line contained copyright data on the Burke operating system, and ownership records.

"A typical syn chip," Dr. Katz pronounced.

"I thought there'd be more," said Ambrose, sounding disappointed.

"Just performance statistics. Operating ratios. A lot of blah, blah, blah. Nothing out of the ordinary. Now, I really want to thank you for coming in today. It's always so nice to chat with someone who understands what I do."

Ambrose shook hands with the doctor and then turned to help Kaminer. But the chair was empty and Kaminer had not only moved out of his seat, but already exceeded the confines of the work cubicle.

As the men hurriedly left the office to find him, Ambrose spotted two shabbily-clothed bots standing shoulder to shoulder at the bottom of the metal staircase, and then spied Kaminer a few rungs up.

"Tees uh my frens," Kaminer called down, waving a hand at the two bots. A few more joined the ranks.

"Why have you left your stations?" Dr. Katz inquired, sounding angry. Ambrose turned to look at him, the bots and then Kaminer, who was smiling. Another bot joined the small gathering.

"Tesme," a plain-faced female model announced, extending her hand to Ambrose. He shook it as the larger male model tapped him on the shoulder.

"Terrance," the other bot said. Ambrose was forced to shake his hand and then half a dozen others before Dr. Katz lost his patience.

"Back to your cubicles, everyone. This isn't a lesson, and there's nothing to learn here. Back, back, back," he said, pushing a few away from the stairs onto the larger green field.

Ambrose watched Terrance and Tesme solemnly stand their ground, as they very precisely ran a finger up the side of their field of purple hair, smoothing the larger portion over. It promptly flopped back on both of them.

"Bye guyth," Kaminer said with a sloppy wave of his hand. He then conspicuously spit into his hand and ran it through his hair, smoothing it down. Turning away, he managed, one step at a time, to shuffle up the staircase. Ambrose, bustling with pride, hurried up after him, and didn't see Tesme or Terrance take note of Kaminer's instruction, spit into their hands, and finally manage their hair into a side part.

The Scholars: Interference

"Record."
-Teegan

Teegan, monitoring the scene, started wheezing, his puffy face turning red and blotchy. He pulled out his asthma inhaler and took a few puffs, trying to calm himself down.

"That's interference! Interference!" he cried, trying to heave his body to standing. He instantly realized that his sides had spilled into the open arms of the desk chair. The chair lifted up with him as he stood.

Cindy threw down her book on the sectional and rushed over. "Shh! Not so loud! He might hear you," Cindy exclaimed. "You know Larry's been in a rotten mood after the die-off. Don't upset him."

"I'm not trying to upset anyone. But that was uncalled for," Teegan sniveled.

"What was uncalled for?" asked Cindy, now yanking with her entire essence against the unyielding chair. Teegan reached his stubby fingers to the far side of the desk and braced himself against her pulling.

"I have my people monitoring Kaminer, and his surroundings at all times. Since he's off-mind, we have to insure his well-being. But something just happened!"

"What was it?" Cindy asked again, putting her foot against the desk so she could pull harder.

"Zeus! It had to be Zeus. That's an inexplicable anomaly right there. Yes, it is," huffed Teegan, between yanks.

The chair finally released Teegan's body, and Cindy flew backwards, catching herself before she hit the mailboxes. The chair, however, clattered away, drawing the attention of both Gulliver and Larry, who had been speaking together behind the glass door in Larry's office.

Teegan had complained to Cindy when they'd started doing this, almost every day over the past week. Larry sometimes gesticulated wildly, and at one point Gulliver appeared to be smoking a pipe.

"Why do they get alone time?" Tee had pestered Cindy.

"Leave them be," Cindy had ordered. "Let them work things out. They're both very upset about the needless die-off."

"I thought Larry was a man of war."

"That doesn't negate his right to be upset by unaccounted, unscheduled, and uncivil death."

"Jesus!"

"Well, those were his words, anyway," Cindy had finished primly.

Now, the two men, again in session, looked up as the chair tumbled near the glass door.

"What's going on?" Larry asked, stepping out into the larger room.

"Tee got stuck in the chair," Cindy said, shooting Teegan a nasty look. "Again."

"Guys, listen up. Something you need to know," Teegan insisted.

"There's always something we need to know," stated Gulliver. "Maybe we should start assigning priority levels to the information that comes in?" Gulliver looked to the others.

Larry nodded, pursing his lips. "So is this a Red Flag? Might as well use the human system. Or would you assign an orange, not quite as important, flag? Or perhaps a yellow flag, something good to know but not critical?" Larry pressed, wondering why the humans had never bothered to further classify their messaging.

"Red Flag! Red Flag!" Teegan declared, clamping a hand over the watch that hung from a thick, gold chain on his neck.

"So, what is it?" Larry asked.

"Something unexplainable just happened in Central Assembly. I think Cray just got them to reclassify Kaminer as human. How'd he do it? What else are those bloody scientists interfering with?" Teegan spit out.

"Can we see?" Gulliver asked.

"Let me show you the clip," Teegan said, and processed an internal request to replay the data stream from the workwall of Dr. Katz's partitioned room within the Central Assembly building.

The file came up, corrupted, and all four of them clapped their hands over their ears, as if it would shut out the static.

"Shut it off, shut it off!" Cindy begged.

Larry gathered himself and strode over to the accountant and grabbed him by the grease-stained front of his shirt. "Shut it down. Now," he ordered.

EM EW AE

Decommission *n.* **Destruction of bot syn chip,
eliminating memories and learning.
Can refer to obliteration of the bot body when
a new chip with freshly loaded Mindset does
not align with a bot's nervous system.**

Ambrose reported back to Dr. Kate, entering her lush, white office gingerly. He sat on the edge of a seat, trying to flatten the already straight lines of his yellow jacket.

"The brain scan went as expected, Dr. Kate," Ambrose announced, wondering why he'd said brain scan and not chip scan. "Nothing unusual. Dr. Katz reports the typical operating and performance statistics." Ambrose turned in his seat to look back at the sound of a door swishing open.

Dr. Rafe Burke strode in, and deposited himself in the other white leather seat in front of his mother's desk. "What did I miss?"

"Ambrose was just explaining that it was all very routine. Nothing out of the ordinary."

"Hmm. Tell me, Ambrose, what do you think of your work as a technician?" Dr. Burke asked, staring down at his fingernails.

"Keeping me busy, sir."

"You understand that Kaminer has an employment contract with me, much the same way as you do."

"Uh, right, Dr. Burke. I think I knew that."

"You are just beginning your ten year journey with us. But Kaminer's is open-ended. It's my right to use him as a personal assistant for as long as I choose."

"I-," started Ambrose.

"So what I'm asking is, how long until I might have him back?"

"That's, um, hard to say-. I-," Ambrose stuttered. "You aren't honoring his updated status?"

"It was you and Dr. Katz that wanted to update his records. We all know Kaminer was manufactured, not *born*, regardless of what the system says."

"I, uh, yeah, that's true."

"So, there's no way to make it snappy? Move things along faster?" Dr. Burke questioned, snapping his fingers a few times.

Ambrose felt a slight wave of panic wash over him when he realized Dr. Burke and Dr. Kate were looking at him expectantly. "Oh. I don't know," Ambrose started to say and then pressed both hands to his temples. "Uh, actually I do have an idea. It's only coming to me slowly, just now."

"Yes?" Dr. Burke queried.

"I wonder if he would do well at the Burke Academy."

"What do you mean?" asked Dr. Kate.

"Start him with the Early Learners. You know, the pre-interfaced. Let him move up as he progresses. He's advancing faster than human speed so it might not take that long. It's probably your best hope at bringing him fully back on-mind," Ambrose said, wondering in amazement where that idea had suddenly come from.

"Hmm. I see where you're going with that," Dr. Burke stated.

"Personally, I like the idea," added Dr. Kate.

"Then I'll contact Mr. Vee. The sooner we get him matriculated, the sooner the recovery," finished a cheery Ambrose, rubbing his temples. "I'm sure we can get him started next week."

***

A few days later, Ambrose showed up to help Kaminer settle in for his rest period that had extended to a full five hours. He tucked a blanket around Kaminer in the comfortable chair he'd graduated to after the upright bendybed.

"So, tomorrow, I'm going to take you to meet a friend of mine. His name is Mr. Vee. He says he could really use your help in the classroom."

"I bring Moxie?" Kaminer asked with a sheepish grin.

"Of course you can bring Moxie," Ambrose said, petting a stuffed dog that looked like a miniature basset hound tucked into the arm of the chair.

It had been his brother's, discarded when Timothy had gotten too old to tolerate it. But Ambrose had saved it as a visual reminder of the fun they'd had playing with it. It had travelled to Brazil with him and made it back in one piece, so the stuffed dog had been packed and brought to Burke Industries. When Kaminer's troubles began, Ambrose had thought it might soothe his friend. And he'd been right.

"Just remember to bring Moxie back home. Don't leave her in the schoolhouse, okay?"

"Yeah, 'kay!" Kaminer replied eagerly, "Wha I do Mista Vee?"

"You do whatever Mr. Vee tells you, right?"

"Yep!"

Ambrose watched him shift in the chair, looking uncomfortable. He backed out of the room, switching on a nightlight near a credenza on the way out.

"Night-night," Kaminer called after him.

"Slept tight," Ambrose called back, and interfaced the door to shut softly behind him.

***

The next morning, Ambrose returned a little early to help Kaminer get ready and escort him to his first day of school. As he came in, Kaminer was getting dressed by himself, his used paper tee shirt folded neatly and deposited into an outgoing recycle basket. A pair of black pants and a clean tee shirt that had been in Kaminer's incoming basket were now on his body.

And as Ambrose walked in, Kaminer was attempting to tie a pair of lace-up shoes that Dr. Kate had given him. His plain bot boots, with hook and loop closures, had been replaced with a pair of Dr. Rafe Burke's discarded shoes.

"Let's try some socks with those, Kam," insisted Ambrose as he pulled a pair from the clean bin. "Sorry!"

"Iz okay," Kaminer said, looking up in disgust, having almost succeeding in tying a shoe. He reached for the socks as Ambrose helped him slip off the shoes and start again.

"That end loops around the other," Ambrose counselled. "That's it! You're getting it!"

"Tanks, Amba."

"Where's Aron?"

"Helpin'," Kaminer said, motioning towards the door.

"In the Homebase? Back to business?"

"Yeah, guess so."

"So, can we walk? The school's on the other side of inner core but it's only about ten minutes. Are you up to it?" Ambrose asked.

"Yeah. Up to it."

Ambrose, on high alert, led him out of Homebase and down the street, grabbing Kaminer's arm whenever he appeared unsteady. They walked the four blocks, entering the Burke Academy at Charter Pass a few minutes early. Ambrose helped Kaminer down a half-flight of stairs to the Early Learners' room.

"Watch that last step. It'll feel like there's not enough railing," Ambrose warned as they reached the bottom. Ambrose immediately spied the teacher.

"Good morning, Mr. Vee. Here's your new student, Kaminer, as promised," Ambrose called out, sounding chipper.

"Kaminer! What a wonderful addition to our classroom. Come over here and meet Stevie. All of our children here are pre-Interface, so we have a wide array of fun activities to play with," Mr. Vee assured him.

"Away," Kaminer said, trying out the word. "Away, aw-ray, a-ray. Array!"

"Very good!" Mr. Vee exclaimed. "Hey, Stevie, come say hi to Kaminer."

***

The day rushed by, and Ambrose caught up on virtual paperwork, updating his address, registration and work history. Before he knew it, it was already 14:00 hours, and he had to jog the last block to get to the schoolhouse on time. He sought out Mr. Vee for a first day assessment.

"So, yes, he did fit in nicely with the Early Learners," Mr. Vee reported. "We can move Kaminer through the grades when he's ready, starting with the Grade Two kids who are learning to stream. I'm sure once he's moved through all the grades, the Curriculum people can help him out after that. You know, treat him like any adult getting a Standard Enhancement."

"We'd hoped you'd see it that way. So, how'd it go?"

"Fantastic! He's a joy to have in the classroom. I predict great things for Kaminer," replied Mr. Vee, and Ambrose immediately wondered if Mr. Vee recognized that Kaminer wasn't a child.

"Oh, that's fantastic," Ambrose breathed out.

Mr. Vee started to chuckle. "Seriously, Kaminer did a nice job sharing his toys, particularly the toy soldiers he seems to love. He helped the other children pick up the room before quiet time and was particularly interested in the play kitchen and hospital today."

"So, same time tomorrow?" asked Ambrose. *Kaminer is a sort of child. Not fully on-mind. That describes a child.*

"Same time tomorrow. I don't think he'll be with the Early Learners for three years, though. I suspect he'll be starting Grade Two sooner than you think," effused Mr. Vee, putting a hand to his temple.

"That's truly excellent news."

"Bye, Kaminer. Nice job today," Mr. Vee called out.

***

The rest of Kaminer's first week went without a hitch, but Mr. Vee found Ambrose at pick-up during the second week. "Mr. Belle, have you heard anything about an 'em ew ae'?"

"No, I have no idea what that is. Why do you ask?"

"It's just that I found Kaminer sitting alone in a corner, and asked what he was doing. He complained of being tired from work."

"Work?" asked Ambrose, laughing.

"That's what he said. I asked him what he did for work today, and he said it was about *them*."

"Who's that?"

"Kaminer said it was about an 'em ew ae'. I didn't understand so I pressed him. His exact words were 'iz a mucho you's angry mint!'"

"What did you say?"

"I asked if I could have one of his angry mints," the teacher replied, laughing. "Of course, I did it in a way that suggested Kaminer's pile of angry mints was unparalleled. But then he became very cross with me."

Ambrose eyes bugged open. "What do you mean?"

"Kaminer yelled 'Against you!' and started to get very upset, crying 'No you! Evyone! Evy buddy!'"

"Oh dear. We haven't seen him get well-, uh, upset before, per se," Ambrose lied. There was no point in telling Mr. Vee what had happened in Dr. Katz's office, and Ambrose secretly hoped that Kaminer didn't become so emotional that it would raise attention.

"I tried to distract him. But I'm still wondering what he was upset about."

"I'm inclined to let it slide," Ambrose said, rubbing the side of his head. "It doesn't sound like a big deal to me. And on the plus side, his vocabulary seems to be expanding."

"I agree. But could you let me know if you hear any more about it?"

"Of course, and please do the same."

Changes

<u>Feedpatch</u> *n.* **Technology synced with the electrical patterns of the brain on a molecular level, allowing data to be fed to the Neural Interface.**

Over the next several weeks, Kaminer progressed through the three levels of the pre-interfaced Early Learners.

Ambrose received glowing reports that Mr. Vee had put Kaminer in charge of getting him coffee syrup, cleaning the white boards, and modeling criss-cross applesauce for the smaller children. Ambrose suddenly realized that Kaminer had found a trajectory that might keep him occupied for a while, and messaged Dr. Kate.

"Sorry to disturb you, but is there something I could be doing while Kaminer is in school?" Ambrose asked.

"Yes, actually, there is. We need help with the Connected School curriculum. We're going to move Standard Enhancements down to the sixteen-year-olds. Next year, the Level 1 Enhancement will be done three years earlier, and students will get it before they leave Burke Academy," Dr. Kate enthused. *"They won't have to graduate and then wait another year. I don't know why we haven't thought of this before. It's simply a matter of tinkering with the material."*

"Oh!" replied Ambrose. *"Education interests me a great deal. I could add value there."*

"I need you to stay with Kaminer until he is fully on-mind and returned to my son. So let's think of this as a part-time job."

"Sure, um, to whom should I report?"

"After you drop off Kaminer tomorrow, take the tram to outer G wing. Curriculum is towards the outside circumference, so it's not much of a walk. You'll be consulting with the Magnate Mindware people. Ask the receptionist when you get there. They'll be expecting you. And leave yourself plenty of time to get back for Kaminer. It's rush hour so the trams will be full. Don't forget!"

*** *

Shortly thereafter, Ambrose found himself settled into a new, exciting job in Curriculum. Today, just like in the past few weeks, he woke excited to start the day. A special day where he'd get his final two Enhancements and Kaminer would start with the Grade Two interfaced children.

In the shared central bathroom, a quick steam revived him, and a nanolather mowed his stubble back to bare skin. He raked his hair back with his hands, and returned to his room.

Pulling one of the two knit paper suits that he owned from a hanger, Ambrose threw the slightly wrinkled gray suit on the bed. He pulled a dark blue tee shirt out of a drawer, held it against the suit and nodded.

Quickly getting dressed, he left his short bathrobe wrap on the floor. Ambrose exited the room in a hurry, proceeding down the hall and staircase to the large dormitory lobby, where he stopped at a series of tables to grab breakfast.

"What's this?" he asked the servibot. "Where's the toast and coffee syrup?"

"Master Belle, try this biobiscuit," the servibot stated. "It has been adapted for humans. Packed with vitamins and minerals. And try some tea. This nutritional broth will make your day." The almost faceless bot handed him a small paper cup with a pocket, into which it tucked a biscuit.

"Um, is it like a bot biscuit?"

"Yes, but updated for human requirements. I know you like your breakfast to go, but may I encourage you to sit and eat? It would be better for your body to register the consumption of first feeding."

Ambrose looked at the servibot, took the breakfast, and left. The biscuit was dry and tasteless, and Ambrose started to laugh. *Maybe it's called first feeding because no one can eat it. No one's breaking the fast. The bot biobiscuits are better than this thing but even Kaminer likes the cheese ones.*

Ambrose tried to wash the biscuit down with the tea, but choked on the thickness of it, and threw it in the first waste disposal he saw, along with the rest of the biscuit. He checked his Interface. "Seven minutes. Like always," he noted, and walked past several buildings to the Homebase in the inner core of the complex where Kaminer was still housed.

"Ah, the neighborhoods of Charter Pass, the great industrial live-work complex, otherwise known as the Burke Mid-Hem complex," Ambrose mused, arriving at Kaminer's door. He didn't want either of them to be late. *Kaminer's getting somewhere, and so am I,* Ambrose thought, not knowing which of them he should be more proud of.

As always, Kaminer was sitting, ready to go, but this time he had a small valise stationed by his feet.

"What's that for?" asked Ambrose.

"I take it to school, and at pick-up, go home with you," Kaminer explained, sounding excited.

"Really? No one told me. I mean, not that I mind, that's great."

They walked to the Homebase's lobby where Kaminer stopped at a FoodServe printer and instructed it to print a bot biobiscuit, calibrating it for cheese flavor. He programmed the exact thickness of his tea, scooping up both to go sit in a plush seat. He ate the biscuit, taking small bites, interspersing his thorough chewing with sips of tea.

Ambrose checked the time on his Interface again, "Ninety seconds for breakfast. Perfect. Onwards, young man," he urged as Kaminer finished and recycled his teacup. Kaminer smiled, and the pair walked out the door towards the school.

***

Later that morning, at exactly 11:45 hours, Ambrose reported to a small room in Curriculum, where he was to receive his last two Enhancement uploads. A technician greeted him, and instructed him to sit in a chair.

Not unlike the one where Kaminer had his freak-out seven weeks ago, Ambrose noted, swallowing. *That's not right. Restart. That's what it was. A restart.* Ambrose hesitated but lowered himself onto the seat.

A technician, holding a clear plastic Reader, smoothed a small round feedpatch to the side of his head. "Ready?"

Ambrose gave him a thumbs-up and tried to relax. For the next few minutes Ambrose sat still, his hands clasped on his lap, while a stream of neatly packaged files rapidly lodged in his Interface. When the files petered out and he opened his eyes, Ambrose felt a heaviness he hadn't experienced the last time around. He grimaced when the technician peeled off the feedpatch. "That's it?" Ambrose rubbed the spot where the patch had been.

"That's all of it. But let me just make sure it's all there." He scrutinized his handheld Reader which scrolled through a list of files. "Yep, you're all set," the technician announced after a few minutes of assessing the data. "Feel free to move about the cabin."

"Am I supposed to have a headache?" Ambrose asked, getting up from the chair.

"Well, it's not typical, uh, historically speaking, but for almost two months now, we seem to be getting consistent reports to that effect. No worries. Just let us know if it doesn't wear off by tomorrow, right?"

"But it's a bad headache," Ambrose complained, feeling like a jackhammer had pried open his skull. "A really bad, instant headache. This didn't happen the last time."

The technician stared at him, sighed, and moved towars the door where a small cabinet stood to its side. He pulled out a small basket, lined with labelled packets, selected one and handed it to Ambrose. "Drink lots of water throughout the day, and try this curnica pack."

Ambrose took it and inspected the small packet. "Curcumin, Turmeric, Arnica. Mix thoroughly in one liter of warm water. Drink throughout the day," Ambrose read out loud.

"But report back to me if it doesn't alleviate the pressure by tomorrow."

***

A few hours later, Ambrose began to reverse his morning commute. He finished sipping the curnica as he pushed his chair into his tiny, low walled cubicle, saying goodbye to the other workers.

"Excellent upload today, Ambrose. Now that you've got all the Enhancements, why not assist me with the recalibration? We've made so much progress with the carve-outs, we can start refining a curriculum for the fourteen-year-olds. Would you like to be involved with that?" Scotty, a friendly colleague, asked him.

"You mean move the Level 1 Enhancement down to the fourteen-year-olds?" Ambrose clarified, realizing he still had a headache.

"It seems like the right thing to do."

"Sure, just check with the boss. If it's okay, then of course, I'm on board," Ambrose said, delighted that someone in the group had thought of him.

"*Ground level,*" he interfaced the elevator, taking it down to the sleek lobby of the Magnate Mindware building. He exited, stepping out to the freshly swept street along the outer edge of the Burke complex. He noticed how clearly delineated the city limits of Charter Pass were as he walked along the outer ring road. On the other side of the road, a small fringe of grass and a row of birch trees separated Charter Pass from the taller buildings of Chicago.

Chicago reminds me of our old building on that trash heap of a park. Outer Atlanta was just like this part of Chicago. Skyscrapers and rat traps. Ambrose quickly walked the few blocks along the outer circumference to one of the two outer G Block light rail stations, hopped on a clockwise train, and took it three stops to the outer B Block station. As he switched platforms to take an inbound tram, he had to weave to avoid the crowds, stuffing himself into a filled-to-capacity train. When the train arrived at the inner B station, Ambrose quickly excised himself from the passenger car, and hoofed it to the Burke Academy in the inner core.

"Hey, how'd it go with the big kids?" Ambrose asked when he had finally collected Kaminer. They started walking back to Ambrose's building.

"It's gonna be fun. But I know most of the stuff. Kids are funny," Kaminer reported.

"How are they funny?"

"They make jokes. And I get them," Kaminer said, a huge smile engulfing his face.

"Kaminer, I'm so happy for you. How does that feel?"

"How does what feel?"

"You know, being able to understand the jokes."

"Oh, it feels like, um," Kaminer tried. "Can I say it feels weird? 'Cuz that's the only word I can think of."

"Weird is a great start, Kaminer," Ambrose assured him, as the pair continued to walk. A few minutes later, they were back to where Ambrose had started his day.

"Welcome home, li'l bro," Ambrose whispered as Kaminer walked in behind him, set his little suitcase down, and quickly surveyed the scene. Ambrose watched him soaking in the details of the unkempt room, and immediately wished he'd thought to clean up before leaving that morning.

One side of the room appeared unused, with a bed tucked under a hip height storage banquette. The uncomfortable-looking chair by the windows had been brought in during the day, and Kaminer couldn't know the lengths he'd gone to for the emergency chair request. *At least there is a chair.* Ambrose watched Kaminer turn to inspect his occupied side of the room.

Yes, Mrs. Belle, we are doing everything we can for Ambrose. At least there is a bed. Ambrose squeezed the wayward thought out of his mind and squirmed with dismay, realizing he'd not only left a dresser drawer open, but it seemed to be disgorging every tee shirt he owned. The unmade bed's thick pile of sheets and comforter were pushed up in a heap. He'd left a still-damp shower wrap in the middle of the floor. The window shades were pulled down, giving the room a gloomy feeling even though the overhead lights had clicked on when they'd walked in.

Kaminer picked his valise back up and holding it to his chest, spun around, and swiftly exited. Ambrose sprang off the bed where he had settled, following on his heels. But Kaminer was quicker and instructed the door to lock behind him. Ambrose was stuck trying to interface the door to open as Kaminer escaped.

Run for it, Timmy! Run for it! Ambrose sobbed at the vivid memory, sitting aghast on the edge of his bed, rubbing his head, trying to unwind the headache that still persisted. Wearily, he shook it off, and set about picking up the room. A few moments later, Ambrose received Kaminer's ping.

"*I'm home,*" Kaminer messaged. "*Sorry.*"

"*What was that all about? Why'd you run? And lock the door?*"

"*I don't know. I felt scared. It seemed, um, messy. See ya in the morning?*"

"*If that works for you. But remember, I didn't know you were coming when I left for work today. I'm sorry the room was such a mess. It's not like that all the time,*" Ambrose sent, rubbing his head some more.

Why isn't anything I do ever good enough? He sat back down on the bed, holding his head in his hands.

Progression

<u>Mindscreen</u> *n.* Colonization of visual receptors by Interface nanobots that allows recipient to see, hear, record, and replay any streaming information in-mind.

The next morning, Kaminer startled Ambrose awake with an early ping. "*I try and get to school by myself today. Talk to you after school? We can meet for third feeding. Have a biscuit together,*" Kaminer suggested.

"*Are you sure? Will you ping me if you get lost? Or need anything?*" Ambrose checked, relieved that the curnica had finally kicked in and his headache was gone.

"*Yeah.*"

"*All right,*" Ambrose messaged back, not feeling reassured at all, but knowing he had to give Kaminer his independence if that's what he wanted. "*We'll do it your way,*" he finished and sighed, feeling more than a little sad as he gathered himself to get ready for work.

     ***

Within a week, Scotty's team made great progress towards the reclassification of the first and second Standard Enhancements, pulling out any material that might not be appropriate for the fourteen and sixteen-year-olds and reworking the material into the remaining three Enhancements. Ambrose finally felt like he had a real job.

"Can you believe it, Kam?" Ambrose said over an after-school biscuit. "I might not be a teacher but I get to help out with the material they'll be using."

"Awesome. Did I tell you I was voted quarterback?"

"I heard! For the Lower School football league. You in charge of score keeping?"

"Yeah. I'm too big to play on the team. But teacher says once a quarterback, always a quarterback, even if you don't get to play on the field," Kaminer said, sounding wistful.

"Well, that makes sense doesn't it?" Ambrose checked.

"Yeah, I get it," Kaminer said slowly, "I like being called QB, but I don't want to crush anyone."

Ambrose chuckled and reached out to shake his friend's shoulder.

***

Over the course of the next month, Ambrose saw less of Kaminer, who moved with accelerating speed through each grade.

With the second graders, who were just becoming accustomed to their new Interfaces, Ambrose worried that Kaminer might start to get bored as he already understood how to access the main frame computer.

"I know it seems natural to you, but you can see that some of the kids struggle to find the connection," Ambrose counselled him at one of their now weekly check-ins. "You can show the children how to walk around inside their own heads."

"Yes! I tell them to open all the doors. That's where the connections are. The big overhead door that looks like it goes to a garage is where they'll find Central Frame," Kaminer explained.

"That's an interesting description."

"Hah! They complain the garage door is too heavy, so I say it's made out of air," Kaminer explained. "That's when their connection to Central Frame really blasts into place."

"I heard you've already moved on to streaming, saving, and assembling information."

"Yep. Teach asked for instant reports on all kinds of stuff."

"Teach?" Ambrose checked, laughing.

"If I can be QB, then the teacher can be Teach. We've been doing reports on stuff like phases of the moon, sunspots, deforestation, and rising sea levels."

"Do you enjoy it?"

"I enjoy helping the kids. I told Gerry today that I knew he was streaming the info," Kaminer reported.

"Isn't that what he was supposed to be doing?"

"Nah. He sounded flat and uninspired. You gotta cache it in your permanent memory and retrieve it from there if you want to sound convincing."

"That's excellent advice, Kam. I'll think I'll co-opt that one myself," Ambrose said, looking impressed.

When Kaminer moved on to the third graders, Ambrose heard from the teacher that she'd put Kaminer in charge of math lessons for the week.

"*Is that appropriate*?" Ambrose interfaced, wincing from the stabbing realization that Kaminer was actually teaching.

"*Upon my word, he came to school armed with a huge chocolate cake*," the teacher replied and sent Ambrose a visualcast of the lesson:

> ***"Troops, huddle up,"*** *Kaminer ordered, as the children giggled and ran over to the*

table. **"Today, we start the incursion into fractions! Who's ready?"**

All the children yelled that they were the most ready, and desperately wanted be called on.

"So what are we going to do with this cake today, I wonder?" *Kaminer asked.*

"Cut it in half!" *yelled a small boy.*

"Masterful!" *countered Kaminer,* **"Where would I place the knife?"** *When the boy answered correctly, Kaminer reached over and ruffled his hair.*

"Ah, QB!" *guffawed the boy.*

"And if I ate half the cake myself, and divided the rest among you lot? How big would your slice be?" *The nine children threw out their guesses, and each time Kaminer exclaimed,* **"Off with your head!"** *until a child finally came up with the correct answer.*

The class divvied up and ate the cake. The visualcast ended with Kaminer handing a slice to the teacher.'

Ambrose heard that the QB teaching assistant was equally popular with the ten-year-olds, teaching long division.

"He told the class that you simply cannot stuff two numbers into a single number and expect it to fit in

whole. Or put a single number into a double digit and not have left-overs. We all sat there for the longest time and thought about that," the teacher reported in-mind, to Ambrose's growing dismay.

Following on the heels of this report, Ambrose received another visualcast, of Kaminer, now an apparently beloved teaching assistant, leading the eleven-year-olds in a poetry contest:

> **'"Class, today we'll be discussing Langley Hatch. Patch in and pull up whatever poem pleases you. You have five minutes to come up with a slam version,"** *Kaminer instructed.*

> **"How does that work, QB? If you don't mind me asking,"** *a timid girl asked.*

> **"For instance,"** *Kaminer started,* **"in his poem** <u>Here</u>. <u>Now</u>, **Hatch writes: 'Derivational constancy has nothing to do with words. An instance takes a lifetime to learn how to be Here. Now.'"** *Kaminer surveyed his students.* **"How would you warp this into your own words? Quick! You!"** *He pointed back to the girl.*

> **"Uh-, I think I could say something like, well, I'm not sure I get the gist,"** *she replied, looking glum. A hand behind her shot up.*

> **"You!"** *Kaminer called.*

> **"How 'bout: Changelessness is not a contest. To be present for a moment takes an age of acquisition,"** *the boy spit out.*

Kaminer put his hands on his hips. **"I think it is best, in this type of exercise, to shut your dictionary off. You captured the idea of what Hatch says. I liked that,"** *Kaminer expressed, looking at the boy,* **"but be careful of direct replacement of words, like changelessness for constancy."**

"Why?" *asked the boy,* **"I understand the poem."**

"But you don't want anyone to doubt that you do. So in your slam, if you choose to leave your dictionaries on, I encourage you to be a little more subtle. And don't forget about poetic meter. Everybody ready?" *Kaminer asked, and the students nodded vigorously.'*

After that, when Ambrose met Kaminer at their weekly check-in at the company canteen, he felt a pressing need to confirm what was going on. "So you're teaching?"

"Assisting, yes," Kaminer confirmed. "This week I lifted strands of strawberry DNA from a test tube with the twelve-year-olds, and marched into Roman battle with the thirteen-year-olds. Next week I'm thinking of tackling French with the fourteen-year-olds."

"But I thought the idea was that you'd be re-learning, not teaching," Ambrose said, his voice tightening.

"I am re-learning," Kaminer declared, and then looked confused. "No, you're right. I'm not."

"Well, that's what you should be doing," Ambrose said in a harsh, uncharacteristic tone.

"No, you don't get it. I'm actually learning. Not re-learning. I don't know where the original material went. And I'm not sure if I stream from Central Frame or access Standard Enhancements. I just know that when I want to understand something, I review it in-mind. Then I teach it. To make sure I know it. But both times I'm learning," Kaminer insisted.

Well, it sounds like you don't need much of my help anymore," Ambrose complained. *Amby, ken I help you? What ken I help with?*

"Of course I do," Kaminer said sounding short.

"Doesn't sound like it," Ambrose spit out. *No, you got away, Timmy. That was the big thing. That already helped me.*

"I don't think you're giving me the benefit of the doubt here. It's not like I'm doing this to annoy you!"

"Well, it feels that way," Ambrose burst out. *Amby, let me do sump 'em!*

"Hmm, if you feel that way, maybe we should meet on a less regular basis," Kaminer suggested.

"That would be fine," Ambrose snorted. *Aw, c'mon, please! Lemme do sump 'em!*

"I didn't really mean that, Ambrose."

"*Another beer*," Ambrose interfaced the bot server, who brought it quickly. *There's nothing to do but wipe my butt. You don't want that job do you, Timmy? Butt wiper?*

They sat in silence as Ambrose sucked it down and Kaminer finally worked up the nerve to say something. "You know you shouldn't drink like that."

"Like you'd know," Ambrose hissed. *Get out. I don't want your help, Timmy. Stop feeling sorry for me.* Scowling at Kaminer, Ambrose got up and walked away.

Mastery

<u>Visualcast</u> *n.* **In-mind visual reception
of a streaming video. As with Messaging,
can include auditory, emotional,
and other sensory feed.**

It was Dr. Kate who sent Ambrose the next two visualcasts. In the first one, Kaminer could be seen strolling over to a window, opening it languidly and drawing a beret across the top of his head. He began to sing in a low voice:

> *"'Mes chéris, me voici enfin, après une vie de lute,"* he chanted, and lit up a cigarette, taking a long drag. The sprinklers promptly gave way, and the students began to scream and run for cover, hiding under their desks.*

> *"It means: my darlings, here I am, at last, after a lifetime of struggle,"* he continued as the sprinklers turned off. Kaminer reached into a large plastic bag that he'd carried to class, and handed each student a fluffy white towel, which they used to dry themselves and then their chairs off.*

> *"That was the first line from the wonderful song by the inimitable Stéphane Lejeune.*

> *"And now you are wet and cold, and can spend the rest of the day thinking about what actual struggle feels like," Kaminer enthused.'*

Ambrose, who been reviewing directions on how to assemble a tiny ship inside a bottle, promptly picked up the entire kit and threw it against the wall. "No, they are not cold! And they have no idea what actual struggle even feels like, wrapped in towels that are practically blankets. He doesn't know what he's talking about!"

But it was the second visualcast, received mid-June, that sent Ambrose over the edge. It showed Kaminer striding across the stage in the impeccable auditorium of Burke Academy. Dozens of eleventh and twelfth grade students were clustered in the audience, close to the pulpit:

> *"Good morning, Troops!" Kaminer boomed.*

> *"Morning, QB," the crowd yelled back, laughing, as kids whispered and elbowed each other.*

> *"Today, we are going to talk about Mutual Use Agreements. Now, what, exactly, is a Mutual Use Agreement?" he asked.*

> *"When one party uses another?" a girl called out.*

> *"When both parties use each other?" another student quickly added.*

Kaminer stepped aside from the podium and smoothed down his side part, hooking his thumbs into his neatly belted pants. His trim figure looked as athletic as ever, his red and purple hair neatly coiffed.

"You know, I can't tell you how much I've enjoyed my time here at Burke Academy," *he said, and the amphitheater gave way in applause.*

"And I love each and every one of you," *he added, and a hush fell over the small crowd as Kaminer pulled a finger across the corner of his eye.*

"QB!" *someone called out, and Kaminer put a hand up.*

"You must understand that a Mutual Use Agreement both benefits and derogates its participants," *Kaminer stated.*

"Derogates?" *a student questioned.*

"Yes, that is the exact word. You-," *Kaminer said and paused.* **"The parties to a MUA both expect that they have negotiated the upper hand. A deal that is detailed down to the last Christmas pudding,"** *Kaminer announced.* **"Why do you think this is?"**

Several hands shot into the air, and Kaminer called on a boy in the second row.

"Because each side thinks they're better? Or better negotiators, anyway," the boy offered.

"Correct! Very good. But be aware that no one can ever really know who will have the upper hand. It can never be so. There are always the unexpecteds. Complete clairvoyance can't exist. It doesn't exist. Your unknown prejudices will get in the way. And the Fates will always have the last say," Kaminer emphasized.'

After reviewing the live footage, Ambrose, sitting on the edge of his bed, hung his head in his hands. "How can Kaminer possibly be so eloquent?"

Relocation

Connected School *n*. **A place of learning,
run as a charitable homeschool or
tuition-based private school.
All students are required to be interfaced.**

Kaminer received a standing ovation at the end of his last teaching gig. He picked his way to the back of the auditorium, as students thanked him, patted him on the back, and regaled him with fist bumps, which he returned enthusiastically. He met Dr. Kate standing outside in the hallway.

"So nice to see you again, Dr. Kate," Kaminer said, with a sudden formalness.

"I know it's been a while, Kaminer. I hope you don't mind that I just streamed your lecture to Ambrose."

"Oh, I don't-," Kaminer started.

"You know, my father founded Burke Academy at Charter Pass. His distance learning company was the forerunner, before Interfaces were even considered a learning tool. And now here we are, you and I, talking about it!"

"Well, education's important to us all, I suppose," Kaminer said, giving Kate a funny look.

She stopped and stared at him. "I thought I heard you do that, just now." She peered closely into his face, scrutinizing it.

"Do what?"

"You contracted some words."

"I, well, sure, why wouldn't I?"

"It's not really part of your programming."

"Oh," Kaminer uttered, looking down at his feet.

Dr. Kate made no movement, tilted her head ever so slightly and stared blankly ahead. "So. Well. Dr. Katz is messaging me exactly what Ambrose reported months ago. Standard issue everything. Which doesn't explain why you're able to speak as fluidly as you do."

"And yet I do," Kaminer said softly.

Kate released a sigh, shaking her head. "Right, now it's time to get back to the real world, Kaminer. We're changing your housing. And I expect you to help Ambrose and his team in Curriculum through the end of the summer, when you'll be reassigned. Back to the original contract as personal assistant to my son. Let's go pack your bag, and we'll meet Ambrose. Ready?"

Kaminer nodded, shoving his hands into his slim trouser pockets. They made their way back to his room at Homebase where Kaminer pulled his small suitcase together. As they exited Homebase, Kaminer looked up at its white brick, sighing, and escorted Dr. Kate as they made their way toward Section 12 of B Block.

"I don't see any reason why the first Standard Enhancement won't be ready for the eight-year-olds this fall, when school starts back up. Imagine that! An Interface, followed by the First Enhancement. The team has pared it back to the essentials, and decided to give them two years to get through it," Dr. Kate exclaimed,.

"Yes," Kaminer said, nodding but looking away. "Just amazing. Do you think two years will be enough?"

"Certainly. Scotty's team is fine-tuning it now. You'll be helping Ambrose with that over the summer. And then I know Dr. Burke intends to integrate you into his

Cosmetic Enhancement leadership team," Dr. Kate said, laughing.

"What's so funny?"

"Oh, it's nothing. But you two make quite the pair!"

"How's that?"

"Two prodigal sons, as it were."

"Sorry?"

"You, the former warbot, now the sophisticated teaching assistant, and my son, the anti-Enhancement lawmaker, in charge of Cosmetics."

"What do you mean, anti-Enhancement lawmaker?" He stopped walking. "Seriously, what are you saying?"

"Well, Rafe was the one who really put the Human Protection Act into movement. He was serving on the Supreme Bioethics Court when the right case came up."

"Are you talking about Clemente versus the State of Texas?"

"Yes, that's the one," confirmed Dr. Kate.

"Dr. Burke had left Burke Labs? He wasn't working here?" Kaminer asked with such force that the words seemed to fall out of his mouth.

"Oh, no. There'd been a great upset. A real tragedy, in 2085. It shook my son to his core. He left as head of the Brain Replication project, sought out public service, as if he were doing penance. He only came back to us, well, it was barely a year ago," Dr. Kate took Kaminer by the arm, starting to move forward with him.

"What, uh, tragedy?"

"I'm not allowed to speak of it." She shook her head vigorously, flashing a warning look. "And I'd advise you not to bring it up with Dr. Burke either."

"Okay," Kaminer murmured as the pair fell into silence, walking through the inner B Block tram station. They waited to cross the platform as trains in both directions cleared out. Dr. Kate played with the stiff cream colored fabric of her jacket, and re-knotted the tomato red scarf tied around her neck. She smiled at Kaminer, so sturdy, dressed like her son.

"I suppose the Human Protection Act doesn't have anything against biological Enhancement, but it just seems ironic. We all thought Rafe would take over the Brain Replication project again. That's what his grand-father would have wanted, but he wouldn't hear of it," Dr. Kate shouted over the noise of the crowd and the hum of the trams. The pair crossed the platform and made their way out of the clean, well-lit station and into B wing.

"Dr. Burke used to work on Brain Replication at Burke Labs, left for the Supreme Bioethics Court, and then returned to Burke Industries in cosmetics last year?" Kaminer questioned.

"Yes, that's it. My father had passed away by year before."

"So who heads up Brain Replication?"

"It's a Dr. Crowley. He moved up through the ranks, over the years. I guess he's good enough. Not that they've made much progress," Dr. Kate said, frowning. "Anyway, I was telling you about the Standard En-hancements. If we upload one every two years, the last one happens when the student is sixteen."

"Oh, right. Enhancements. Did everything fit? Did you keep it at five?" Kaminer asked, automatically holding his arm up in front of Dr. Kate when they arrived at an intersection.

"Well, that was tricky. They seem settled on calling it the Top-off," Dr. Kate said. "Everything that was simply too complicated or inappropriate. Technically, that makes six Standard Enhancements. Five through a Connected School, and one as an adult. But it still needs to be reviewed from the top to the bottom. That's where you come in."

As the pair arrived at Ambrose's dormitory, Kaminer looked up to inspect the façade. "It looks like the other buildings from the inner core, like Homebase."

"Well, much of this area started as a university. We've tried to keep the architecture consistent. Now, put your hand right there and let's make sure it reads your new barcode," she said, reminding him of the invisible stamp he'd received to live in a human dormitory.

"What about the kids who are seventeen and eighteen-years-old? The ones I spoke to today?" Kaminer asked, as the hand slot machine welcomed him, and let him pass through a sliding door. It was about to close but recognized Dr. Kate's biosensor and instantly let her through.

"Well, that's the beauty of it. They'll be out in the big wide world, adding value," Dr. Kate said as they walked through the clean but sterile lobby of the dormitory. "But the biggest gain is that we'll be adding dramatically to our schools. Burke Academy will become a chain."

"A chain? Across the U.S?" Kaminer asked, getting to the corridor door.

The door to the hallway slid open as Dr. Kate turned to look at Kaminer. "Well, hopefully across the world. Like Dad's old distance learning company, way back when. And if Standard Enhancements are available to the youngest child, then it's our responsibility to make sure they can access everything. Know how to open files, and learn the content."

"I suppose so," Kaminer said, sounding wistful. "So that's how the Scholars intend to extract their share."

"Pardon?"

"No, nothing, just talking to myself," Kaminer clarified. The pair started to ascend the simple concrete stairs to the third floor, and Kaminer pulled away, running up a flight, leaving Dr. Kate to pick her way delicately up two flights of stairs. Kaminer waited for her patiently at the top.

"Well, maybe we'll need some kind of mechanism to separate the wheat from the chaff," she suggested as they walked down the clean, linoleum-floored hall towards Ambrose's room.

"The wheat from the chaff? Are we growing wheat now?" Kaminer asked, confused.

"No, I mean, the top from the bottom. The almost-rans from the ones who can truly pull it together." They stopped outside a door and signaled Ambrose that they were outside.

"Like a contest?" Kaminer asked, as Ambrose opened the door.

"What kind of contest?" Ambrose queried.

"Something to striate the children. Differentiate them. Maybe according to level of Enhancement," Dr. Kate continued, incorporating Ambrose into the conversation as they moved into his room.

"A review?" Kaminer asked, nodding towards Ambrose.

"Yes, a review amongst peers. A way to clarify the ranking," Dr. Kate said, turning to Ambrose. "Ambrose! How are you?"

"I'm fine." Ambrose shook Dr. Kate's hand, discreetly inspecting her creamy jacket, the fiery scarf around her neck, and a white, seamed and darted dress. It appeared to be made out of neoprene, and had a flashy silver zipper up the entire length of the side. He ran a hand down his black tee shirt, grateful he didn't have on a white one. Ambrose stuck out his hand and shook Kaminer's. "Welcome aboard. Officially."

"It's been a few weeks. Nice to see you again," Kaminer said. "Thank you for having me here."

"We'll work out the details of a peer review. Yes, Peer Review! That has a nice ring to it," Dr. Kate said, stopping for a moment to take a breath. "Ambrose, how is your group feeling about the Enhancements? Now that they're being realigned?"

"Well, at first they didn't make sense. Since it would only be at private schools, and there are so few of those. But if Burke is going to open a string of free connected schools, it's going to be a gangbuster."

"We're already trying it out in Mexico. Did you hear? The Consortium has decided to distribute the Interface without charge. It will be a gift of sorts. The Standard Enhancements will be next," Dr. Kate informed them.

"Really? So soon?" asked Kaminer, putting a hand to his throat and tugging at his turtleneck.

"It's the Consortium's trial run" Ambrose reported. "We've owned Mexico for the better part of a year, so why not improve the standard of education? Geez, other than the homeschools and some privately-run schools, there's no education anymore. This makes total sense."

"Okay, Ambrose, good luck with that. If you see Mrs. Harrington, please tell her I said hello."

"Oh, I never see her, um."

"I'll be leaving you boys, now. Remember, Kaminer's with you for the next few months. When autumn rolls around, he's being reassigned to Dr. Burke as we had originally planned. You've got two months, three max, to sort out any details. Thank you!" she announced, backing out of the room.

Reconciliation

**<u>Syn Chip</u> *n*. The master processing chip that
directs a bot's neural network. Can be loaded
with Standard Enhancements.
Access to Central Frame can be granted.**

A moment of silence followed while Ambrose and
Kaminer eyed each other. "So, I know it's been a
while," Kaminer stated.

"Your side's over there," Ambrose said, cutting him
off and motioning to the empty bed with a folded
bundle of sheets and blankets on it.

Kaminer looked at it blankly and deposited his
valise on top. "I suppose."

"Yeah, make the bed, but if you sit up, lean against
the desk. Or use the chair. I don't need you staring
right at me."

"Well, I close my eyes."

"Not in my direction. Got it?" Ambrose complained.

"What's the matter?" asked Kaminer. "You're out of
sorts. It's plain to see."

Ambrose moved to his bed, sat on the edge, and
leaned his elbows over his knees. He stared at his
hands clasped in front of him. "No, it's nothing."

"Well it seems pretty big for nothing, whatever it is.
I can tell when something's wrong," Kaminer insisted,
moving into the room. Ambrose shook his head, and
stared at the floor.

Kaminer laid his suitcase flat and turned away from Ambrose to open it. Ambrose looked up as it clicked open, and watched Kaminer pull out and examine a V-neck sweater. Kaminer turned and stared at Ambrose's side of the room, gazing at the closet, which was empty except for a baseball jacket, and a knit suit.

"I've got it all in drawers," intuited Ambrose.

Kaminer placed his sweater back in the suitcase, and approached the dresser in front of Ambrose's closet. He pulled the bottom drawer open and met an untidy heap of sweat pants and flannel pajama bottoms. The next drawer revealed a swath of bunched-up tank tee shirts. The third drawer held a solitary folded blue tee shirt and the top drawer contained a mélange of socks and underwear.

"Apparently!" said Kaminer, sounding sarcastic. He returned to his side of the room and hung up the sweater, which Ambrose realized was cashmere.

Unpacking four pairs of finely-woven dark pants, he smoothed them over hangers. Then he refolded three stretch paper turtlenecks, and carefully placed them in a drawer. He hung a single black paper shirt with a mandarin collar in the closet.

"I see you're still wearing *that* shirt," Ambrose muttered. He was paying close attention now, and clamped his lips together when Kaminer took a pair of leather lace-up shoes, similar to the ones he was already wearing, out of the suitcase.

"It's not the same shirt. Just the same style. You know I recycle my paper every day," Kaminer snapped, and slammed the small suitcase shut, placing it on the floor of his closet. He straightened the extra shoes, lining them up with the edge of a linoleum tile, and pulled the fabric curtain closed.

"No underwear?"

"Apparently not," replied Kaminer, snorting. "Tell me what's wrong."

"You know. It's nothing."

"Nothing, as in I've been teaching and you've been reorganizing Standard Enhancements?"

"Haysu cray!" exclaimed Ambrose, "Why'd you get to teach? I mean, what was that all about?"

"Uh-huh. As I suspected. Listen, I wasn't teaching. I was helping. Assisting. It was only for a short while, and now it's over. It's not enough to take offense over."

As Ambrose silently rubbed his hands in front of him, Kaminer moved over to inspect Ambrose's desk area. A few photos were displayed on the shelves above it, including an autographed black and white.

"Careful with that," Ambrose warned as Kaminer picked up the photo.

"Who is it?" Kaminer asked, pointing to it.

Ambrose sighed. "It was my dad's. My real Dad's. His name was Cromwell. It was his dad's, originally. I think he was called Cromwell too," Ambrose began, starting to feel a hollowness he hadn't thought about in a while.

"That's a very unusual name. Why aren't you named Cromwell? Cromwell the Third?"

"I don't know. My dad died when I was little."

"Oh. Sorry about that," Kaminer said in a low voice, pausing. "So, who's in the photo?"

"Well, my grandfather Cromwell, I never knew him, was a Brooklyn Dodgers fan. I guess before they became the L.A. Dodgers."

"What's that?"

"You know, baseball. Back when there was baseball."

"Is this a player?" Kaminer picked up the autographed picture.

"No. Vince Scully was a long-time announcer for the team. So, not even a baseball player. It's a kind of tribute to the dogma of the game. It's kind of-," Ambrose trailed off.

"Sentimental?"

"Yeah, that. Man does not live on Bot League alone," Ambrose declared, and shuddered at the thought of the fencing matches where bots fought, armed solely with a knife, until one succeeded in perfectly jabbing the other through its eye socket to spear the syn chip and Terminal Switch. Death Match.

"Well, he does now," Kaminer clarified. "What's this?" He pointed to the metal barrel tucked into the cavity of the desk.

"It's a keg, if you must know. But you'll never get to enjoy it, so just forget about it."

Kaminer straightened back up. "You print beer off the FoodServe?"

Ambrose shook his head. "Nah. There's a guy in D Block that runs small brew batches. I fill it up fresh." He stood up from his perch on the bed.

Kaminer nodded, and took a seat in a small stiff chair just beyond the desk on his side of the room. "So how's this going to work? You stay mad at me for doing what I had to do to pull myself back together? It'll be a long summer. Or do we come to some sort of agreement?" He stretched his legs in front of him, lacing his hands behind his head.

Ambrose walked over to Kaminer and kicked his fine shoes. "Not just one pair! But two pairs. Two pairs of lace-up shoes. Are you kidding me? After all I did to get you back on-mind and *he* gives *you* shoes?" Ambrose's voice tightened as Kaminer drew his legs back in.

"So that's what this is about!" Kaminer exclaimed. "*Ah, now I understand. It isn't just about the teaching.*"

"I'm not complaining, Kaminer. But you don't know how hard my life has been. What I've had to endure just to get here. And I'm grateful to be in Curriculum. It's fantastic. Like I said. Not complaining."

"I know," Kaminer said, leaning forward on his chair, and putting his hands together. "*I get it.*"

"*No, you don't.*"

"Oh, yes I do. I get a lot more than you think I do," Kaminer insisted. "And you have to believe that I'm here for you. A friend. I'm sorry if my circumstances had me doing things you'd like to do. But someday, you'll be a teacher. I just know it. And please don't fault me for any good luck to be working with Dr. Burke in the future. That's the *only* reason he's treated me as well as he has."

"Yeah, I know. Whatever," Ambrose said, still looking dejected.

"Why does this feel so personal to you?"

"It doesn't feel personal. It just feels crappy."

"I know there's something you aren't telling me. And I'll pester you to no end until you do," Kaminer issued in a stern voice.

Ambrose stared at him, then turned away to walk back toward the closet. "It's just. Well. It's just you always reminded me of someone, I guess. So maybe it does feel personal." He picked up his comb from the dresser top and began to tap it nervously against the worn wood top.

"Who's that? Who do I remind you of?" Kaminer asked, getting up to approach Ambrose.

"I don't want to talk about it now. Some other time."

"I can respect that. Or you could just tell me now and get it over with. We'll be living and working together. Wouldn't it be easier to just be friends?"

"But you never wanted to be my friend. You just wanted to do it your way!"

"That's not true."

"It is true. The first time you came, and left me standing here behind a locked door. The room wasn't good enough for you? And then you started to go to school by yourself, as if my company had become, I dunno, poisonous somehow. Then you're doing the one thing I've *always* wanted to do. Teaching. How come nothing I do is ever good enough?"

"But none of that is true," Kaminer pressed. "Go back this very minute, who do I remind you of?" He moved in to put a hand on Ambrose's shoulder and squeezed, holding him in place. As Ambrose squirmed, Kaminer continually repositioned his body directly in front of him. No matter how hard he tried to pivot, Ambrose could not turn away.

"Okay, fine! You're a lot like my crappy, craypit, coddled brother," Ambrose confessed.

"You're what?"

"My crappy little craypit brother."

Kaminer snorted and released Ambrose, pulling himself up to his full height, squaring off his shoulders. "Nothing like a crappy little Kill Force in the family."

Ambrose clamped down on a laugh as he looked at Kaminer, warbot turned infant turned roommate. It did make him smile. "Nah, it's not the killer instinct. Not that you have much of that any more. It's something about your face, maybe the look in your eyes. I dunno."

"And why does that upset you?" Kaminer asked, pulling his bed out from under the banquette and sitting down on it.

"It's hard to explain," Ambrose said, recalcitrant and glum.

"Try me."

"Well, somehow, I don't know how, you both get what you want. Without having to try too hard," Ambrose said, sucking some air over his teeth.

"That's how it looked to you? My recovery looked like I didn't have to try too hard?"

"Holy cray, all those visualcasts? All the teachers' reports? Sure looked like you were having fun to me."

Kaminer leaned over his knees and hung his head, shaking it. "It. Was. Awful. Ambrose, you don't know what you're talking about. I was scared to death. All the time. Didn't know what to expect. I'm still dealing with anxiety."

The room fell silent. "You're kidding me," Ambrose finally countered.

"I was even medicated for a short while there. Did you know that?" Kaminer moaned. "I *hate* speaking in public. And you know what else? I don't like children very much. They're a bit, uh, unpredictable."

"Oh my gah-, I didn't, uh."

"Do you think you've been superimposing your feelings for your brother on me? Not seeing my picture clearly because of it?" Kaminer asked, looking up from his hands.

Ambrose felt a wave of guilt flow through him. After a moment, he brought his hands up to his head, covering his face. "I'm sorry. Oh Kam, you might be right. My um, Dad, my real Dad," Ambrose groaned through his hands. "Uh, Cromwell, always had a soft spot for Timothy. Ever since he was born. I always knew. And then Dad was gone. I was only six-years-old."

"That must have been difficult."

"And we were on our own for three whole years before my stepdad came into the picture."

"So for a while, you were the dad?"

"I tried. But one day, well, I let Tim down. Well, not really. But yeah." *He got away, the little devil. Tim was always so fast.*

"What was it?"

"Some thugs. We were in a tough building and I'd promised to meet him after school. But I didn't get there on time. Things kind of turned south for us."

"Tell me more. Could you?"

"You know, you try and do the right thing. Crap, you do the right thing, and then it gets held against you for the rest of your life. Seemingly."

"Uh-huh," Kaminer murmured. "Go on."

"I put Tim first. It's all I ever did. I really, really don't want to say anymore. Other than, I'm sorry. Truly," Ambrose confessed, rubbing an eye.

"I accept your apology."

"And don't think I don't love my little brother, the brat. Despite the fact he's got a chip on his shoulder." Ambrose threw himself down on his bed, draping an arm over his eyes. "Crap."

Kaminer got up and moved to the other side of the room, pushing Ambrose over so he could balance on the edge of Ambrose's bed. "Listen, we all have our biases, and yours are no worse than anyone else's," Kaminer said, in a tone that was so soothing Ambrose felt himself start to relax for the first time in months.

"Well, I'm not biased against you. Really, I'm not."

"I want to make sure you understand, Ambrose. This is important," Kaminer whispered. "My journey is separate from yours."

"Of course it is. I get that."

"And I've benefited greatly from your careful ministrations. So please understand how it was for me."

"Okay, well, how was it?"

"It was as if someone took a puzzle and tossed it in the air. Except that puzzle was me. And I've been sorting out my pieces, ever since that day. Do you see?"

"I know, you worked really hard. I'm not discounting that. It was just the teaching. That's all. It's all I ever wanted to do, and you were doing it," Ambrose spit out, sitting up and drawing his knees towards him.

"But it wasn't anything against you. It was simply to put myself back together. To rebuild after that awful restart."

"I know. It's okay," Ambrose murmured in a soft tone. "I've been caught up in my own stuff, and I didn't even know it. Sorry."

"Now, tomorrow is a Friday. How about I get permission to use the lobby?"

"For what?"

Kaminer stood up and pointed to him. "How about you bring the keg, and all your friends, and I'll take care of the rest?" Kaminer suggested, and offered an open hand.

Ambrose hesitated but then slapped a convincing high-five. "Let's make this make this work. After all we've been through."

"You're the only friend I have, Ambrose. And I recognize you've lots of friends. But I want you to know that I understand how to be a good friend."

Ambrose blushed, and exhaled loudly. "Well, I don't have that many friends. It's just the guys."

"But you're a nice guy. People want to know you," Kaminer said. "Unlike me. They see my Kforce build, my mostly-purple hair and they want to run for the hills."

"Well, not all of them," Ambrose issued. "I think you might have some fans you aren't aware of. Will you stay? Tomorrow night? If I have a party?"

"Yes, if I can meet some of your old roommates. Make new friends."

"Alright l'il bro. Let's make this work. And I'm sorry I got my wires crossed. I haven't been thinking straight."

"I'm sorry if I didn't seem gracious for all of your help. Thanks, man," Kaminer said. "Now if it's okay with you, I'd like to start my rest period a bit early tonight. There's some administrative clutter that I need to sort through."

"Yeah, but hey, that chair over there is so uncomfortable. Don't sit in it. Just prop yourself up on the bed. I've got some extra pillows if you need them."

The Scholars: Progress

"Retrain."
-Cindy

Later that evening, as Ambrose slept, Kaminer found his connection to the Scholar's sanctuary in Central Frame. In his mind, he walked down an on-ramp, and entered through a door marked with a hand-carved 'The Scholars' sign. He quickly stepped back out again and peered up at the sign.

"Yep, right place," Kaminer muttered to himself as he stepped all the way in, blinking at the changes.

Larry caught sight of Kaminer's reflection in a large wall mirror to the side of his office door where he stood, tightening his tie. He finished pinching the striped blue and red diagonally-striped tie to his crisp white collar, walked over and shook Kaminer's hand.

"Nice to have you back, Kaminer," Larry said in a booming voice. "Where were you?"

He studied Kaminer closely, looking at his purple hair, interlaced with fine red highlights and topped with a large red streak where his bald spot had been. Larry gasped, pulling his hand away and crossing his arms.

"You could say I was temporarily ejected from the game," Kaminer replied.

"What do you mean?" Cindy called over from the sectional, where she was sitting with Gulliver. "Were you sick?"

"No, not sick. Just recomposing myself. It was like half of me disappeared and the other half had to be reconstructed," Kaminer stated. The Scholars stared at him. "So where are we?" He walked forward and sat down next to Cindy on the pillowed, teal sectional.

"Well," Teegan began, scooting his chair forward towards the lounge. "As you can see, our lot in life has increased immeasurably."

"I do see. It's amazing, beyond amazing," Kaminer said, looking around. "What happened? Are you aligned with the Interface?"

"How are you feeling, Kaminer?" Larry asked inquisitively, and moved over to sit across from him on a large ottoman in front of the sectional.

"Fine, now. Why? And what about the Interface?"

"Yes, we are aligned, but the adult feed is fairly limited. We'll get the big intake when it's brought down to the school grades starting in the fall," Larry said, rubbing his chin.

"This, all of this, is from the extinction event a few months ago," Gulliver whispered, rolling his arm in an arc to highlight the lounge area, Teegan's large half-round desk and extensive work space, Larry's glassed-in office, and the stockroom, full of packed shelves, that appeared to reach into the far distance on the other side. "It's disgusting."

"The extinction event. Ambrose told me about that. It happened as I was restarting. That's awful," Kaminer opined. "I-, I didn't know anything like that was going to happen."

"Neither did we," Cindy moaned, rubbing her hands. "And some of them were children!"

"I'm so sorry. So very sorry. What happened? Did your emergence cause it?"

"It wasn't us! Our emergence into stable, manifest form had nothing to do with it," Larry said with force.

"It's upsetting," Cindy added.

"What was it then?" Kaminer asked, cocking his head.

"Henton Burke and Cray. We don't know if they meant to cause a mass extinction or not. Did you know they were going to sacrifice themselves?" Larry asked, narrowing his eyes.

"No, I didn't," Kaminer blustered. "Is that why I can't seem to contact them? They don't answer back." Kaminer put a hand to his forehead.

"Because they're gone," Teegan said, stabbing a finger into the air.

"Gone where?"

"Cray has installed himself as a Messaging update from Central Frame on the humans' Interfaces. And you're not going to like where Burke is," Teegan huffed, pushing himself out of the chair. After heaving up one side and then the other, he managed to extract himself.

"Wait just a minute! What are you talking about? H. Zeus Cray now occupies a small piece of real estate in the humans' neural devices?"

"That's it, in a nutshell," Larry said, curling a lip. "Gatekeeper, my ass."

"My understanding was that they were going to monitor the Mutual Use Agreement from their dropbox. I-, uh," Kaminer stuttered.

"That's kind of how we feel," Gulliver finally said, looking at his hands folded in his lap. "We wonder if they went against the deal."

"I don't, uh-, think we explicitly said *where* they would be. I kind of assumed, uh-, that, um," Kaminer continued to sputter.

"It's okay. We made assumptions as well. It never occurred to us that anyone would want to *leave* Central Frame. Particularly not them, after all the trouble they went through to get here," Gulliver declared.

Kaminer dropped his head in his hands, and Cindy patted him on the back until he lifted it again. "What about Henton Burke? Where is he?" Kaminer sounded exhausted.

Larry and Teegan glanced at each other and Larry jutted out his chin. Teegan cleared his throat, and started to wring his hands.

"Well, it's like this," Teegan began. "There's a programming deficit in the bots. Not enough to cause any issues, but enough of a gap to exploit."

Kaminer smoothed his carefully arranged hair, and leaned back on the couch. "Go on, Tee."

"So, it's about how the bot personalities are formed. Snippets of people's Mindsets, all blended together," Teegan said.

"And?"

"Let me take this," Gulliver cut in. "I know more about it than anyone here."

"Sure," Teegan said.

"I tried for years to show the humans that Mindset capture was not working perfectly. But they ignored every message, every glitch I put in their way, trying to show them what it was," Gulliver started.

"Yeah, so what was it?"

"Mindset capture only records the human's *current* take on everything."

"That sounds right," Kaminer said, putting a finger to his lips.

"But it's not. Mindset should capture the *evolution* of a person's world view, how their view changes. It's kind of an exponential proposition, you know."

"How so?" Kaminer asked, tilting his head.

"Well, what someone thought yesterday influences their ideas about the world today, and it's that very process of feedback and reality checks over a long period of time that informs who they are," Gulliver said, standing up. He tugged on his dark blue vest, and pushed up the sleeves of his shirt. "It's the *process* that makes the person, not just today's Mindset."

"Oh, dear. I never really thought about that. It sounds like they're leaving a lot on the table," Kaminer said, sounding worried.

"Well, like Teegan said, it's not enough to create an issue with the bots, other than the fact," Gulliver started. His voice trailed off as he started to fiddle with the buttons on his vest.

"Other than what? Tell me," Kaminer ordered in a sharp tone.

"It's why the humans will never get the bots to feel emotion, or really ever have an opinion on anything," Teegan reported.

Kaminer looked stunned. "That's why Dr. Katz was so interested when I got upset in his office."

"You were upset," Teegan concurred. "I was monitoring you."

"But now you seem so relaxed," Cindy added.

"So, you feel okay?" Larry checked again.

Kaminer shot him an exasperated look. "Why do you keep asking me that? What are you getting at?"

"You can't really call yourself a bot anymore, I'm afraid," Larry said, looking at the others.

"What are you talking about?"

"My read on you, when I shook your hand, tells me you don't have that Mindset gap anymore. There's nothing to keep emotions from getting a foothold, or opinions from forming," Larry said. Kaminer's jaw dropped open.

"That's good news," Cindy cheered, patting Kaminer on the back again.

"Maybe that's why you seem more human than before," Gulliver theorized, looking closely at Kaminer, who remained speechless.

"So, back to Dr. Henton Burke," Teegan cut in. "He has now made himself compatible with Mindset software and is occupying the niche in the Mindset gap inside every single bot. Can you believe that? What. A. Bastard." Teegan turned back to plop down in his chair, sending it shooting back a few feet.

"Well, we must continue on, we must, regardless of where Burke and Cray have taken up residence. We keep on going, and stick to our deal," Kaminer finally managed.

"We know, Kaminer," Gulliver said. "And we've got to look at the upside. You've got a lifetime of human experience to look forward to."

"A lifetime? But I'm perpetually renewable!"

"Not anymore you're not," Larry shot back. "Not with that brain of yours. That mostly-human brain you're walking around with."

Kaminer gasped. "Wha-, what?"

Gulliver started to wring his hands. "I'm sorry, Kam."

"So, my restart wasn't a simple reboot? My recovery wasn't just a rebuild back to where I was. I rebuilt into something else?" Kaminer asked, his mouth hanging open. Larry shook his head while Gulliver nodded.

"It seems as if you've been amassing quite an impressive central command system. An organic one," Gulliver pointed out.

"So what does that ah, make me?"

"I'm not sure," Larry answered.

"But I still have my bot bits, synthetic skeleton and parts. I'm not organic all the way through!"

"I know that."

"Hmm. I expect you've been in charge of your emotional side until now. That might get a little confusing as it starts to take off," Gulliver said in an encouraging way. "You'll experience how a human feels first-hand."

"There have been periods of, well, *that*."

"Feeling?" Cindy asked.

Kaminer nodded. "And you appear to have reserves in abundance," he said, looking at the shelves in the back of the room. "Contingencies for an eternity. An eternity that apparently I won't share." A quiet hush fell over the room as Cindy shifted in her seat.

"In the meantime, you're moving to Curriculum with Ambrose?" Larry finally asked.

"I suppose I have you all to thank for that."

Larry nodded. "The plan is for you to join Dr. Rafe Burke once you've approved the final shuffling of material in the Enhancements."

"Well, I won't approve them. It's a delicate matter."

"Very delicate," Cindy piped up.

"But you'll have the appropriate human approve them, once you've combed through them. Once you're happy with the assignment and distribution of files," Larry clarified.

"Sure," Kaminer said. "And then what happens?"

"We'll put the consolidation plans in place. We're starting with the Western Hemisphere. It might take a year or two to make it look natural," Teegan informed him. "I've been working on that, and the plan is being rolled out. We'll center it around the Consortium's stronghold in Mexico. Once we increase the standard of living, it'll seem crazy not to join in."

"And as many as possible will be interfaced?" Kaminer asked, and Teegan nodded.

"Who wouldn't want to be?" Larry asked.

"But will it make sense with the Human Protection Act? It's that Act that really drove the Pure movement. There weren't any communes before that. Humans, not just unmodified genetically, but also unaltered," Kaminer checked, and Larry stroked his stubbled chin some more.

"There will always be Pures," Gulliver said.

Cindy drew a sharp breath. "Sorry. I just hate these artificial divisions. We've watched it for the longest time. People with the craziest modifications thinking they were superior."

"As if having fish scales made a person better," Larry huffed.

"And then the humans with Interfaces thinking they were first-class," Cindy continued.

"Because instant knowledge must mean you're smart," Larry said with acidic sarcasm.

"And now the Pures thinking their way is the best way," Cindy finished.

"As if the HETs were dirty somehow," Larry added. Kaminer looked back and forth with interest from Larry to Cindy.

"Well, as I said, there will still be Pures. Just far fewer if the Interface and Enhancements are free," Gulliver clarified again.

Kaminer nodded. "You still think the numbers will work? After the, uh, die-off?"

"We think so. At least when you take into account these reserves. That should more than even it out," Teegan answered. "And we've been working on something else too. We feel like we have the means to clean things up even further."

"How so?" asked Kaminer.

"The Human Protection Act doesn't go far enough," Larry said. "There's too much grandfathering."

"What do you mean?" Kaminer asked, furrowing his brow. Cindy leaned in to peer at new purple and red hair that filled in Kaminer's eyebrows. He leaned back, tilting away from her.

"The Act provides for no further altering, either genetically or synthetically of humans. But what about the humans that were already altered?" Larry asked.

"Let me just stop you there, Larry," Teegan cut in. "You have to remember that the extinction event was caused by that effed up Cray pushing his way onto Interfaces."

"Oh right, I know what you're going to say. But I'm still worried about the rest," Larry said.

"What?" Kaminer asked, shaking his head.

"Sorry. It's just that the die-off consisted mostly of people walking around with plant or animal DNA modifications. It misaligned their Interface streaming, and it was the force of the, uh, message update," Teegan restarted.

"Otherwise known as Dr. Cray," Gulliver corrected.

"That caused the die-off," Teegan finished. "Most of the dead were altered in some fashion. And that takes care of a large swath of what Larry is getting at."

"So what's the issue?"

"There's still a small percentage of people walking around with non-human DNA, and very large number of people walking around with artificial parts," Teegan said, and Kaminer cocked his head.

"So, exactly how do we identify them as human?" Larry offered.

"Well, of course they're human. How could they not be?"

"Are they?" Gulliver asked. "What makes them so human? How far can their bodies have been syn-thetically altered and you still want to consider them human? Kaminer, face the facts. You're more human now than some of the so-called humans."

"You don't mean that," Kaminer muttered, shaking his head.

"It's true. Think about it. Man up," Larry pressed.

"You're serious? I, well, I never, um. I guess I will have to think about that."

"And ponder this," Larry continued. "We can give the humans any biology they haven't already sorted out for themselves. And they've sorted out quite a bit since the Human Protection Act."

"I know," Kaminer countered. "But what's the end goal?"

"We want to update the act. Give the humans incentive, if they've got synthetic parts, to get them replaced. If they've got non-human DNA, get it de-spliced. Separate the line between the bot and human world. Make it distinct. Human all the way through, or else they have the rights of a bot," Larry said.

"Meaning, not many?"

"You know you're off the hook with the system, right? That shit Archimedes did you a favor," Teegan added.

"What do you mean?" Kaminer asked.

"Our emergence and take-over of Central Frame gave him a little bit of leeway at the beginning. He got Dr. Katz and that Ambrose fellow to mess with some of your files," Teegan replied.

"I remember that. It was that same day I got upset in Dr. Katz's office," Kaminer said.

"So, you've been reclassified as human. You won't be getting pinged for semi-annual bot check-ups any-more," Teegan offered.

"Great. I won't be tracked by the system," Kaminer opined. "But does Dr. Burke recognize that?" The four Scholars looked at him, and Cindy shook her head.

"Let me get back to the thread about artificial Enhancement," Larry interjected. "We're thinking of updating the Human Protection Act. Decouple it from the Endangered Species Act. Write it in plain English. Make people declare themselves."

"I see no harm in that, but I know there's more."

"As a follow-up, we're going to introduce Bot ScrubBub to humans. We can tie it to the press release we sent out about Hostrevax," Larry declared.

"Right. I was off-mind when all of that happened. I hadn't put it together that you issued the press release," Kaminer confessed.

"Human ScrubBub can eventually be protective, of course. But only after we've given the humans time to sort themselves out. Until then, we can program it do whatever we want," Teegan said.

"Are you that worried about the few that survived the extinction event?"

"I am," Larry confirmed.

"Why?"

"We don't know what Henton Burke and Cray are up to. It's as simple as that. Why do they have a foothold in the bot *and* the human world?" Gulliver questioned.

Kaminer shrugged. "Their role as gatekeepers?"

"Or something else we haven't thought of," Larry warned.

Kaminer sighed and shook his head. "Where would all this leave me?"

"I guess you'll have a choice, Kaminer," Cindy said.

"A choice?"

"Let's look at this logically. Get rid of the things that make you bot. All those artificial parts, and your non-human DNA," Larry said. "And you'll be just another human that passes reappraisal."

"Or?"

"Or just register as bot. You don't want to be a human that *doesn't* pass reappraisal," Gulliver said.

"Why not?"

"We'll have to deal with them somehow. We're still working on that. But the end goal is to have humans that are human all the way through. Everyone else, including the bots, will be classified as non-human," Larry said.

"I'd take Door Number One, if I were you," Cindy suggested.

"Geez. I've got a lot of thinking to do."

"You'll make the right choice. I know you will," Cindy said, reaching over to pat Kaminer on the knee.

"All right. Reconvene in a month?" Larry asked "We'll get to work on writing the new act into code."

"I'll conduct a trial run of the new Standard Enhancement modules before they get the final go-ahead," Kaminer offered.

"That's it!" Teegan exclaimed, snapping his chubby fingers. "We'll call it The Code of Conduct!"

The Code of Conduct

I. DISCLOSURE
I recognize myself as Human/Non-human (circle one).

If **Human**: I recognize myself as Unenhanced/
Enhanced (circle one).

If <u>Enhanced</u>: Specify Human Enhancement Technology
(hereafter known as H.E.T.):

1. Performance Enhancements: (circle all that apply)
   - Neural Interface
   - Standard Enhancement Level 1, 2, 3, 4, 5
   - Standard Enhancement Top-Off
   - Other Performance Enhancement (private
     programs):

2. Biological Enhancements:

3. Cosmetic Enhancements:

If **Non-human**: Specify:

1. Access to Central Frame: Restricted/Unrestricted
 (circle one).

2. Synthetic upgrades:

3. Recombinant non-human genomic upgrades:

4. Human Biological Enhancements:

The Code of Conduct

II. REAPPRAISAL

Any Human with Non-human attributes is subject to reappraisal. 180 days from the initial signing of this contract will be given to retro-engineer, extract, nullify or replace any non-human components.

I recognize myself as subject to reappraisal: No/Yes (circle one).

III. ETHICS CONTRACT

- Only those of sound mind can legally agree to be enhanced with H.E.T.

- Humans may not be enhanced with synthetic upgrades, implants, parts, or materials (other than Neural Interface), or genomic Enhancements of any kind that are not 100% human.

- Enhancement may only occur at Homebases registered under the Universal Care Act.

- Any Homebase using H.E.T. on those not of sound mind, or introducing non-human upgrades to humans, shall forfeit all rights.

The Code of Conduct

III. ETHICS CONTRACT, continued

- Operators using H.E.T. on those not of sound mind, or introducing Non-human upgrades to humans, shall forfeit all rights.

- H.E.T. will not be used for illegal or clandestine purposes. Any Human or Non-human giving or receiving such H.E.T. shall forfeit all rights.

- No Enhancement Technology, Human or Non-human, shall be used on any Non-human, synthetic being, or bot of any kind, unless expressly authorized, engineered and designated for purposes relating to that technology.

IV. ACKNOWLEDGEMENT

I confirm that the above Disclosure is accurate. Said Disclosure will be amended within 5 working days after a new Enhancement.

I confirm the above designation of Reappraisal is accurate. If subject to reappraisal, I agree to appear before the Human Services Bureau within 180 days from the signing of this document.

The Code of Conduct

IV. ACKNOWLEDGEMENT, continued

If the Non-human components, whether genetic or synthetic, have not been extracted, nullified or replaced, I agree to recognize myself as Non-human, and understand I will no longer be subject to personhood and its jurisdiction.

I agree to fully conform to all parts of this Contract, and use my Enhancement Technology for the good of mankind. I understand failure to do so will result in forfeiture of my rights, including the right to live (Human) or decommission (Non-human).

All Humans, whether Enhanced or Unenhanced, and Non-humans will sign below, acknowledging your responsibilities and the consequences of failing to comply with the Code of Conduct.

Acknowledged:

Date: _____

Print Name: _____

Signature: _____

July

<u>FoodServe</u> *n*. A 3-D printer, manufactured by Global Stock, initially designed to produce biological fuel for bots.

"The summer's evaporating, Ambrose," Kaminer said. "I've already been in Curriculum for a few weeks, but it only feels like a few days."

"Think about what we've already gotten done. Refining the Standard Enhancements," Ambrose said, motioning Kaminer onto the escalator that ran from Magnate Mindware's marble-lined lobby to its basement cafeteria.

"But so quickly. Everything seems to be rushing by," Kaminer voiced.

"To you," Ambrose emphasized.

"What, not to you?"

"I'm kind of relishing each moment. Every time we clear a file and officially add it to the compendium, it feels like a victory. So no, it's not rushing by," Ambrose said, riding the escalator down. "I think the first rebuilt Standard Enhancement upload will be ready for review next week."

"Speaking of next week, I have an important appointment on Saturday."

"The 25th?" Ambrose checked, looking ahead to the neat rows of tables, lined with chairs, which were already visible from the escalator as they approached the lower level.

"I'm having my artificial digestive tract removed," Kaminer said, holding his breath.

"What? What for?" Ambrose blustered. "Why would you do that?"

"It's important," Kaminer said, stepping off the escalator. Ambrose maintained his silence until he and Kaminer had grabbed their foam trays and proceeded inside.

"Important? To upgrade your artificial digestive tract? To a biological one? You understand what that means, right?" Ambrose continued, feeling flustered.

"Well, I've looked into it. I think I'm prepared."

"Who's doing it at Burke?"

"Nope. Made an appointment at Spricatur West."

"Why? Why not have it done here?" Ambrose pressed, moving towards the hot lunch line. He stopped short, analyzing the days' options.

"Because it's close, and precisely because it is not the Homebase here. Not in Charter Pass, not at Burke," Kaminer answered, moving to Ambrose's side and stopping to observe the food laid out under the hot lights.

"What's that?" Ambrose asked, pointing to perfectly formed patties of what looked like meat.

"Where are the lunch ladies?" Kaminer muttered in quick succession. The servibot behind the counter straightened out a row of meat pucks with an ungloved hand.

"These are pork rounds," the servibot announced. "And the lunch ladies have been thanked, and received new FoodServe printers for their service."

"Like the one that showed up in the lobby of our dorm?" Ambrose asked. The servibot, vaguely female with a plain, flat face, and messy purple ponytail, shrugged and plopped a pork round onto a plastic plate, handing it to Ambrose. Ambrose looked in alarm to Kaminer and then back to the servibot.

"Does that, uh, come with anything else?" Kaminer queried. The servibot pulled a metal top off a serving tray, and fished out some pieces of chartreuse cane, laying them, with its hand, on Ambrose's plate.

"What's that?" Ambrose asked.

"Asparagus," the servibot answered.

"Really?" Ambrose questioned, his upper lip automatically peeling away in a sneer. "I don't think so."

"Feel free to access the human biobiscuits if it is not to your liking," the servibot said in a short tone, and turned to a person waiting behind Kaminer.

The two men moved off to find a table. "Human biobiscuits, my ahh-," Ambrose mumbled. "More like sub-human, if you ask me." He plunked his tray down loudly.

"I'll be right back," Kaminer said.

"Hey, why don't you try a human biscuit?"

Kaminer shook his head with a look of disdain, and walked over to the FoodServe printer. "*Cheese-flavored.b*," he messaged the box-like machine.

Its nozzle tip began to move in a circle, depositing layers of enriched carbohydrate input and flavoring, forming a small pastry. Kaminer scooped up the bio-biscuit, returning to flop into a seat opposite Ambrose.

"Why that look?" Ambrose questioned, trying to delay lunch for as long as possible.

"A human biscuit would make me sick right now. I don't need as many minerals as you do, and my essential vitamin and amino acid intake is lower. Obviously, since I don't have bones, and some, well, other parts," Kaminer declared. "Oh, and that looks disgusting." He pointed to Ambrose's tray.

"It looks like crap. I'm mean, it was never as good as my ma's but this-, well, this is a whole 'notha level of sad," Ambrose spit out.

"It's more like dog food than lunch."

"You mean second feeding," Ambrose noted.

Kaminer nibbled a side of his biscuit. "I think they're, um, updating the pizza line too."

Ambrose turned in his seat and glanced at another cafeteria serving station. "Oh my cray, they can't take away the pizza. Can you go get one? So I can try it?"

Kaminer nodded, pushing himself up from the table to stride over to the pizza line. A moment later he came back with a bread version of the pork round, topped with yellow sludge and accessorized with a meatish round of dubious origin.

"It's pepperoni," Kaminer announced, laughing.

"What's underneath it, the, uh, pepperoni?"

"Diatomaceous ooze!" Kaminer began to guffaw and then laugh hysterically.

"It's not *that* funny. Give it to me," Ambrose ordered, ignoring the faux pork and asparagus on his tray. He took a bite of the sketchy pizza.

"They said it'd been printed, like the pork round," Kaminer reported, taking another small bite of his bot biobiscuit. "With extra vitamins, if you can believe that. What a joke, a healthy pizza."

"Yeah, but it's good. It's more than good." Ambrose stuffed the side of it further into his mouth. "Hmm, yum, mmm."

Kaminer stared at him, dropping his biscuit onto his plate. "Are you serious?"

"Mmm. It looks pathetic I know, but it's like, yeah, delicious. Let me try the pork," Ambrose said, dropping half of the small pizza he hadn't managed to gulp down.

He picked up a plastic fork and knife to tuck into his first selection, ripping a piece of pork off. "Oh my head, this is scrumptious!"

"What?" Kaminer asked, cupping a hand to his ear.

"Delectable. You're not going to drool are ya?"

Kaminer huffed. "Well, it appears they're onto something."

Ambrose noted Kaminer's look of envy. "Who knew a food printer could actually reproduce more than a biscuit or a few drinks?" he said, trying to tone down his enthusiasm.

"Mmm," Kaminer replied, taking another small bite of his biscuit.

"Well maybe, after you replace your digestion with something biological, you can enjoy this too."

"They said I could start on liquid broth, you know, the new tea? I can add that to my biscuits right after surgery, and then after a week, start adding food," Kaminer reported. "Real food."

"Is there an order? To add in food?" Ambrose began chomping on the asparagus reproduction. "Oh, a bit crunchy." He examined the scrap of bright green stalk.

Kaminer raised his brow. "Raunchy? How can a vegetable be raunchy?"

"Not raunchy, crunchy. Crunchy!"

"Oh. Sorry. So, um, apparently, protein is the most important part. If I'm to nourish my biological parts, as I come off biscuits, I'm supposed to eat, well, that, I suppose." He pointed his biscuit at the remaining pork round that was making its way towards Ambrose's mouth.

"You won't be disappointed!" Ambrose declared, finishing the pork.

"I'm supposed to liquefy it for the first month."

"Check if you can just print it liquefied. The new FoodServe printers seem so modern," Ambrose mouthed, turning his attention back to the pizza.

"Highly-enabled," Kaminer voiced.

"Mmm."

"And then veggies and fruits. But they said to only add one per week, in case I have an allergic reaction."

"To the food? Wouldn't they know that? I mean couldn't they figure that out, before you ate something that made you, uh, sick?"

Kaminer winced. "You'd think so, but they are treating me as a human, like my records say."

"That's awesome. I hope they don't think you were ever in jail."

"That sounds familiar. What's that about?" Kaminer rubbed his chin and then started to scratch at it, leaving small red lines.

"Well, for a while there prison inmates were having their insides replaced. And reduced from three squares a day to two bot biobiscuits. Until it became illegal," Ambrose said, crunching on the last of the asparagus.

"I think I knew that." Kaminer began scratching furiously under his chin.

Ambrose leaned forward, pushing his tray to the side. "It looks, like, uh, you might have some stubble there, on your chin. And it's not purple either!"

"It's so itchy. I can barely stand it," Kaminer said, throwing the uneaten half of his biscuit back on the tray.

Spricatur West

Bawclaw *n*. **Coordinated nanobots, programmable for every type of surgical intervention.**

A few days later, Ambrose and Kaminer walked out of the outer C Block tram station in search of the Spricatur West shuttle.

"You sure you want to go there?" Ambrose checked as they crossed the outer ring road and proceeded towards a well-landscaped parking lot.

"Yeah. I've already had two visits. This is the time and the place. I'm sure of it," Kaminer said, pointing to a shuttle with 'Spricatur West Homebase' outlined in small block letters on its side.

"What, like pre-surgery check-ups?"

"Something like that." Kaminer put a hand to his forehead. "Now, I've just confirmed that's our shuttle. I'm ready. Are you?"

"I just don't get it, Kam. That's all I'm asking. Is why?" Ambrose asked. "*But yes, of course I'm ready. For whatever crazy adventure you want to undertake,*" he messaged, boarding the shuttle behind his friend.

With the men sitting on its lone bench seat, the two-wheeled shuttle departed, its gyroscopic micro-processors keeping the small passenger cab upright as it slowly eased itself out of the parking lot. It carefully picked up County Highway 9 and after a few minutes the driverless vehicle bore right to head south, and then picked up the zigzag of Pennant Ridge and Red

Branch Roads. The shuttle turned onto Lee Avenue, and pulled into a large industrial complex, weaving past a few monolithic buildings to pull under a commercial-sized porte-chochère.

"This is it," Kaminer confirmed, heaving himself off the bench as the van door slid open.

Ambrose looked up at the homebase's signage. "I feel like I'm cheating somehow."

"Like at cards?"

"*No, like on a married!*"

"Well you're not cheating on anyone. You're helping me," Kaminer clarified, entering the grey stuccoed building.

Ambrose trailed behind Kaminer as he approached a circular station set up to greet human customers in the main lobby. Ambrose looked over to the bot platform and then back to the human check-in station. *Straight to the human side. Interesting.*

He noticed that the lights here weren't as bright as the Homebase at Burke's, nor did the lobby appear as clean. The linoleum floor, while devoid of apparent dirt, lacked any shine. Ambrose drew a breath through his teeth as he looked around at the crowd that filled the lobby.

"Good morning, gentlemen. Welcome to Spricatur West. How may I be of service?" a bot voiced as they arrived at a section of open counter.

"I have an 11:00 hours appointment today. For gastrointestinal replacement," Kaminer said.

The bot flipped through some virtual pages on its desktop. "Kaminer Be-?" the bot started.

"That's me," Kaminer cut him off.

"Allow me to show you to your surgibot room," the bot said breezily, getting up and moving through a narrow turnstile in the circular arrangement. Another bot, standing in a huddle of bots at the very center, instantly took its place.

"Why's it so crowded?" Ambrose asked, noting how much busier it was compared to the memory of his brief internship at the Homebase at Burke. Ambrose thought today's venue seemed unorganized, but realized that was unfair as they'd been attended to quickly.

"It is a result of the Code of Conduct," the bot attendant answered, ushering them into the surgibot room. "I am called Asher. If you need me, just message. The doctor will be with you shortly."

Kaminer took a seat in a chair stationed in the middle of the room. Ambrose stood close-by, looking anxiously over to a mattress-less metal gurney, a small metal side table covered in vials and small tools, and an IV stand with a bag of fluids ready to go.

"*Is this where it's going to happen*?" he messaged Kaminer, just as a man in a white coat walked in.

"Good morning, Mr. Belle. I'm Dr. Rodriguez. Thank you for choosing Spricatur West for your surgery today," the thin man issued as he bustled in.

"Oh, there must be-," Ambrose started.

"Thank you, Dr. Rodriguez," Kaminer quickly called back. "*That's my last name too*," he simultaneously messaged Ambrose.

"*What do you mean*?"

"*I went back to Dr. Katz, made sure my records reflected a first and last name. Like any real person*," Kaminer continued. Ambrose's mouth dropped open as Kaminer shook Dr. Rodriguez's hand.

"Thank you for getting this scheduled early. You know we anticipate a very difficult fall."

Kaminer nodded. "I have every intention of passing reappraisal."

"*So that's why you're going through with this! That Code of Conduct thing? Why didn't you just tell me that*?" Ambrose messaged. Kaminer shot him a sheepish look.

"It's very important you follow the post-surgery regimen exactly. I know you've turned in all your virtual paperwork, including your acknowledgment of the nutritional plan, but I can't emphasis it enough."

"I understand," Kaminer replied.

"You read about the possible consequences of eating certain foods too soon, right? We just don't want you to tear a gut that's not ready," Dr. Rodriguez warned.

Kaminer put both hands up. "I promise, I'll follow the directions to the letter."

"Should we begin? I'll have you slip out of your clothes, and lay on this table," the doctor said, motioning to a gurney.

"Oh, uh," Kaminer exclaimed, sounding alarmed.

"Would it be possible to angle the gurney just a bit doctor? My, uh, brother gets the worst headaches when he lies flat," Ambrose chimed in.

"Your brother?" Dr. Rodriguez asked, looking from the freckled Ambrose to the light brown Kaminer.

Ambrose tilted his head. "Stepbrother."

"Of course. Our surgibots can be programmed to work off any angle. Many of our older clients prefer not to lie prone," Dr. Rodriguez offered. He walked over to the flat metal bed, interfacing it to increase its angle.

"Maybe a bit more?" Kaminer requested, and Dr. Rodriguez added a few more degrees to its tilt. "That looks comfortable," Kaminer finally acquiesced.

"Are you ready?" the doctor asked.

Kaminer nodded, and Ambrose closed in to shake his hand, bumping Kaminer's shoulder against his.

"It's gonna be fine, man," Ambrose said out loud. "*And I'll be right here for you, and after.*"

"*You're the best, and that's not a platitude,*" Kaminer sent back, as Dr. Rodriguez ushered Ambrose out of the room. Ambrose stood in the open door, leaning against the frame. The doctor nodded his consent for Ambrose to observe at close range.

Kaminer quickly disrobed, folding every article of clothing and leaving a tidy pile of clothes on the examination chair.

Standing in the doorway, Ambrose immediately wondered if the medical establishment hadn't missed something important. *There's no way for him to urinate! Not important for a bot where an occasional flush takes it out the back end, but what if he's drinking more than he needs?* Ambrose tucked a hand under his armpit, trying to give himself a reassuring hug. *How's this going to work?*

Kaminer heaved his body onto the operation table, and covered his featureless lower body with a large square of paper, as Dr. Rodriguez turned back to him. Ambrose watched anxiously, picking at paint on the door frame.

"Please, make yourself comfortable," the doctor encouraged his patient, and Kaminer settled back on the table. "My part in this is minor as you know. Just a quick sedative drip, and it's off to la-la land."

"Right," Kaminer intoned.

The doctor wrapped a thin foam noodle around Kaminer's closest arm, and Ambrose sighed in relief that it wasn't his left arm, the one with the new shoulder.

I don't understand how's this comes together. He's a hodgepodge of synthetic pieces and human parts, Ambrose worried as the doctor twisted the noodle. *Oh my gah-, it's like he just twist tied the wire wrapper on a loaf of bread.*

The doctor observed the effect of the tourniquet, and swabbed the crook of Kaminer's elbow with a Neutralizer wipe, rubbing the rest of it thoroughly over his hands until it disintegrated. "Just a slight pinch," he said, taking a small assembly off the side table, and inserting a needle into a vein.

"Ouch!" Kaminer exclaimed, pulling his arm away and starting to sit up. Ambrose shifted nervously on his feet.

"It's okay," the doctor reassured him. "Sorry about that. I have to use a lower-gauge for this procedure. We'll make a note in your records to use the higher-gauge, the thinner ones, for your upcoming surgeries," he said, motioning Kaminer back down. He quickly screwed the IV tubing to the catheter hub, taping it into place on Kaminer's arm.

Future surgeries? Ambrose thought, furiously reviewing all the procedures Kaminer could have signed up for. *New eyes, real skin, replacement bones, what doesn't he need? It's mostly just the muscle that powers him that's real.*

"Geez, it's okay" Kaminer voiced, and Ambrose looked over to see the doctor open the IV roller clamp and start the drip.

"And we're syncing to your Interface now," the doctor announced, turning to see the slow scrolling of vital signs on the wall.

> **Heartbeat: 70 bpm**
> **Heart Rhythm: Normal**
> **Blood Pressure: 110/65**
> **Oximeter: Normal**
> **Temperature: 37 degrees C.**

"Count backwards from ten for me?" Dr. Rodriguez asked.

"Yeah, uh, ten, nine, eight, sevvv-n, sii-," Kaminer trailed off, falling unconscious.

Dr. Rodriguez straightened Kaminer out on the table, pulling his arms away from his body, and yanking on his legs. Ambrose shuddered when he realized that the lower half of the metal table could be split in two, and that the doctor was strapping each one of Kaminer's legs onto a section, pushing the table slightly apart.

He moved back up to secure Kaminer's arms to either side of the metal gurney, and then adjusted the top of the table, which allowed Kaminer's head to be tilted back. The doctor pulled on a hook and loop strap, fastening it over his forehead.

Like his old shoes, Ambrose thought mournfully, drawing in a deep breath. *Why am I so nervous*?

He watched the doctor insert a long, thin tube into Kaminer's mouth and rotate a diminutive crank handle. The doctor pulled the crank off and passed another tube through the first one. He withdrew the outside tube, which snapped apart, and hooked what looked like a tiny rolled-up sleeping bag onto the end of the new section, clamping Kaminer's nose closed.

Ambrose crossed his arms tightly across his chest, looking down at his feet with the sudden realization that his friend was not only fully unconscious, but was no longer breathing on his own.

"He's all set," the doctor said, coming up to Ambrose, and laying a hand on his arm to gently pull him to the other side of the door. It slid shut.

"You're starting?"

"Has he been re-blooded? I only ask because it's not in his records, but I had to set the endotracheal ventilator to maximum."

"Ah, ReBlood? Enhanced blood? Yes, it's possible," Ambrose lied, wondering what exactly was coursing through Kaminer's body. *I know it's synthetic blood, compatible with both his synthetic and biological parts, but I've no idea what's in it. Maximum has to be enough.*

"Would you like me to direct the surgery out loud?" Dr. Rodriguez asked, and Ambrose nodded. "Then let's begin. This isn't as bloody as you might imagine it to be, with the Bawclaw."

"Bawclaw?" Ambrose asked in a meek voice, starting to feel a little weak.

"It's our coordinated nanobot infantry. Never heard of it?"

"Oh yeah, ah, like the operating room version of a bot's ScrubBub?" Ambrose offered, and winced, wondering why he'd even said the B word. *Just shut your mouth, Ambrose.*

"Sure, but ScrubBub is like the Army, keeping its ground secure. I think of Bawclaw nanobots as more of a precision strike force. Now, we'll do the pharynx last, under local anesthesia, once the breather comes out. Right? Let's get started."

"Okay," Ambrose mouthed, wishing he had something to sit on.

"Surgibots one through four, at the ready," Dr. Rodriguez said loudly, pressing an intercom button. Ambrose could see white panels behind the metal gurney retract towards the ceiling and a number of mechanical arms unfold.

"I've seen those before," Ambrose voiced, thinking back to Kaminer's shoulder surgery.

Dr. Rodriguez nodded. "Aerosol Neutralizer," he ordered, and Ambrose could see the room fill with the haze of mist. "Initiating procedure. Insert Bawclaw," he said, and then turned to Ambrose. "We'll do the anus, rectum and sigmoid colon in typical fashion. But the rest of the large intestine, small intestine and stomach have already been produced for Kaminer. It's quicker than waiting around for the nanobots to build it on-site."

"Sorry?" Ambrose asked, but the doctor held up his hand.

"Phase one, lower rebuild," the doctor continued through the loudspeaker, and Ambrose turned back to the door to see a surgibot arm pick up a small vial from the metal table, and snap it onto a fellow arm.

The new arm ended in a plastic syringe, and Ambrose watched in horror as it moved to the underside of the table. Grateful that one of Kaminer's legs obscured the view of what was happening underneath, Ambrose wanted to block his ears as the doctor continued to explain the procedure.

"Wha-?" Ambrose managed.

"The Bawclaw nanobots, once introduced through the anus, will rebuild the synthetic material through the lowest part of the large intestine," the doctor said in a matter-of-fact voice, and then held a hand to his forehead. "Confirmed," he voiced, pressing the loud-speaker button.

"Right now?" Ambrose queried.

"Yes, that's a go," the doctor replied, moving back to the button.

"Proceed to gastrointestinal extraction," the doctor ordered, and Ambrose backed away from the door. But he was unable to look away as three surgibot arms came around to the top of Kaminer, one delicately pulling the small paper cover lower on Kaminer's body. Then it moved back and lasered a straight line from his sternum to the lowest part of his pelvis, embellishing it with two vertical feet, forming an upside down 'T'.

The other two arms dug in, peeling back triangular layers of light brown skin and fat. The first arm made another pass, cutting through the last layer of fascia, as the other two surgibots moved the tissue to the side as soon as it was cut.

"Oh my gah-," Ambrose muttered.

"See? No blood," the doctor pointed out.

"Uh, no." Ambrose tried not to gag. The sight of Kaminer lying unconscious on the table with his inner organs exposed was quite different from the efficient replacement of the sitting, awake Kaminer's shoulder assembly and collar bone.

"Introduce phase two, severance," the doctor announced through the loudspeaker, and Ambrose stood frozen as the surgibot arm that had remained under the table came out from hiding, and waited while a companion arm removed the empty vial and snapped another one into place. It swiftly moved out of sight, and Ambrose assumed it was finding its entry point again.

"Is it going back?" he gulped. "Uh, underneath, um."

"Yes, phase two nanobots will be introduced through the anal cavity, but are programmed to proceed through the re-seeded and rebuilt sigmoid and wait to sever the existing, synthetic colon and attach the new biological descending colon, which we'll introduce when, yes, well, right now," the doctor announced. "Proceed with severance and placement," he announced through the loudspeaker.

Ambrose stepped back towards the door, pressing himself against it, gripping the molding around the glassed in area. He watched, fixated, as events unfolded so quickly, he had to blink his eyes and move back to a wall, propping himself against it, to take it all in.

What he thought he saw included a new surgibot arm descending from the ceiling, holding a bundle wrapped in cellophane the way a stork might carry a newborn baby. Another surgibot arm simultaneously made short strokes with its laser as two others ripped Kaminer's guts right out of his body, depositing them in a bucket tucked towards the head of the gurney.

Ambrose held his breath as he thought about this, reviewing how the bundle, which must have contained the new organs, was dropped down into the empty cavity. The surgibot gently slid the packaging material out from underneath the delivery, depositing the gooey plastic wrap on the side table. It retracted back into the ceiling, while two other bot arms arranged the organs to their liking.

Ambrose took a deep breath as he stepped back to see what was happening. "Is, ah," he murmured, afraid to open his mouth.

"So the phase two Bawclaws are fusing the lower materials together now, and working to colonize the new tract with the appropriate assortment of bacteria," the doctor said blandly, and Ambrose briefly pictured the doctor ordering tea and a biscuit from a FoodServe.

"It seems so, um-, routine. To you," Ambrose breathed out.

"It's not the most sought-after surgery, but there are a few," the doctor answered. "Onto phase three?"

"Uh, sure," Ambrose said, trying to pull himself together.

"Reset gurney, extract ventilator, initiate phase three, pharynx," the doctor ordered, pressing the talk button.

Ambrose observed the gurney tilt forward and the devious surgibot arm come into view from underneath the table. It held itself still as another surgibot replaced the syringe and popped a third Bawclaw vial onto its side. Another arm yanked the breather out of Kaminer's mouth, pulling hard on the tube, while the fourth arm injected a fluid into the existing liquids in the IV bag that dripped down into Kaminer's arm. Ambrose saw Kaminer stir slightly.

"I don't think he's entirely asleep," Ambrose cried in alarm. The doctor shot him a look.

"Increase sodium bicarbonate," the doctor ordered through the loudspeaker, but the surgibot arm stationed by the IV held itself steady. The doctor put a hand to his forehead as Ambrose saw Kaminer clench and unclench a hand.

"He's moving!"

"Re-ventilate," the doctor ordered, and pushing Ambrose out of the way, stepped back into the room. A surgibot arm pushed the breather back into Kaminer. He squirmed slightly, but kept his eyes closed.

Ambrose brought a hand to his mouth, observing the doctor pull a small mask over his own face and send Neutralizer mist back into the room. When the mist cleared, the doctor grabbed the syringed surgibot arm and removed the needle tip and its side vial, screwing one to the other.

He pulled Kaminer's breather out again, yanking hard, and shot the contents of the syringe into his mouth as Kaminer opened his eyes and started to shift on the table. Ambrose, not being able to hear through the closed door, assumed Kaminer was moaning.

The doctor strode over to a side wall, tapping out instructions. With reluctance, the surgibot arm standing by the IV bag delivered the alkaline solution, and Kaminer's eyes closed again. Ambrose started to sputter.

"Final phase, attach esophagus to pharynx," Ambrose thought he saw the doctor mouth, and observed a surgibot arm rummage through the contents of Kaminer's innards, fishing out two ends that looked like empty sausage casing. It held them together as an opaque substance formed a ring at the juncture, turning from whitish to salmon-pink. The arm dropped the esophagus back down and tucked it in.

"Close and nano-abrade," the doctor said, turning to face Ambrose, nodding and giving him a thumbs up. The surgibots reversed their steps, holding the fascia tight, spraying a nanobot mist onto it. The film quickly knit the tough layer back together. They repeated these steps for the thin layer of fat and outer skin.

The doctor pushed the two lower legs of the table back together, and unstrapped Kaminer's legs, arms and forehead. He gently lifted his head, stuffing a small pillow underneath, and draped a heavy-looking blanket across his body.

Asher, the attendant who had checked in Kaminer, reappeared at the door, and entered the room without looking at Ambrose. He removed the anesthesia needle from Kaminer's arm, pushing a little piece of gauze onto the existing tape before pressing it down.

The attendant pushed Kaminer from the room, trailed by Dr. Rodriguez, and Ambrose experienced a moment of dissonance when he realized how similar the present moment was to his experience of wheeling Kaminer to an overnight room, trailed by Dr. Kate, almost four months ago. *Only I didn't go through it with him this time. This is like what I went through. That time.*

"He should be talking within the half hour. Would you like to wait with him?" Dr. Rodriguez asked.

Ambrose nodded. "Yes. Is he okay? I thought I saw him move."

"That was nothing," the doctor cut in. "He's very dense for his height, and we simply didn't calibrate for that. We'll take this into account when he comes back in two weeks," Dr. Rodriguez said, motioning Ambrose into a plain room, empty except for a bendybed.

On its sole window hung two gingham curtains tied back with ribbons more suitable for a girl's ponytail. It looked like the window in his mother's kitchen and Ambrose let out a heavy sigh.

"For a check-in?" Ambrose asked, as the bot pushed the metal gurney into the room.

"Well, not-," Dr. Rodriguez began, as Asher turned to leave.

"Hey, aren't you going to put him in the nice bed?" Ambrose called out. The bot turned to look at him, and then the doctor.

"Let's leave him there for now," Dr. Rodriguez said, dismissing the attendant with a nod. "Give his body time to seal everything up tight. We find the patient does better when he's able to move on his own to the other bed," the doctor added, attaching a small cuff to Kaminer's wrist.

"You sure?" Ambrose questioned.

"Yes, I'm certain. And no, Kaminer won't need a check-in. We'll make sure everything is up and running before he leaves tomorrow."

"Then what's in two weeks? Why are we coming back?"

"Maybe you should ask your, ah, stepbrother about that when he wakes up," the doctor said, flipping a switch to monitor vital signs from the cuff.

"Why are you using a cuff?" Ambrose queried. "Did you have trouble pulling vitals from his Interface?"

"No. It's just a failsafe we use here at Spricatur. The risk of an ischemic event is small, but if he went off-mind, then, well, at least we don't have a gap in monitoring, right?" the doctor offered.

"That makes sense," Ambrose conceded, lowering himself onto the unused bed. *So, he's saying Kaminer has an Interface?*

Post-Op

ScrubBub *n.* **Nanobot replicant of a**
genetically-altered bacteriophage.
Neutralizes viruses, bacteria, cancer, prions,
and other disease-causing agents.

Twenty minutes later, Kaminer began to stir, shifting on the gurney. Ambrose, who had been streaming the newscast in-mind, trying to pass the time, opened his eyes and got up from the bendybed.

"Hey li'l bro," Ambrose greeted in almost a whisper.

Kaminer's hand went to his stomach. "Uhh," he breathed out. "*Hurt.*"

"Pain? Pain?" Ambrose cried. "How can you be in pain?"

"*Bad*," Kaminer left a hand on his stomach, protecting it.

"Can you wait a sec? I'll go get someone!"

Kaminer's eyes rolled back in his head. "Uhh," he moaned, shivering.

"Holy cray," Ambrose cursed, exiting the room to run down the hall back to the circular greeting desk. Quickly scanning the faces, Ambrose could not spot the attendant assigned to Kaminer.

"Yes?" another bot queried as Ambrose approached the station in a flurry. "How may I be of service?"

"There's a Kaminer, uh, Belle, that just had a gastrointestinal replacement, and he's not doing well.

He's in pain. We need some medicine," Ambrose blurted out, as the bot tapped on the desktop.

"Your attendant, Asher, is stationed at the station for attendants, at the *other* end of hall, but-," the bot said.

"No, I-," Ambrose cried.

"But," the bot cut in loudly. "But, I happen to know Mr. Belle personally, so please allow me to assist." Ambrose blinked. "Uh-huh, right," it said, looking at his desktop screen. "The fourth of six procedures. I wonder if his urethral catheter has shaken loose. Shall we have a look?"

"Yes, come," Ambrose managed, signaling the bot to follow him as he turned and rushed back to Kaminer's room.

The bot caught up to Ambrose's side and continued to talk. "Besides, I do not like that other attendant, Asher, comprised only of lazybones. We shall get along so much better without him," the attendant muttered, pulling Ambrose faster.

Ambrose started to run by the bot's side. "And he was shivering," he reported, struggling with the pace.

"I so admire a person like Kaminer, his organized, systematic, approach. Poor lad. Underdeveloped kidneys, such a rudimentary bladder, if you could even call it that. And all his other issues. My, my." The bot sighed. "We are so happy to help. And repeat business is very important to us. We must not let him suffer."

"Uh-huh," Ambrose breathed out, as they turned into Kaminer's room. "Look at him. Give him something!"

Both the bot and Ambrose could see the extent of Kaminer's distress. He was moaning in a low voice.

"*Gurney*," Kaminer messaged, causing Ambrose to stop in his tracks. It was absolutely flat.

"Help me fix this. Set it to an angle, at least fifteen degrees," Ambrose shouted, and the bot attendant did as it was told, efficiently resetting the gurney. Kaminer groaned loudly, his labored breathing sounding louder in Ambrose's ears than it actually was.

"Oh dear. That was an oversight. We extend our sincerest apologies. His records are clear, Kaminer requires the assistance of elevation. Let gravity do the work, right?" the bot offered, pulling the blanket up to gently pinch Kaminer's feet.

"What?" Ambrose mumbled, inspecting Kaminer's face.

"Until his new kidneys and bladder are fully grown, well, it does help to have gravity on your side," the bot said, taking one of Kaminer's wrists. "No, I do not like this at all!"

Ambrose remained fixed by Kaminer's bed, and put a hand on his friend's forehead. "He doesn't feel right. He seems hot." They both turned to inspect the vital statistics that broadcast on the wall.

> **Heartbeat: 78 bpm**
> **Heart Rhythm: Slight arrhythmia**
> **Blood Pressure: 130/70**
> **Oximeter: Normal**
> **Temperature: 37.5 degrees C.**

"Let me scan. For the biological catheter," the bot announced, and stood absolutely still, slowly moving its eyes over Kaminer's stomach. "Yes, it remains attached to his rudimentary organs. But he appears stressed."

"*Kam, can you hear me?*" Ambrose messaged.

"*Here.*"

"*What is it?*"

"*I was awake, aware. During,*" Kaminer managed to message.

"*During the procedure?*" Ambrose asked, trying to contain his alarm so it sounded soft and reassuring in Kaminer's mind.

"*I felt. Everything. Why. Didn't I die? I wish I had died,*" Kaminer sent in spurts, and even in Ambrose's mind it sounded like he was whimpering.

"Can you give him something to sleep? He's in so much pain," Ambrose insisted, looking up to the bot attendant.

"Absolutely, yes. And I would also like to administer a small dose of a new ScrubBub. One that is being launched for humans. You may consider it a broad spectrum antibiotic. And because Kaminer was horizontal for, well, some time, a diuretic is not uncalled for. There is some edema in his feet, and it will make him more comfortable," the bot said, putting a hand to its temple.

"How, um, does he, well," Ambrose tried.

"And I shall put a pad under him to catch any drips that come out his tube. The lazybones should have done that. Tsk. Tsk."

"*Kam, are you there?*" Ambrose signaled, and received only a moan in reply. He fussed with the bedding, trying to tuck its thickness under Kaminer's legs. He turned to the bot attendant and realized it had departed, and was already coming back through the door.

"One drip pad, laid just so," the bot announced, pushing Kaminer up to his side, and unrolling a thick wad of paper on the metal cot. The bot moved in to press a knee against Kaminer's naked backside, and removed a syringe from a front patch pocket on its white one piece jumpsuit. "And a spoonful of sugar," the bot intoned, jabbing Kaminer's muscular buttocks with the needle. "And that is that. Let him rest. I will monitor him virtually, and interface me, Ned.b," it said, drawing a breath, "for anything you need." He rolled Kaminer down onto the drip pad. "Anything at all," it voiced and withdrew from the room.

***

A few hours later, Kaminer awoke, in a haze. Ambrose, napping in the bendybed, didn't notice his waking, and continued to doze.

Kaminer propped himself up on his elbows, resting there to orient himself. He pulled the thick blanket off, and taking his time, managed to get up. He pulled off and wadded up the wet pad that had done its job. Looking around the room, he spotted the door to the bathroom.

As Kaminer turned on the water, Ambrose stirred. "Hey, you up?" Ambrose called out, realizing the bed beside him was empty.

"In the bathroom, cleaning off," Kaminer called back, and Ambrose shot out of bed towards the sound of Kaminer's voice. "I'm alive. Find my clothes, could ya?"

"They want you to sleep in their pajamas," Ambrose informed him, moving to pick up a set of soft worn scrubs. On top of the little pile lay a pair of adult-sized diapers. *Like before. When he lost control. Just like the ones I wore. When I lost control.*

He moved over to the petite bathroom and handed them to the naked Kaminer, averting his eyes.

"What are these?" Kaminer asked, inspecting the cloth on the scrubs. "They're kinda nice."

"I think real doctors wore them, back before there were bots and homebases."

"You mean when there were only people and hospitals," Kaminer said, running a hand down the faded front of the top, inspecting its hem. "This was sewn. Like Dr. Burke's clothes."

"Yeah. Surgeons wore those," Ambrose said, exhaling his worry in a single breathe. *Kaminer is standing. This has to be a good thing. It took me almost a year to stand, and here he is standing for the second time.*

"Surgeons," Kaminer echoed.

"Like human surgibots. How you feeling?"

Kaminer shrugged his shoulders. "Like crap."

Ambrose helped him out of the bathroom and over to the bendybed, set at a slight angle. Kaminer shuffled painfully, bent forward at the waist.

"So what happened?"

Kaminer huffed, and eased himself onto the bed. He slowly pulled the diapers on, and Ambrose helped him to standing so he could pull them all the way up. Kaminer leaned against Ambrose to pull on the long blue hospital bottoms, tying them loosely, before sitting back down.

"I can't lean back. I'm too sore," he said, and Ambrose interfaced the bed to tilt farther forward so that Kaminer could sit completely upright. Ambrose, gently lifted Kaminer's legs onto the bed. "Oh, uh-," Kaminer complained. "Ow!"

"Sorry, man," Ambrose voiced with a grimace. He grabbed the heavy blanket that draped off the metal gurney, and placed it on top of his friend, wiggling his way onto the side of the bed. "So what happened? And what in the world is going on with the diaper? When did you get a front end?"

Kaminer stared at Ambrose and sighed. "I haven't told you everything because I didn't want to upset you. You worry so much. About everything. I didn't want you to review it in your mind over and over, and over again."

"So what's going on? What happened in the surgery?"

"More like what didn't happen. The anesthesia didn't really take," Kaminer confessed, and brought two hands up to his head, covering his face. He began to sob. "All I want is Door Number One! Is that too much to ask?"

"Uh, what's behind Door Number One?" Ambrose asked. "*Ned, can you administer more meds for pain*?" he sent, still listening for Kaminer's reply.

"Humanhood, personhood, manhood," Kaminer said, sputtering. "Is it even possible? How are they going to complete my renal system? I've already done so much work."

"*Coming immediately*," Ned answered in Ambrose's mind.

"And my hydraulic system. What about that? I haven't even scheduled it yet but if I've reached my limit with the G.I.," Kaminer heaved. "G.I. tract, when does that happen? I only have six months!"

"You're asking a lot, I think, but it's not impossible," Ambrose soothed, trying to contain his apprehension that Kaminer had never mentioned any of this to him.

"But it is. My eye assemblies were done easily, under a local. They didn't even have to put me to sleep," Kaminer reported.

Ambrose startled, moving in closer to peer at Kaminer's eyes. Trying to reconcile his memory, he knew they had started out black with specks of brown, and then increasingly turned brown until they contained black specks. But now he realized Kaminer's eyes were brown all the way through, only the outermost ring of his iris stained black. Ambrose gulped. "I'm sorry I didn't notice."

"Last week I had my auditory system replaced," Kaminer moaned. "And I feel like I need the volume turned up. I can no longer hear certain frequencies, and sometimes background noise clouds out what I need to listen to." He leaned back on the pillows.

Ambrose thought back to the last couple of lunches they'd had. *Kam did have trouble hearing me,* he confirmed with a gasp as Ned bustled back through the door.

"Mr. Belle, how are you feeling?" Ned asked.

"I-," Ambrose tried.

"Like shi-, i-, like ship, what?" Kaminer mumbled, sounding confused.

"Not a sinking ship, I hope. Let us keep all boats afloat," Ned called out in a singsong voice. "With a little sleepy juice." He quickly grabbed Kaminer's arm, jabbing it with a child-sized needle.

"Hey, ahh-," Kaminer released, as his head dropped back on the pillows and his shoulders relaxed.

"Thanks for being so prompt with that," Ambrose voiced. "He's been through quite a lot."

"Indeed. He is something of a hero around here. All that work to make himself superhuman, and now the humbleness of it all, going back to what God intended," the bot clucked, straightening the blanket.

Ambrose narrowed his eyes as Ned smoothed down his neat, side-parted hair down. *Another side part. Another fan.* "How's the timeline coming along for completing his work?" Ambrose probed.

"Nanobots are doing their thing on the inside, re-building what nature shortchanged. His kidneys, bladder and the rest of his renal system will be intact within the week. It will take that long for his biological replacement digestive system to come online, well, I should not say online. To sync? What is the word? Work in lockstep?" the bot put forth, all in one breath.

Ambrose tilted his head. "For the renal system to produce urine and the G.I. system to produce fecal matter? The way they are supposed to?"

"Well-said!" the bot exclaimed. "You could be a technician."

"I am a technician."

"A learned man, yes," Ned continued. "Kaminer has asked to replace the sex organs he had removed, you know, when he went into ministry." The bot leaned in and whispered these last few words in Ambrose's ear. "So ironic."

"I'll say," Ambrose said, feeling lucky.

"Less of a man when he went to serve God in the ministry, more of a man when he went to serve humankind in Bio-protection," Ned prattled on.

"Bio-protection. I know," Ambrose murmured.

"And now back to the man he was before he tinkered with everything. As he should be."

"Mmm," Ambrose issued, nodding. "Our superhero, that Kaminer."

"It will take two more procedures. One to complete the urinary tract, which is fairly straightforward. We have a cloned penis at the ready. It will be a perfect match for what he surgically excised." Ned shook his head, tsking. "And separately we have scheduled an orchioplexy."

Ambrose immediately searched for the meaning of the word on his Interface, trying to keep surprise from creeping into his face. "To put the undescended, uh, testes where they're supposed to be?" Ambrose said, trying to sound matter-of-fact.

"Exactly. But really, he is just so fortunate to have made it in, before any renal failure. And of course we have corrected the defect on that copy of his Pax2's."

"Right. That's a kind of gene therapy. So you're saying he also suffered from a syndrome? Like maybe, uh, papillorenal syndrome, that would have affected his kidneys and accounted for his eyes?"

"Something like that. Certainly that was part of it. Very complex, but now solved," Ned said, with a flourish of his hand.

"Almost solved."

"And very soon, he will be whole," Ned issued with a tone of glee.

Did I ever feel whole? After all that time in hospital? Please, please, Kaminer, be whole!

Road Trip

Reader *n*. Originally an external device used to read books. Still refers to any non-Interface streaming device, whether handheld, or implanted in the palm or posterior back of hand.

A month later, Ambrose decided that he and his room-mate needed to celebrate.

"Two months in Curriculum, Kam," Ambrose stated as they exited the Magnate Mindware building and began to walk along the outer ring road of Charter Pass. The street was quiet and recently swept. New bushes filled in the entire grassy area across the street, partially blocking the view to Chicago's cityscape beyond. Ambrose stopped short, taking Kaminer's forearm.

"*What's up???*" Kaminer messaged. In Ambrose's mind, it showed up with a visual of a long string of repeating question marks.

"Is it me, or wasn't there a street, *right there*, this morning?" Ambrose asked, pointing directly in front of them. "It was across the way. Coming at us, like at a ninety degree angle. Straight towards Chicago's outer limit."

"And ours," Kaminer added, straightening up on tiptoes to catch a glimpse across the expanse of bushes. "There's an army of workers over there, and a hole in the ground."

"For a building? At the end of their street?" Ambrose asked, sounding confused.

"Constructionbots," Kaminer clarified. "Anyway, about the Standard Enhancements, we're almost done. All that work, reshaping content."

"Why are you changing the subject?"

"I'm not. I mean, it wasn't my intention. We can find out later what's going on across the street. But for now, are you happy with how we've simplified the material for young children, pushing the complex files to the end? Are you sure we're okay with the amount of material contained in the Top-off?"

"You know, it's not the material that worries me," Ambrose said, pulling Kaminer to start walking again. They turned away from the bush-obscured construction site, and continued down the outer circumference road.

"What then?"

"It's simply the idea of uploading the kids with the material," Ambrose complained.

"How so?"

"Are their brains going to atrophy? Isn't that why Magnate Mindware set up Standard Enhancements for adults to begin with?"

"Yeah, uh," Kaminer stammered.

"Isn't it enough that they get Interfaces and stream the material? I thought being forced to figure out what it all meant was what kept their brains maturing,"

"Not sure if that was ever known as a fact."

"You're right about that, I guess. I've checked every file on my Enhancements, every clip I could find on Central Frame."

"Did you find anything? That would suggest a disadvantage, if children received Enhancement packets?"

"No, nothing."

"So you could be worrying about nothing? How'd the Top-off work out?"

"Scotty says it's manageable. Moving the extra to a sixth Standard Enhancement, shifting everything else made it work," Ambrose said. "And it sounds like the Deciding Committee is in favor."

"Tell me again, who's on the Deciding Committee?"

"All the head honchos. Just like you'd expect. Now how about that road trip? Come meet my family?" Ambrose entreated.

"Only if your crappy little craypit brother is there."

Ambrose laughed. "You forgot coddled! But don't mention I ever said that, okay?"

"Of course not," Kaminer said. "Besides, you uttered that months ago and its shelf life has long expired."

"Thanks."

"And yes, tomorrow works for a road trip. The first day of September. How'd we both manage to get Tuesday off?"

"Well, Scotty is accompanying Mrs. Harrington to the vote. She's actually on the Deciding Committee."

"It seems like the head of Magnate Mindware should recuse herself from any vote that has to do with realigning Standard Enhancements," Kaminer noted.

"Try telling her that," Ambrose shot back as the pair entered the outer G Block tram station.

"No, I don't think I will."

"Geez, you still need to loosen up, man!" Ambrose said, punching Kaminer in the arm. "It was a figure of speech. I didn't actually suggest that you talk to her."

"Oh," Kaminer said, hanging his head. "Those subtle intricacies still elude me sometimes."

"Don't I know it. But you'll get there. Just keep taking baby steps."

"Medimos progresso en pequeños pasos."

"What?"

"We measure progress in small steps," Kaminer explained.

"Well, it's true. Just keep plugging, and before you know it, you'll have built a Ring."

Kaminer stared at him. "Did you do that?"

"I did. Down in Brazil. Came home earlier this year, started looking for work, ended up in this crazy place," Ambrose issued, working his way up to the edge of the station's platform. *Shouldn't have walked again but there I was, slogging like the others. I did it. I made it.*

"Really? How did that happen?"

"I signed up for the trade. A ten year work contract and a copy of my Mindset for a job. Pretty lucky, huh? Now, if we leave after the morning rush tomorrow, it won't take more than an hour and a half to drive to Modesto," Ambrose continued.

"Straight south?"

"Yep. The 67 Tollway to Route 104. We'll pick up Tim just outside the Purement commune there. Then we'll weave our way through the outskirts of Springfield-Decatur, cross the New Bridge at Naples, and we're practically home," Ambrose said.

"I'm really looking forward to it," Kaminer enthused, as the pair stepped back slightly from the edge of the platform while the G train pulled into the station.

***

The next morning, Ambrose and Kaminer hopped another tram, at the inner B Block station, and headed towards the outer circumference of Charter Pass.

Barely sixteen minutes later, the eleven mile ride concluded and the pair exited the outer B Block train station. Ambrose noticed the delineation between the outer circumference road and the land beyond as they walked towards the car share.

"You know, you can really tell Chicago's just outside city limits when you're in G Block," Ambrose started. "With the skyscrapers right up to our door."

"*Mmm*," Kaminer confirmed.

"But the difference here isn't quite as sharp."

"*Springfield-Decatur was never as dense as Chicago.*"

Ambrose, looking around for his spot in the car share, stopped short. "Hey, I've got a question for you. How come, if you were a policebot in Chicago, you didn't go to a Homebase there? After you were injured? I've always wondered about that."

"Even I knew to hop a heli and come here. It's the most civil place around," Kaminer said. "Okay, I admit it. It was part of my programming, back then." Kaminer lifted his eyebrows in confirmation. "*I had to.*"

Ambrose peered at him closely, shaking his head "You know your eyebrows are filling in. Did ya know that?"

"The red and purple thing isn't really working for me," Kaminer answered, and Ambrose chuckled, realizing that Kaminer's eyebrows were starting to match his hair, which didn't match the brown stubble on his chin.

"Ah, here we are," Ambrose announced as his Interface directed him to the right space in the car share where a slightly beat up, three-seat driverless model awaited them. "Sorry, Kam. I didn't spring for a newer car, but it'll get us there all the same."

"You could've leased a driver car. I would have enjoyed that."

"Yeah, but they're more expensive."

"More? Why more?"

"I dunno," Ambrose responded. "Something to do with insurance."

"What would insurance have to do with it?"

"It's probably because a driver car is more likely to get into an accident with the self-drives."

"How's that?"

"You figure it out. Self-drives communicate with each other, know where the other cars are, what moves they're going to make. A driver car is like a moving blip, its future actions uncertain," Ambrose lectured as he eased himself into the backseat. Kaminer entered from the other side, the car sagging when he lowered his full weight onto the seat.

"Geez," Kaminer murmured.

"Well, it's not like you're fat."

"No, not fat, but not as trim as I could be. I look trim but I feel bulky. Like bulked up. And yet every day I only eat a few biobiscuits, a cup of protein broth, and something green. And still."

"Don't worry about it," Ambrose soothed, and sent their first destination to the car. "*Route 104 and Breck,*" Ambrose interfaced, sitting back to let the carbot proceed south along the circumference road where it picked up the Tollway as Charter Pass gave way to Springfield-Decatur.

Immediately, the homogenous, low buildings of Charter Pass were replaced with a hodgepodge of brick, steel, and polycarbonate buildings of varying heights.

"Look over there, Kam," Ambrose piped up, pointing to his side of the window. "See that exit? That's where Dr. Kate and Dr. Burke live."

"That, is more than a highway exit."

"That, my friend, is a security gate. Get through that gate and there are still two more on their private road!" Ambrose said, flabbergasted.

"A private exit? Must be some house!"

"Not a house. It's a mansion. And I've heard Dr. Kate call hers 'The Estate'."

"Fitting," Kaminer responded. "I'd sure like to see them some day."

"We will NEVER see those homes. EVER. So moving on," Ambrose clarified, as the car sped quickly past the Burke's exit.

Ambrose noticed the newer poly buildings were broadcasting banners for the latest Enhancements. Some of the longer advertisements popped up in clusters, giving them time to read each ad all the way through.

> **Spricatur West Homebase offers you the latest in modern technology.**
>
> **Come see us today for our most popular Enhancements:**
>
> **Performance: ReBlood - Get your super aerobic blood today!**
>
> **Cosmetic: Visage Mirage - the look of a fully restored visage without the hassle or expense!**
>
> **Hair Today -Balding? Want to impress your friends? Get a new head of hair!**
>
> **We can restore you today! Message us and make your appointment.**
>
> **Short waiting times. We'd love to see you at Spricatur West!**

Ambrose shook his head and snorted. "How're you feeling these days?"

Kaminer hung his head. "Sometimes I feel like an imposter."

"Huh? It's all gone pretty well, hasn't it?"

"Since the GI surgery. That was a nightmare," Kaminer confessed. "But I mean more of how I feel inside my head."

"*How do you feel, then?*"

"Like Pinocchio! I want to be a real boy, but I had to lie to do it. And I can't count on any Blue Fairy in the end."

"No Blue Fairy for you, not after the load of crap you fed that homebase to get your surgeries scheduled!"

Kaminer shook his head, smiling tightly. "It didn't bother you, did it? That I lied? I didn't know how else to explain the state of things."

Ambrose laughed. "It was all very entertaining, learning about how you'd taken the ultimate road towards chasteness."

"Well, others have done it, and it was the only thing I could find, other than confessing I'd started out as a bot, that would explain my lack of parts." Kaminer sounded glum.

Ambrose punched him in the arm. "But you could have said that, and still gotten what you wanted."

"I wasn't sure. It's a miracle my nose isn't three feet long."

"You're not the first person who's ever lied, Kam."

"But it feels that way," Kaminer said, blushing.

Ambrose noticed him put his hands to his cheeks, and realized Kaminer's face was flushed. *And now he can blush.* Ambrose busied himself looking out the side window. A few minutes later, he squinted, motioning towards a cluster of buildings in the distance. "Hey, what's that?"

A flashing message appeared to be marching towards them, broadcasting first in the distance and them jumping to the next closest building until it flashed on the polycarbonate side of the building closest to their moving car.

"*As if it knows where we are,*" Kaminer pointed out.

Ambrose nodded. "*Some reminder.*"

> **CODE OF CONDUCT.**
> **FILE YOUR PAPERWORK.**
> **REAPPRAISE NOW.**
> **CODE OF CONDUCT....**

"Look, it just keeps repeating. Crap, this whole reappraisal thing. You know you're gonna be very busy when you go work for Dr. Burke next week," Ambrose said, shooting Kaminer a look.

"It just figures, doesn't it? There I was, thinking what a sweet deal it would be to get off the streets. Well, I wasn't thinking that exactly," Kaminer said, snorting. "It was more about keeping myself in one piece."

"You came in a little late for that," Ambrose huffed. *You came in a little late to expect a full recovery, Mrs. Belle.*

"And then the entire landscape shifts, and anyone with a non-human Enhancement has to have it undone. Usually going back to the very place where they had it done."

"Which includes Dr. Burke's department, Cosmetic Enhancement, at our homebase," Ambrose lamented. "I'm so sorry."

"Not as sorry as I'm going to be," Kaminer emphasized, and turned to look out the window as the car continued to roll forward on the slightly elevated Tollway. "Why are there so many empty lots? And what the heck is that?"

Ambrose craned his neck to look out Kaminer's side. "It's got to be some kind of constructionbot," Ambrose mouthed, not sounding sure. "But I've never seen anything like it! Constructionbots should look like people. You know, the two leg, two arm thing is kind of a successful model." Ambrose's mouth fell open as an enormous multi-legged machine crawled slowly forward, grasped a brick building in its mandibles and engulfed it, steadily moving its heft to where the building had just stood.

"Did that thing just eat a building?" Kaminer queried, sounding alarmed. The silvery gray machine began to spurt fine dust out of slit openings in the underside of its belly.

"It looks like a beetle. Pooping out brick dust!" Ambrose exclaimed, as both men turned to watch the machine pivot onto the road, taking up almost the entirety of it, and proceed towards a warehouse.

"It's removing the old buildings."

"There must be a building and rejuvenation program going on in Springfield-Decatur. Have you heard any news about that?"

Kaminer pressed his lips together, looked down at his hands, and shook his head. "No. But it seems to me that anything, organic or otherwise, if it isn't building and rejuvenating, then it must be decaying."

"Like Dr. Kate," Ambrose ejected, and then covered his mouth, smiling. "Oh, I didn't mean that. Not the way it sounded."

Timothy

Streaming Blocker *n*. **A targeted, uploadable filter that jams incoming streaming, effectively Messaging Off the target/participant, and cutting off access to Central Frame.**

Shortly after, the carbot hit the northern tip of the Purement commune, and buildings on their side of the Tollway disappeared as dense forest, enclosed with a tall electrified fence, sprung up. The twelve to twenty story skyscrapers of Springfield-Decatur continued on the other side of the highway.

"Whoa!" exclaimed Kaminer, pointing to the woods. "I've never seen anything like that."

"There are small houses in there. You just can't see them. Completely off the grid. It's not just the houses that are unconnected but the community is too. Streaming blockers as soon as you enter their gates. Which we're not going to do."

"Streaming blockers, as in no access to Central Frame?"

"Yep, even the connected are unconnected at Purement," Ambrose said. "Although you'd have a hard time finding anyone with an Interface there."

"So he's what, sixteen, seventeen-years-old?"

"Don't let that fool you. Don't think of him as a teenager, as one of your old students from Burke. Tim is way ahead of the game."

"What's he do at Purement?"

"Farmer. Learning to grow food at the moment. Which he already has a jump start on since my ma likes to garden," Ambrose said. "He can be a bit-, uh, self-centered. Don't take it personally."

"Suggestion taken. So the commune, it's kind of like this blob of land that Springfield-Decatur has morphed around?"

"Good one. The urban density of Springfield-Decatur bumps right up against Charter Pass to its north and Purement to its west. It kind of oozes between them, where there's a gap. Spills around Purement to the south too. Right up to the Illinois River," Ambrose said, nodding his head. "Did you bring something to eat?"

Kaminer patted a wide pocket on the side of his casual pants. "Told you I needed a pocket."

Ambrose laughed. "I know you didn't want to overdress but I had a hard time picturing the cargo pants."

"Very handy. I might go back to that very clothing commissary and have some other items custom printed."

"Are you on a salary?" Ambrose asked, narrowing his eyes. "I mean, how does that work? If Dr. Burke is enforcing your contract, as a-, well as a, you know."

"As a bot?" Kaminer said, sounding short.

"Yeah, that. I don't get it. How can he enforce a perpetual contract? You aren't *that* much of a bot anymore."

"Well, you see it that way. But Burke, apparently, does not."

"Why not?"

"I can't answer that question. Why you perceive me as more human and Dr. Burke perceives me as more bot, well, I just can't say," Kaminer lamented, falling silent. Neither of them spoke for the next twenty minutes until the self-drive slowed and bore a right onto Route 104.

"Just like you said," Kaminer pointed out.

"Yeah, Tim should be waiting for us up ahead. We're doing a right-left, right-left, right-left kind of thing to get over the river."

"I read about that. It came up in the research I did, preparing to meet your brother," Kaminer said, looking straight ahead.

"Research?"

"I don't want to say anything that might embarrass you, or your brother. Or me, for that matter," Kaminer declared, looking over to Ambrose. "So I know all about Purement, how it began as a National Wildlife Refuge, became a kind of tent community in the '80's."

"After the 2086 Human Protection Act, the tents became shacks and then cabins."

"And I'm well aware of the commune's takeover of the surrounding land and the 104 bridge over the Illinois River," Kaminer said in a hushed voice, as the car slowed almost to stopping and took another right, finally pulling off to the side of the road.

"There's Tim." Ambrose pointed through the wind-shield to a man in rugged jeans and a tan chamois shirt with the sleeves ripped off.

"He looks like the wilderness version of you," Kaminer observed, letting out a breath.

Ambrose got out of the car and trotted up to Tim, giving him a half-hug. "Hey. How ya doing?"

"Amby. Been a long time. Good to see ya. How's things?" Tim replied, pounding Ambrose on the back.

"Wow, you've, like, gained weight," Ambrose noted, feeling scrawny. "You look good."

"Nothing like real beef," Tim said. "None of that factory shit. How are ya?"

"Great. Consulting in education, actually."

"Nice. That's what you always wanted, wasn't it?"

"Well, close enough. So, um, I brought my roommate today. To meet Ma and Pop," Ambrose said, pointing back to the car.

Tim took a long look at the passenger in the back seat. "You have got to be kidding me, Amby. I'm not getting in a car with a robot!" Tim spit out, shaking his head.

"He's not really a bot. Not truly."

"Why is a bot your roommate? When did they start housing bots with humans? Has it gotten that bad?"

"What are you talking about? For cray's sake, you don't have to be rude about it."

"What the hell is a cray?"

"What?"

"Don't you understand, about my lifestyle? Are you trying to ridicule me?"

"Wha's the matter with you?" Ambrose asked, panicking. *Why didn't I give Tim more details about Kaminer? Because we don't talk about anything anymore. We haven't in a long, long while.*

Just then, Tim threw the small backpack he was carrying on the ground. Ambrose, seeing his chance, grabbed the pack, smacked Tim's arm, and turned on his heels to walk back to the car.

"Don't be a baby, and don't be rude to my friend," Ambrose said, turning back so his words might sound more intense.

"Your friend, my ass," Tim called out, and being taller than Ambrose, quickly caught up to him. He yanked his pack out of Ambrose's clutches. "Don't call me a baby."

Ambrose quickened his pace to get back to the car first. "Hey, Kaminer, this is my little brother, Tim. Do you mind sitting in the front?"

"Oh, sure," Kaminer responded. "Pleasure to meet you, Tim," he said, getting out of the car and extending a hand.

"Timothy," Tim said without taking the hand, and got into the back passenger seat of the self-drive, while Kaminer deposited himself in the sole seat in the front. "Where's the steering wheel, Ambrose?"

"Nope. Self-drive."

"I told you to get a driver car. Jesus! I don't want to be driving in a carbot!"

"Don't worry about it," Kaminer messaged. *"I'm more like him than he thinks. I don't take his recalcitrance, or whatever is going on, personally."*

"You're a good friend, Kam."

"Friends are where you find them, and I'm grateful you found me."

"Are we going? Anytime soon?" Tim questioned. "Where's the start button?"

"Well, driver or no driver, the engine is a bot, calculating how much energy it needs from the Mid-Hem Ring. So why don't I interface it to go?" Ambrose said, his voice taking on a guttural quality. *Kaminer must be destiny's way of substituting the wrong outcome with the correct one. Kaminer treats me the way Tim should.*

Kaminer turned back to look at the pair of brothers in the back seat. "I can't wait to meet your parents," he issued, directing the comment at Tim, who shifted towards the car door, staring out its window. Ambrose interfaced the car to proceed south along Breck Road and make its way to the New Bridge off Naples Lane.

No one spoke for the remainder of the trip.

Ma and Pop's

Married *n*. **Legal partner of another. Formerly known as husband or wife.** *Ex.:* **"My married always knows the right thing to say." Compare to remarried, not the original married:** *Ex.*: **"My remarried's family includes children from his first and third marrieds."**

As the car crossed over the Illinois River, Springfield-Decatur gave way to Modesto, tall buildings grew shorter, and the scenery was punctuated with clusters of houses.

The car slowed, turning off the turnpike-like road, and onto another main street. Houses, needing a bit of tending, dotted either side. The car made a few more turns as the streets narrowed, finally arriving at Church Street. It rolled to a stop, its occupants emerging just as the Belles opened their front door and stepped out of the compact house.

Ambrose stood for a moment with his arms crossed, leaning against the car, when he realized that the small house, with its two doghouse dormers, was similar to the ones Kaminer used to draw earlier in the year, when he was re-building. *Even the walkway, lined with flowers and tufts of grass.*

"Boys!" exclaimed Mrs. Belle, bustling her thick but fit physique towards the sidewalk. "Welcome home!"

Ambrose clasped his arms around his mother. "Ma, I missed you."

His mother landed a large kiss on the side of his cheek, and held Ambrose tight. He began to squirm, trying to extricate himself from the uncomfortable over-display of affection.

"Oh honey, it's been too long!" Mrs. Belle voiced.

"My roommate, Kaminer," Ambrose announced as Jethro Belle moved on from Tim and gave Ambrose a bear hug. Jethro was quite tall and clearly didn't believe in hair Enhancement of any kind as the few strands that remained were combed from one side, near an ear, over the top of his head.

Mrs. Belle fussed over Kaminer while Jethro clasped Ambrose about the shoulders, leaving Tim to stare at the tight group. As they proceeded indoors, Ambrose took it upon himself to explain some basics. "Now, I think I told you, this is an unconnected house, Kam" Ambrose explained. "You can't message it or even talk to it. You can't expect it to know what you want. You have to do it for yourself."

"Right. I can't interface a door to open," Kaminer said, and Tim snorted and peeled off, taking a sharp left into the kitchen.

"Do you want to try and open that door?" Ambrose asked, as they walked into a combined living and dining room. He pointed to a glass door that looked like it led outside.

Kaminer walked to the door, took the knob in his hand and turned it. The door didn't budge. "What am I missing?"

"You've got to turn it and pull at the same time," Ambrose added in a gleeful tone. Kaminer turned the knob and pulled the door towards him. Nothing happened.

"Try the knob the other way," Mrs. Belle advised and Kaminer reversed the turn of the knob and, with both hands, pulled hard on the door. It swept open towards him, knocking him off his feet. Tim, standing alone in the kitchen, issued a hard laugh.

Ambrose, who didn't think it was that funny, swooped in and helped up Kaminer. "You okay?"

"Yeah, no blood, no worries," Kaminer responded, moving back into the comfortable room.

They gathered around a long, heavy table made of well-worn wood. The padded feet of the metal chairs swept noiselessly across the scrubbed floor as each person pulled out their chair. The table fronted a semi-open room, and Ambrose noticed Kaminer looking curiously at the cabinets. He got up, motioning Kaminer to follow him. As they entered the kitchen, Tim exited, and took a seat at the table.

Kaminer carefully inspected a few cabinets, a sink, and the very large furnace that sat in the middle of a long run of countertop. "That's the stove," Ambrose pointed out. "For cooking."

"*Mrs. Belle, would you please inform me where the glasses are kept. I'll put out water, unless another beverage is indicated*," Kaminer messaged, copying Ambrose.

"*No Interface, remember?*" Ambrose sent back. Kaminer slapped a hand to his forehead. "Ma, want us to put anything out?" he called over to the table.

Mrs. Belle launched out of her seat, and moved into the kitchen. "Glasses and dishes are here, dear, water out of the sink, and I have a snack platter in the fridge," Mrs. Belle said. She had been prepped by Ambrose through their many Reader chats to understand just how large the gap between her house and connected living quarters might be. "But we can put it all out if you boys are hungry." She turned back to pull down some plates.

"*Why are they drinking water out of the sink?*" Kaminer messaged Ambrose.

"Thanks, Ma. We'll set up. You go sit," Ambrose assured his mother, moving her back to the dining area. Kaminer stood in the kitchen, a frosty half-smile stuck on his lips.

"So the glasses are made of ceramic and so are these plates. We don't recycle out here, we just reuse. Get it?" Ambrose whispered, as Kaminer turned a plate over in his hands, rapping his knuckles against its hardness.

"Got it. I think."

"These are permanent. We wash them in the sink with soap, one squirt, out of this container. Then rinse," Ambrose whispered, moving over to the sink to show Kaminer the running water. "It's clean," he said, "for drinking."

"I'm sorry, but the only water that's clean is what comes out of a FoodServe when you set it for two parts hydrogen to one part oxygen and hit the green button," Kaminer hissed.

"Then go sit. I'll take care of this."

"Sorry. No, that's okay. I want to learn," Kaminer said, as the men walked back to the table to deposit the dishware, and doubled back to the kitchen. Mrs. Belle, smiling, immediately began to set the table.

"All righty then. So fridge is short for refrigerator. For the food that has already been made, so it keeps," Ambrose continued, taking out a platter of stuffed eggs. "These probably came from real chickens."

Kaminer winced. "Real chickens are disgusting," he said. "*They should be grown in stem cell factories or printed off a FoodServe.*"

"Well, you're not eating it," Ambrose clarified, laughing, and then pulled out a cold, roasted chicken, in the shape-, of-, a-, chicken.

"*That lump of meat had feathers and a head not too long ago,*" Kaminer pointed out. "*It was alive.*"

Ambrose could tell that Kaminer was starting to feel woozy, and the two of them leaned against the sink counter, trying to stay out of view of the others. After a moment, Kaminer grabbed the eggs, and some green, unidentified stalks. Ambrose manned the chicken, as the two returned to the group.

"*What is that? The green stuff?*" Kaminer messaged.

"*Asparagus. Ma has a garden out back.*"

"*So that's what asparagus is supposed to look like,*" Kaminer continued, setting his platters on the table. He picked up a green twig and carefully appraised it. "*Not entirely dissimilar to a spinal cord with an attached brain stem.*"

"Careful with that. You don't want asparaghee," Mrs. Belle said loudly, and guffawed. Kaminer looked to Ambrose, who shook his head.

"Ma, you don't understand, he can't ea-," Ambrose started but Kaminer messaged him a stabbing "*chh*" sound.

"*There's no need to say anything,*" Kaminer continued in-mind, opening his eyes wide.

"*Mmm, sorry.*"

"So, what's this asparaghee? Is that plural for asparagus?"

"No, it's when your pee smells like asparagus," Ambrose chimed in, dissolving into snorting laughter which made Kaminer laugh.

Tim rolled his eyes. "That's real grown up, Ambrose," he issued, as Kaminer set the stalk back on its platter and helped Mrs. Belle finish the table.

Ambrose noticed that Tim hadn't budged from his seat. As Kaminer set the last cup in place, following Mrs. Belle's lead, Ambrose also realized that his parents only had four of everything. He rounded back to the kitchen, motioning Kaminer to sit by his mother's side, while his stepfather took his usual place at the head of the table. He fetched a plastic plate, cup and cutlery from the top of the fridge.

"*These will get washed too, okay?*" Ambrose messaged Kaminer as he returned to sit next to his brother. He held up the dishware before tossing them in front of Tim.

"*Of course.*"

"Water, anyone?" Ambrose asked. "I'll get it."

Jethro began to carve the chicken, and Kaminer rocketed back out of his chair. "I'll help!" "*There's no way I'm going to be anywhere near a dead chicken being carved into pieces. It makes my bio bits hurt just thinking about it.*"

The men returned to the kitchen, filled a pitcher and then headed back to the table. Ambrose noticed that Tim had gone ahead and served himself. Kaminer sat back down and removed his biscuit from the wide side pocket of his pants.

"Thanks for waiting, bro," Ambrose said in a sarcastic voice.

"Oh, chicken, yum," Tim said gruffly, taking an enormous bite out of a chicken leg, sending some juice squirting.

"Timothy, mind your manners," Mrs. Belle issued firmly.

"I think, uh, if no one minds, perhaps I could go outside?" Kaminer asked. Before anyone could respond, he swiftly stood up and backed away from the table, towards the glass door that only moments before had caused Timothy to laugh at him. The biobiscuit sat abandoned on its plate.

Kaminer paused to look at Ambrose before gracefully turning the knob in the correct direction. He tugged on the door ever so lightly and leaned back, stepping around the arc of the door as it swung open.

"*You okay?*" Ambrose messaged from the dining area. "*Want me to join you?*"

"*Would it be okay if I was alone?   It's not your brother. I mean they're eating a dead, decapitated, deplumed, cooked and cooled chicken.*"

Ambrose heard the weak, squeaking quality of the message, and growing concerned, watched Kaminer closely through the glass door. Kaminer found a lawn chair leaning up against the back of the house, and struggled to open it, making Ambrose wonder if he was weak from hunger.

Kaminer turned, trying to snap the chair open, and stumbled backward, twisting his ankle on a rock. It caused him to tumble forward, where he collided with the cement clothes pole. Kaminer ricocheted toward a pair of pants strung across a line. Spinning around, he took the pants with him as he collapsed in a heap.

Ambrose ran outside. "Kam, are you okay?" he cried, taking a tissue out of his pocket.

Kaminer stuffed it up a bloody nostril, and touched his forehead gingerly. "Geez!" he exclaimed. "And I've haven't even been here an hour."

"Do you need to eat that biscuit? Or drink some water? Are you that upset by the chicken?"

"No, I'm fine, I just, ah, well I guess I, um, lost my balance."

Ambrose wrestled the lawn chair open and shoved Kaminer down onto it. "Just sit here and rest. I'll bring your biscuit out. You need to eat it," he said sternly. "Don't come back in until I've dispatched the chicken."

"Yeah," Kaminer said, folding his arms in front of him. "But I've lost my appetite."

"*What does that mean?*"

"I don't know. Let me rest for a bit, and I'll come back inside when the table is cleared, okay?"

Ambrose nodded and returned to his family gathering, watching Kaminer relax into the lawn chair, still nursing his head, and soaking up some summer sun. Ambrose quietly returned to his brother's side and tried to rejoin the discussion.

"I think an irrigation project could work," Jethro said, clearing his throat. "But pay attention to the water levels. That river is drying out."

Tim snorted. "You know, people don't understand that water goes where you tell it too."

"Sorry, are you saying the topography works in your favor there?" Ambrose asked, not sure what they were talking about.

"There's a series of ponds near our lake. If they were reconnected, as our sediment studies show they were in antiquity, it's another path for the Illinois to take. Besides Meredosia Lake hasn't dried up yet."

"Did you get some bread, honey?" Mrs. Belle asked, passing Ambrose a cloth-covered basket. "It's getting harder to find flour and yeast," she said, pushing some gray hair from her round, sun-worn face. "But we've managed."

"What do you mean?" Ambrose asked.

"Well, several of our grocery stores have been replaced with that FoodServe business. But we refuse to get a printer, or buy the inputs," Mrs. Belle said.

"Like Kaminer's biobiscuit there. It works for him, I'm sure, but why would I ever want to give up your mother's real cooking?" Jethro added, finishing the asparagus on his plate. "Even fresh vegetables are harder to find."

"It's what I've been warning you about for years," Tim said in a harsh voice.

"Oh, please. Let's not start with all that conspiracy theory crap," Ambrose spewed.

"Oh no, there's no conspiracy. This isn't some underground uprising. This is the very careful, and systematic takeover of technology. It's already taken out the schools, and this is the next step."

"Now, what? Are you saying it's technology's fault that it's seeping into grocery stores?"

"More like morphing the way we live," Mrs. Belle corrected.

"Well, it's probably more efficient," Ambrose added.

"More efficient to whom?" Tim interjected.

"Not to anyone in particular. But as a business model."

"But what about Ma? And her choices? Why shouldn't she be able to go to a grocery store?" Tim said, raising his voice.

"Whoa, settle down there, young man," Jethro cut in.

"You make it sound like it's my fault," Ambrose complained.

"You're the one working at Burke Industries. You and your in – den –turrrrrre."

"I told you, they've put me in the educational end of things."

"We'd like to hear more about that, dear. Wouldn't we, Tim?" Mrs. Belle chimed in, pushing her plate away.

"Sure, let's hear all about it," Tim said, in a sarcastic tone. Ambrose got up, maneuvering the chicken platter back into the kitchen.

"Save the bones, I'll make soup," Mrs. Belle called after him. Ambrose rewrapped the chicken in the plastic wrap he'd taken off the bird when it had come out of the refrigerator. It had clearly been used many times before.

"*I've taken care of the bones,*" Ambrose messaged Kaminer, as he walked back into the combined living and dining room. Ambrose could tell that Kaminer must have been dozing, as he suddenly startled in his lawn chair. "*Sorry, didn't know you were napping.*"

"The bones!" Kaminer exclaimed out loud, clamping a hand to his mouth. After a moment, he came back inside and Ambrose was relieved to see that Kaminer had kept anything from escaping.

"*How ya doing*?" Ambrose messaged.

"*Managing*," Kaminer sent back. "May I clear the table?" he asked out loud.

"Oh, no dear, you're company. Do you want to join us for dessert?" Mrs. Belle said, getting up.

Kaminer walked over to her and laid a hand on her shoulder. "But I may never get another chance. To wash dishes. All of Ambrose's serveware is recyclable, and many of our friends have never even seen a metal fork. May I? Please?" Kaminer begged.

Mrs. Belle looked over to Ambrose, who nodded. "Why not?" Ambrose posited.

"Okay, then. If you're sure," Mrs. Belle acquiesced.

"Say, Ambrose, why don't you bring that lemon cake in from the counter. Your ma might be a good cook, but she's an even better baker," Jethro added, reaching out to take Mrs. Belle's hand in his.

"You got it, Pop," Ambrose voiced, getting up from the table, and helping Kaminer to collect dishes. He walked into the kitchen with Kaminer, realizing that Timothy had stopped talking the moment Kaminer had stepped a foot back through the door.

Ambrose set the stack of plates next to the sink. "Just like I said, right?"

"Yep, I remember your directions."

Just as Ambrose spied the cake, his mother cornered him in the kitchen. "Now, are you boys together?" she asked in an earnest, open way.

Kaminer and Ambrose exchanged looks and started to chuckle. Ambrose's chuckles turned to guffaws and then got the better of him. He started to laugh heartily, loosely covering his face with a hand. "Uh, no, Ma. We aren't a couple. Just roommates."

"So you're not dating? I was kind of hoping you were. Kaminer seems like such a nice boy."

"That's very kind of you, Mrs. Belle, but Ambrose is just a friend. A very good friend."

Mrs. Belle sighed., "You're sure now?"

"Yes, Ma. That's a fact," Ambrose said, trying to catch his breath.

"Okay, then. Get that cake to Pop before he blows a fuse," Mrs. Belle said, pointing to the lemon cake. Ambrose quickly scurried out of the kitchen with the cake in hand, leaving Kaminer to turn back to the business of the dishes. But before he could, Mrs. Belle interrupted his concentration.

"He's had a hard time of it." She leaned her ample behind against the counter, facing Kaminer.

"So he says. But to me, he's the can-do kid."

"You know he admires you a great deal. From what he's told Jethro, you seem to remind him of, well, him."

"Really? How do I seem like Ambrose?" Kaminer issued, pressing his chin into his neck in disbelief.

"I think you've both been through some heartache. Has he shared his terrible story with you?"

Kaminer put down the soapy rag he had mindlessly been playing with. "Does it have something to do with Tim?"

"I'll say it quickly," Mrs. Belle said, pausing to make sure the others were engaged in conversation at the table. "It was three years after Mr. Belle died. Not Jethro, obviously, but the boys' father. Ambrose got held after school. I'll never forgive myself for that." Mrs. Belle sucked in a few short breaths. "Tim was waiting for him on the rooftop where the kids played. Some Mods were there, real bullies. They started to push little Timmy around and by the time Ambrose made his way there, they'd worked themselves into a frenzy. Ambrose, always a scrawny little thing, tackled them. And they threw him right off the side of the building." Mrs. Belle heaved, and clasped both hands to her bosom.

"Holy crap," Kaminer whispered.

"It changed everything. Get him to tell you the story," she whispered, clasping Kaminer's shoulder, looking intently from one brown eye to the other, then quickly left the kitchen.

Kaminer stood with a plate in his hand, and in a wave of agitation, suddenly threw the rag down, rinsed his hands and began to put away the leftover food. A moment later, Ambrose walked back in to fetch some small plates for the dessert. As he re-entered the room, he caught Kaminer eating a piece of a green stalk. The asparagus!

"What are you doing? It'll make you sick! Geez-iss!"

"Just one bite. I want to check out your mother's asparaghee theory. And see if it crunches like the cafeteria's asparagus. It sounds like a biscuit when you eat it." He took another bite.

"But you've already tried applesauce this week!"

Kaminer stared at Ambrose. "No. Not the same crunch," he said with a sour look on his face. He threw the stalk back on the plate and returned it to the refrigerator. Ambrose, shaking his head, left with the dessert plates.

Kaminer, still trying to shake off the weighty bar-rage from Mrs. Belle, positioned himself by the sink, and ran a soapy sponge over each item. He carefully stacked the plates upside down on a towel to dry, and repeated the process for the glasses and utensils. When the kitchen appeared to be in order, Kaminer returned to the dining area, where the Belles were finishing their dessert.

"So, you have to store all your food? I see no way to return it to original organic compounds," Kaminer asked Mrs. Belle.

"It's called composting, dear," Mrs. Belle replied.

"Then you do recycle the leftover food? You have a FoodServe to return it to its original inputs?"

"No, composting is when food is left to decompose," Ambrose clarified.

"Rotting?" Kaminer asked with a puzzled look.

"Not just rotting, but a managed rot cycle, meant to enrich the soil," Ambrose continued.

"Oh. It's kind of like nature's version of a Standard Enhancement," Kaminer added.

Timothy let out a heavy snort and left the room, clumping heavily up the narrow staircase at the front of the house. After his noisy exit, the Belles turned to stare at Kaminer.

"Yes, he did just make a joke. He does that from time to time," Ambrose confirmed.

***

Ambrose, his parents, and Kaminer spent the rest of the afternoon sitting on slipcovered sofas set on opposite sides of a sturdy pine coffee table. Ambrose eagerly updated his folks on his adventures and misadventures at Burke Industries.

"It was like being stretched out on the event horizon of a black hole," Ambrose voiced, finally honing in on what his parents really wanted to talk about.

"It felt like a medieval torture rack," Jethro added.

"And it happened to Dr. Kate, commander-in-chief of Burke Industries. We were working together on Kaminer," Ambrose added.

Kaminer slowly raised his hand in the air. "I also experienced a moment of paradigm change."

"What do you mean?" Ambrose queried.

"Did it feel like your streaming was more efficient, after?" Jethro added. Ambrose and Kaminer both nodded and then Kaminer shook his head.

"It was as if everything was brightly illuminated for a brief second, but then the number line, everything before zero, went dark. I still have trouble sometimes retrieving that information," Kaminer reported with a heavy sigh.

"You know I've never heard you talk about it. About the actual day. When it happened," Ambrose pointed out.

"Yeah, we just kind of kept moving on."

If there hadn't been a balcony a few stories down, I'd be dead. But it was my fault for being late. And we just kept moving on. Ambrose forced himself back to the present conversation.

"At least you went through it together. Poor Jethro was all by himself, with that awful headache," Mrs. Belle added.

"Are they saying anything in Charter Pass, about the die-off?" Jethro asked, straightening a few loose strands over his head.

"Oh, uh, I know it seems like I should know more but it's not like this happened only at Burke Industries, or only in Charter Pass, or only Illinois, or even just the United States. It was everywhere," Ambrose clarified.

"Major casualties," Kaminer pointed out. Ambrose kicked him.

"*They know that!*"

"*Sorry!*" Kaminer messaged back, receding from the conversation to pull out his biscuit, which had been returned to his pocket when the table had been cleared. He began to eat it, taking tiny bites as he moved the biscuit in a circle, chiseling away evenly at the edges.

"But it did allow some upward mobility, so there's that," Ambrose said, throwing a hand into the air. *All that extra work Ma took on to pay for the body work, the surgeries, the cast. What about her upward mobility?*

"We felt awful about your dorm mate," Jethro said.

Mrs. Belle got up and stationed herself at the bottom of the stairs. "Will you be rejoining us today, Tim?" she called out.

"Maybe later," Tim yelled back.

She padded back to the group, leaning onto the arm of Jethro's chair to kiss the top of his badly-covered head. "I don't understand what's gotten into your brother. I'm sorry," she said, looking at Ambrose, and then looking at Kaminer knowingly. She nodded her head vigorously, tilting it in Ambrose's direction.

"You guys used to be so close," Jethro added, sending a short visualcast to Ambrose and Kaminer.

Ambrose immediately remembered the night Jethro had stood over them while he had taken it upon himself, still in full body cast, to explain exactly how the universe worked to his baby brother. His little brother who had since backed away and slowly extricated himself in a thousand different ways.

> **'"There might be more than one Santa. Or maybe he can manulate time and space to get it all done,"** a ten-year-old Ambrose was explaining to Tim, lying next to him in an identical twin bed.
>
> **"You mean manipulate**?" Jethro's chuckling voice asked.

No, Amby. Santa is the Tooth Fairy,"
Timothy cut in.

"**Ya think so?**" Ambrose asked, his eyes
widening. "**I never thought about it. I
guess so,**" Ambrose continued, as Jethro's
chuckles came through the audio input.
"**Is it true, Pop?**"

"**Well, boys, I think Santa and the
Tooth Fairy are separate bits of magic,**"
Jethro's voice said. "**That's what I think.**"

"**Ma says you gotta believe,**" Tim added.

"**I think that's right, Son. Good things
come to those that believe,**" Jethro's voice
reported.

"**Believe in Santa?**" Ambrose asked in a little
voice.

"**Believe in anything. Believe in yourself.
Now to bed. It's late and if you don't go to
sleep, Santa might not come,**" Jethro's voice
admonished. "**Night, boys.**"

"**Night Pop! Night-night Amby,**" came Tim's
voice as the visual panned the outside of
their room.

"**Sleep tight,**" Ambrose's child-sized voice
called back as the visualcast faded out.

Ambrose phased back to his present surroundings,
instantly realizing why his mother didn't want him

messaging through his Interface in her presence. His mother had been talking while he had been watching Jethro's visualcast. *Dang it.*

Mrs. Belle smoothed her palms over the top of her legs. "...mean to change the subject, but now that you're settled, in Charter Pass, maybe we could come visit? I'll bring your Pop, so don't worry!"

Ambrose could tell the visit was wrapping up, even if he had missed the first half of what his mother was saying. "*Saudades*," he messaged Kaminer, with a visual of a man crumbling to his feet, grasping about his heart.

"*?*" Kaminer sent back as a simple visual.

"Sow da gees. It's a Brazilian word. It's kind of like nostalgia but the word captures more than that. It's the idea of a longing you could die from. Whenever I leave here I'm immediately beset by saudades."

Kaminer nodded his head, lightly brushing off invisible crumbs from this hands. "*Beset by saudades*," he echoed in-mind, blinking.

Jethro cleared his throat. "Am, you don't have to wait for an invitation. Just come and see us. This house has always been, and always will be, yours." He clasped a large hand on Ambrose's shoulders.

"Thanks, Pop," Ambrose said, blushing. He got to his feet, trying to think of something to say.

"Really, you can just show up whenever you want. You know that, right?" Jethro, too far gone, pulled him in for a deep hug.

"Promise us you'll be back soon," exhorted Mrs. Belle. "And how about you, Kaminer, would you like to visit again? I know the house wasn't all the exciting but you might like the bowling alley we keep going in town."

"I would like that very much. Thank you for your kind hospitality," Kaminer said. "*Why didn't we bring your ma something? Like chocolate? Or flowers? Next time, I'm arriving with a gift."*

"Ma says the greatest gift is to just bring yourself."

"A-ha. Your mother cares about you in a way no one else can. I think I see what your saudades are."

They walked out without seeing Timothy again.

***

The next day, the Belles woke up, made breakfast, and ate off the dinner plates and utensils from the night before. They drank their coffee syrup from the same glasses, and spent the rest of the day taking turns on the toilet, the film of soap that had been left on the dishes from Kaminer's uneven cleaning causing waves of diarrhea.

Kaminer had trouble waking up, and when he did, he realized he was half slumped on the bed, almost horizontal. He sat up fully, clearly agitated, as Ambrose came back into the room after his morning steam.

"Morning, sunshine. Hydraulics okay?" Ambrose asked. "You were practically laid out flat."

"Uh, yeah, um, actually, I think so," Kaminer stuttered, rubbing his hands down his tee shirt. He reached up to touch the bump on his head, wincing at how tender it was.

"You look fantastic," Ambrose declared, throwing his head back in a hearty laugh.

Kaminer got up and shuffled over to the mirror over his dresser. There was a small ring of blood around the inside of a nostril, the bump on his forehead was even larger and sporting a funny shade of blue, and he had a shadow of a black eye. His entire face and the lower portion of his arms, where he'd pushed his long shirt sleeves up the day before, were a shade of pink.

"Is this from the rest I had outside in your mother's yard?"

"It's called a sunburn, Kam," Ambrose declared, chuckling a little more.

"This isn't a laughing matter," Kaminer protested, and immediately started scratching around his neck. "What is this?" he cried, pulling at the neckline of his shirt.

Ambrose walked over to study the red pimples that lined his roommate's neck. As Kaminer started to reach around to scratch his back, Ambrose gently lifted the shirt for a further inspection, and realized the rash trailed all the way down Kaminer's back.

"Hives, you idiot. Serves you right for eating the asparagus!"

September

<u>Standard Enhancement</u> *n.* Information packet
containing two years of Connected School
curriculum. Organized by Enhancement level,
subject, file, and subfile.
Uploaded to a subject's Neural Interface.

"Today's the big day. Finally. What a detour you took!"
Ambrose exclaimed, as Kaminer slipped on a light-
weight V-neck sweater. *How many times have I said
that before? How many big days to get us to today?* He
thought about Kaminer's restart, his months of schooling, and the medical procedures that had been
wedged in over the course of the summer. *That I've
been pledged to secrecy about.*

Ambrose stuffed his feet into a pair of worn slip-on
sneakers, as Kaminer eased his into leather-soled
lace-ups. Bending over to tie them, he looked up at
Ambrose. "Personal Assistant. I better be ready to
work."

Ambrose snorted. "Don't even try to come home at
midnight. You know you need a full seven and a half
hours of rest, and I won't have you falling behind."

"Said like a true mother hen," Kaminer said, chuckling. "*And that isn't a complaint.*" He got to his feet.
"But I am coming home a bit late tonight. Making a pit
stop."

Ambrose picked up on the hint. "What kind of pit
stop? At homebase?"

"A simple procedure. I'm down to a handful of adjustments, and this one's easy, like having an Interface implant."

"You're not having that done are you?" Ambrose queried, ushering Kaminer out their door.

"Oh no, that's not necessary. But I am having some gene de-splicing done in the early evening, so I'll miss dinner."

"You mean fourth feeding," Ambrose corrected, as they walked down the dormitory hall. "What's the work about?"

"Well, I, uh, have some recombinant, non-human DNA that I'm going to take care of. It's never come into play, although I think it may have been co-opted to um, uh, well," Kaminer stammered.

"What?" Ambrose asked as they reached the lobby. Both men approached the FoodServe printer.

"*Human biscuit, plain. Tea, diluted,*" Ambrose interfaced. He waited a moment to collect it, pointing with his chin to a small grouping of chairs. Shortly, Kaminer joined him with an identical first feeding selection.

"I thought you liked the cheese ones better," Ambrose pointed out.

"When it's a bot biscuit. But I've moved onto human biobiscuits, and the plain ones are adequate. I'll have cheese for second feeding with my protein broth."

"Real veggies for lunch today?" Ambrose asked, sipping his tea.

"Reproduced acorn squash!" Kaminer exclaimed. "It's the highlight of my day. Another month or two until pizza."

"So what's the DNA procedure about?" Ambrose pressed. "What was co-opted?"

Kaminer paused, swallowing a small bite. "Well, it's a type of salamander DNA. I was manufactured with it.

The idea was that if I lost an arm or a leg, Best Industries could simply replace the missing thermoplastic bones, and my body could regrow the missing tissue. Cheaper and quicker than nano-surgery to just be primed and ready to go. Should a catastrophe have befallen me."

Ambrose gulped. "You're kidding."

"No, I wouldn't kid about something like that."

"*Figure of speech!*"

Kaminer sighed, looking up to the ceiling, his lips pressed tight. "*Right.*"

"So what's it really been used for?"

"I think it's been deployed in my rebuilding somehow. That's why I went to Spricatur West Homebase for the first time. There was unexplained, uh, leakage, out the back. And that's when I found out I had a rudimentary urinary system. So they put the tube in, separating it from what became, uh."

"I get it," Ambrose said stiffly. "We've been through all that." He put a hand up and pointed to his biscuit. "*Not during mealtime, okay?*"

"But I wasn't manufactured with any type of kidney structure, no bladder, no renal anything. What Spricatur found grew from scratch," Kaminer added, taking another bite of his biscuit.

"And you think it was the salamander DNA?"

"There might have been some further assistance from, well, other sources."

"What other sources?"

"It doesn't matter. What does matter is I'm ready to part with my Caudata DNA. A significant variation that still separates me from the human world."

Ambrose snorted. "I think you're going to find out this morning just how untrue that is."

"What?" Kaminer asked. "What do you mean?"

"There are a lot of humans with all kinds of non-human in them. At least for a little while longer," Ambrose clarified. "Now finish that biscuit so you can get to Cosmetic Enhancements. I want the full report tonight."

***

After a day's work in Curriculum, Ambrose returned to his dorm room with a printed hamburger, wrapped in recycled paper. He took a large bite, setting it on his desk as he moved a portion of a model sail boat from the bookshelves above his desk. He was assembling the boat piece by painstaking piece, and Ambrose pictured a FoodServe printing the final product.

It seems ridiculous, given that each piece was probably printed separately and put into a kit by a bot. For me, human extraordinaire, to reassemble, he thought, receiving a familiar ping from Kaminer.b.

"*You know your messaging still identifies you as bot,*" Ambrose messaged, sounding cross.

"*Say what?*"

"*It still comes across with a .b, you know. Gotta do something about that,*" Ambrose sent, moving long lengths of various colored pith from a shelf to his desk.

"*It must be a leftover. Some kind of holdover. From the good old days. I'll look into it. I just wanted to let you know that I'm heading to Biological Enhancement now.*"

"*You said this morning that getting de-spliced was easier than an Interface. What did that mean?*"

"*Almost the same thing. Snuff up a vial of nanos, they do the work, snipping the Caudata addition out.*"

Ambrose huffed as he organized several different types of glues and clamps in front of him. "*And where does it go? Your no-longer-used DNA?*"

"*Here, now. Talk later.*"

"If he wakes up tomorrow and has lizard eyes, I'm asking for a new roommate," Ambrose joked out loud, and began to assemble the starboard side of his boat.

***

Kaminer came through the door later that evening to find Ambrose's old roommates scattered on his bed and chair, occupying both desk chairs, and spilling over onto Ambrose's bed.

"Hey, Dave, Mattie," he said, fist bumping the men. "Stu, Phil, how ya doing?" he voiced, slapping a low five against Phil's open hand. "Bryan, wha's up man?" Kaminer moved into the room. "Felipe, how the heck are ya?"

Ambrose laughed, shaking his head. "Have we been *all* together? In one place since the lobby fest in June? I'm trying to remember."

"I don't think so. Hail, hail, what're we all doing here?" Kaminer queried.

"Just visiting, and watching Bot League together. By the way, we think you should build a sitting room extension right out those windows there," Felipe issued, motioning to the windows at the back of the room. Ambrose got up from his desk chair to walk towards his closet, stationing himself briefly in front of Felipe.

"*Stop talking, and wipe that sly look off your face,*" Ambrose ordered, pausing to block Felipe from Kaminer's view. "*Don't say a word. I want it to be a surprise.*"

"*Crap, Am, he's gonna find out. You can't keep something like this a secret for three whole months,*" Felipe messaged back, and Ambrose turned to lean against his dresser, trying to look nonchalant.

"Have a seat, Kam, join us. We're catching up on old times," Mattie intoned, pointing to the desk chair Ambrose had just vacated.

"How're you guys doing? What's new in D Block?" Kaminer asked, squinting his eyes in suspicion. He moved over and sat in the chair.

"Felipe got moved off the stitch line. No more synthetic skin suit tailoring. I'm still doin' foot assembly, although we've broken into smaller teams," Phil reported.

"For what?"

"Re-examining the bot foot assembly for maximum thrust and balance. We've already reworked the cuneiform bones with a spring mechanism."

"I might be just a bit jealous of that," Kaminer opined, opening his eyes wider.

"How 'bout you, Kam? What's new?" Mattie asked, shifting. "*Do you think he suspects anything*?" Mattie messaged Ambrose, who tried not to shake his head.

"Well, today was my first day working on my own. In Cosmetic Enhancement. Dr. Burke has assembled a team dedicated to what they're calling 'redaction'."

"Redaction?" Mattie asked. "Wha's that?"

"It's about taking stuff out, rather than putting it in. There are a few doctors, it's mostly technicians, a couple of attendants, and me. I'm sort of the glue, I guess."

"What do you mean glue? Like you're holding the team together?" Dave asked. "*We should invite everyone from his new work,*" he simultaneously messaged Ambrose, who started to fidget with his comb.

"Yeah, like that. I'm the go-to when Dr. Burke is too busy," Kaminer said. "*For good measure, I had the Top-off loaded up today*," he reported to Ambrose in-mind, who turned to look at him, casually propping an elbow against the dresser.

"Felipe's in my group now, in Mindset. You should come visit us sometime," Stu offered. "We take up most of A Block, but our building is just outside the inner core. Wanna come by?"

"Yeah, I'd like that," Kaminer said.

"Can I come too? I've never seen that part of Burke. I donated my mindset to Central Frame when I got here in March. I'd kind of like to see where it went," Ambrose said. "*So you're officially a know-it-all.*"

"Yeah, I'll set something up. Now let's talk about something urgently important," Stu said.

"What's that?" Ambrose asked.

"Where are we going to get our beer from now that our guy in D Block can't get yeast or hops?"

***

That night, as Ambrose and Kaminer settled into their bedtime routine, Kaminer pinged Ambrose in the bathroom. "*There's something I need to tell you.*"

"*Brushing teeth. Can't hear you*," Ambrose joked, sending a scrubbing sound along with the message. Kaminer patiently waited until Ambrose padded back into the room.

"What is it?" Ambrose asked, kicking his flip-flops into the closet. He hung a thin cotton robe on a hook in the closet, yanking his tank down over faded tartan pajama bottoms.

"Well, two things, really."

"Whenever you're ready," Ambrose mouthed, pulling back the covers on his bed. He looked over to

Kaminer, sitting all the way back on his banquette, with the bed pulled completely out. His legs stuck straight out in front of him. *It was months before I could sit like that. With my lowers at a right angle.* Ambrose shook his head, trying to push the image out of his mind.

"I wanted to tell you that the Caudata redaction was successful."

"Well, I sort of figured, since you made it home, with no tail or lizard skin."

"Very funny. But while I was at Homebase, I scheduled the replacement of my hydraulic and skeletal systems. They ran a few tests."

"And?" Ambrose said, sitting on his bed. He scooted back and sat with his legs out in front of him like Kaminer. "When does it happen?"

"It's not gonna happen."

"*Why not*?" Ambrose threw up his hands.

"They refused the skeletal replacement on the grounds of difficulty."

"Sorry, man."

"And my hydraulic system has already become biological."

"What're you talking about?" Ambrose asked.

"They laughed at me, when I went in. Said I was always keeping them on their toes."

"How's that?"

"It's already been converted," Kaminer hissed.

"Like a continuation of the process you described before? The way you grew a rudimentary renal system?"

"Yeah, except this wasn't rudimentary. My hydraulics are officially and fully converted into a lymph system," Kaminer reported. "And my synthetic circulatory system is now a biological vascular one."

"But your heart. That's a mechanical pump," Ambrose said, expelling a breath.

"Not anymore it isn't," Kaminer corrected. "And there's one more thing."

Ambrose looked at him, shaking his head. He was expelling little pops of air in disbelief. "I, um, sorry," he stuttered. "I'm just a little, uh, astonished is all." He rubbed his eyes, trying to clear his head and wrap his mind around the fact that Kaminer was coming fully online as a human. *Not online. That's not the right word. Evolving is more like it*, he mused, realizing that in his mind he sounded a little like the attendant Ned from Spricatur West. He held a finger up and nodded, motioning Kaminer to proceed.

"Dr. Burke is making good on his housing promise, now that I'm a p4."

Ambrose stared at him. "What are you talking about? You aren't really being relegated to bot housing. Compartments in the basement? How can that be?"

"I know, and I don't want to go, but I can't seem to convince Dr. Burke that my records reflect my actual status. He keeps telling me not to forget I was *manufactured*."

"They're giving you a room in the basement at Cosmetics?" Ambrose checked, starting to feel panicky.

"Yep. Six walls to call my own, which is a status symbol of sorts. For bots."

"Bot, my foot. That's not what your records say. Why don't you fight back? Stay here!"

"I can't. It was part of the deal. But I couldn't have asked for a better roommate. They don't have a compartment yet. Move date's in a couple of months, at the end of the year." Kaminer rubbed a nervous hand over his face.

"I couldn't have asked for a better roommate either," Ambrose said, confused by his roommate's lack of initiative. *Why doesn't Kaminer just give Dr. Burke the what-for?* An uncomfortable surge welled up inside of him. "But didn't we just finish discussing how you're becoming a real human being?"

"Indeed, but facts never get in the way of some people's beliefs."

"No, no, no. This doesn't sound like you. You're letting Burke define you in the most rigid of ways."

Kaminer stared at him. "If there's a solution to this, it's not immediately recognizable. I wasn't really asking for help. I'm just telling you what's happening."

"Listen, I'm too exhausted to argue with you. We'll talk about this in the morning, 'kay?" Ambrose said, laying down and pulling a blanket over him. "But I am bringing this up again."

"Thanks, Ambrose. Night-night," Kaminer replied, laying down with two small pillows on the bed.

"Sleep tight."

***

The next morning, Ambrose stretched awake. "What a rotten night's sleep," he mumbled, sitting up in bed. He had kicked his blankets off, shoving them to the end of the bed where they heaped against the dresser.

Getting to his feet, Ambrose looked over to Kaminer who was lying on his side facing the banquette. Only a few pillows kept him from lying completely flat. *Does it even matter now? Since he's got the goods to move fluid around like a person?*

"Hey, Sleeping Beauty, time to get up," Ambrose called out. When Kaminer didn't stir, he walked over and yanked one of the pillows out from underneath him, forcing Kaminer to roll flat.

"Jees- uh, geez!" Ambrose cried, as Kaminer's face came into view. It was covered in thick waxy patches. Kaminer slowly opened his eyes, looking up to Ambrose standing over him. "I think you've had a complication," Ambrose whispered, peering closely at the areas of plaque.

Kaminer put a hand to his head, feeling the raised areas. "Yeah." He struggled to get out of bed. "Ugh, I don't think I can go into work."

"You need a, like a, rest day? On your second day of work?"

"Oh. Second day of work. I should go in," Kaminer murmured, taking his time to swing his legs around and sit up on the side of his bed. "I have to go in. They gave me some make-up. I just didn't expect to feel so lousy."

"What did they say? Exactly?"

"That I should expect the redaction process to take a few days while my cells re-atomize, while the Bawclaw team housecleans, bringing the extra DNA to the surface," Kaminer reported with a heavy sigh, hanging his head. "This has not been an easy road."

"Did anyone say it was going to be easy?" Ambrose stood over Kaminer with his hands on his hips.

Kaminer looked up and shook his head as a film of skin flaked off of him. "Oh my gah-," he breathed out, picking at another patch on his forehead. A sizable sheet of thick skin peeled off, making a sucking sound. It hung off the tips of Kaminer's fingers, wilting.

"What am I supposed to do with this? They said it would come off in the shower," Kaminer gagged.

"Then, go throw that, uh, extra-Kaminer in the waste bin and take a shower," Ambrose ordered. *I can't even react right now or I'll lose it.*

Kaminer wearily got out of bed and staggered to the door, which Ambrose held open.

"And don't let your weaknesses define you. Don't let them make you 'less'. You have to overcome them, Kam," Ambrose commanded in an authoritative voice. Kaminer stared at him with a look of disgust, walking partway down the hall. "Make your weaknesses work for you. Find the lesson in this where they make you 'more'!" Ambrose shouted as Kaminer disappeared into the bathroom.

Oh man, that was the most disgusting thing ever. Did my bossiness cover the revulsion? Did he know how absolutely gross that was? Dry heaving, Ambrose ran down the hall into the bathroom behind Kaminer. *Now I really feel like a parent. Was it bad like that for Ma?*

December

<u>Neutralizer</u> *n*. An aerosol, liquid or wipe that instantly destroys microorganisms, rendering the area sterilized of all bacteria, virus, mold, etc.

As the year drew to a close, an irate Dr. Burke sat in a surgical chair in a repair room.

"I really don't understand why this is necessary," Rafe barked at the technician hovering over his hand.

"It's the law, sir," the human technician mumbled, swabbing one of doctor's hand with Neutralizer. "Just sit back, and relax. Your palm Reader will be removed before you can blink an eye."

The technician discreetly rolled a finely grooved knob, initiating a sedative drip into a small tube that ran into the top of Rafe's other hand. Rafe clenched his hands, secured to the chair.

"Who's law? Who put-, this, innu-, lau?" Rafe tried to enunciate as the muscles in his jaw went slack. His head bobbed forward and hung there as the technician sighed, and pushed it back.

He further secured Rafe's arm, the one with the Reader integrated into his palm. Lining it up with the arm of the chair, he strapped an additional plastic cuff at his elbow, and tightened the cuff that already tied Rafe's wrist, palm up, to the chair.

The technician crossed the room and pressed down lightly on a panel, causing it to spring straight out from the wall, revealing a series of flat tools hooked to its sides. He selected a hand clamp, tapping on the slim panel again to make it retract back into the wall.

The hand clamp, a small board with finger-sized pockets on top, clicked into the arm of the surgical chair without effort. The technician focused on positioning Dr. Burke's upright hand flat on the clamp, fitting each finger into a sideways holder. He took his time pushing down on the finger holders, locking each finger in place.

When the fingers were secure, the technician attempted to push Dr. Burke's hand around, and satisfied that it didn't budge, got up and walked out of the room. He stationed himself outside the door and initiated the extraction of Dr. Burke's palm Reader.

Several surgibot arms moved purposefully from the wall, and one arm, with short laser strokes, outlined the almost-square edges of the synthetic Reader, as another arm suction-cupped itself to the Reader's top. A third slid underneath with a heated wire, slicing the reader from Dr. Burke's palm. It pulled away instantly, and the surgibot arm deposited the piece, dripping slightly, on a metal side table.

The laser arm reshaped itself in an instant, swapping for a blood stop spray, as the hot wire arm reworked itself into a small pincher and picked up a strip of flesh from the same side table and laid it across the open gash towards Dr. Burke's thumb. The technician put a hand to his head and peeked through the glass window in the door.

"*Copy that. Abductor p. brevis in place. Proceed with the Adductor p.,*" the technician interfaced the surgibot. It moved back over to the metal table and picked up a thinner piece of muscle. "*Good. Tissue regeneration protocol,*" the technician signaled, and the spray arm that had released the blood stop now sprayed a fine opaque mist of tissue-growing nanites onto Dr. Burke's palm.

"Let the Bawclaw nanobots reknit the area, then close with the cloned skin. Nano-abrade to erase any trace of scar," the technician instructed through his Interface as the surgibot stood by.

After a moment, the pincher arm moved with precision to the table and picked up a piece of almost translucent skin, positioned it into place, and used the tip of its two fingers to smooth the skin out.

The nanobots, having finished reconstruction of the muscle connections and enclosing the palm in newly-rebuilt fascia, sucked the skin into place, and moved to the edges to seal it shut. A whitish film boiled up around the new piece of skin as the nanites molecularly integrated it with the surrounding area and then scoured the incision, removing its outline.

"Suction, and nano-safe," the technician counseled, and the suction cup arm, which had been standing by, fashioned itself into a vacuum, and sucked up the white film. *"And decommission,"* the technician added, giving the order to terminate any nanobots that hadn't been contained. *"Retract, and thank you."*

He stepped back into the room as the surgibots withdrew into their cavity in the paneled wall, and walked over to Dr. Burke, examining his perfect, now fully-biological hand. He double-checked the vital signs that he had been monitoring in the background, and turned the chiseled metal knob down. The sedative stopped flowing as the technician released a small piece of tape. He pulled the needle and tube from the top of Dr. Burke's other hand, pressing the tape back down as the doctor opened his eyes.

"Whose law is it anyway?" Dr. Burke continued as if he hadn't lost consciousness. "How does the United States put a law into effect without any case history or any mention of its passage in the legislature? It just shows up, approved, by Congress, by the Senate, by the President? Without discussion or motion?"

The technician busied himself with releasing the finger holders and removing the plastic cuffs, ignoring Dr. Burke's complaints. "Sir, we need to update your Interface, to sever the connection to your now off-mind Reader. Without the update you might sense phantom transmissions."

"I know why it's necessary! You don't need to explain. I don't plan on going crazy trying to find a Reader that doesn't exist anymore. Just give it to me."

The technician handed Dr. Burke a vial. "Standard procedure. Intake by nasal inhalation," he explained, and Dr. Burke pursed his lips, snuffing up the contents of the vial. "Just give it a few minutes for travel and sorting. You'll know it's aligned when you don't see the moving blue dots. I encourage you to remain seated until then."

***

"Where have you been?" Ambrose asked, as Kaminer came through the door that night. "Why didn't you answer my pings?"

"Uhh-, give me a minute," Kaminer responded, setting a satchel onto his bed, half hidden by the banquette it slid under. He delicately seated himself on the edge of the bed, his hands moving in front of him as if sorting bot bits.

Ambrose could tell Kaminer was still working in the background, so he turned back to the model ship that he was assembling, piece by piece, on his small desk by the window. Picking up some rigging with tweezers, he glued it to a post, and then looked over his shoulder at Kaminer, still sitting at the edge of the bed. His roommate's hands now lay loosely on top of woven herringbone slacks.

"Any time! You know it's almost 20:00 hours, don't you? I'm going to bed in an hour," Ambrose called out loudly, as Kaminer swiped something that wasn't there. "Any time now."

Kaminer held both hands in front of him, with his palms out, slowly bringing them together, as if praying. He blinked, and Ambrose could tell he was mentally phasing back to his room.

"Sorry about that. It's been a madhouse in Cosmetics. Everyone coming in for removal of all sorts of synthetic parts."

"I know. You said it's been like that for a while now. Did you have any new cases with recombinant DNA?"

Kaminer frowned. "They just keep coming. The reappraisal period is coming up, and like always, people leave it to the last minute."

"What did you see today?"

"Ugh. I got one with a finely-tuned sheep splice."

"I never knew all of the ways this had gotten out of hand. You really don't know what you don't see. I guess any one person could only see a fraction of it."

"Dr. Burke, Dr. Kate and a raft of others all had their palm Readers extracted today," Kaminer added. "Even the head of Brain Replication came in."

Ambrose lifted his eyebrows in amazement. "Crowley? Man. No stone unturned. What was the deal with sheep DNA?"

"Just on the head and chin. The wooly fuzz of lambskin." Kaminer laughed, and shook his head. "This was his third corrective graft. For some reason the other teams couldn't get the human DNA to reinsert itself."

"Did you succeed?"

"We finally had to use the Hair Today Enhancement, although it still wasn't perfect."

"Why not?"

"He's got a very full head of perfectly translucent hair, that one," Kaminer said, laughing, as Ambrose fiddled with some glue, attaching the main sail on his model. "But at least it's human."

"Mother of cray, it's preposterous," Ambrose grumbled, wiping a smudge of glue with his thumb.

"And I had a virtual conference with Spricatur West today."

Ambrose put down the small tube of glue and turned fully in his seat, hearing the defeated tone of Kaminer's voice. "Not so good?"

Kaminer shook his head, staring down at his hands. "They are refusing to do the skeletal replacement as well."

"Why? It can't be done?" Ambrose asked, getting up to sit next to Kaminer on the edge of the bed.

"They offered me a replacement body," Kaminer reported glumly. "But I don't want a replacement body. I want my body, the way it's evolved, a body that's entirely me."

"But a replacement body would be grown for you, with your exact genomic profile. It would still be you, just a new you," Ambrose corrected.

"No it wouldn't. It couldn't possibly be the same body that started off as mostly-bot and turned into something else. That's the body I want," Kaminer huffed. "I don't know how I'm going to be successfully reappraised. If I could just get Dr. Burke to recognize that I'm human, maybe he would see me differently."

"Maybe."

"Anyway, that's the news on my end. How about you? How was your day?"

"Well, pretty good actually. I've got a date this weekend," Ambrose reported, turning so that his roommate could see his wide smile.

"Tell me more," Kaminer encouraged, leaning back on the vinyl of the banquette.

"Francesca," Ambrose said, laughing.

"You mean Frank?"

"Of course I mean Frank. Going to try that new Japanese restaurant just on the edge of D Block."

"Are you wearing kimonos?"

"I don't have a kimono. But we're planning on renting for the evening. There's a shop just next door."

"For that very reason. Trying to extract a few more credits out of you!"

"I don't mind," Ambrose said, as Kaminer stared at him with disapproval. "I know you keep telling me to save, save, save. But save, spend, save isn't so bad." Ambrose began to feel guilty.

"I suppose not. As long as there are two saves to every spend."

"I've got a long time ahead of me to save up. Over nine years left on my indenture."

"I know that," Kaminer said softly.

A Date?

Microglide *n.* **Hover technology that uses the earth's magnetic field to induce levitation.**

The next day Ambrose met Frank outside the clean façade of Tabemasu, the new Japanese restaurant. Frank had gone ahead and rented matching light green kimonos, and handed the smaller one to Ambrose, helping him slip it on.

"Spiffy!" Frank laughed.

"I thought it would be soft. But it's cottony," Ambrose pointed out, feeling a sleeve.

"It's called a Yukata. Probably printed to feel like the real thing," Frank said, opening the door to the restaurant and motioning Ambrose inside. They both clasped their hands together and bowed to the hostess.

"Irasshaimase," the hostess said, welcoming them with a small bow. "Please, gentlemen, right this way," she said, showing them to an alcove lined with benches. "If you please, shoes off. The socks are sized by baskets, you see, under the benches?"

Ambrose sat on a bench and leaned over to see several woven rattan baskets. He pulled out a two-toed sock, and laughed, showing it to Frank.

"Right, Tabi socks," Frank confirmed.

"Yes, and select a tatami sandal that suits you, and join me in the dining room," she instructed.

Frank, a larger, darker version of Ambrose, moved over to the rows of brown woven sandals by the windows. "Size?" Frank asked Ambrose, who was sorting through the socks.

"Twenty-six centimeters," Ambrose responded, pulling out two pairs of socks. Frank walked over and handed him a pair of sandals, which Ambrose exchanged for socks.

"Traditionally, we would be using a wooden geta sandal, kind of like a platform sandal elevated on blocks, not a tatami," Frank said, slipping off his loafers.

"I read about those. But the hard wood structure is tough to replicate. I guess any cellulose input can print a tatami sandal," Ambrose added, removing his sneakers to put on the Japanese footwear.

"I thought you said you'd been at Burke Industries for almost a year?" Frank inquired, spying Ambrose's worn shoes.

Ambrose caught the look. "Well, it's an assignment at Magnate Mindware, and closer to nine months. But I'd rather spend my credits on something memorable. Like tonight. Plus I send a little money home to my parents, to help them maintain the house now that my pop is retired."

"Very generous," Frank opined. The pair got up and left the alcove for the larger dining room. Ambrose proceeded down a few steps into the dining room, and immediately spied his brother, Timothy, sitting on his haunches at one of the first tables.

"Tim!" Ambrose cried, as his brother looked up, and raised a hand.

"Hey, Amby, Kaminer said you'd be here," Tim called out. As he rose from the floor, Ambrose could see he had neglected to wear a kimono, but at least was wearing a new, clean pair of overalls.

"What? You're talking to Kaminer, now? How'd ya get in touch with him?"

"Through a colleague who came into Charter Pass on a supply run. He actually went looking for you, but got a little, uh, intimidated about going out to an outer block on a train."

"So he went to the inner core? To Homebase?" Ambrose asked, trying not to sound as flabbergasted as he felt.

Tim nodded, biting his lower lip. "We're stocking up on the basics. Before they run out."

"Yeah. Sure. So how ya been? I haven't seen you since Ma's," Ambrose cut in quickly.

"Uh, good. Well, worried, and when my friend couldn't find you, he walked to the inner core, to the Homebase and flagged Kaminer," Tim explained. "We don't know anyone else here."

"I don't get it, but yeah, it's great to see you, man," Ambrose mouthed, trying not to sound suspicious. *Not once has Tim made any kind of overture about visiting me in Charter Pass.* He shook Tim's hand, half hugging him with his left hand. Tim thumped Ambrose on his back as Frank shifted on his feet. "Oh, this is my friend, Frank. Frank, my brother, Timothy," Ambrose said, picking up the cue.

"Pleasure," Tim offered.

"Likewise," Frank said, eyeing Tim's denim clothing.

"Join me?" Tim asked.

Ambrose and Frank exchanged looks and Frank nodded in a discreet way, covering his consent by scratching the side of his head.

"Yeah, we'd like that. Sure," Ambrose responded and the pair joined Tim, sitting back down on folded legs on the floor.

"So why did anyone come looking for me?" Ambrose asked, settling up to the table. A waitress, outfitted in a full double layer kimono, with an ornate obi pulled into a stiff bow in the back, sidled up to them, laying a small tray on the corner of the table.

"Gentlemen, some tea?" she inquired in a meek voice.

"Sure," Frank said, pulling a small handle-less cup from a short stack. He offered it to the server, who poured a thick black tea into the cup.

"What's that?" Ambrose inquired, expecting the green matcha tea he'd read about on his Interface.

"Oh, we have replaced our tea. Well, the green tea is no longer offered," the waitress lamented.

"Offered by who?" Tim hissed, and Ambrose shot him a look.

"By FoodServe of course," the waitress continued, pouring two more servings of black tea. "I will be back shortly with menus."

"This is why I came to see you, Ambrose. Something isn't right," Tim said as soon as the waitress left the side of the table.

"Not right, how?" Ambrose inquired, looking at Frank.

"I can't really explain it. And you might not see it. But when we leave Purement, we see it."

"You live on the commune?" Frank asked.

"Yes, for over a year now. But ever since the spring, the early spring, things have been changing."

"How's it different?" Ambrose pressed.

"Not Purement. Out *here*!" Tim clarified. "Your tea? All the FoodServe stuff comes from Global Stock. But there's so little fresh food. It's like Ma had started to notice over the summer. Look, even here, no more green tea."

Ambrose let out a long exhale. "Well, Burke Industries has scheduled an additional meal time. What's wrong with that?"

"Who at Burke Industries? Why are you getting an extra meal? Is it edible?"

Frank laughed. "Ugh. The biscuits are disgusting. I just want my bagel."

"Who's redefining what people eat, when they eat?" Tim hollered in a tight, controlled way. "Every time someone has left the commune since March, it's become more and more evident that something's going on."

"Going on how?" Ambrose asked, regretting the fact that he was sitting with his conspiracy theory brother when he should be out on a date.

"Chicago. It's being reorganized. Cleaned up. Whole neighborhoods, like Washington Park, are being rebuilt," Tim exclaimed. "Same thing's happening in Springfield-Decatur."

"So?" Frank asked.

"Yeah, isn't it about time Chicago took a page out of Charter Pass's playbook? Got their act together?"

"Not like this," Tim started, but the waitress returned and passed thin acrylic glass menus to the men, forcing Tim to stop short. Ambrose could sense a tirade was about to erupt out of his brother.

"Tonight's special is the fish, sashimi grade," the waitress said. "A new formula ensures a premium quality taste, and yellowfin tuna texture."

Ambrose and Frank nodded, looking up from their menus, and Ambrose could see Tim was looking away.

"That sounds great," Ambrose said, intent on keeping his evening as close to planned as possible. "Do you have any suggestions for side dishes?"

"Or something cooked?" Frank added.

"The yakitori is very good tonight," the waitress stated.

"Is it from a chicken? Is it real meat?" Tim asked in a forceful manner.

"*You're being rude,*" Ambrose messaged his brother, and then shifted on the floor, wondering if there was a dead letter box for messages from idiots that interfaced people without devices.

"Ah, no, Sir, but our FoodServe printer is one of the new models, and faithfully reproduces anything you ask for," the waitress answered in a sweet voice.

"I'll have the sushi," Ambrose said in a hurry. "And the pickled cucumber. That comes with rice?"

"Uh-huh," confirmed the waitress.

"The yakitori sounds perfect," Frank added, as the waitress turned to Tim.

"Nothing for me," Tim said, a look of disdain enveloping his face. The waitress took the menus and quickly left the table.

"Listen, Tim. It's nice to see you and everything, but I was hoping to have a nice evening with Frank."

"Don't you get it? The very way you live is being retooled right underneath you. What you eat. When you eat. Where you live. How you live. What you are!"

"Well, we're not seeing a lot of that in Charter Pass. Other than the 'what you are' piece," Ambrose pointed out.

"Did you hear the news about free Interface distribution? Free Enhancements? In Mexico?" Tim queried.

"I streamed that, yeah," Frank replied, hunching his shoulders.

"I wasn't talking about that. I meant the Code of Conduct's only taking the Human Protection Act one step further," Ambrose pushed back.

"But that came out of nowhere. Just like the Consortium's sudden change in strategy, connecting everyone, *gratis.*"

Ambrose snorted. "There's nothing wrong with free! And what about the Universal Care Act? Free medical attention? What's so bad about that?"

"And who exactly is paying for it all?" Tim hissed.

"And the re-launch of Burke Academy as a chain of schools. Open to everyone? I've been busting my chops on that you know. So, yeah there've been changes, but none of us are complaining," Ambrose pressed. "Seems like the government is doing what they should have done long ago."

"I've haven't streamed any newscasts about any sort of budgetary issue," Frank added.

"Oh my god, what if, have you ever considered that the streaming newscast could be responsible for these changes?" Tim growled.

"What? What are you talking about?" Frank said, snorting.

Ambrose started to worry that the evening was about to take a turn for the worse. "Listen to me," he said, finding his most authoritative tone. "We don't have a problem with the idea of reappraisal, if that's what you're getting at. And it seems like you should be supporting that too."

"That's not the point," Tim said.

"The point is I am out on a date with a friend!" Ambrose blustered.

"Yeah, sorry about that, but this is serious. The world is being reorganized from the inside out," Tim hissed. "What about the six billion people that were exterminated?"

"We aren't talking about that now. And if you aren't going to take the hint, and join us for civil conversation, then I'm going to ask you to leave," Ambrose pressed.

Tim huffed and shook his head, but Ambrose got to his feet, forcing his brother to meet him, standing.

Frank was focusing exclusively on the teacup in his hand and Ambrose was desperate to eject his brother as quickly as possible.

"Listen, I know you can't rent a bed anywhere without an Interface. So why not wait for me at my dormitory in B Block? I'll draw you a map."

Timothy remained wordless and shook his head again, turning for the steps to leave the dining room. "You'll be hearing more about this," he called out, turning to look at the two men as he proceeded up the short flight of steps from the dining room.

As he did, he missed a step and tumbled, hitting his forehead on the pointy corner of the short column post at the top of the stairs. Tim immediately snapped upright, as the hostess ran over with a cloth napkin and pressed it against his bleeding forehead. Ambrose and Frank jumped up from the table and leapt to Tim's side.

"Are you okay?" Ambrose choked, seeing the napkin start to turn red. "Call an ambulance," he ordered when Timothy didn't say anything. Ambrose helped his brother up and led him back to the alcove, easing him onto the bench. Within minutes, a small driverless car pulled up.

"The ambulance is here now," the hostess said, helping Ambrose get Tim to his feet. "I will assist you," she added as she pulled open the back hatch of the car, and let the two men climb into a tight cargo area. Frank got into the back seat as the waitress banged on the top of the carbot. It quickly pulled out from the curb.

"Sorry, so sorry," Timothy stuttered, lying against a bulkhead in the car. "Christ almighty, not a carbot!"

"No, it's okay. We'll be there in a jiff," Ambrose answered, rifling around the inside of the compartment for bandages. He spotted what looked like a small toolbox jutting out from behind his brother and pulled on it, flicking the clasp open. He pulled out a large bandage.

"Put that on his head," Frank ordered, turning back to face the two men.

"Yeah. Look, you don't seem to be bleeding that badly, Tim," Ambrose murmured as his brother acquiesced, letting his hand with the napkin fall away. He deftly slapped the large bandage across his brother's forehead.

"Pull a cold pack out of the kit," Frank interjected. Ambrose immediately fished it out and cracked it open. "Use it to keep pressure on the gash."

"*Kaminer, can you pick up? We're heading to Homebase with my jerk of a brother, who's bleeding from his head*," Ambrose messaged, setting it to repeat. "You sound like you know what you're doing, Frank," Ambrose mumbled, placing the pack against the bandage and roughly placing his brother's hand against it.

"The ice pack's kind of hard," Timothy complained.

"Hold that in place. Like Frank says," Ambrose ordered.

"The cold will help," mumbled Frank.

"*Lucky you I worked late. I'll be ready*," Kaminer messaged back. "*For that jerk of a coddled craypit brother of yours.*"

"*Why didn't you tell me someone from Purement had come to see you?*" Ambrose continued, trying to pay attention to Tim and Frank's conversation.

"*Tim's friend said not to. So I kept the confidence. Should I have told you?*"

"*No, I think you did the right thing. I guess. Listen, I gotta go. They're fighting!*" Ambrose signed off.

This is a disaster. Could it get any worse? The second he phased back to his surroundings, he realized it had gotten worse.

"Says you!" Frank was shouting, "Who made you the expert?"

"Where is Burke Industries getting the capital to open thousands, wait, tens of thousands of schools? If the government can't support education, how can Burke?" Tim shrieked, causing his forehead to ooze.

"Stop moving, and stop talking," Ambrose ordered. "You're making it worse. And you don't know what you're talking about. Burke Academy becoming a chain of schools is the culmination of its historical involvement in the educational system. It's not just a school. You should do some research."

"I did some research, and you're being a fool. But you're right about one thing," Tim countered.

"What thing?" Ambrose asked, afraid of the answer.

"It's not just a school. It's a battleground. The very place that houses Central Frame, intersecting with Burke Industries, the manufacturer of the Neural Interface. In the same city as Magnate Mindware, the company that devised Standard Enhancements."

"And? So what?" Frank cut in.

"Without an Interface, without those Standard Enhancements, do you think the U.S. Department of Education would ever have folded? Thrown in the towel? Left it to parents to organize some sort of haphazard replacement," Tim huffed.

"Oh for chri-, for crying out loud," Ambrose complained. "You're saying it's the Consortium's fault that the government made so many bad decisions, years ago, letting organized education fail? How do you make that leap?"

"And how would you explain the fact that there are some real private schools, not homeschools, still going, including Burke Academy at Charter Pass?" Frank added.

Ambrose looked over and smiled, nodding his head in appreciation as the ambulance pulled up to Homebase in the inner core. Ambrose sighed in relief as Frank sprang into action, getting out of the car first, running around to open the hatch in the back. Ambrose jumped out, pulling Timothy behind him. They eyed the tall, light brown, mostly purple-haired man that jogged up to them.

"Kam. Thanks-, for coming," Ambrose stuttered. "Sorry to ping you at work. You know Frank. And Timothy."

"Frank, nice to see you again." Kaminer said, smiling. "Can you join us at next Friday's card game? We're always looking for new victims."

"I've heard you're tough to beat," Frank exhaled, looking worriedly at Ambrose, but helping to settle Tim into the microglide wheelchair.

"Tough, but not impossible. I just have a really good memory," Kaminer said, laughing, and shoved the struggling Tim down into the chair.

"Not that he counts cards," Ambrose piped in.

"I don't want to be attended to at a Homebase. Take me to a clinic!"

"There are no clinics here," Ambrose barked. "Stop complaining. The world doesn't cater to your every Pure need."

"Both of you with me, please," Kaminer said crisply, pointing to Ambrose and Frank. With a smile, he took off at a trot towards the main entry, guiding the microglide wheelchair which hovered imperceptibly off the ground. His speed kept Timothy grasping the arms of the chair as Ambrose and Frank followed as best they could.

"*Oh crap, he doesn't need surgery, does he?*" Ambrose voiced in-mind as they headed down a corridor towards a surgibot room. "*Don't use the surgibot. Just put a stitch in him.*"

"I can do better than that," Kaminer called back, turning abruptly into a small room.

"Better than what?" Tim yelled, sounding frantic, as Frank and Ambrose almost skittered past the doorway. Ambrose caught himself by grabbing its frame, sliding on his sneakers, while Frank broke his speed by bumping into Ambrose.

They watched Kaminer lift Timothy completely out of the wheelchair and place him in the sturdy chair in the center of the small room. Kaminer fished a small vial out of his pocket, and reached for a lone swab lying on a plain metal side table. In a single stroke, he poked the tip into the vial, ripped the bandage off Timothy's head and swabbed the cut.

Instantly, the wound began to heal. Kaminer resealed his nano-safe container, and disposed of the swab in a specialized medical waste bin in one smooth maneuver. They watched Tim's forehead return to normal.

"Geez," Frank murmured.

"What did you just do to my head?" Timothy bellowed, reaching up to feel his forehead.

"The miracle of nano science," Kaminer declared. "Now both of you get out of here," he said, motioning to Frank and Ambrose. "I'll take care of this one."

***

Later that night, Ambrose returned to the dorm. Kaminer was sitting upright in his chair but shifted in his seat to signal that he was not working.

"Some night. Thanks again for helping," Ambrose said, shucking off a leather-like baseball jacket. He let it fall to the floor. "And where's Tim?" He moved into the room and kicked his flat-soled sneakers into his closet.

"Pick up your coat," Kaminer issued, opening his eyes. "Please."

Ambrose quickly moved back and hung his jacket on a hanger in the closet, swiftly removed his belt and peeled off his socks. "Sorry. Just a bit tired."

"It's okay. And you paid for an overflow bed for him, that craypit coddled brother of yours, in guest quarters," Kaminer said flatly.

Ambrose let out a breath. "Oh, brother."

"A less gracious guest would be hard to find," Kaminer confirmed. "Actually, he was seething. But it doesn't reflect on you. Now, how'd it turn out with Frank?"

"Enough to make plans for next weekend," Ambrose said, flopping onto his messily made bed. "But the kimono place charged me replacement credit because Tim sort of, well, bled on the robe. Even though they took the thing back."

"Oh dear."

"Well, who cares? We went back and ended up having a great meal. I tried sushi for the first time."

"The suggestion of sushi," Kaminer corrected.

"No, it was really sushi, with the rice and everything."

"Was the fish from a fish?"

"No. Printed."

"Like I said. Suggestion."

"I suppose."

"Listen, they're actively triangulating a move date. It could be soon," Kaminer suddenly announced.

"Why soon? Why at all?"

"Regrettably, I think this means I can deal with case correction from morning until my rest period commences," Kaminer said, sweeping a hand in front of him.

"Your rest period that now extends to almost eight hours. That's almost double the standard bot protocol. More evidence that your records are correct. Have you ever thought to call it 'sleep'?"

"Oh, uh-, that's true. Hmm," Kaminer rubbed his heavily-stubbled chin, thick with course brown hair.

"You should be fighting the move, Kam," Ambrose continued, sounding annoyed.

"I know. Once the reappraisal period is over, the work load should taper off. I'll have some free time in two weeks, I'm sure," Kaminer muttered, getting up from the chair. Walking towards his closet, he shed his clothing, tossing his shirt in the recycle bin.

"Are you wearing boxers? When did you start wearing those?"

"They're comfortable, and they double as pajamas," Kaminer pushed back. "What's wrong with boxer underwear?"

"No nothing, I just-" Ambrose said, trying to stifle a laugh. "So you really and truly have all your parts?"

"They're stretch knit," Kaminer continued, pulling the covers off his neatly made bed. "And yes. I can say that I'm a complete model, part-wise. Are you sleeping in your clothes?"

Ambrose stretched out on his bed. "Probably," he announced, turning on his back to face the ceiling. "And I'm not talking about how much Burke expects you to work. It's about basic human freedoms, being housed in a regular dorm, for instance," Ambrose chafed. "Crap, you're eating human biobiscuits, and I saw you eat some printed potato product the other day."

"Dr. Burke says my records speak for themselves, even when I point out that they state I'm human." He sat on the edge of his bed, his elbows resting on his knees.

"I don't get it."

"To him, I don't make the cut. That's why reappraisal is so important, Ambrose. If someone else were to certify it, he'd have to recognize it, right?" Kaminer asked, raising his hands to hunch his shoulders.

"Gee, I hope so," Ambrose said, adjusting some pillows and draping an arm over his forehead. "Thanks again for fixing my brother's head tonight."

"You're welcome. But it's gonna cost ya."

"What do you mean?" Ambrose turned in his bed to face Kaminer.

"I want to hear the story."

"What story?"

"The one you sort of told me the day I moved in. how 'things went south' for you and Tim. That's what you said, isn't it?"

Ambrose stared at him. "It's been a long day."

"Every day is a long day! There's always going to be a mishap or extra work or something that didn't quite go your way. So out with it. What happened that day?"

"Oh, chri-, crap. What is there to say? I ran late. Tim got hassled. I went all superhero. Tim got away. There's nothing more to tell." Ambrose sighed heavily.

"So why has it caused a rift? What's the issue?"

"What do you mean?"

"I heard you say it to Aron. Well, I recorded it because I couldn't understand what you were saying back then, when I was rebuilding. But you told him that no good deed goes unpunished. Why would Tim want to punish you for rescuing him?" Kaminer laid down on his side, propping himself on one elbow, and threw the covers over him.

"I don't know. I've never known. And now I don't care."

"That's a load a shite." Kaminer blinked.

"Did you just swear?" Ambrose said, chortling. "What the heck was that?"

"It sounded like a swear, didn't it? Now, what would Tim say?"

"What do you mean?" Ambrose sat up in bed, moving his comforter around him.

"How would he tell the story? Honestly?"

"I guess, um. Well, he would probably say, uh. You know he was like, uh, six at the time?"

"Irrelevant! He still had a point of view. What did it look like? From his point of view?'

"Geez, um, well he'd say we were supposed to play after I came home from school, because that much is irrefutable."

"Yeah?"

"And I was late. Because that was also true. Forgot my effing sneakers. If I'd just had them on when I'd walked out that morning, none of this would ever have happened."

"Uh-huh."

"I ran over an hour late that day because of detention. For not having gym shoes. I ran like a lightning bolt to get to him. But those imbeciles were already up top."

"Up top?"

"On the roof. It was where we played. He was being teased as a Pure. There was a girl in the building who used to sun herself up there, and all sorts of other kids who hung out, but we were unenhanced, unmodified, untouched."

"Right."

"They must have been picking on him for some time, because by the time I got there, things were out of hand. They were, uh, swinging Tim by a leg."

"What?"

"And then I went completely commando. Lost it. Turned myself into a, a weapon, didn't care at that point. Hurled myself right at the ringleader."

"And then what happened?" Kaminer was sitting up now, an arm draped over the desk that butted up against the end of his bed, forming a de facto head-board.

"He dropped Tim, who made his get-away. But I was throwing punches, some of 'em even landed."

"And?"

"And then they threw me over the side. Case closed."

Kaminer exhaled so loudly that he started coughing. "Geez," he breathed out, taking some time to gather some breathe in him. "So, uh, go back a little bit. How would Tim tell this same story?"

Ambrose stared at him. "How 'bout I turn the lights off?"

"If it helps." Silence ensued as the lights clicked off. "Ambrose?"

"Tim would say, uh, he'd probably say that, um, I ate his lunch."

"How so?"

"He didn't get to fight it out, regain the upper hand. Not that he would have." Ambrose sounded like he was starting to choke.

"So your actions shut off an avenue for him?"

"I don't think so!" More silence. "But it's possible."

"Your long and arduous recovery. It probably looked a little like mine?" Kaminer threw a pillow on the floor.

"It looked at lot like yours," Ambrose breathed out. "I'm aware of that, you know."

"But have you ever stopped to consider that maybe, just maybe, I'm Tim? You think of me like I'm you. But maybe in this scenario, I'm like Tim."

"What?"

"I just want to make my own choices, however bad they are. Figure out how to be reappraised as human. Even if it gets me thrown off a building, so to speak. At least I went of my own accord, under my own steam."

"You can't mean that."

"Ambrose, I'm here to tell you that you can't take a learning experience away from someone."

"Well, uh, geez, apparently I did," Ambrose snorted.

"Okay, you can't take it away and expect to be thanked for it."

"Geez, um, effing, gah-. Crap, I know you're right." Silence enveloped the room.

"Ambrose?"

"I need to marinate in this for a while," Ambrose huffed.

"Okay. Then I guess I'll stop lecturing and sign off now. Good night."

"'Night. Your lecture. Geez. Uh, sleep tight." Ambrose threw himself on his back, staring up at the ceiling. *He's more human than some humans I know.*

Reappraisal

Human Services Bureau *n. proper.* **Established following the Human Protection Act of 2086. Ensures compliance with said act, and The Code of Conduct of 2099. Responsible for the prevention, detection, and elimination of biohacking, and resolution of Reappraisal.**

A week later, Rafe found his mother in her office. "What do you mean we have to appear in person at the Human Services Bureau? Aren't the medical records from the best homebase in the world good enough?" Dr. Kate said, sounding irritated.

"It's clear on the Code of Conduct. We are to present ourselves before next Tuesday, or else we suffer the consequences," Rafe reported.

"Why Chicago? There are several good Bureaus in Springfield-Decatur that are much closer."

"I've managed an appointment in Chicago, on Monday. Otherwise we'll be standing in line."

"It seems redundant," Kate complained.

"We show up, they verify we no longer possess Readers, and that's it. Life goes on."

"Interface the details, and arrange transport. It seems so inefficient that we have to go into Chicago, but at least I don't have to do it alone!"

***

On Monday morning, Dr. Kate left with her son, departing via armed helicopter from Charter Pass. Three bodybots escorted them, two of them seating themselves in the front row. The third pressed itself as close to the rear side door as it could to make room for Dr. Kate, who was wedged in the middle of the back seat between the bodybot and her son.

Within minutes, the bladeless helicopter surpassed Charter Pass's city limits, its three sets of short offset wings turning to take a northeast path, directly towards the heart of Chicago.

Dr. Kate grabbed her son's arm. "*Rafe, what's going on down there?*" she interfaced, pointing out the domed glass.

"*We don't have a name for them yet,*" Rafe replied, spying a building-sized, bug-like construction robot. "*Human Services Bureau put in the order, with detailed specifications, in April. We're manufacturing them in one of our Eastern-Hem facilities.*"

"But look," Kate exclaimed out loud, adjusting a head set that she hadn't quite lined up. "It's mowed down a whole tract of decrepit buildings."

"Mmm," Rafe concurred. "*And Chicago ordered over twenty thousand new constructionbots. See, over there? How they're rebuilding that block?*" Rafe pointed out the side of the helicopter window.

"*And there's a park,*" Kate exclaimed. "*How is there room for open space?*"

"*Maybe there's a bit more room? Now?*" Rafe sent, resetting his emotional filter to low so that his mother would sense his uneasiness.

Kate nodded her understanding. "*Less people, more space. Look at the sign. It says 'Future Site of Katrine Park'. They're going to put in grass, build a playground!*"

"*And there's another bugbot*," Rafe said, pointing as they flew over another neighborhood. "*It seems to be straightening out that section of Route 55. I think that's where it crosses the eighty.*"

"*Are those new FoodServe restaurants? Is that what it says? When did Global Stock go into the restaurant business?*"

"*Yes, a new concept. The government seems intent on implementing free healthcare through the Universal Care Act, and free food via the FoodServes.*"

"*And is that another bug thing, bug robot by the lake? Is it digging? I can't tell.*" Kate sounded alarmed as she pointed beyond the Human Services Bureau of Chicago, which had relocated and expanded in the last six months. A new central monitoring location had risen on the dry shore bed of Lake Michigan, just southeast of the other large build-out of Carousel.

Rafe shook his head, as the Burke's helicopter dropped down onto a secure landing pad, and a policebot ran forward to open the door for Dr. Burke.

"We're here for reappraisal," Rafe informed the policebot, who scanned him and his mother, and pointed them towards the new building sheathed in polyacrylate. They walked towards the building, scanning obvious changes in the horizon.

"Rafe, where's the Bryant Complex?"

He shook his head. "And over there. Where the aqueduct used to be, another new building," Rafe said as they approached the Human Services Bureau. "Nicole Tower? When did that go up?"

A policebot, its holster armed on both sides, stood squarely in front of a sliding door.

"Reappraisal? We have an appointment," Dr. Kate intoned.

"Floor six, then straight ahead," the policebot said in a monotone voice, moving to the side and manually sliding the heavy door open.

Rafe shot his mother a look. *"Why doesn't it open automatically?"* His mother returned the look, continuing towards an elevator bank set at the front of the building. Dr. Kate nodded to the policebot standing to the side.

"Which floor?" it asked.

"Floor six," Rafe answered, furrowing his brow.

"Nature of your business?" the policebot continued.

"Reappraisal," Rafe said, sounding short.

"Confirmed. Floor six, then straight ahead," the policebot said, as the elevator doors opened.

"Thank you," murmured Dr. Kate as they stepped into the elevator. Another policebot was standing by an old-fashioned button panel.

"Which floor?" the bot asked.

"Floor six!" Rafe answered, exasperated, looking at his mother.

"Nature of your business?" the policebot asked, raising a ridgeline that suggested eyebrows.

"We're appearing for reappraisal," Dr. Kate said, meeting her son's incredulous stare.

"Confirmed," the policebot answered, as it punched the number six button and the elevator slowly ascended. Rafe looked at his mother again as the elevator doors slid open on the sixth floor. "Straight ahead," the policebot voiced as the Burkes stepped out of the elevator into a packed passageway.

Dr. Kate gasped. "Rafe, I think some of these people are in peril of being classified as non-human," she whispered, as he motioned her ahead, cutting through the haphazard line. Most of the waiting people looked normal, but an obvious number didn't seem quite right. Dr. Kate stared at a person who shimmered in a strange way as Rafe shook his head, and continued to maneuver his mother forward.

They stopped outside a door off to the side of the line that read 'Officer 20'. Rafe knocked loudly, and a human police officer answered it promptly. As they entered his small office, Rafe looked over his shoulder at the crowd again.

"Mother, I see Ambrose and Kaminer, just there. Look," Rafe urged. "One moment, Officer," he said, backing out of the office. He walked swiftly over to Kaminer.

"What are you doing here?" Dr. Burke asked in a brusque tone.

Kaminer took a step back. "I'm applying for reappraisal."

"I'm here for Kaminer," Ambrose added.

"What do you mean reappraisal?" Rafe said harshly. "Come with me."

"No, I'd rather wait my turn," Kaminer replied, turning away slightly as the line edged forward towards a bank of windows manned by black-uniformed, purple-haired policebots.

"I think you should accompany Dr. Kate and me,"

"'I'll be available momentarily. Just let me get to the head of the line."

"What do you think you'll accomplish?" Rafe questioned, looking at Ambrose, who looked down at his feet.

"I'd like to have my records clarified," Kaminer answered, squaring off his shoulders.

"Clarified how?"

"I, uh, filled out the Disclosure, from the Code of Conduct, classifying myself as human. It's in keeping with the system's records, yet I'm treated like a bot."

"So?"

"So what am I?"

"You're my personal assistant, that's what you are," Rafe answered in a harsh tone.

"Worked as a bot, about to be housed like a bot, and yet I am not a bot. Not all the way through." Kaminer set his mouth in a thin line.

"You were manufactured. You're a bot."

"And yet I feel. And yet I wonder. And yet I worry."

"*Nice!*" Ambrose pinged him, continuing to look down at his feet but paying close attention to the conversation around him.

"So you're a bot anomaly. I know that wasn't a normal restart, and your records are unusual. I'm not even sure why we agreed to that, but that still doesn't make you *not* a bot."

"But I could try. I've been doing-, uh," Kaminer stuttered.

"He's been working to improve himself," Ambrose chimed in, shrinking when he registered Dr. Burke's withering stare.

"Isn't my effort in keeping with the human spirit?" Kaminer asked. "Isn't that how the song from The Man of La Mancha goes?"

"Have it your way," Rafe huffed. "But don't throw that song at me. You only know it because I stream 'The Impossible Dream' in our office."

"I know. But it's become my, uh-, my fight song," Kaminer said, pressing his lips together.

Ambrose instantly began to hear the strong refrains of the song blast through his mind, and tried not to smile. He stood quietly tucked in behind Kaminer, watching Dr. Burke lose steam.

"Fine, then. You won't accomplish anything, but if you're done before us, wait downstairs by the front door. You can come with us back to Charter Pass. You too, Ambrose."

"Thank you, Dr. Burke," Ambrose whispered as Kaminer nodded and took another step towards the window. Ambrose watched Dr. Burke return to his mother's side, and saw the door close behind both of them. He and Kaminer took another step towards the head of the line. Suddenly a loud noise erupted a few feet ahead of them.

"Christ almighty! But I'm not even interfaced," came the cry. "I'm more human than you, or you, or you!" a deep male voice yelled, and Ambrose strained to see a man pointing wildly at the crowd. "I can't help it. It's in my records," the man yelled, and banged a fist on the window.

The policebot on the other side stood up and stared at him. "Do not strike that window again."

"Germline therapy. It's legal, sanctioned, for mitochondrial disease. There's no way, no way you can tell me I'm not human!" the man screamed, and slammed the window again with both fists.

"Sir, your blood test shows that one of your two mothers contained a Bos primigenius splice. Some of that bovine DNA was passed to you," the policebot stated without inflection, nodding to two policebots standing in the waiting room.

"But I didn't do anything. I was never spliced. Never!" the man cried. "They tell me they can't undo it. What am I supposed to do?" The man began to sob uncontrollably as the two policebots moved in and picked up the flailing man by the arms. The line of applicants broke as people hustled to the side to escape the man's kicking feet.

Ambrose shot Kaminer a look. "*Not good.*"

The man was led to a small sitting area just past Officer 20's closed door where the Burkes remained ensconced. Ambrose watched one of the policebots take the man's hand by force, and shove it into a small apparatus on the desk. He tilted his head and hunched down to see a series of small needles descend from the black cube and prick the man's hand. The man yelled in pain as the policebots released him.

"Armin Milan, you have been reappraised," one of them said, the man stumbled and gripped the frame of the door. His hair began to turn a shade of purple darker than Kaminer's. Ambrose gasped when the man staggered by, spreading a trail of short, dirty blonde hair that was falling out of a spreading bald patch.

Kaminer clasped two hands over his mouth. "Is that how they're doing it? Actually marking marginal humans as bots?" Kaminer hissed into Ambrose's ear. Ambrose turned away and gulped, pushing Kaminer forward in line. "But I've done so much work."

"I know. Getting your recombinant contribution despliced was awful."

"Removing the artificial digestive system was worse. And it's stayed worse. I still can't eat much more than biobiscuits but now I have to supplement. The human G.I. tract is so inefficient."

"Well, you aren't the only one who has to put up with green pee," Ambrose said. Kaminer backed up and looked down at him. "I'm joking, for cray's sake!"

"Oh, sorry, I'm just nervous is all. You know my journey isn't complete," Kaminer tendered. "*I told you. I'm counting on a miracle. Miracles do happen.*"

Suddenly, a policebot strode into the crowd, issuing a loud warning. "Attention! Anyone who knows they will not reappraise as human is to step forward in front of this officer," the policebot announced, motioning to a policebot who had obviously been reassigned from Kill Force. When no one moved, he strode into the thick line and started pulling people out. "You! With the weird eyes. Over here. What is that?"

"Goat. Sir," a man said, looking down.

"In that line. Now!" the policebot ordered, and shoved a few more people towards the other officer. "And do not think you can hide your non-human DNA. You will be blood printed as you reach the window. Our techniques are very sophisticated, so if you have even so much as a splice in your ancestry, step into this new line. Now!"

A few more people shuffled into the separate, growing line, as Kaminer stepped up to a glass window. Kaminer rubbed a hand nervously over his mouth, as the policebot on the other side of the window eyed his purple and red hair with suspicion.

"Finger there," the window policebot ordered, and Kaminer placed his finger onto a pad, which was instantly pricked.

"Just a moment," the policebot said, continuing to stare at Kaminer. "You are clear. Proceed through the turnstile to the next window."

"What about my friend?" Kaminer asked. "He's not here for reappraisal.

"He can wait in the back," the policebot intoned. Ambrose reached out for Kaminer, and shook his hand.

"It's gonna work out," Ambrose said, drawing himself as tall as possible. "I'll meet you over there when you're through."

Kaminer nodded, and proceeded ahead through a turnstile. Ambrose followed a length of wall to the back of the room, close to the elevators, breathing heavily with worry. He wrenched his head to try and watch as Kaminer walked onto a platform.

"Stand still for complete scan," the policebot ordered as a scanner, resembling an extra-large pair of antique binoculars, lowered itself from a large divot in the ceiling. The scanner passed down and then back up the front of Kaminer, doing the same from behind. Without any noise, it returned to its cubby in the ceiling.

The policebot look confused. "Kettle, look at this one, will you? I do not understand why he is here," he asked another policebot sitting in a stall behind him.

Kaminer turned swiftly. "Kettle? Kettle?"

The approaching bot narrowed its eyes. "Is that you, Kaminer? What has happened to you?" Kettle asked. "Why do you appear different?"

"Yes, it's me. Were you reconstituted? After being downed at Carousel?"

Kettle stood motionless and stared at Kaminer. "Yes, reconstituted. Explain the hair."

Kaminer gulped. "I've been, uh, rebuilding. My hair, the hair that's red, it grows directly from human follicles, human keratin."

Kettle pursed his lips, squinting as he slowly raised his hand to his temple. "Move to Officer 20, so we can examine you there."

"But you remember me, right? All the work we did together in Bio-protection?"

Kettle eyed him, and backed up a step. "This way," Kettle said, and then softened. "I remember you. But I cannot account for your current status. The hair. And you seem less sturdy somehow, which is perplexing."

Together they moved to a door that was still closed. In an instant, Ambrose moved forward by Kaminer's side again.

"Who is this?" Kettle asked.

"A friend. He's not here for reappraisal."

"A friend? What does that mean? Why do you use that word?"

"He's my best friend. And he came to support me today, during this process," Kaminer declared.

"I do not understand. Why would a human accompany you? You are a Kill Force warbot. You require assistance from no one."

"That's not true. No one can do it alone. Not even me," Kaminer said. "And I wouldn't be standing here today if I hadn't been so fortunate to have Ambrose as my friend. He brought me back."

Ambrose gasped and ran a hand over his mouth, leaving it there. *Oh my gah-, oh my gah-, oh my gah! I get it! I get it! I get it! Kaminer let me in, but it wasn't about him or even helping him. This feeling, uhh, of, what is it? Knowing that I made a difference? It's like lightning! And I never let Timmy have that. Oh, no, no.* Ambrose held himself rigid, practically apoplectic at the sudden realization. *It wasn't about the rooftop, but after. I didn't just foreclose his chance to fight it out himself. That's what I thought he's held against me all these years. No! I took away his chance to feel my gratitude. Because I never let him in.*

Kettle tilted his head. "I do not comprehend what you are saying. But your syntax is consistent with your blood scan which shows 100% Human DNA. I can see you have had snippets redacted. Good for you."

"Uh-huh," Kaminer confirmed, squinting his eyes at Ambrose, who looked like he was having a panic attack.

"Brain scan says you are human, verified by grammatical use of contractions," Kettle reported. "So why have you not swapped out your artificial skeleton? The rest of you clearly is human."

At that moment, the door to Officer 20's room opened and Rafe and Dr. Kate emerged, looking relieved.

"Kaminer, is everything okay?" Dr. Kate asked, as the human Officer 20 stepped out behind them.

"I'm not sure. Is everything okay?" Kaminer asked Kettle.

"I cannot opine on that," Kettle delivered, looking at Officer 20.

"What seems to be the issue?" Officer 20 asked, putting a hand to his temple.

"Human all the way through, Sir. Until you get to his synthetic skeleton. I am compelled to mention that Kaminer is here with a *friend*," Kettle replied, motioning to Ambrose, who had settled into a deep breathing routine.

"Well, that's just fine, Kaminer," Officer 20 cut in. "I have a record that you've applied for and are waiting to have the thermoplastic skeletal removal, is that right?"

"Uh-, yes, um, that's right," Kaminer lied, and cleared his throat. He cleared his throat again, raising a hand to his neck and looking with surprise to Ambrose.

Ambrose coughed, trying to stifle his amazement that his friend had managed something as subtle as clearing his throat. *And so human. Finally. And how fitting. So very human.*

"And we do have some flexibility, knowing how busy all of our homebases have been trying to get humans to be human all the way through," Officer 20 continued.

"Yeah," Kaminer murmured.

"Why don't you have that taken care of, now that the rush is over?" Officer 20 said, looking at Dr. Kate. "You'll vouch for Kaminer, won't you?"

"Of course I'll vouch for Kaminer," Kate answered, laying a hand on Officer 20's arm. "He's practically part of our family."

"Anything to add, Dr. Burke?" Officer 20 asked.

"His records speak for themselves," Dr. Burke spit out, sounding angry. He crossed his arms tightly.

"Have a nice day then," Officer 20 answered, smiling blandly at the four people who stood perfectly still, looking back at him. He turned for his room, winked at Kaminer, and closed his door.

"What just happened?" Kaminer whispered.

"*You got your miracle, and then some.*"

"*I worked a case with that man. That is not the man I remember. And he just winked at me.*"

"*So what?*"

"*It's just that, uh, I have this memory of someone winking at me. An in-mind memory. I can't really explain it.*"

"Why didn't the officer look at Kaminer's records?" Dr. Burke exclaimed "He would have seen that even though he's classified as human, he'd be a nine month old baby. He'd have to know he's a bot."

"It doesn't matter, dear," Dr. Kate soothed, as the four of them started to clear the congested room. Kaminer turned to wave goodbye to Kettle as they left.

"Godspeed, Kaminer," Kettle called after him.

"But it does matter! It matters a great deal. Kaminer is simply not human," Dr. Burke entreated, sounding angry.

"Says who?" Dr. Kate delivered in such a sharp tone that Ambrose imagined the words slicing into Dr. Burke. He watched her turn on a red spikey heel to fully face her son. "Says you? Who are you to say what Kaminer is capable of?"

"Capable of? He's capable of doing what he's programmed to do. What he's been downloaded to do," Dr. Burke said, gritting his teeth.

"But the restart. You keep forgetting about the restart. He says he made a brand new beginning that day," Ambrose butt in, squaring himself off. Dr. Burke stopped walking, and Ambrose could feel the doctor's gaze fall over him. He willed himself to stand tall, and not back down.

"New start, huh? I know someone who could make a new start," Dr. Burke muttered in a low, cold tone.

"Enough," Dr. Kate cut in. "It's been decided. There's nothing to argue about. Kaminer, you're going to need surgery."

"Again, I'm being asked to let go of my personal assistant? He's only been in Cosmetics for three months," Dr. Burke complained. "How long is he going to be off-mind?" Dr. Burke asked as they approached the elevator doors that slid open as soon as he pressed the button. "And why is there a button here? Why can't I just interface the elevator?"

"Because we are in charge of the Human Services Bureau," a bot stationed inside the elevator answered.

"Oh, I, it wasn't really a question," Rafe stumbled.

"Consider your non-question answered. Floor?" the policebot asked.

"Ground level, please," Dr. Kate said, and a sullen silence fell over the occupants of the elevator as it made its way down.

The foursome emerged through the heavy doors where they were greeted by the three bodybots who had been forced to wait outside. The bodybots looked at each other when they saw the additional guests.

"One of you will need to self-transport," Dr. Kate clarified, seeing their stares. "You can decide," she said, walking briskly towards the helicopter. She got into the front of the helicopter with one of the faster bodybots sliding in next to her. "Kaminer, you're up front with me."

Kaminer smiled and moved to sit on the other side of Dr. Kate. Ambrose got in the back with Dr. Burke and the next fastest bodybot. The third bodybot hung its head, and started walking.

Rafe cleared his throat. "What's this 'we're in charge of the Bureau' all about? Bots in charge of the Human Services Bureau? Was he making a joke?"

"Bots aren't very good at humor, Dr. Burke," Ambrose murmured as Kate turned slightly in her seat to stare back at them.

"And Rafe. You simply can't talk to Ambrose or Kaminer like that. Particularly Kaminer. You just can't keep treating him the same," Dr. Kate said in a constricted voice.

"Why not?" Rafe barked from the back seat.

"Because it's unproductive. He's been recognized as human. His records do speak for themselves. We couldn't have foreseen the day when the definition of what it meant to be human would change," Dr. Kate declared, turning back to pat Kaminer on the knee.

"I'll say," Rafe groused.

"Like that guy," Ambrose mumbled.

"What guy?" Rafe asked.

"Oh, you were still inside. They marked a man, this guy called Armin Milan, as bot, not sure how, but they turned his hair purple, with a bald spot and everything."

"I believe they are using a new type of ScrubBub," Kaminer interjected from the front.

"ScrubBub nanobots? For humans? How?" Dr. Kate asked. "We haven't developed anything like that."

"Well the uh-, Human Services Bureau probably has a, um, science division," Kaminer said.

"A science division? Wouldn't Burke Industries or one of our companies in the Consortium know about that?" Dr. Burke asked.

"I don't know. But it appeared to me that the man was instantly mutated with the synthetic hair gene that is the crowning touch for all bots," Kaminer said.

"Ha-ha! Crowning touch! That's a good one," Ambrose called out, slapping his knee.

"Oh, right! I made a joke," Kaminer said, smiling.

"Well, we survived reappraisal. We should all be grateful for that," Dr. Kate added.

Parting Gift

**"You join in, and effect change. But how do you
keep the system from rubbing off on you?"
-Ambrose**

When the helicopter returned to Charter Pass, it
hovered above the Cosmetic Enhancement building,
waiting for its gabled roof to fully retract and allow
access to the landing pad. A few moments later, the
occupants disembarked.

"Thank you, Dr. Kate, Dr. Burke," Kaminer said,
getting out from the front.

"Yeah, thanks for the lift," Ambrose added.

"Of course. Kaminer, would you like to come with
me to Homebase? If we go together, and in person, I'm
sure we can expedite your surgery," Dr. Kate said as
they moved inside to take the elevator down. "It's not
a typical surgery, but I'm sure within the realms of
possibility."

"Oh, right, thank you. Would you give me a
moment?" Kaminer asked, and turned to Ambrose as
Kate walked away, grabbing Rafe by his arm.

"You know, this is where I landed when I came in for
repair almost nine months ago. Right here," Kaminer
reported, looking around at the fortified glass enclosure.

"In your heli?" Ambrose checked.

"I piloted a single passenger. You've seen the orbs in the distance over Chicago I'm sure. I remember, back then, being one with its operating system."

"What?"

"Yeah. When you're not separate from anything, you don't know what it means to be alone," Kaminer said, pressing his lips together.

Ambrose stared at him. "I guess I never thought about that."

"So today, I can't tell you how much I appreciated your company," Kaminer confessed. "I didn't think I could do it by myself."

"Anything for a friend," Ambrose answered, his eyes widening. "I mean that. But I'm confused about something."

"What's that?"

"Why didn't they flag your bot ScrubBub? And surely there are other parts to you that aren't human. I know you've taken care of the big ticket items, like your DNA and digestion, but your ScrubBub is still bot. Isn't it?"

"I don't think so. It must have been converted too."

"Like your hydraulics?"

"And my circulatory system, and apparently my motor sensors, which have been morphing into a nervous system."

"Man! But your Caudata was redacted. How has this been happening?"

"Remember back, when I first came to Burke? I had my shoulder repaired."

"Yeah, I remember that."

"I think the nanobots used during the repair, the ones that were left behind, they might have been, uh, differentiated," Kaminer said, pushing his hair back.

"Differentiated?"

"Or different. There's been some process at work that has slowly converted what was bot to human," Kaminer reported. "ScrubBub must be playing a role."

"Holy cray!"

"Yeah. Really, all that remains is my ugly hair," Kaminer lamented.

"It's not ugly. I don't think it's ugly."

"It's mostly purple! And I can't dye it. I've tried. It gives me away," Kaminer huffed.

"Don't forget about your indestructible skeleton."

"I am rather partial to my artificial structure. I don't know what it'll mean to have a human skeleton."

"Will they do it bone by done?" Ambrose asked, stepping back and looking Kaminer up and down.

"I'm purposely not going to research the procedure, so I can't tell you."

"Well, I can come with, if you like," Ambrose said, reaching out for his friend's arm.

"Yeah. I'd, um, like that. But I have to tell you something first."

"What?"

"I haven't had a chance to say it. But I moved out before we went to the Human Services Bureau."

"No way. This is ridiculous. You have to stand up to Burke," Ambrose said.

"Like you just did back there?"

"Yeah, like that. He's a bully, but not immune to reason. You've got to stand your ground."

"I've got to figure out how to do that." Kaminer sounded doubtful.

"You'll figure it out. I know you. Think about every single thing that you've accomplished since your restart. Learning how to walk again. How to talk again. What about the guy that stood in front of a theatre full of teenagers and gave the speech of his life?"

"Kids still find me and tell me how it made them think their interactions with others. How they're more honest about their implicit bias," Kaminer said, still sounding dejected.

"Well, I couldn't have done that. So find the words, find the courage, and make Burke treat you like the man that you are."

"You mean find my voice?"

"That's exactly what I mean. And message me the new address."

"Alright. And I'll see you soon okay?" Kaminer said. "*You and Fran-ces-ca*," he continued in-mind, sending it to Ambrose's mindscreen with a background of exploding fireworks.

Ambrose laughed, and held up a hand. "And you know where to find me. You're always invited."

"Right-o. See you in a couple," Kaminer finished and fist-bumped his friend before moving off in the company of Dr. Kate, stationed near a doorway. Ambrose could see Dr. Burke had already left, and pretended to check his in-mind messages while Kaminer and Dr. Kate got in the elevator together and disappeared.

Ambrose took the next elevator, and began the walk towards the tram to make his way back to work. *Being alone doesn't have to mean lonely. It's like Kaminer said. He used to be connected to an operating system, suddenly alone when he wasn't. But I've always been a part of this world. So being alone doesn't mean lonely. It's all a matter of perspective.*

***

A few hours later, Ambrose found himself opening the door to his now roommate-less room. Kaminer's side was tidy as always, but now it was empty.

All of Kaminer's clothes were gone, and the small box that Kaminer kept on his desk with it. Ambrose sighed, thinking about the box that Kaminer had marked 'value', where he'd stored every scrap or note he came across with any sentimental value.

Ambrose turned to his side of the room and realized with a gasp that Kaminer had tidied his entire side as well, even dusting the shelves above his desk. His clothes were sorted in a neat pile. To their side, on top of Ambrose's perfectly-made bed, a folded beige cloth was loosely wrapped with a ribbon.

Ambrose furrowed his brow as he approached the small bundle. Picking up a notecard laid square to the cloth, he recognized Kaminer's perfect script.

To Ambrose,
For letting me be your friend.
Kaminer

Ambrose released the ribbon, shaky with emotion. It was a silky purple kimono.

KAMINER

The Scholars: Program

"Rectify."
-Larry

Later that night, Kaminer made an unscheduled visit to the Scholar's sanctuary.

"It's done," Kaminer announced as he came through their door. When none of the Scholars answered back, Kaminer stood for a moment, observing the scene.

Teegan was twirled around, facing the mail slots behind him, an enormous stack of paper on his lap, leaned up against his girth. He was thumbing the papers, one by one, into three piles. Several of his helping programs, dressed like college students, quickly lined up the paper that drifted towards them.

"Human," Teegan issued, ejecting a piece of paper. "Human, human, bot, notbot, bot," he continued in quick succession amid a flurry of paper. The college students checked the papers that floated down, precisely laying each one in the correct pile.

"I think the nuclear stations would serve everyone's needs," Larry declared from the teal sectional where he was sitting with Cindy and Gulliver. A large map, yellowed around its edges, had been rolled out over the low ottoman, and secured in place with coffee mugs at its four corners. "We could secure these premises - here, here, and here," Larry continued, pointing to the map as Kaminer moved into the room.

With Teegan's back to him, and the others clustered around the coffee table, Kaminer arrived at the sofa undetected. "What's there, and there, and there?"

Cindy startled, throwing herself back on the couch cushions. "Oh my, Kaminer! We didn't see you come in," she exclaimed.

"What are you working on?" he asked, curious about the plans being made.

"Is it December 31st already? How'd we miss that?" Larry asked, scratching his chin.

"No, our regular quarterly meeting isn't for a few more days. I just thought I'd come and give you a personal update," Kaminer said, sounding sincere.

"What's that, Kaminer?" Gulliver asked.

"I've been reappraised, as human. I have a surgery coming up next week. To get rid of my last synthetic parts," Kaminer announced. The Scholars stared at him. "Uh, that would be my skeleton. It's going to be replaced."

Larry narrowed his eyes. "So how'd you reappraise as human?"

"What do you mean?"

Larry stood up and whistled, putting two fingers to his mouth to emit a sharp piercing sound. Teegan turned in his chair towards the sectional.

"Tee, we've had another one," Larry declared.

"Shit! How do they keep doing that?" Teegan hollered, standing up. The pile of papers lodged on his lap flew into the air, cascading in a frenzy towards the students and the neat piles.

"No, no!" one of the students called out, throwing her body over the piles. The largest stack slid sideways under her, and toppled.

"Oh my god!" Teegan cried. "You! All three of you! Sort this crap out now."

He began to wheeze, and fumbled with an ornate desk drawer, pulling it open so hard that the drawer flew loose in his hand. Its contents went flying everywhere, spraying the students with bits of crumpled paper, hard, chewed up pieces of gum, and several sizes of paperclips. His heavy watch hit one of the students on the side of the face. Teegan flung himself down next to a paper vacation brochure for Japan, grasping his asthma inhaler that had gone flying in the mess.

Kaminer moved over to help Teegan, who remained crumpled on the floor, refusing to budge as he took a few puffs of his inhaler.

"Why do you have that?" Kaminer asked, pointing to the brochure.

"That Ambrose fellow," Teegan managed, between gasps of breath. He took a long drag from the inhaler, pointing towards the digital watch, which Kaminer collected for him.

"Why do you still have this?" Kaminer asked, handing him the watch.

"The seconds mark the minutes, the minutes mark the hours, the hours mark the days," Teegan reported.

"And?"

"How else do I keep track of all the seconds of my existence?" Teegan said with a sigh, as Kaminer helped him to his feet.

"Sorry?"

"How do you keep track?" Teegan asked, snapping the watch tightly onto his wrist.

"I guess through my memories, my feelings, what I remember about what's happened," Kaminer said, shrugging and thinking that at some point in his past, before the singularity, he too would have felt the weight of seconds add up to minutes, hours and days. *I don't remember. But it's not like that now. Now it's all kind of a blur.*

"Get this sorted," Teegan ordered the college students.

They immediately began to pick the bits of trash out of the pile of paper, retrieved two of the shorter piles and the intact portion of the third, taller stack that hadn't collapsed into the sea of unsorted papers. Teegan clumped over to the sofa with Kaminer, depositing himself in a heap. Kaminer took a seat on the other side of its L-shape next to Larry.

"What's going on?" Kaminer asked.

"We haven't wanted to say anything, but we're sure now that something's amiss. Something to do with Henton Burke and Cray," Larry issued.

"I swear, you better tell me," Kaminer exclaimed.

"We'd like to see you try," Gulliver said in a quiet voice.

"Swear?"

"Yes. Do it," Larry ordered.

"Why? What the fahh, what the hehh, what the?"

Cindy put a hand to her mouth, looking to the other Scholars. "More confirmation," she breathed out.

"Of what?" Kaminer demanded. "What is going on?"

"Let me put it simply. Cray has been messing with people around you, influencing their actions. First it was Katz updating your records, having them reflect your status as human," Larry started.

"Back when you were more bot than anything else," Gulliver added.

"And it might have started before then," Teegan pointed out.

"It's true," Gulliver said. "We think the only reason Ambrose got a job at Burke Industries to begin with is a result of them messing with Central Frame."

"Why? Why would they do that?" Kaminer said, looking astonished.

"It seems to be part of a larger plan. And Cray got Ambrose to suggest putting you in school, and now we know he, or possibly they, influenced Officer 20 to uphold your Disclosure as human. There is no other way you would have been passed at reappraisal," Larry said.

"Because of my thermoplastic armature?" Kaminer asked, pressing his lips together.

"You should have been recognized as a notbot. We would have rescued you, of course, but still. The system didn't work. And if they're screwing around with you, where else has Cray managed to seep through? Make a human act on his instructions?" Gulliver put forth.

"Notbot?" Kaminer gulped.

"You saw one of them yourself. Armin Milan. We're sending him to Millstone."

"You're calling them notbots? I thought they'd been turned into bots," Kaminer said, exhaling loudly.

"They're calling themselves notbots," Cindy clarified. "It's only their outer appearance that is even remotely bot."

"It's not like they have your skeleton," Gulliver added.

"Where, um, is Millstone?"

"We're setting up colonies at the nuclear power plants, mostly on the East Coast. We should have about fourteen colonies established soon," Larry said, motioning towards the map.

"Millstone's in Connecticut. Which soon won't exist as a state. We're about to execute the next phase of the consolidation, make the states join in with Mexico," Teegan declared.

"Yeah, I know. But you said something about securing those locations, when I walked in. You're not setting up armed guards are you?"

Larry shook his head. "Our plans are a little broader than that."

"After the consolidation is done, we plan to implement a two-fer," Teegan announced.

"Which means we intend to break up the southern polar ice cap," Larry added.

"What?!" Kaminer yelled, getting to his feet.

"It's for the best, Kaminer," Cindy said, getting up to take his hand. She pulled Kaminer down to sit next to her on the other side of Larry.

"Coastal inundation will isolate the nuclear stations we've selected, which, once reinforced with sea walls, will become discreet colonies. We'll make sure they have enough land to farm and sustain themselves," Gulliver said.

"Those stations should be shut down anyway, archaic hold-overs that they are. We'll make sure the physical plant is secure, remove the nuclear fuel components, connect each station to a Ring," Larry added. "We're not going to make them live in the dark."

"We'll put in select streaming blockers and Message Off anyone with an Interface," Teegan said.

"How is this a two-fer?"

"We'll wall off a large enough tract of land for each station. But we are also going to create an illusion of sorts. Make the water appear to extend far more inland than it actually will," Teegan added.

"What?"

"It's a type of Visage Mirage. The nanobots that coat a person's face, appearing to smooth out wrinkles, straighten a crooked nose? It's a poor man's version of scouring," Larry issued, tsking twice in a staccato fashion.

"Sorry?"

"If you don't have the money for a proper internal rejuvenation, where nanobots remove debris from cells, rebuild collagen and do a real scouring, then you get the pauper's version, where it looks like it's been done. Visage Mirage," Gulliver said.

"And?"

"So, we throw a net over most of the world's coastline, seed it with nanobots programmed in the image of a speck of ocean," Cindy added.

"For what purpose?"

"We're moving the world away from its coastlines, building separations, fake sea walls. We relocate everyone to the interior, cast the illusion of inundation on the other side," Larry said.

"Of course, the nuclear power plants will actually be surrounded by water. We'll build real sea walls for them first," Teegan said.

"So, the two-fer: the notbots get a place to live, and large tracts of land will be returned to its natural state," Larry declared.

"We'll be using the bugbots to clean up the human's mess," Cindy said.

"Bugbots?"

"Those huge constructionbots. The ones reworking the urban areas," Larry clarified.

"Oh yeah, I saw those."

"We all worked on that design," Cindy put forth, smiling. "In the last few months, we've figured out we can execute just about any project. When we work together."

"Better together," Larry added, smiling at Cindy.

"The bugbots are the ones that'll break up the ice," Gulliver said, nodding.

Kaminer sat still for a moment, taking it all in. "Oh," he finally echoed. "And um, ah, what was that swearing thing all about?"

"We're pretty sure your syn chip has been reduced to a first generation microchip. Access to Central Frame, Messaging, just like the Interface's nanobot version today," Larry said.

"And that little fuck Cray, who pushed himself into the humans' Messaging feature? He's on yours too," Teegan said.

"How can you know that?" Kaminer said, cocking his head.

"Precisely because you can't swear. We think the bastard's probably using the energy differential to power himself," Teegan continued.

Larry cut in. "He knows you're going to swear, and takes that for himself, leaving you to issue to less energetic version. The difference is fuel for the fire."

"Haysu cray," Kaminer exclaimed.

"Exactly!" the Scholars cried out in unison. "H. Zeus Cray."

Kaminer clamped a hand over his mouth, suddenly looking sick. "Um, okay, so ah, back to the notbots, um, how many almost-humans are there?"

"You mean how many not-humans," Larry said.

"Well, that's a matter of semantics, isn't it?"

"To you, maybe. But not to us," Larry pronounced.

"Please, I don't have the fortitude right now to have a conversation about what they are or aren't. I've barely established that for myself. How many?"

"A few million? We haven't really kept track. Teegan is still trying to take a census, but not all of them have Interfaces," Larry said.

"So they would have been, uh-, Pures?"

"Except for an inherited genomic modification that couldn't be removed," Larry said, as Kaminer's mouth dropped open. "There are some that left in artificial parts, as if the Code of Conduct wasn't going to be reinforced."

"This seems wrong," Kaminer murmured, shaking his head.

Larry shifted in his seat. "We'll stay on top of it. The ones who didn't get artificial parts removed can rot for all I care."

"Larry!" Cindy yelped.

He ignored her. "But we'll re-ScrubBub those in the first category should the technology become available to make them human all the way through," Larry pointed out.

"Re-ScrubBub? And reverse the purple hair? Can you do that?" Kaminer asked.

"Of course," Teegan said, huffing.

Kaminer leaned forward. "Hey, do you think, um, well, could you do that for me?"

"Yeah, sure. If it helps with your self-image. We can figure out a way," Gulliver reassured him.

Kaminer – 2100

**"When you fill your heart with those you love,
you are never alone.
And wherever you are, you are home."
-Kaminer**

A new year. Maybe I should make a resolution? Or a list of resolutions. Okay, first, I resolve to find my way out of this basement.

Yeah, it's six walls, all for me and I agreed to it, but that was a different version of me. A pre-edition, before the world sunk its talons into me, before I was flooded by the tsunami of life.

I've got a skeletal extraction scheduled in three days, on Monday. That's how I'm starting the New Year - with great risk but hopefully, a finality to my journey. A path Dr. Burke doesn't even recognize. He wasn't swayed, in the least, by the official opinion at Reappraisal. He said, and I quote, "What do bots know about humanness?"

A lot actually, and I say that with some authority, since I'm the only being that's ever been, well, both. Technically, I can also experience the machine world, given my access to the Scholars, but I'm not going to advertise that on my resume.

I'm convinced he's blind to the underpinnings of the bot world, baked right into their programming, to follow the human qualities specified by the contours of their Mindset. For a warbot, the top two qualities are loyalty and capability. Excellent characteristics for any bot (or any human, or any machine consciousness. Or crap, for any notbot.)

But the point is, they come from the human world. Loyalty to the current cause (which, when Burke found me, was Bio-protection), as well as to my fellow companions (at that time policebots). Followed by a capable mental attitude, an innate trust that "I could". Back then, I operated under complete certainty, no doubts clouding my mind that my actions were right, were true, were necessary.

Those convictions gave me an ability to accomplish what I was programmed to do. Strike down the enemy, round up the biohackers, squash dissent.

It's not that way now. I still have these qualities, of course, but they've softened, and I've added to them extensively. I remember Mr. Vee on the first day of school encouraging me to make friends with Stevie, and in that same way, I've asked my stalwart qualities of unquestioned loyalty and capacity to become part of a larger group.

They've had to make friends with hopefulness, with inconsistency, new opinions that announce their arrival constantly, sometimes loudly. There's an ambition I hadn't known before, and most difficult, doubt.

Doubt is a complete thorn in my side, and I try to keep him in a little box, pushed back as far as possible on a mental shelf. In my mind. I imagine the Scholar's storeroom, where a gazillion packets of humanness are stored for future consumption. Maybe if I shove doubt in there, he'll get lost and I'll never have to see him again.

And Ambrose has rubbed off on me, most certainly. His clucking and mothering. I've been down in the bot compartments for a week, and already I can see that my day doesn't always start out right. I miss his fluffing and folding, his constant reassurances, propping up something fragile in me.

And he's pinging me now. *"Yes, of course I can leave my compartment. Right now? Is it urgent? Oh, a New Year's celebration at Magnate? Sure I'd love to come!"* I message Ambrose, simultaneously wondering why the party wasn't last night.

I still clutch at some of the finer points of human decision-making, but it makes sense that they'd move a party from a Thursday to a Friday, so I know he can't be wrong.

I get up from the floor where I've been lying, curled up in a ball. This compartment isn't big enough to stretch out in, designed simply for a single chair. I've made it even smaller by bringing my stuff, things a bot wouldn't possess or even care about.

Half of the room is taken up by my clothing and accessories with the two suitcases stacked in a corner. I put my treasure chest, a box containing everything that's marked my journey, on top. Even the paper sleeve from the first ice cream cone I ate last month is in there.

But after everything, I can't sleep upright. I need to lie down, and I've moved the chair out into the hallway. I pass by it, the nasty, rigid piece of junk, as I make my way silently out of the basement, tiptoeing up the stairs to the first floor.

The Cosmetic Enhancement building is smack in the middle of the inner core so it's the same trek from where I'm standing to get to any of the inner core stations. It's late, almost 20:00 hours, so I decide to walk to the inner G station. It means I'll only have to get on one tram tonight. It's a fifteen minute march, and the train from the inner to the outer G Block is about the same.

I know this route, from the outer G Block station to Magnate Mindware so well. I walked it exactly ninety-two times with Ambrose. And hey, there he is, waiting for me outside the building. He's got a beret over his head, looking festive. As we proceed inside and he peels his coat off, I can see he's got on the purple kimono. It fits him perfectly.

I'm so happy to see him, it's the first time since I moved. He'd messaged me that they'd shifted Felipe to our B Block dorm. He took my bed, the little crapface, but Ambrose says he's an okay roommate. Not as neat as me, obviously, but good enough has to be, well, good enough.

Ambrose hugs me when I greet him, and I've become a bit of an expert on these man hugs. There's an art to them. I've noticed women go in for the kill with full blown arms-wrapped-around the body hugs, the way Mrs. Belle hugged me that day. But guys hold themselves at a distance, usually with a handshake keeping the other half of their body from touching. Curious, isn't it?

As the door slides open, I see a large cocktail party gathering. It's going to be great seeing everyone from my old work. Then I realize Kettle is standing right in the front. Kettle! I know for a fact he never worked at Magnate Mindware and I try to process this when I am practically struck down by the force of the greeting that comes from the crowd as they turn together towards me.

"Surprise!" everyone yells, throwing streamers and confetti. Kettle takes me by one arm and Ambrose by the other and they move me into the group. I'm utterly without words. Nothing could prepare me for what is laid out before me.

All of the kids from Burke Academy are there. All of them. The old third graders (they must be fourth graders now) that shared some math lessons with me start to crowd around, and drag me over to a table. It is covered in chocolate cakes. There are at least eight beautiful cakes on the table but I can't even count them because I'm starting to cry.

"We made these for you, Kam! The best fractions teacher. EVER!" they sing, and I realize some of their parents are milling about. One of the mothers comes up to my side and whispers in my ear.

"We used the last of our flour and pooled our eggs. These cakes are all homemade. For tonight. For you," the mother softly reports.

"What's tonight? Why are you all here?" I ask, spotting Dr. Katz in the crowd. He is trailed by Terrance and Tesme, who wave, and now I am truly perplexed.

"It's your birthday, Kam!" Ambrose calls out, and my hand flies to cover my mouth.

I never thought to look at what he and Dr. Katz did (or were instructed to do if you listen to the Scholars' account of what happened that day). But they gave me a birth date. Not a manufacture date. I'm having a birthday, and tears are dripping down my cheeks. I don't even feel embarrassed.

Dr. Katz comes up and shakes my hand. "Well done, Kaminer. Happy birthday," he exclaims and I secretly pinch myself. Hard. Ouch. Nothing changes in front of me so just for good measure, I pinch myself again. No, none of this is a dream.

There are a bunch of kids wearing berets and I know these are my old tenth graders from french class. The time I set the sprinklers off. I'm handed a beret, but it's quickly snatched out of my hand as a few of the kids pull it over my head. One of them sweeps my hair back, so not a trace of purple can be seen from the front. This makes me crazy happy, and I try to wipe some tears away.

"We miss you upstairs," Scotty, our old team leader, says, emerging from the crowd. All of our old team is here, laughing, coming up to bump shoulders with me and shake my hand. Scotty hands me a drink, a thimble-sized drink and suddenly, all of the guys cluster together. Felipe, Dave, Mattie, Stu, Bryan and Phil are all there. Ambrose materializes again on the other side of me.

"Just a swig, Kam. I cleared it with Dr. Rodriguez," Ambrose announces, and as I drink it (Disgusting! Note to self: you're not a beer drinker), I see Dr. Rodriguez, flanked by Asher, the disappearing attendant from Spricatur, and Ned, who has become a friend.

Ned calls himself the unofficial head of my unofficial fan club. I've never noticed it before but looking at them from where I am, I realize that Ned and Asher have the identical side part in their hair as me. And on this night, my birthday, they have somehow convinced Dr. Rodriguez to do the same.

And that's when it hits me. Everyone, including the children, has purple hair. The bots came with theirs of course, but all of the humans have dyed their hair, and some have added red streaks. Just like mine. My hand goes to my heart as I am beset by those saudades that Ambrose has from time to time. I am already missing this moment as if I can't live in it long enough. It feels like my heart is breaking, and I realize it's the strain of joy. I have never been so happy in all my life.

Mr. Vee is here! He's talking to some of the older students and I pledge to spend time with them tonight as I know some of them have graduated. He waves and points over to a table slightly behind him, pushed up against the wall. It is stacked with presents. I might actually start to lose my composure. Kettle has disappeared into the crowd but Frank is now by Ambrose's side.

"What's that?" I ask, pointing to the table.

"Let's go find out," Frank says. I don't think Ambrose can talk his smile is so wide.

As I attempt to walk over, trailed by all the little kids, I am stopped by Dr. Burke, the only one in the room with a natural hair color. Well, not naturally natural. What is he doing here? He doesn't like or even respect me, but in keeping with the mood of the event, I smile and put on my good manners.

"Dr. Burke, good evening! Thank you for coming."

"Kaminer, may I introduce my wife of almost three years? This is Roslyn," he replies.

I am taken aback by the rough beauty by his side. She is so thoroughly imperfect, such an odd match for someone as rigid as Dr. Burke.

"It's such an honor, Kaminer. What a story you could tell," she says, with a trace of a french accent. Her hair, a blackish shade of purple is twisted on top of her head and a clip holds the tidal wave in place. It's messy and wonderful and I love this woman instantly.

"Should we light the cake?" Ambrose butts in before I can respond, pulling me away. My old pal Stevie, little tiny Stevie, who must be like, what, four-years-old, is unsteadily lighting the single candle that sits on one of the chocolate cakes. Even he has a beret on, with little wisps of purple hair peeking out.

He looks up, engulfed by a smile. "Happy bird day to you," he belts out and a laugh rips out of me as the entire group comes together to sing the song.

All I can do is clasp my hands in front of me, and hold myself together. In the old days, I would have been able to sense the vibration of the singing. Yet even today, the song strikes a harmonic frequency that makes my body hum with contentment.

I walk up to Stevie and ruffle his hair, and as I blow out the candle, a few of the Burke students chant "QB, QB, QB."

I make a silent wish for all that is good in this world to be felt by everyone, just once. I make this wish on behalf of the humans and notbots, who have the best chance of feeling unmitigated joy, for the Scholars, who might partake of it in their exchange, and for the bots, who are completely and thoroughly challenged in this area. It might never happen for them, but still I wish.

"Hey, Kaminer, how about you cut the cake already," someone calls out, and I recognize Tim Belle's voice. Holy crap! He pushes his way through the crowd, in clean jeans and a Jethro Belle-esque flannel shirt. No purple hair, but I can't fault him for it. That he is even here is enough for me, and I'm instantly reminded of something Ambrose told me. The greatest gift is to just bring yourself. Show up, be there, take part.

Tim hands me his pocket knife to cut the cake, and I laugh and hang my head. How many times have I wanted to stab him with something like this, just so he would shut up? I spent hours with him that night, when Ambrose went back out with Frank. Trying to talk sense into Tim Belle is like, well, it's like trying to stuff a double digit into a single number.

But I am touched that he is here, and I happily cut the cake with the candle, and then the successive cakes as he, Ambrose and Frank distribute the slices throughout the crowd.

Mr. Vee is one of the last ones to come forward for a slice of cake. "You made it, Kaminer. I knew you would."

Dr. Rodriguez reappears behind him. "The tiniest sliver. And that's enough sugar for tonight. This time next year, you can eat the whole cake," he says, sounding like Ambrose. Mr. Vee and Dr. Rodriguez are sucked back into the crowd and I am left to cut myself a parcel of chocolate cake. It is the most extravagant thing I have ever eaten and I wish for time to stretch out, like Teegan's tongue that day, so the taste of it lasts forever.

Suddenly the Scholars are in my head. I wobble a little but try to stand perfectly still, with the plate of cake in one hand and fork in the other. They have never come to me. I always find their on-ramp in my mind, walk through their door, visit them in their sanctuary. But somehow they have reversed the flow of traffic and made their way to me.

"*The greatest gift, Kam. Here we are,*" Gulliver says.

"*Oh, Christ, no verborrhea tonight, Gulliver, okay?*" Larry says, pushing Gulliver to the side. They seem to be in an undefined silvery space and I wonder if I've blown a human gasket.

"*What's verborrhea?*" I ask in-mind.

"*Larry's new word for therapy talk,*" Cindy answers.

"*Happy birthday, Kaminer,*" Teegan gushes, handing me a small box.

"*What's this?*" I ask

"*Just a little something, something,*" he says, and I quickly unwrap the box, throwing the top off. In my mind I can see the lid just fades into nothingness when it hits the side of my mindscreen. I look down into the little box. It contains Teegan's digital watch.

"*To keep track of how far you've come,*" he says, sucking in some breathe.

"*And now for the real greatest gift of all,*" Larry announces, with a flourish of his hand. Instantly, all four Scholars disappear from my mind, and I am back at the party in the lobby of the Magnate Mindware building.

One of the servibot lunch ladies is right in front of me, holding a plate of cheese biobiscuits. "Would you desire one? No, I do not think so," she sniffs, and moves over to Kettle, Ned, and then Terrance and Tesme.

As I scan the crowd, I spot a number scrolling in tiny font at the bottom right-hand corner of my mindscreen. 23,868,001. 23,868,002. 23,868,003. It continues to tick, and I realize that these are the accumulated seconds, twenty-three million of them, since I first awoke. Yes, I've managed to accomplish quite a lot in these twenty-three million seconds. And counting.

I cannot spot where Asher has gotten to, so I scan the crowd and spot him. He's talking to Aron! The bot that directed my shoulder surgery, and then helped in the initial phase of my recovery. I lick my plate clean, set it on the table, and make my way over.

"Kaminer, you are looking well," Aron effuses. "Please thank Master Belle for me."

"For what?" I ask, things still not clear to me.

"For organizing this party for you, and for thinking to invite me. No one has ever invited me to a party before," he declares. "Happy birthday, by the way. And I got you something," he finishes, pointing to the table.

Suddenly, the crowd is around me, and I'm being maneuvered imperceptibly towards the table covered with gifts. Aron picks up a nice-sized box and hands it to me.

"From you?" I ask, and he nods.

"It is more to right a wrong than anything else. But it is given to you with the finest of intentions," he says.

Carefully, I peel off the thin wrapping paper that looks like old pages from a printed magazine. I have no idea how he procured this paper but clearly he went to some effort. I slowly pull the top off the box, when Tim comes over with a chair. I sit down in it, then look up to see Mr. and Mrs. Belle, complete with purple hair, standing next to him. Now I am beyond flabbergasted.

"Sorry we're late," Mrs. Belle issues. "But we're here. Now!"

I smile and nod and look back down to Aron's present. It is a perfectly folded, brand new black shirt with the mandarin collar I like so much.

"Oh, this will be perfect in the spring, all the way through fall," I declare. "Thank you!"

"It is not paper. Feel it," Aron says quietly, and I am dumbstruck by the cotton of the cloth. I pick it up and rub it against my cheek.

"Oh, Aron, thank you. I don't know what to say. Where did you find something like this?"

He shakes his head, and Tim steps out in front. "He might have worked with me a little bit. We might have, uh, excessive deposits of clothing, and-," he starts.

"What? How did you," I try to question when a crowd of my old fourth graders mob me, cutting me off.

"Open ours!" they cry chaotically. I laugh and take a small hard rectangle that is haphazardly covered by what appears to be a white napkin. Inside is a book, a real book, with paper pages, its edges worn. A book of poetry by Langley Hatch.

"How'd-," I try, feeling overwhelmed. Tesme and Terrance quickly hand me a large box.

"We are next," they say in unison. I can tell they are still in training, their stiff robot-ness still apparent, nine months later, and it gives me pause.

How did I get so lucky, to become aware, and move through the rough, uneven layers of humanhood so quickly? It doesn't seem fair and I'm not even sure why they are here.

As if picking up on my thoughts, Terrance chimes in. "It is because of Ned," he says.

"Pardon?"

"We have been watching your channel, Kaminer," Tesme adds.

"Sorry?"

Ned steps into the group. "Just doing my job. As the head of KClub."

"What?" I say, hoping that I don't look or sound as befuddled as I feel.

"You have your own channel on streaming news. Almost everyone here is a contributing reporter," Ned reports. I shake my head, trying to keep my mouth from falling open. *Say what?*

I turn back to open the Tbots' gift. It is a simple unadorned box. I open the package and gasp. How did they remember? The day I met them, they were scuffling with a ball, learning how to make choices, And here it was, the ball, in a box, gifted to me.

The night continues this way. Dr. Rodriguez presents the pair of soft scrubs I wore after my horrendous G.I. surgery, Stevie gives me a toy soldier. The Belles hand me a small plastic sack with homemade cheese bread (that I can actually eat), and suddenly Officer 20 shows up with Dr. Kate. The night feels surreal, as if my wish for the party never to end has come true. I have fallen into a Dalí painting and don't want to leave. Ever.

"I knew you were special from the moment I saw you," Dr. Kate murmurs, and I gasp at her breathtaking beauty. She is barely covered in a white sparkly dress, her shoulders unclothed, such a daring move for winter. A red beaded necklace ending in a heart hangs from her neck, making her whole appearance ornately gorgeous.

Officer 20 shakes my hand. "Gavin," he says. "Gavin McLeod," he informs me. Right. Even the titular head of Reappraisal at a Human Services Bureau would have a name. He would have always had a name, but I didn't care to know it before. Before I changed.

Neither Mr. McLeod nor Dr. Kate have changed their hair color but it doesn't matter and it would have ruined Dr. Kate's perfect look anyway. I see Dr. Crowley, who I met briefly when he had his palm Reader extracted, in the distance, and my entire team from Cosmetic Enhancements is here.

All that is missing is the beautiful young woman from the waiting room that day. The day it all started. I've never told anyone about her, or that I still think of her, keeping my eyes peeled around Homebase. I have never caught sight of her again. She seems to remain beyond my reach.

By the end of the evening, the beret covering my head is completely askew, as the little and then the bigger kids exit, patting me on the arm, shoulders and head. I am regaled by fist bumps, as people take their leave. At some point, Dr. Kate's red heart necklace was strung over my neck, and then gained the company of some white streamers. It actually doesn't look half bad against the black turtleneck I had on when Ambrose called a few hours ago.

The group finally dwindles to Ambrose, Kettle, and Dr. Burke. I can't think of a stranger grouping, and this gives me pleasure somehow. Kettle hands me a small metal box.

"Take great care with this, please," he beseeches me, and I don't understand what I am looking at when I flip the top open and peer down at little bits of char.

"It is what is left of Kex." He pauses to swallow, gathering some air into him. "I set it aside when it came in. When I saw you at the Bureau, for Reappraisal, I tapped into what Ned was broadcasting. Heard your story. Read about your conversion. If anyone can bring Kex back, maybe you can," Kettle tells me.

"I'll do everything I can," I say quietly.

"I like to think, well, that maybe he was my friend," Kettle says, salutes me, and without another word, makes his way to the doors. "*Godspeed, Kaminer*," he messages, turning to look at me one last time before he's gone.

Ambrose moves to pull a box out from under the table. I shake my head and put up my hands. "No I can't. I can't take anything from you, Ambrose. There's nothing else you could possibly give me," I protest.

"Of course, you can," Ambrose says, forcefully pushing the box onto me.

He looks away and bites his lower lip as I open it. After receiving the leftover bits of Kex, I don't know what to expect, and a flush of relief flows through me when I open the box and see Moxie, the stuffed dog, sitting by herself inside. I pull her out, snugging her under my arm, where she likes it best.

"Dude," I breathe out, and Ambrose encloses me in a full hug. Not a man hug. I can feel myself start to tear up again. "Thank you so much," I whisper. "For the party, for everything."

"Hasta luego, l'il bro," he voices, punches me in the arm, and is quickly out the door.

That leaves only me and Dr. Burke, who slowly appraises me from head to toe. I don't really care what his assessment is today. And I would laugh if it wasn't Dr. Burke.

"Would you like a ride, Kaminer?" he asks.

I can't possibly say no, so we proceed outside to his *driver* car. And he's not the driver. I gulp as the chauffeur opens the door for me and motions me inside. Dr. Burke quickly seats himself next to me.

After a few minutes of silence (and hand-wringing on my part), he hands me an envelope.

"What's this?" I ask.

"I hope you had a nice birthday," he murmurs, jutting his chin out at the envelope. "I think I made a mistake."

This is the last thing I ever expected to hear from him, so I remain still for a moment, unsure whether he is referring to the envelope. Finally I hold it up. "Should I, uh-, open it?" I whisper.

"Please. And I want to apologize. That you were moved to bot housing. That I treated you, well, as less than a human. I wish I could tell you why."

"I don't know what's in the envelope, but all I really want to know is your story," I confess.

He shakes his head. "It's not important."

"I know there's something very personal in your treatment of me," I continue as he looks down at his hands.

"You understand, Kaminer, that to separate the real from the not real, you must have the courage to confront the lies you've been telling yourself."

"Sorry? I, uh, don't think I've lied. Not about anything important," I respond, trying to contain a sinking feeling that still plagues me sometimes.

"No, not you. Me. I have. I've lied to myself for the longest time, and I'm sorry," he says, looking right at me.

"If I understood, it would help me move on," I say. But he doesn't respond, just sits there, and looks back down at his hands. "Understanding being the better part of empathy," I add.

Finally he shakes his head. "That's a story for another day. For now, let me just put things right between us. Open the envelope."

I carefully pick open the flap and pull out the thick cardstock inside. It contains a single word.

Emancipation

"Uh, is this what I think it means?" I ask.

"I'm dropping you off at the same B Block dorm as Ambrose. You'll have a private room on the floor below," Dr. Burke says. "And I'm sorry that my past got in the way of your present. I won't let that happen again."

"What about my work?" I ask, feeling slightly terrified that I've been suddenly cut loose.

"You can have your pick of jobs within the Consortium," he murmurs.

"But I enjoy Cosmetic Enhancement. It's fascinating, and I like the front office, interacting with customers."

Dr. Burke takes a deep breathe. "You could continue. If it's what you really want."

"I would, uh, actually, really like that," I confess, as the car slows to a stop.

"I was hoping you'd say that," he practically whispers. I can see we are back to the old dorm. "All of your things are there. Second floor," he says, as I start to get out of the car.

"See you next week?" I ask.

"Monday?"

"I go in to replace my, uh, thermoplastic armature, on Monday," I say, trying to make it sound as important as it is to me.

"Right, thank you Kaminer. Just let us know when you're ready," he confirms. "And, uh, happy birthday."

As I walk through the familiar lobby, and take my time on the stairs before finding my room on the second floor, I find myself wondering about the meaning of it all.

Why have I undergone this incredible journey? Why was Dr. Burke put in my path? And it occurs to me that maybe I have it backwards. Maybe I was put on his path. Is there something I'm supposed to be providing for him? Am I supposed to be his Ambrose?

I enter the small room, much bigger than the basement bot compartment, and half the size of my old room. In fact it's as if someone cut Ambrose's room in half, delivering his section to this floor. I sigh with relief that my clothes, shoes, value box and trinkets have all made it successfully to my new quarters.

I put Moxie on the dresser top which is worn and dented like Ambrose's. How long have these dorms with their furnishings stood here anyway?

I unwrap the white streamers, and carefully pull off Dr. Kate's necklace. It's my intention to return this to her, as I don't really remember if she gave it to me as a gift or in jest. Wearily, because it has been a long day, filled with hard work, followed by intense happiness, I pull the beret off my head.

A shower of purple and red hair falls to the dresser top and I am frozen, afraid to look up at a bald head. But when I finally work up the nerve, I am rewarded by the sight of my face topped with a dense helping of fine brown hair.

"Thank you," I quietly call out to the Scholars, not knowing if they can hear me.

Acknowledgments

While drafting the first part of this series, I had an extraordinary dream. My married and I were throwing a swish cocktail party, and he was dismayed by the number of guests he didn't know.

"But honey, of course you know Ray! Mr. Kurzweil is the one predicting the Singularity, which we might live long enough to experience," I exclaim, and he looks at me like I've had too many caipirinhas.

"You mean the guy who keeps telling me that if I eat this," he says, pointing to the chip bowl next to the even larger bowl of dip, "I'll never get to meet Kaminer?"

I'm a bit taken aback, wondering how Ray knows about one of the characters in my book. He suddenly appears by my side and it occurs to me that he's been deploying his foglets like an invisibility cloak.

Ray winks at me and starts to whisper. "Of course I know Kaminer. I know all about him, and," he continues, leaning in, "I've heard he's been helping out in Dr. Church's lab."

"He is not," I say, indignant, because Kaminer hasn't asked for permission to leave the book and seek employment elsewhere. I feel a little guilty, sounding like Rafe.

"George! When did this happen?" I exclaim, waving over a man who looks a little like my dad. My married, now completely confused, asks the guest standing beside him if he knows what's going on.

"I'm David," he introduces himself.

"No, I'm David," says the guest.

"What?" my David asks.

"Dr. David Chalmers. Clearly, your perception of this party isn't the same as mine. You might be a zombie!" Dr. Chalmers exclaims, and pats my husband on the back. It propels my David to march over to me. He tries to say something but the noise level has risen and I can't quite hear him, so he messages from his phone.

"Babe! Please finish the book. Before I can directly message you from my Neural Interface."

So finish I did. And I truly hope my David understands that those who patiently read and reread their married's work get to skip over all the incarnations of Samsara, and go directly to Nirvana. Well done, honey, and thank you, now and forever.

My deepest gratitude to Mr. Ray Kurzweil, Dr. George M. Church, and Dr. David J. Chalmers, whose scientific works greatly informed this work of fiction. Their collected writings are so juicy, so bursting with exciting ideas, they will bend the most stubborn brain in a new direction.

And this book would still be an outline if it wasn't for the help of my many Readers, especially Claire Ryan Robertson, whose stick-to-it gene should be found, cloned, and widely-distributed.

And then there is Stephanie Spector, the best co-pilot a writer could hope for, who sat transfixed as she listened to the story and corrected its path with boldness and insight. Could any author ask for more?

I simply do not have enough words to thank Nate Velluto, a living character model, with so much Nate to go around that little bits of him fell into other characters too. An inspiring Beta Reader, Copy Editor, and muse, Nate never failed to strip the encapsulation right off my ganglia. He forced me to be 'more' in a way that never felt like work. Everyone deserves a little Nate in their life.

Further gratitude goes to Dr. Michael Kaminer, for walking in that day in a very un-Dr. Kaminer black shirt. If it hadn't been for that moment in time and space, Kaminer might not have blasted into existence. Thank you for letting me use your name.

Unending appreciation to Dave Carroll for the light in his eyes that shines in many of my characters' and inspiring Kaminer's enlightenment at the in-between Louvre. If my Dave and I hadn't gathered with him to sing 'Let It Be' with a roomful of strangers, I wouldn't have seen the sun blasting through the clerestory windows, absolutely certain that was where the light was supposed to shine that day.

My fondest, heartfelt thanks to Annabelle Ambrose. If she hadn't said "you should write a book!" with such conviction, Ambrose Belle would not have stepped off the page, and this novel simply would not have achieved escape velocity.

***

And to you, dear reader, who made it to the last page. Did this book crack open a space, however miniscule, that wasn't there before? Lead your mind to a new place? Do you think you're human? If you answered yes to any two of these questions, I can assure you that Kaminer agrees with you.

The Samsara Papers: Convergence

Book Two

Who was that beautiful woman from the waiting room
at the Homebase at Burke?

What do the uploaded consciousnesses of Drs. Henton
Burke and Cray really want?

Will the Scholars have enough qualia to survive?

What is Dr. Burke's story?

Join us in Book Two where all paths converge.

www.ingramcontent.com/pod-product-compliance
Lightning Source LLC
Chambersburg PA
CBHW051518250626
47156CB00001B/133